Tom Fox's storytelling emerges out of many years spent in academia, working on the history of the Christian Church. A respected authority on that subject, he has recently turned his attentions toward exploring the new stories that can be drawn out of its mysterious dimensions. *Dominus* is Tom's first novel.

TOM FOX
DOMINUS

TOM FOX
DOMINUS

Quercus

New York • London

Quercus

New York • London

© 2016 by Tom Fox
First published in the United States by Quercus in 2016

ISBN 978-1-68144-451-2

Library of Congress Control Number: 2016933367

Distributed in the United States and Canada by
Hachette Book Group
1290 Avenue of the Americas
New York, NY 10104

Manufactured in the United States

10 9 8 7 6 5 4 3 2 1

www.quercus.com

To Alex and Megan, who always ask the most delightfully provocative questions

Behold, he cometh with the clouds, and every eye shall see him, even those that pierced him. And all the tribes of the earth shall wail because of him. So it is to be. Amen.

Revelation 1:7

Lo, I come unexpected, like a thief. And blessed is he that keepeth watch . . .

Revelation 16:15

PRIMO

1

St. Peter's Basilica, Vatican City: Sunday, 8:22 a.m.

He did not come with trumpets from heaven. Angels did not burst into song. There was no darkening of the sun, and the fabric of the ancient basilica remained unscathed.

He entered quietly, without fanfare, though with every footstep he took, the world began to change.

Not that his outward appearance gave any indication of what was to come. An unassuming man in worn jeans. A gray button-down shirt, slightly wrinkled. His shoes, mildly tattered. In every visible way he was unremarkable.

Later, no one was able to recollect seeing him enter St. Peter's. Not one of the thousands gathered there observed him pass through the vast western doors or step into the great expanse of space designed to reflect the glorious meeting of heaven and earth. All they could remember was the way his silent walk through the interior had gradually drawn their attention once he was in their midst.

But of his demeanor, there in the centuries-old heart of Christendom, they remembered every detail. The way he'd moved calmly down the central aisle during the pontifical High Mass. The way men and women had unconsciously parted to create a path while their children had clambered toward him, inexplicably drawn. The way they'd all hushed as he drew near, and how their gazes had lingered on him as he'd moved by. They remembered that.

He had a posture that spoke of purpose, though he walked almost casually through the throngs. His hair, only a few inches in length, slightly wavy and with a gold-brown tone, seemed oddly bright in the orange light of the ancient church. As he strode toward Bernini's great baldachin, his eyes were ever forward. Gentle and serene, yet strong.

They all remembered his eyes.

At the far end of the 211-meter-long nave, the Mass's chief celebrant stood albed in white, bent at the high altar. Though his bodily infirmity would have conveyed the message effectively on its own, the design of the massive bronzework above him reinforced the fact that, for all the pontiff's worldly fame and power, he was yet a tiny figure before the majesty of God.

He was surrounded by two cardinal concelebrants, and between them and him were the customary assistants who went everywhere with the beleaguered Pope, holding his twisted form upright by the elbows for those parts of the service that required him to stand. He was far from an old man, but the specific type of spinal stenosis he had suffered from since childhood left him permanently disfigured and unable to stand under his own power. The lingering results of that infirmity, however, had never weakened his spirit. They had only strengthened it, and the man the media had cruelly termed "the crippled Pope" was loved all the more by his flock for the weak body that made his inner spiritual convictions so evident.

The Pope and his assistants were flanked by a suite of priests and a full cohort of servers decked out in their liturgical fineries. Behind them, on specially constructed risers, the red-robed choristers of the Sistine Chapel choir filled the space with the angelic Latin of the Sanctus. The angels themselves, one elderly woman would later recall, could have produced no more glorious a sound.

Sanctus, Sanctus, Sanctus
Dominus Deus Sabaoth . . .
Benedictus qui venit in nomine Domini.

Holy, Holy, Holy
Lord God of Sabaoth . . .
Blessed is he who comes in the name of the Lord.

The stranger walked slowly forward.

The Pope glanced up from the instruments of the bloodless sacrifice—the chalice and paten of hammered gold—his face beaming the glory he felt at every celebration of the sacred service. It was clear, as he craned a pained neck and gazed out over the faithful, his hazel eyes reflecting the shimmer of the crimson wine in the chalice, that the inheritor of the office of the Apostle Peter was wholly enrapt in the sacrosanct liturgical rite.

It was as he looked over his flock that the pontiff caught his first sight of the stranger's approach.

And it was then that the inexplicable began to take place.

At the front of the rows of chairs in the basilica's central nave, just beyond the red ropes that kept the faithful at a respectful distance from the clerical centerpiece, the vivid blue, red and orange ceremonial uniforms of the Swiss Guard formed a crescent before the high altar. The men within the costumes, who looked like something out of a Renaissance carnival, were among the most highly trained and devoted military protective details in the world.

As the stranger approached the periphery, the guardsmen were the last bodies before the baldacchino and the clerics beneath it. By tradition and honor, as well as by the oath each had sworn when they were commissioned in the Cortile di San Domaso, theirs was a line they would allow no man to pass. Holiness incited hatred as well as reverence, and for centuries the Swiss Guard's ranks had ensured that, at least in practical terms, hate did not win out over love.

But as the stranger continued to approach, it was clear that the path he intended to follow did not end at their cordon. The two guards closest to the central aisle stiffened, their position blocking his route, hands clutched tightly at their ceremonial halberds. Behind the approaching man it was as if the whole basilica had gone silent and stiff. The space was electric with focus. The thousands were staring at this man, totally enthralled.

The stranger slowed, his blue-jeaned appearance all the more out of place as he came before the ancient uniforms erroneously attributed to a design by Michelangelo. He drew to a stop only a few feet from the guards. He said nothing. He kept his eyes only on the Pope, beyond and elevated several steps above.

The stalwart guards tensed, devotion and tireless training calling them toward their sacred duty.

And then, as the stranger stood before them, they knelt.

The whole troop of elite soldiers, the de facto standing military of the Vatican, fell to their knees in almost perfect unison. The two closest to the stranger skirted aside, obeisantly poised, allowing him an unobstructed path.

Muffled gasps from the crowd were audible as the stranger resumed his progress, stepping softly around the entrance to the crypt of St. Peter. A few paces later, he began his ascent to the high altar.

The corpulent red-robed director of the choir glanced over his shoulder, shocked, then spun away from his choristers. His fat arms were still suspended in a conductor's pose as behind him the choir faltered, then went silent.

The sudden absence of sound in the basilica was overwhelming. The man's footsteps could now be clearly heard, echoing through the mesmerized space as he mounted the final steps.

At last he stood face to face with the Holy Father across the laden altar. The Pope's body was bent sharply to his right, his assistants firmly gripping his upper arms in support. He stood frozen in place, his fingertips still touching the shimmering chalice, and locked eyes with the stranger.

"Who are you?" His familiar, sonorous voice trembled.

The man gazed peacefully into the pontiff's eyes. While the people would remember the mysteriousness of the silence that filled the vast space during their long, interlocked glance, the Pope would recollect that it had been as if he was staring into eternity, his heart filled with the same sense of wonder and majesty that it formerly had equated only with gazing out over the undulating waves of the sea and contemplating the vastness of God's glory.

Then, in a gentle voice, holding out two upturned hands, the stranger finally spoke.

"Do you not know me, Peter?"

Gasps filled the basilica. Stillness gave way to a wave of sibilant tension as the man's answer was whispered through the rows of faithful. The casual visitors in the throng struggled to comprehend what it meant, but the meaning of the words was apparent to men and women of faith. Apparent, and explosive. Peter was the name of the first holder of the papal office—the man who had denied Christ three times.

These were words the Savior would speak to his own.

Camera flashes began to ignite the space in their hundreds. But the Pope only stared at the stranger's extended hands. The pontifical eyes welled with unexpected tears.

"My faithful servant," the stranger said a moment later, his voice rich and oddly soothing. He placed one of his hands upon the trembling pontiff's shoulder. The assistant holding the Pope's right arm reinforced his grip, but the stranger kept his gentle gaze on the Holy Father, absent of any menace.

"Do not be afraid. It is I."

The Pope's eyes were like glass, his breath weak. In the distance, the stranger's latest words had been heard and their even more direct contents ignited the faithful, who snapped images with their cameras, filming the scene with their phones, dozens dropping to their knees in prayer. The dozens became a hundred, and a hundred became two. But the pontiff gazed straight into the man's face. His whole body trembled.

And then the miracle happened.

"You are a man of faith," the stranger said softly to the Pope, "and your faith has made you whole." He reached out his other arm, grabbed the hands of both the assistants from the shoulders of the pontiff and pulled them gently aside. They resisted only a moment, then silently let the man draw their hands away from their charge.

The Pope stood, unsupported and bent, wavering.

"Stand, Peter," the stranger said. "That which was crooked has been made straight."

The Pope stared at him, his eyes wide. He took a breath. Swallowed.

And then the Holy Father stood upright for the first time in his life.

Neither man seemed to notice the cries of wonder from the cardinals and clerics surrounding them, or from the awestruck masses behind as the crowd beheld the healing of their spiritual leader.

The Pope's own eyes were glazed with a film of wonder and gratitude.

With his right hand, the stranger lifted the golden chalice and placed it back into the Pope's grasp, ensuring that the pontiff's grip was tight.

"Now, Your Holiness, finish what you came here to do."

Without saying another word, he walked around the altar table to the pontiff's left and took one of the clerical seats behind him.

And then, closing his eyes and folding his hands calmly on his jeans, the stranger began to pray.

Fidene Municipal District, Rome: 8:36 a.m.

Six kilometers to the north, at a sharp isolated bend in the Tiber river, a body floated face down in the cold water. The golden hair on its head swirled almost beautifully in the gentle current. At this early hour, no one lamented his absence. No one was out searching. No one even knew he was gone.

In fewer than forty-eight hours, the whole nation would know this dead man's face. It would spark controversy. It would incite anger and mistrust and prompt cries of deception. It would shatter faith on an unthinkable scale.

But at this moment the corpse bobbed in the river in solitude, its face concealed in the cloudy waters. The murder that had taken the man's life was a thing of the past, the chains at his ankles insufficient to submerge the body as his killer had hoped. And so his corpse floated steadily toward the center of the city. As if it knew that more was to come.

2

Headquarters of La Repubblica newspaper, Rome: 9:28 a.m.

Silver smoke curled upward, its tendrils bending back on themselves in plumes that dissipated slowly in the stagnant air. Those that fell downward reached fingernail and skin and joint, caressing flesh and leaving their unmistakable mark: yellow and faint, the hint of congealed tar and breath.

The problem with chain smoking was the damned yellow fingers.

Over the years, Alexander Trecchio had tried a thousand different postures for propping his favored MS Filtro in his hands to avoid the smoky recoil and the sticky yellow build-up that invariably formed around his knuckles, but nothing worked. His doctor had told him even more times than this that yellowed skin was the least of his worries. But Trecchio was a man who based his actions, and especially his habits, on concrete facts. The possibilities of emphysema or a short-ened lifespan were frightening, but dismissably hypotheti-cal. The fact that his fingers were yellow, by contrast, was inescapable.

He drew a long, constrained breath through the thin paper and tightly packed tobacco, his eyes closed. He visualized the red coal singeing its burrow deeper into the shredded fragments of dried, cured leaf and the smoke wending its way through its tiny conduit, racing to meet him. As the familiar richness rolled over the buds of his tongue and into his lungs, Alexander realized that at the end of the day he didn't really care about any of the inconveniences, even the fingers. His bad habit was one little thing that brought comfort and calm when so little else did. He'd take it.

"You were late last week."

Speaking of things that bring little comfort or calm.

The annoying, Chihuahua-like voice of Alexander's line editor broke through the serenity of the moment. He held the smoke in his lungs longer than usual, hoping that when he finally exhaled, the man would evaporate with it. But that kind of luck was not with Alexander Trecchio this morning. Sundays brought blessings and peace to many, but rarely to the staff of a newspaper that printed a Monday-morning edition.

"You know the filing deadlines. You sit ten meters from my office," Antonio Laterza continued like a barking rat. Alexander opened his eyes and stared up at the other man.

Laterza was medium height, with a fair build, fair face and all the signs of being completely obsessed with his physical appearance. His chestnut hair flowed neatly toward his neck, its swirls fixed with spray and ends lightened to ensure that the highlights and shades of sunshine were as vividly contrasting indoors as they were out. The suit draped over him compensated for an average body build with more than average style: an immaculate monument to fine tailoring, washed in light brown silk, accentuated with a belt and matching shoes—overpriced memorials to the alligator they had formerly been.

Twenty-seven-year-olds with money, ambition and subscriptions to *GQ*: if they came shrink-wrapped and prefabricated, they would look like Antonio Laterza.

"You have no excuse, Alexander," the polished man continued. His expression and tone were disapproving, like a scolding parent. Never mind the fact that he was more than a decade and a half Trecchio's junior.

"I needed to check a few facts."

"That's why we give you seven days. You're not writing a daily column, *coglione*. What the hell were you doing all week?"

Alexander took another drag from his wilting cigarette and blew the smoke demonstratively in Laterza's direction, ignoring the overused Italian insult. He'd been called worse things than a set of bull's testicles. The truth was, Alexander had no idea what he'd been doing all week. Talking to a priest on the phone? Looking into the finances of some-or-other local parish? Sifting like an obsessed stalker through an inconsequential youth worker's Facebook timeline? Maybe one of those. Maybe all of them. It was all the same, and it was all so *boring*.

"I had some sources I had to confirm," he finally muttered, plucking out a probable-sounding excuse. He was good at that, the result of years of practice. And there were always plenty to choose from. "You're aware of the occasional necessity."

"Bullshit." Laterza glowered down at him. Alexander had known he wouldn't buy the explanation, but he also knew the overly ambitious and vastly overcologned editor couldn't fire him. Local religious affairs was not a section of the paper for which reporters climbed over each other to gain the few column inches on page eleven that came with the job. And Alexander had two distinct advantages: he'd had one big story a few years back that had proved he wasn't completely worthless, and he was old friends with *La Repubblica*'s owner, Niccolò Marre. His job was about as secure as they came in the business.

"You're getting lazy," Laterza continued. He had something close to post-teenage spite on his face, and Alexander wondered now, as he had done more regularly lately, whether twenty-somethings were getting younger or he was just getting stodgier. Forty-four wasn't that old, but next to Laterza, Alexander felt prehistoric.

"You have no ambition, and your work is tired," Laterza snorted.

"Yet you publish it every week. Rome isn't Rome without the Church, and a Roman paper isn't worth its salt without a few column inches of Vatican scandal-reporting. Especially *La Repubblica.*"

That felt good. A little snapping back at the diminutive shit, especially if he could make the man look like he didn't know his own turf. Ever since Eugenio Scalfari had founded it in 1976, *La Repubblica* had held a reputation for being a harsh critic of the Catholic Church. It wasn't a paper that was going to give up religious reporting, however tired it became.

"That story you kept us waiting for last week," Laterza sneered back. "It was about two parishes going over budget on their renovation costs. *Over budget.* You think this counts as Vatican scandal? You think our readers give two shits about such nonsense?"

He gesticulated broadly as he spoke, raising his voice to a well-practiced almost-yell. It was clear he wanted the scolding to be noticed by the bullpen, though few beyond the cubicle partition seemed to be paying any attention to the exchange.

Alexander sighed, slumped back into his chair and drew his cigarette close. He'd be so much more eager to fight, to kick up an energetic response and retaliation, if at his core he didn't agree with the kid's points. No one cared about these stories, least of all him. Alexander had wound his way into the paper not out of zeal but availability. A man entering his forties and lumbering toward middle age with two degrees in theology and a short career as a parish priest in his pocket wasn't exactly vocationally primed for the twenty-first century. When he had finally tossed his dog collar aside and left the life he'd prepared for since his childhood— disillusioned at the irreconcilable conflict between an institution that was meant to be holy and the men who ran it, who so often were anything but—he'd discovered a limited set of options. He wasn't a programmer leaving Apple for Google. He was a priest leaving the church for a world that, with every passing year, was less and less sure just what the Church was, and increasingly convinced that it was out of date, out of touch, and didn't matter.

But Alexander had always been a strong communicator. As long as he didn't aim at any of the high-visibility or competitive areas of journalism—the kind that twenty-year-olds fought for and senior reporters clutched close to their chest— the paper provided a viable option. Add in the journalistically sexy angle of the ex-cleric with a chip on his shoulder and he'd been a natural enough fit for *La Repubblica*'s Church Life section, which amounted chiefly to a gossip column on whatever could be dug up from the murky depths of current ecclesiastical affairs.

And that had been that. For three years he'd probed the lower limits of what human attention could be persuaded to care about. Yes, occasionally there were sex scandals, and the election of a new pope, which had taken place only eleven months before, always brought excitement and attention. But the rest of the time . . . the rest of the time, "mildly interesting" was a height to which he could only hope to climb. And most days he was perfectly willing to sit at the base of that mountain, caring just as little about these things as the paper's average reader.

He gazed up from his desk. Depressingly, his editor was still there. Alexander waited for the next barrage of choreographed abuse, but Laterza's reddened face was gradually fading to a normal color. He looked for an instant like a child who'd been told by his parents that he had to do something

nice for the boy next door, even though he'd much rather tie
him to a flagpole and steal his bicycle.

"I'm giving you an assignment, Trecchio." The words came
out as if it disgusted Laterza to say them.

Alexander was startled. Management was generally happy
to let him troll for stories himself.

"What sort of assignment?"

Laterza scowled. "There's been some sort of activity over
at St. Peter's—something about the cripple standing upright.
Quite the buzz online since the end of this morning's Mass.
Surely you've heard?"

"Online buzz doesn't do much for me," Alexander
answered. "The bastion of idiots and gossips."

"Well, those idiots and gossips have been hopping for the
past two hours, and their hype is spreading." Laterza gave
him a pitying look. "Some of them have footage. Surely even
you can make a story out of that."

The Vatican: 9:31 a.m.

"Seal the doors. Do it now."

The voice of Cardinal Secretary of State Donato Viteri
was rich and resonant. He'd held his post, the highest in the
Vatican city state apart from the pontiff himself, for twenty-
three years, through the reigns of three different popes. The
tall, broad-shouldered man was known for being neither
friendly nor verbose: the kind of elderly clerical adminis-
trator that anyone who knew the Vatican considered old
school and the droves of faithful everywhere else rarely
encountered. Viteri was a man whose spirituality resided
within, never bubbling to the surface in shows of piety or
overt reverence—a prelate more at home behind a desk
than an altar, who prayed with the same businesslike tones
in which he conducted meetings or oversaw political func-
tions. His love for the Church, he occasionally said, was

manifest in a commanding, untiring practicality in overseeing its affairs. He did not give sermons but orders; and when he spoke, he expected to be obeyed.

"Which doors?" The commandant of the Swiss Guard, Christoph Raber, stood next to him, still in his colorful ceremonial attire from the Mass that had concluded only minutes before. Holding the rank of *oberst*, colonel, the highest of all military ranks in the Holy See and held by only one man, Raber was a bulky officer, pure muscle over firm bone, which even the billows of the formal attire could not make look less than fiercely imposing. In the hierarchical world of the Vatican, only the Pope and Cardinal Viteri himself were in a position to give Raber orders.

"All of them," the cardinal completed his command.

A pause, long and awkward. But then, Raber thought to himself, everything that morning had been awkward. Inexplicable. The commandant, despite his long years of experience, had not yet fully regained his composure from the Mass.

"All of them?"

Viteri repeated the command, his voice exuding a finality that was not open to question. He rested his aging eyes directly on Raber. In this moment they were not the stalwart windows into an unflappable soul they were renowned to be. The cardinal's brown eyes were troubled, the deep crow's feet at their corners furrowed into trenches, as if the gravity of his instruction had affected the deliverer as much as the recipient.

Oberst Raber's own expression only gave indication of his surprise for a fraction of a second. He'd had too many years of training to permit it to linger any longer. But underneath, the commandant's surprise was overwhelming. In all his decades of service, such an order had never been issued.

"The whole basilica?"

St. Peter's was a vast structure. Built to the aggrandizing standards of a pope who had inadvertently fostered the

Protestant Reformation by seeking to pay for it by selling indulgences to the masses, it covered over five acres of land, with more than 163,000 square feet of floor space and one of the largest worshipping enclosures on the planet, where a walk from the main doors to the chancel was more than an eighth of a mile beneath soaring, gilded ceilings. And though parts of it were at various times closed to the public and lesser members of the clergy, it was unheard of for the whole complex to be locked down. St. Peter's was the heart of Christendom, the seat of the Lord's reign on earth, and it would not shut its doors until the end of time.

"No," Cardinal Viteri answered, "not the basilica."

Despite his best efforts at stoicism, Raber could feel the features change on his face. Even legendary Swiss unflappability had its limits. If the Cardinal Secretary of State had not meant St. Peter's, then Viteri could only have intended his instruction to relate to one thing.

"Your Eminence, you mean the . . ." Raber's voice trailed off.

"Every gate. Every street. Every point of entry," Cardinal Viteri confirmed.

He placed an old hand on the commander's shoulder, his gold episcopal ring shimmering in the basilica's orange light. Viteri's grip was as firm as his stare.

"Clear the remaining people out of here," he said, motioning toward the worshippers and tourists still filling the church, "then shut down the Vatican."

3

Polizia di Stato, Monteverde XVI Station, Rome: 9:34 a.m.

The Monteverde XVI branch of the Italian Polizia di Stato is an uninspiring building perched midway through a residential block in an urban district near the center of the city. Most who pass it by do so without knowing that the unimpressive facade conceals one of Rome's most active police departments, its members working in concert with the Carabinieri and the Guardia di Finanza to complete the local infrastructure of Italy's fantastically complex national policing system.

Within the bowels of the station, in an office even more uninspiring than the building that housed it, Ispettore Gabriella Fierro sighed a long, frustrated breath. The desk at which she sat was factory-produced metal, and to say that it favored functionality over form would be to commit an act of spectacular understatement. It was ugly, as were the crooked metal shelves along one wall and the two aluminum filing cabinets on another, both of which looked like they'd been battered and tired since the day they were made. There were no windows, and Gabriella had never bothered to decorate the walls with plaques or posters. It had never seemed worth the effort. No one came to Inspector Fierro to be impressed with credentials. Few entered her office at all. And ugly was ugly, even if you threw a poster over it.

Gabriella glanced down at her diminutive Bulova watch, one of the few luxuries in her otherwise rather plain life. She had a rumbling in her stomach. For normal people, lunch would only be a few hours away, but she knew that wasn't going to be her lot. Not today. If she was going to get a lunch break at all, it was going to have to come much later. She was buried beneath a pile of paperwork that would make Atlas himself cower, and every time she risked getting through it, her repugnant supervisor, Sostituto Commissario Enzo D'Antonio, added more to the pile.

It was going to be a long, long day.

Gabriella Fierro had been with the Polizia di Stato for over four years, and each of those had been a battle with her boss. When she'd initially graduated out of cadet status, D'Antonio had kept her at the base rank of *agente* far longer than would have been normal. For a time Gabriella had wondered whether she would retire from the force at the same rank she held when she entered; but eventually D'Antonio had granted her a promotion, forced into the act when a case she'd led two years ago had made the national news. He'd given her that file as a write-off—a gift intended to humiliate and disappoint. But sometimes gifts surprise the giver. The case had turned out to be major news: financial scandals in the Church, a murdered cardinal overseas. Her supervisor hadn't been able to prevent her earning a few stripes from the affair, but he'd given them grudgingly.

The source of D'Antonio's animosity toward her remained a mystery to Gabriella, though she had her ideas. The fact that she was a woman clearly rubbed him the wrong way, in a predictably misogynist manner. That alone was probably enough to account for his hostility—a woman daring to stick her toes into a man's territory. Add in that she knew she was fairly good-looking and it made matters worse. If she had to be a woman, at least she could have done D'Antonio the courtesy of being as ugly a woman as he was a man. And then there was the fact that she had grown up a pious Catholic, and managed somehow to remain one in her adulthood. An individual as openly antagonistic toward belief of any kind as D'Antonio wasn't going to count her faith as a strong point.

Maybe they were all factors; maybe it was something else entirely. At the end of the day, the only sure thing was that the Deputy Commissioner of the Monteverde XVI station loathed his subordinate inspector and made no attempt to hide it.

Take the fact that she was here, in the office, today. Gabriella had been assigned to work Sundays every week for the past two years. There was nothing coincidental in this. Attending Sunday Mass—once a cherished tradition—had become only a memory, wiped out of present experience by her boss. She now had to settle for weekday services and lunch breaks on a Sunday, when at least she could go and reflect quietly by herself.

Generally, about throttling her boss. Though occasionally she did try to pray.

Today, if she was to get the chance, she was going to have to buckle down and focus on the extra work. And that meant ignoring the louder-than-usual chatter taking place in the station's kitchen-cum-coffee-break-room, just beyond her office door. There had been a bustle around the station for the past hour, giving the normally quiet morning air something of a buzz. "Something's going on at the Vatican," was all Gabriella had been able to make out through the thin walls—but she'd heard it multiple times, spoken each time with increasing vigor. Her personal interest in church matters was enough to propel her toward her internet connection a few minutes ago, just to find out what it was. And yet—fates be damned—at precisely the moment her finger hovered before the desktop's power button, her supervisor had appeared in the doorway. D'Antonio himself, in all his greasy glory, with a stack of documents under his arm. Three new files. Time-critical. "Report back to me within thirty minutes with a status update."

Time-critical.

If that wasn't the joke of the week. Nothing that D'Antonio handed to Inspector Fierro was ever critical, time- or other-wise.

But he was still her boss. Gabriella drew her finger away from the computer. Its screen remained dark. The bustle outside would have to wait.

Headquarters of La Repubblica newspaper: 9:40 a.m.

At first glance, the story looked like a let-down to Alexander and he immediately began to suspect his editor was using it to punish him. In terms of public interest, there was far more activity online about the recent surfing death of Abigaille Zola, a rising teen actress whose world of fandom was taking to the internet to express its grief. That was the kind of material, inconsequential as it was, that was on the front pages in this country. Fashionistas and celebrities, even dead, made great cover.

By contrast, the first reports coming in about the "buzz" to which Alexander's editor had referred seemed to indicate nothing more than a man who'd disrupted the Sunday morning papal Mass.

Chrissakes, let's rush to press.

An intrusion on normal Vatican propriety might, perhaps, be worth a mention in the paper—the kind of interestingly uninteresting dross that caused people to read articles on Coca-Cola shipping centers being disrupted in India, or soap production plants in Mexico suffering power shortages, despite the fact that these had no conceivable bearing or impact on their everyday lives. But a story this was not. Had the murmurs been that the man had walked into church stark naked, chanting anti-Western rants or speaking in tongues, preferably carrying a banner that read "Screw the capitalist agenda," Alexander might have the chance of making something of him.

But then new phrases had started to emerge on his web search. Accounts of impromptu silences amongst the faithful. Talk of strange behavior from the Swiss Guard. And when Alexander read the words "healing" and "Pope" in the same sentence on the tiny screen of his phone, he knew that more research was going to be necessary, if only to set his mind at rest that there really was no story here.

He fired up the surprisingly new computer on an otherwise entirely out-of-date desk. The old brown phone at its corner had barely blazed its way out of the rotary-dial generation, the ashtray had a faded enamel image celebrating the 1989 ascension of Giulio Andreotti to the office of prime minister, and the newest of the books piled up at the edges of a mess of papers were published decades before e-books had digitized their way into existence. By contrast, the Acer Aspire S7 laptop was shiny and new. Alexander had much preferred its dinosaur of a predecessor, with its green screen and advanced electronics capable of only two modes: "word processor" and "off." That was his kind of dinosaur. But he'd been forced into the internet age and the requirement of a new computer when hand-held cameras and video phones had transferred news-gathering into the reach of the general populace. He, like every other reporter in the world, needed a computer capable of looking at it. He even had a "smartphone," a word almost too ridiculous to be said aloud in serious company.

But it meant he could keep tabs on what the internet was up to, which was what he needed to do now. The events at St. Peter's had made their way on to the net through various camera clips that had instantly become YouTube and Vimeo videos. At the very least he owed the story the time it took to watch the incident.

He clicked one of the links from a search engine. There were at least twenty at the top of the results, which for the first time gave Alexander pause. Whatever else might be said of the incident he was investigating, it had obviously attracted public attention, and far more of it than he would have expected. Which meant his editor had been at least partially correct.

Shit.

The video began to play, and Alexander tried to swallow his annoyance and pay attention. It was a square-framed, low-resolution recording taken from a camera phone. There was a jumble of noise coming from his speakers—a choir in the background, the Mass obviously in progress.

In an instant, he was transported. He was there: vested, abluted, standing before the altar, a young priest once again. He could smell the incense, see the familiar instruments of the office set out before him. His maternal uncle, the beloved Cardinal Rinaldo Trecchio, who had helped him make his way into the life of the Church, stood at his side, beaming with pride. Everything was familiar. *Known.* And in that moment he again had a solid faith.

The memory shook him. Everything in Alexander's life had once been so firm, so stable. Even as far back as high school his faith seemed to grow year by year, and with his uncle's help he'd entered the seminary the summer after graduation. He'd had that family support every step of the way as he'd been ordained deacon and then priest, traveling with his uncle to Rome for the occasion, then back to New York to settle into his first parish assignment. He'd begun a life of holy work. A life he intended to maintain until he died.

But his faith was not as sturdy as he'd assumed. Within a few years it had started to falter. The longer Alexander was involved in church life as a priest, the more he'd come to realize how deeply he struggled with the actions of the men around him. He'd always believed that those called to serve the Church were meant to be bastions of virtue, examples of piety and morality. When he'd discovered that they often had dark secrets, sometimes far deeper than other men, it had torn at his faith.

But in this instant, as he heard the music of St. Peter's waft through his diminutive computer speakers, it all returned. He was there once again. He had not grown disillusioned; he did not battle his conscience. He simply allowed the beauty to overwhelm him, to inspire him, to fill him with . . .

The instant passed, as it always did, and Alexander was back. He pulled deeply on his cigarette, shaking off the unwelcome feeling. It was said that familiar memories lost their sting, that time healed wounds, but in Alexander's experience these were just trite lies. Old memories remained as traumatic as ever.

He forced his attention back to the video clip. Over the heads of worshippers the angle panned to the left, toward the central aisle of the cathedral. There, though a clear view was obscured by countless bodies, the attention of the crowd had coalesced on a man walking slowly toward the front of the church.

Alexander's left eyebrow rose, its motion always taking the lead over the right. It was his usual reaction when something took him by surprise.

Even through the blockish granularity of the video, something about the man was . . . compelling. Alexander leaned in toward the monitor as the scene continued to unfold. Suddenly he found the low resolution of the recording immensely frustrating and wished he could be seeing this in clearer tones.

The noises crackling through the minuscule speakers faded as a hush overcame the crowd. As the man walked, he seemed to be accompanied only by the angelic sounds of the choir.

The Swiss Guard fell to the ground, the choir faltered. And then came a scene he never could have imagined. Alexander Trecchio, who had been ordained eleven years before in that same basilica, his face pressed against the cold stone floor as his body lay prostrate in the form of a cross, watched as the man approached the Pope across the altar. He gazed into his face and spoke softly, words that Alexander could not hear.

When, a moment later, the crippled Pope stood upright, Alexander felt his skin go cold.

There had been many intruders into the Vatican in the past, many men claiming to be angels or prophets or even Christ returned. But never had one infiltrated a Mass, much less so quietly, peacefully. Never had one brought the Swiss Guard to their knees.

And never, never had one healed a pope who stood before the throne of God.

4

Rome: 9:42 a.m.

Across the city, the morning sun shone a golden light through the office window of an underpaid, aging professor by the name of Salvatore Tosi. The light shimmered across leather book spines, custom-made picture frames and the surroundings of a man who had less than ten minutes to live.

The two figures that had walked into Tosi's office a few minutes before, unannounced and most certainly unwelcome, knew that this morning's death was to be the first of many. Death came to every man—that could not be changed. They simply helped it along, when required. It was necessary work, sacred in its own way, and they undertook it with devotion.

This morning's task had come upon them suddenly, the scope of their commissioned work potentially extensive, though they knew neither its full contours nor its intended ends. They rarely did—they were passed solely the data they needed to get the job done.

It was background work, they'd been informed, to ensure "the advent of a miracle."

"We've told you already," one of the figures said to the trembling Salvatore, now tied fast to his wooden chair, "that your silence will bring only torment. Tell us what you know. Everything you were planning to use to expose the Messiah." It was a strange term to use, but they'd been told that was the image at play. "The quicker you tell us what you know, the less painful this will be."

Salvatore's bound wrists were already bleeding. Sweat soaked the skinny middle-aged man's armpits, tears stinging his vision as his attention moved back and forth between the two intruders. Their strange calmness was designed to upset him and was having its intended effect.

"I've told you before, I know nothing!" he cried, spittle streaming from his mouth as the panicked words escaped his throat. "I don't know why you've come to me!"

"Lies, Salvatore, will get you nowhere. They will merely bring you more pain. Only the truth can set you free."

Salvatore blanched. "I'm not lying! I don't know your 'Messiah.' *I don't know what you're talking about!* Please!"

"If you won't cooperate, then this is going to have to be . . . difficult," the second figure answered. The gleam in his eye suggested that this did not disappoint him.

Salvatore pleaded. "Tell me what you want. I can help you. Maybe I can give you something!" He waved his head desperately at the surroundings of his office. The small academic chamber was filled with a collection of artifacts that looked to be worth a decent sum—the accumulated trappings of a moderately successful professional life. Some small, apparently ancient statuary. Carved figurines. A few examples of original artwork.

The two intruders' stoic calm persisted. It was clear they were not interested in his trinkets.

"Who are you?" Salvatore asked, his terror now complete.

"You'd be surprised how many people ask that question," the first intruder answered, "but does it really ever matter? We could be men, or demons, or angels. Is there any answer that would comfort you?" There was a slight twist at the edge of his lips. Was it a smile? *Did men such as this smile?* "I can tell you," he added wryly, "it's never comforted anyone else."

Salvatore's expression was panicked, though bitterness crept in at the man's words. There was a hint of piety in him and these men offended it. He felt his anger growing. "Angels don't come with ties and threats and . . . knives." He tried not to stare at the sheathed blade conspicuously present on the left man's hip.

"I've been told they come in many forms." The response was emotionless. "But I'm no theologian." The man allowed his eyes to lock with Salvatore's, transmitting his meaning through the tense space, already filled with the stench of terrified sweat.

Then he broke eye contact, reached down toward the knife and released it from its leather hold.

"But I do like that imagery. Angels, the messengers of God," he said. "You seem a religious man. Maybe the thought will aid you." He abruptly took a step closer to the trembling Salvatore, the knife blade coming up to his chest as he leaned in and breathed into his sweat-covered face.

"Because by God, these messengers are going to make you speak."

5

Headquarters of La Repubblica newspaper: 10:40 a.m.

However scarred I might be, I still have enough respect to expose a fraud. Even a fraud in the Church.

The thought came vividly into Alexander Trecchio's mind. There were many ways to describe a broken relationship, but no term perfectly fitted his lingering relationship to the Church. He usually characterized it as dysfunctional: he didn't hate the Church, but he didn't love it. He certainly would no longer describe himself as a man of faith, but he was not without the lingering tendrils of respect. At least enough respect to expose a quack.

And a quack was exactly what Alexander knew the stranger at St. Peter's had to be, despite what he'd seen on the screen. After the strange entrancement of his first video-based vision of the man's appearance had been supplemented by five additional online clips, Alexander had puffed through a new cigarette and determined three things in quick succession.

First, there was nothing supernatural about the stranger, despite the online hype and rampant speculation. He was a man, plain and simple. All other considerations aside, and mundane as the fact might be, the video clearly showed him to be wearing jeans with a label over the back pocket. Alexander doubted that Levi Strauss had a manufacturing branch in the Great Beyond.

Second, he was obviously charismatic, which explained the mesmerized reaction of the crowd and the clergy—indeed, even the strange entrancement Alexander had felt when watching the footage. This made the man even more loathsome in Trecchio's eyes. Charisma was an easy tool to wield against the unwary, and one never had to look far to find examples of charismatic men leading others to do deplorable things.

And third, this was a story after all. Alexander could no longer pretend it wasn't, or that interest in it would dissipate on its own. The most visible man in Christendom had been "healed," by all appearances, and in plain view. This would reverberate worldwide. Already the internet had taken flight, the posted videos starting off a chain reaction of social media activity that was consuming the digitized generation throughout Rome and spreading outside the city. The Twitter hashtags #StrangerInTheVatican and #PopeHealed had been trending for over an hour. There were already three community pages established on Facebook to assess whether the man who had affected the pontiff was an insane vagrant or a divine visitor. Unsurprisingly, opinion was about evenly split. People were just as anxious to believe in the supernatural as they were to mock the sub-par. The human condition at its finest, made all the more fragmentary and divisive when questions of faith came into view.

And it was that ingredient that made this story troubling. Alexander was a man who had struggled long with his own faith before finally letting it go. He'd grown up far too Catholic for him to consider God's existence as anything other than a fact, and even today he wouldn't risk the audacity of saying he didn't believe in God at all. He was too close to his uncle, the cardinal who had tolerated Alexander's wandering but would never put up with "that kind of defeatist nonsense." But Alexander certainly didn't believe in the Church. He'd been too intimately involved in ecclesiastical life not to be scathed by it, and the psychological scars that resulted gave evidence of being just as permanent as the physical variety. He'd seen the worst of men claiming the best of God, and it had driven him further and further away.

Still, what lingered wasn't hate. He'd left the clergy, walked away from the embrace of an institution that millions called Mother, and his faith—whatever that really was—had dissipated until it was only a memory. Yet some faint tendril of an attachment remained. And the man who had taken the helm since his departure seemed a decent and well-intentioned pontiff. Too bad he hadn't been around sooner.

But that very fact brought out a fourth curiosity, one that made Alexander far more uncomfortable than the other three: what was the Pope's involvement in this? Alexander had watched the man stand upright with his own eyes—an action the whole world knew was impossible. But this was the Pope, not a swindling faith healer's audience plant. Catholics in every nation on the globe knew of his childhood illness, knew the story of his struggles against physical restriction to climb higher and higher in church life. He had been in the public eye for decades. Always crippled. Always physically broken.

What the hell is going on?

Whatever it was, it stank of deception. Alexander had watched too many sick people die in his years as a priest to believe that God spontaneously healed the suffering. Those things he'd witnessed and been willing to call miracles had always been interior: the transformation of sorrow into peace, the calming of hearts torn by grief. God tended to be a quiet actor in Alexander's experience, not a showman who performed parlor tricks, even if the backdrop was the Vatican.

All of which meant something was afoot. Alexander knew instinctively that his chances of getting anywhere with the curia were non-existent. The church wasn't known for talking to the press, even on a good day. That meant no line to the magisterium, which in turn meant that focusing squarely on the Pope would get him nowhere.

He had to go after the stranger, and see what he could dig up on the man.

Strangely, that task inspired a powerful zeal within him. He almost didn't know what to make of it. But for the first time he could remember, Alexander felt enthusiastic about his job.

6

The Apostolic Palace, Vatican City: 11:09 a.m.

"Cardinal Viteri, come in," the Pope announced, speaking loudly so that his voice would carry to the far side of the large room. A few seconds later, a wooden door slid open and the familiar shape of his Secretary of State stepped into the office, closing the door behind him. Viteri said nothing, but walked solemnly toward the pontiff. The Pope observed his approach in contemplative silence.

His Holiness Pope Gregory XVII of Rome had sat upon the throne of St. Peter for less than twelve months, and already his life had changed more times than he could articulate. It had changed at that moment in the conclave's third round of voting, the frescos of Michelangelo's Sistine Chapel soaring majestically above them and the scents of antiquity filling the space, when the deciding vote had been read aloud by the Cardinal Dean from a slip of paper deposited in the chalice. The much-speculated possibility of his being named the next

Bishop of Rome and Supreme Pontiff of the Church had, in that instant, become reality.

It had changed in the moment they had first lain the white robes upon him, veiled his shoulders in scarlet and led him to the balcony of St. Peter's to address his people. The moment when Cardinal Antonio Pavesi, as he had been before the conclave, had vanished and the world had been introduced to Pope Gregory. He had set his eyes on the vast crowd that afternoon, itself only a tiny fraction of his billion-strong flock, and felt the weight of the awesome responsibility God had given him.

It had changed in those first weeks of his papacy, as he had come to know the inner workings of the curia more intimately—the good as well as the bad—and had become aware that it was down to him to call it toward a higher standard of life.

It had changed, too, the morning he had celebrated his first papal High Mass over the bones of the chief of the Apostles, St. Peter, entombed in glory beneath the majestic dome of the basilica that bore his name. The church had been packed, the whole world watching, and in that moment Gregory had felt closer to heaven than ever before in his thirty-nine years of ministry.

And it had changed this morning, when during the angelic service he had met . . . him.

The Pope didn't know what to call the man who had appeared before him during the Mass. He didn't know what to think of him. He didn't know how to interpret the strange, unexplained fire burning in his heart. He only knew that at this moment he sat upright, which he had never before done. That he'd walked himself into his apartments, alone, for the first time in his life. That he could stand straight. Whole. *Healed*.

That God was somehow speaking to him. It was terrifying, and it was awe-inspiring.

"I want all the cardinals summoned back to the Vatican," he announced to his Secretary of State as the towering man reached his desk. "I want them here within twenty four hours, if not sooner."

"Your Holiness," Cardinal Viteri answered, shaking his balding head, seemingly startled by the sudden command, "it will take longer than that for such arrangements to be made."

"Exercise expediency, Donato," the pontiff replied. "I want them here now." He did not feel the urge to explain himself further to the older cardinal.

"As Your Holiness wishes." A long, tense silence passed.

"I have already isolated Vatican City," Viteri eventually added. "We shall be alone within these walls for as long as you see fit."

"Good," the Pope muttered. His eyes were elsewhere.

"Would you like anyone else brought in?"

"No." He looked to the Secretary of State. "Have the bishops tend to the functioning of the churches. Issue an instruction for all parishes throughout the world to celebrate a daily Mass of intention."

Viteri hesitated. A global call for Masses dedicated to specific causes was not made lightly, or often.

"For what intention precisely, Holiness?"

Pope Gregory looked past him to a gilded wooden crucifix on the far wall of his office. That was the question. *For what?* He sighed softly. For now, there could be only one answer.

"For the will of God to be revealed."

7

Above Rome: 12:17 p.m.

Drago Lazzari gazed out from the curved Plexiglas of the Radio-
televisione Italiana RAI 2 news helicopter, scanning the territory beneath him through the viewfinder of his ARRI Amira
camera. He never tired of the spectacular scenery and up-
close aerial views that few people had the privilege to see.
Drago considered his post as airborne videographer one of
the best at the station, and he felt intimately familiar with
every corner of Rome. At least, from above.

The Roman skyline always looked majestic, and there
were few sights to rival the view from the vantage points of
the Eternal City's famed seven hills. But from the air it was
something else entirely: an undulating sea of ancient brickwork and even more ancient roads, punctuated by domes
and towers that shimmered orange beneath the large Mediterranean sun. It was an image of the past, painted out like
a great canvas from the hands of one of the Renaissance artists it had housed. The haze from the automobiles crowding

its streets provided a glow that made the vast city look even more like a dreamscape.

But little of that interested Drago today. His focus was solely on a singular, narrow plot of land: the 110-acre expanse of the world's smallest city state.

Vatican City had sealed its walls less than an hour after the appearance at St. Peter's of what people were already calling "the stranger." The world had seen a miracle, and then the doors had been closed. Had been *slammed* closed. Church officials had given no reason for the action. They seemed intent on keeping the public in the dark as to what was taking place internally in response to the inexplicable transformation of the Holy Father. *And the identity of the man who had wrought it.* And with a few notable exceptions, the Vatican had a pretty good track record of keeping secrets and closing out public scrutiny when it chose to.

But they could not seal off the skies.

Drago scoped out the walled compound through the camera's powerful telephoto lens. The helicopter's pilot maintained the legally mandated sovereignty of the Vatican's airspace, keeping the craft outside the immediate vertical territory above the state, which meant a necessarily oblique camera angle. But this could be worked around. Drago had worked under such conditions before.

He swept the lens from one courtyard to another, each pause in the viewfinder's path framing a scene that was printed on a million postcards sold in the shops below. The Vatican was so small that every public corner was known the world over. Yet despite its tiny size, nearly half of its interior space was closed off to the public, rarely seen by any but the Church's innermost circle and the holders of its highest offices. And what was hidden was as beautiful as what was revealed. Behind gates and walls were narrow cobblestone pathways that ran through manicured gardens into palaces and offices that had housed some of the greatest religious figures of Europe.

Drago panned the frame to his left. A bustle of activity caught his eye on a balcony near the Apostolic Palace, but as he increased the zoom he saw it was only a domestic worker, sweeping away dust and debris from the orange-tiled surface.

A few dozen meters to the right, a large tree swayed in the gentle breeze. Drago swung slowly in its direction, his senses at their height.

Then he caught it. The sight he needed—and something well beyond anything he could have hoped for.

The Santa Anna garden was tiny, barely more than a bench on a patch of well-watered grass surrounded by flowers and containing a minuscule, if artistic, fountain. It was a private escape within a private world. But at this moment, to Drago, it was the most glorious spot on earth. For it was surrounded by far more of a Swiss Guard presence than could ever be thought normal—they were at every exit, even along the walls. And bizarrely, they were all facing inward, interested not so much in those who might invade this small space, as in keeping an eye on those who were already within it.

The Pope himself sat on the solitary bench at its center. His white cassock and zucchetto marked him out with perfect clarity, even from so far above.

And beside him was the man that Drago recognized as the stranger.

They were talking, nestled in this intimate surrounding, seemingly oblivious to anything beyond the tiny expanse and its walls.

And then—by the blissful fortune of divine providence, a moment after Drago thumbed the record button—the Pope leaned down and kissed the other man's hand.

The skin of his guest's hand felt soft against Gregory's lips. As a Catholic since birth, he had kissed bishops' and cardinals' hands a thousand times in his life, but since ascending the throne of St. Peter, that had changed. Today, though, in this moment, the sign of affection and humility felt right.

The man sitting next to him on the bench had a warmth about his person that had nothing to do with the sunshine of the early afternoon. He gripped the Pope's hand in return, smiling. In the distance, a guardsman appeared to tense at the gesture. But the Pope had instructed them not to interrupt his discussion.

"You realize," the stranger said softly, a thumping noise beating in the air high above, "that your world is about to become far less calm."

Pope Gregory sighed. It was not exasperation, simply acceptance. "So be it." He wasn't sure why he felt so confident accepting what lay before him. He had more questions than a mind could contain. Doubts. Anxieties. Fears. Yet they all, somehow, seemed to give way to an unexpected trust.

"You're ready to face a storm?"

Gregory reflected silently. "My predecessor in this office," he finally answered, gazing out at the serene landscape, "the first to hold it, was once called to step out of a boat and walk on a stormy sea."

The stranger smiled softly. "Your point, Your Holiness?"

"My point is that he had to step on to the water whether he was ready or not."

"St. Peter had help," the stranger answered.

The Pope turned to face his guest. Their eyes locked long before he finally spoke.

"So do I."

The frenzy that broke out in Rome twenty minutes later consumed the city. For all that the ancient capital seemed, on a day-to-day basis, unconcerned by the affairs of the church headquartered on the plot of land at her heart, it loved nothing more than those rare occasions when two thousand years of tradition confronted a moment of singular irregularity and the strange life of the Church suddenly took center stage.

When RAI 2 broadcast the live footage of His Holiness the Pope kissing the hand of the man who only hours earlier had stood at the high altar of St. Peter's and, by all accounts, healed him, that craving exploded into a storm of attention. Drago Lazzari's footage broke through the afternoon news, streaming live on to tens of thousands of televisions. Within minutes it was the fastest-trending video on YouTube within Italy.

Within twenty minutes, it was trending internationally.

Before an hour had passed, it was the most watched online video anywhere in the world.

8

The way into a story is research. Research requires sources. And chasing up sources is a skill at which every reporter, however meager his remit, is forced by necessity to excel.

When live feeds of the Pope kissing the hand of the stranger in the Vatican gardens started to roll out across television channels throughout Rome, Alexander realized he was going to have to switch into a far faster gear than that in which he usually worked. He needed sources to talk to, and he needed them now. The little story he'd been handed was fast turning into the biggest news event in recent memory.

But so far, no one was willing to talk.

A stranger in the Vatican was interesting. The healing of a pope was impressive. The pontiff's act of reverence toward another man was unusual. But as yet it was all something that hard-and-fast sources—people with credentials, with substantive things to offer that papers and editors counted as credible and therefore printed—wouldn't touch. It was *sensational*.

Line up a conclave to elect a new pope and scholars and politicians would trip over their robes to offer expert opinions on historical precedents, future pathways of moral leadership or any other matter, however incidental, that might put their name in the press as expert commentators or talking heads.

But set up a situation where a man the internet buzz was calling "a divine visitor" works an inexplicable miracle and heals the unhealable, in a *church*, no less, and those same experts didn't want to come near the story. Conversations about God and miracles might be the stuff of wonder for the religious, but they were tantamount to a leper's touch to credentialed commentators.

Alexander lit up a new cigarette in frustration. At least a dozen phone calls over the past twenty minutes had resulted in the same disappointment. He was getting nowhere.

In front of him, his Twitter feed raced through refreshes at a speed he'd never before seen. Ironic. None of the people he wanted to speak to were talking, but it seemed like everyone else was.

Santa Maria in Trastevere, Rome: 2:04 p.m.

What does it mean to truly believe? To know beyond doubt that you are here, that you are never far from my side? O Lord, I believe. Help my disbelief.

Gabriella Fierro whispered her prayers silently from her customary perch at the end of the sixth pew in Santa Maria in Trastevere. Her lunch break had finally come, a good two hours into the afternoon, and she'd immediately made her way to her preferred spot in all of Rome. She'd at last escaped the clutches of her boss, wholly deprived of any interaction with the buzz going on outside her office door all morning. But she hadn't arrived here ready to curse him, as she'd thought she might. She was genuinely in need of refreshment. Of spiritual strength. And D'Antonio had no part to play in that.

Gabriella had discovered the Santa Maria in Trastevere church in her teens and it had been her personal sanctuary ever since—despite an encounter two years ago in which it had suddenly become anything but peaceful. Gunshots and death in an ancient shrine were hard to put from one's mind, but she'd not allowed them to rob her of her one place of solace.

She sat with the creases of her beige slacks running in neatly parallel lines down her legs, pressed together with her hands folded on her lap. Her hazel eyes stayed open as she stared up at the shimmering mosaic that covered the apse behind the altar. She knew that most people prayed with their eyes closed, but what were these glorious scenes for, if not to help a heart draw closer to God? And in a life as demarcated by the lonely lines of the struggle for advancement as hers, such closeness was precisely what she desired. If she couldn't find it with another human being, she would take it with God.

Gabriella supposed she'd always believed in God in some way or another. That had been true even in the long years of her difficult childhood, before her family had discovered the Church. She wouldn't have known what to call him, or what to make of him, back then. But then she and her parents had undergone a kind of family conversion, and no one had taken their entrance into the Catholic faith more seriously than Gabriella. For a while, in her late teens, she'd even considered becoming a nun. She'd spent a summer as a postulant at the Convent of Our Lady of Perpetual Mercy, living with the sisters and waiting for God to call her fully into the habit. But that call hadn't come.

She'd been disappointed at the result, but it hadn't dulled her piety. Now, looking back through her thirty-one-year-old life, she could see that her faith had always stayed with her—which in the midst of so many other trials was a source of comfort.

Still, that didn't make it straightforward. As Gabriella experienced more of life, she was coming to appreciate the scripture's strange statement all the more personally. *Lord, I believe. Help my disbelief.* How strange a mystery, the human heart, that it could contain belief and disbelief in apparently equal measure. That it could be afraid of that which supposedly did away with fear.

The crooked orange light that beamed through the high windows of the church glinted on the colored tiles of the thirteenth-century mosaics. Christ sat enthroned on his marble seat wearing white and flowing gold. The Blessed Virgin was at his right, while around them a host of apostles and bishops gathered in pious council. Beneath Christ's feet were a flock of sheep, artfully produced from white stone and keeping their gaze upon their chief shepherd. High above, blue and white rays of mosaic light poured down from the Holy Spirit, represented by a tiny dove.

Gabriella gazed longingly at the image. The picture was perfect. It was the vision of a harmony and peace so rarely echoed in the world she knew outside.

As if on cue, the tiny Nokia in her breast pocket started to buzz. For the first time since entering the space, Gabriella closed her eyes, forcing herself not to capstone her moment of retreat with anger at the intrusion. Work was work. It was going to break through the silence eventually. Her boss would make sure of that.

Opening her eyes once again, she made the sign of the cross and slid out of the side of the old pew into the church's center aisle. Genuflecting toward the altar, she turned and walked to the exit. With each step the pious, humble woman was transformed into the professional that Gabriella Fierro had to be at all times outside these walls.

As she approached the door, she reached into her jacket
pocket and retrieved the tiny buzzing phone. She'd been left
alone for nearly forty-five minutes. That was far longer than
she usually got. Maybe miracles really did happen.

She flipped open the phone. The station's familiar number
flashed on the display.

Pulling the thin floral silk scarf from the top of her head
and bundling it into her bag, she shook loose her golden-
blond hair. She stepped through the doors into the colon-
naded portico that led to the Piazza di Santa Maria. The
afternoon hour in the popular quarter meant that, as usual,
it was buzzing with young, fashionable types filling the cafés
that poured out on to street-side tables.

She took a refreshing breath. Her break was over. The
phone was at her ear, and over the bustle around her she
began to speak.

"Hello, this is Inspector Fierro."

Another woman's voice sounded from the far end of the
line. Agente Flora Costanzo was one of the few members of
the Monteverde XVI station whom Gabriella considered a
close friend. A fellow woman battling it out in a man's pro-
fession in a man's universe, and under the same oppressive
thumb of the man they both called boss. And Flora was still
several rungs down the ladder, poor thing.

"Gabriella, where are you?" she asked.

"Where am I always at around this time?"

"You're in church? Holy shit, it's Sunday. I forgot."

Gabriella cringed at her friend's irreverent language. Flora
wasn't a believer, though she did Gabriella the favor of treating church matters with as much reverence as she could
muster. Which wasn't all that much.

Her next words were less irreverent than puzzling.

"I take it you've heard, then?"

Gabriella's movement hesitated before the steps of the
massive fountain at the center of the piazza.

"Heard what?"

"Christ, Gabriella! You, of all people! I thought you prayed to the man, after all!"

Another cringe, but now Gabriella was confused. "Flora, who are you talking about? *What* are you talking about?"

"The Pope!" her friend cried down the line. "Your Supreme Leader, or Excellent Holiness, or whatever you call him."

The tightening at Gabriella's shoulders this time was more pronounced.

"What about him?" she snapped.

"He's been healed. In front of the whole damned world! And Gabriella, you won't believe who people are saying did it."

9

Headquarters of Global Capital Italia, Rome: 2:48 p.m.

The two assassins walked through the head office with impunity, a right reserved for a select few. None of the three secre-
taries en route to the corner suite so much as spoke to them
as they approached, the third only pressing a small red button
at her desk, illuminating a light in the room beyond, which
gave indication to its inhabitant that visitors were imminent.

"You're late."

The words came in a cold, almost robotic tone. The CEO
didn't look up at the brothers as they entered. Umberto and
Tommaso, who was always known as Maso and had the servile
habit of calling his elder brother "boss," were familiar figures.

"We came when we'd finished our task. Tosi is out of the
picture. So is the other one."

The two men stood before the vast glass desk in the thoroughly modern office, but—as always in these meetings—
only Umberto spoke. He, like Maso, was dressed in a sleekly
fitted black Armani suit, and was cleanly shaven and

groomed to an impeccable degree. His chin was heavyset but not obtrusive, giving his face the angular proportions of a Soviet statue, bold and sleek and strangely disconcerting. His eyelashes were so thick they risked appearing fake, and behind them were blue eyes that seemed to glisten, even in the dim professional lighting of the office.

"The academics can't be the full extent of things," the CEO answered. "The list we gave you was only a beginning."

"We're following your instructions. We'll get to the other names, and we'll add more if we turn up new individuals who might pose problems."

"How many are on your list now?"

"As of this moment, four," Umberto answered. "But Tosi and his counterpart were the most vocal threats. The others are minor, at worst."

A long silence. The firm's chief officer still hadn't looked up.

"Don't delay with them, all the same. And don't report back until they're all finished. If you need more men, you only have to say the word."

"We'll manage ourselves." There was an edge to Umberto's voice. He and Maso were considered amongst the most elite killers for hire in all of Italy; indeed, they were known beyond the borders in that strange, dark, illicit circle of people who knew about such things. They'd been all but exclusively contracted to this new employer for over four years now, but their propensity for not having others involved in their work clearly hadn't settled fully in to their employer's mind.

At last the CEO's eyes lifted upward and bore directly into his. They were somewhere between blue and hazel, but he'd never been able to look directly into them long enough to satisfy himself with a final determination. Despite his years of service and the blood in which he routinely soaked his hands, Umberto found the stare intimidating and quickly averted his gaze. He knew the reputation for brutality that lay behind it.

"I hope it's understood," the CEO said slowly, "that the reputation of this 'Messiah' must be preserved at all costs. Now that this has begun, nothing must be allowed to interfere with that directive."

"Understood."

Another long pause, then the CEO's eyes fell back to the papers on the desk.

"Then there's no more to say. Go and do your jobs."

Umberto departed the office, Maso behind him, with the mixture of emotions he always felt when he left the CEO's presence. There was work to be done, starting with making a call into their contact with the State Police to ensure that their handiwork from the morning was handled discreetly. His employer's contacts gave Umberto powerful friends, and he enjoyed wielding influence over them.

And there was the general anticipation he felt with his job as a whole. He'd worked with his brother his whole life, and though Maso was eight years his junior and far more a ruffian than a clone of Umberto's brand of sophistication, they both regarded their occupation with devotion. But this project was something special. He could sense wonders in the air. Their tasks were, he'd been told, going to generate miracles. It wasn't every day that kind of language came along in his line of work.

But there was disgust—and more immediately, annoyance—mixed with that pleasure and awe. Even after four years in the firm's employ, having taken care of work that had sent him across Italy and Europe, he still hated his meetings with the CEO. Something about them would never sit right.

It was not good for a man of his stature, of his purpose, to take orders from a woman.

The two men finally gone, Caterina Amato at last sat back in her chair, folding her hands across her lap. The firm she ran was an empire, which she had crafted from the ground up. And while the chair of any major corporation always held power, the CEO of Global Capital Italia had a kind of power few could ever dream of.

Like every empire, there was far more that went on here than met the public eye. To all outside appearances, her company was a multinational conglomerate that dealt in capital investment and finance, just like a hundred others in Italy. And ninety-nine percent of the people who worked for Global Capital Italia itself did so without any awareness of anything darker beneath the veneer—legitimate businessmen and women engaged in legitimate business.

Precisely as she wanted them to be seen. Caterina had learned the importance of covering vice in the fine veneer of legitimacy from her parents in the youngest years of her childhood. They'd taught her by example. Covering their own vice—a propensity for controlling and domineering her and her brother Davide's every move—with the outward appearance of fine culture and just the right level of class had been their chief skills.

Her father had barely noticed their existence. Her mother, an abusive woman with an internal fire fueled by an uberreligious zeal, had wanted them around only long enough to gain the image of being a good mother amongst her socialite friends. Caterina and Davide had been sent off to boarding school as soon as the image had been attained, when she was eleven and her brother fifteen. "As good Christian parents of our station have always done."

Terrible parents they may have been, but they'd taught Caterina a valuable lesson: a person can get away with just about whatever the hell he wants, so long as what he shows the world is proper, well-formed and shines with the factory-standard trappings of the legitimate.

So ninety-nine percent of Global Capital Italia was Caterina Amato's factory-standard show: the equivalent of the social club membership held by her mother to conceal the fact that when she wasn't at the club she'd hurl wine bottles at her children and steal funds from the charities she so kindly ran. A cover.

That left the other one percent of the company. They were Caterina's true colleagues. These were men—she'd always felt more comfortable around men—with the resources and power to do, and to get, what they wanted. And what they wanted was always money: incomprehensible amounts of money, but always *more,* however high the numbers rose. Some would call their attitude greedy, some obsessive. Caterina didn't really care what others termed it. Money was power, and power was like a drug. That she was addicted to this drug did not concern her. Of course she was—*of course she would be.* That was what happened when the drug was so good. She had the power to get what she wanted, and to get others to do what she wanted them to do. She could influence politicians, she could buy police. She could hire security guards that constituted small armies. All were at her disposal. All *hers.*

But with power came enemies, and if Caterina's company was an empire, then its enemies needed to be handled with brutal swiftness. Absolute destruction. Scorched earth and salted fields and bones left rotting in the street. You find an enemy and you crush him. And while certain foes couldn't simply be eliminated in traditional ways, every enemy was destined to meet its fate.

That lesson, too, she'd learned from her parents. Her mother would go to the limits of her power to eliminate from her path those she deemed a threat to her way of life, and so would Caterina. Any enemy. Every enemy.

Including those that wore white zucchettos.

Caterina Amato sat back in her leather desk chair, swiveled and gazed out over the Roman landscape beneath her. In the distance, the massive dome of St. Peter's rose over the rooftops, marking out the skyline as it had done for so many centuries.

Just the sight of it brought the familiar, biting flavor of bile into Caterina's mouth. It was the monument to her greatest hatred—one far greater than that she harbored for her parents, both now long since dead. She'd learned to manipulate, to seek control, from her mother. But from the Church Caterina had learned evil. No, not learned: experienced. She would never forget what she'd seen that holy institution do to her brother, to his peaceful spirit . . .

She forced her memories to a halt. Hatred was the automatic reflex that rose within her at the sight of the ancient basilica with its attached palaces and halls. If her company was an empire, her offices her castle, then the Vatican was the other castle on the other hill: the one whose very existence was a thorn in her side.

But today, for the first time in her life, the sight of St. Peter's didn't disgust her. Today Caterina knew with an unspeakable certainty that she would finally have her way there too.

Even with all her power, Caterina Amato couldn't just walk up and kill the Pope, an approach she'd taken with many others in her time. He was not an enemy who could be dealt with in such a way.

But sometimes there were better ways to eliminate a foe.

10

Quartiere San Lorenzo, Rome: 5:11 p.m.

Alexander shuffled slowly up the stone steps to 1118 Via Tiburtina, not far from the Roma Termini railway station. It was the location where the lone voice of any merit willing to speak about the recent events in the Vatican had indicated he was prepared to meet him, between 5:00 and 5:30 p.m. He flicked aside the smoldering end of a cigarette as he approached.

One man. That was all Alexander had been able to pluck from a not unsizeable Rolodex and a lengthy search online. Not that he could blame the others. At this point the story smelled more like fodder for tabloid media than scholarly comment, despite the Pope's apparent involvement. But it would become more, that much was certain, and Alexander had finally found one voice. Via Twitter, of all places.

The American-born Professor Marcus Crossler had a reputation for sitting at the edge of scholarly credibility, studying esoteric Christian traditions and fringe spiritual movements.

His brief bio on the Sapienza University's website listed him as Visiting Professor in Expressive Spirituality, a strange title that befitted the reputation Alexander had learned he had. Even the tiny headshot in his Twitter profile reinforced the impression. The thirty-something professor wore an inexplicable amount of tweed for a young man working in a Mediterranean climate. His tufts of yellow-brown hair shot out from an almost perfectly spherical head in random, disorganized directions. "Crazy" would have been the word used to describe the look in most social contexts. "Eccentric" was the accepted equivalent in academic circles.

When Alexander had phoned Crossler a few hours previously, the eccentric professor had seemed only too pleased to have his Twitter interactions lead to a telephone contact. Almost thrilled. He'd suggested he could "make a compelling case for the contours of this particular fraudulent show, which is more manipulative and perfidious than people might think," which Alexander took as academic-speak for "prove it's all a hoax." He'd hung up the phone at the end of their conversation satisfied but annoyed. Alexander harbored a particular dislike of scholars and their unnecessarily elevated speech, but at least this one was saying something interesting. More importantly, he was willing to say it to him.

The fact that the door to Crossler's town house was ajar was Alexander's first sign that something was amiss. The professor was expecting him, but no one in Rome—even a foreign scholar, unfamiliar with local customs—left a street-level door standing open in the center of the city.

"Hello," Alexander announced, his voice slightly elevated. "Professor Crossler? It's Alexander Trecchio from *La Repubblica*."

Silence. Alexander waited a moment and announced himself again. Nothing.

An innate sense of caution pressed him to depart, to phone the police or seek help. But then he felt the foolishness of premature suspicion. To call the police out for nothing . . . He didn't need the conversations about cowardice and hesitancy that would bring on back at the office. Not when he could have at least checked for himself.

He leaned forward and nudged open the door. A tiny hallway led straight back into the narrow house. No lights were on.

"Dr. Crossler?" Alexander repeated, taking a tentative step inside. He silently wondered whether this constituted breaking and entering, if he hadn't actually done any breaking.

Silence met his latest words, just as it had met his first. Alexander walked a little more boldly into the narrow corridor. It was lined with bookshelves, a few photographs in cheap frames on the wall. The professor's former college friends, by the look of them. Evidence of a few world travels over the years. The face he recognized from the website bio was there, standing before the pyramids in Giza, then before the Eiffel Tower in Paris, looking just as out of touch and eccentric in its twenty-something-year-old version as it did today.

There was a familiar smell of cigarette smoke in the air and it had a soothing effect on Alexander's nerves. Perhaps the young professor wasn't all bad. Anyone who'd resisted the current social push to view smoking as a singular source of evil had to have hit at least one mark right. There were few days that Alexander didn't arrive home to light up a smoke, collapse into a chair with a drink and nap for a good hour. Perhaps he'd find Crossler in that comfortably reclined pose he knew only too well. He supposed that university professors worked hard during the day, though for the life of him he couldn't imagine how.

Ahead, a door opened to the right, and he could already make out a tired rug over the cheap wooden floor—probably the sitting room, by the location of it. At the very least, it looked to have the aura of a well-lived-in space. He turned through the door and stepped into the small, den-like retreat.

The blood covering the two-seater settee was a bold crimson, contrasting starkly with the otherwise pale colors of the traditionally decorated room. As Alexander's stomach clenched and the shock of adrenalin burst into his system, he thought he could smell urine and bile over the sickening metallic scent of so much blood.

His eyes wouldn't move. The body of Professor Marcus Crossler lay sprawled out, only half on the settee. His throat was cut from ear to ear, his expression terrified, and now, everlasting.

11

Pescara, Italy: 5:15 p.m.

Dr. Alberto Russo pinched a metal clipboard under his arm, striving to manipulate an overly hot mug of coffee in one hand and an overly full keychain in the other. He was not a nimble man, and his lack of coordination was showing.

The dim lighting of the Salvator Mundi Hospital in Pescara didn't help. It always left the sanitized laminate corridors looking eerie, almost as if they'd been constructed for a bad B-grade horror film. Russo wasn't sure he would ever grow used to the economically mandated dimness of the surroundings. He certainly hadn't become any more comfortable with it over the seven years he'd worked at the facility.

But then, he knew, he was one of the few people within these walls who noticed.

He shook the keychain in his left hand, aiming for the small brass number that would open the glass doors to Wing C. Russo enjoyed the peace and quiet of Sunday evenings. The children needed looking after just like every other day, but most of the hospital employees had the day off. It was one of the few opportunities each week he had to make his rounds of the residential institution in solitude.

The brass key wasn't cooperating, caught in the teeth of two others and refusing to shake free. The coffee mug in the doctor's other hand lurched as he tried to manipulate his grip, slopping its scalding contents on to his white laboratory coat.

"Merda!" he exclaimed, too loudly. He regretted the word choice immediately. His patients here might not be able to see, but they could hear perfectly well, and Dr. Russo was a respectable man, raised in the good traditions of the old country. Profanities were for teenagers at football matches, and he didn't want the children beyond these doors to think he was the sort who approved of such language. Or of football matches.

He finally set down the coffee at his feet, used both hands to sort through his keys, and unlocked the door. Wing C was the first of two dormitories in the hospital. Twenty-six children slept soundly in beds that the Salvator Mundi's staff made as comfortable and homey as their limited funding would allow. Russo smiled as he rose from collecting his coffee, gazing into the dark room with its three rows of beds. His ward—his wards—in the midst of a siesta following an afternoon filled with exercises and play. He was profoundly protective of the children his experiments were designed to help, even as he knew that such help would never directly affect these pre-teens. His research was longer-term than that. But these children were part of something greater, and one day their condition might not plague others as it plagued them. He felt a grandfatherly affection for each and every one of them.

Russo stepped into the dormitory. It was even darker here than in the corridor, but he knew his way to the wall panel by memory. The children still had another fifteen minutes to sleep before the bell sounded that would raise them for evening activities and supper, but Russo didn't hesitate in flipping the switch. He knew the bright fluorescent lights would disturb none of them. The blindness caused by Leber congenital amaurosis was absolute and complete. These children had never seen light, and never would.

The long bulbs high above flickered to life and the dark room became a bright, electric white. The children were mostly sprawled out on their metal beds, sleeping soundly over teal blue and mauve blankets. Between the rows the floor was textured with ridges and bumps, designed and carefully positioned to help their sightless navigation of the space when they woke. Beyond the far wall, through a pair of automatic doors, the first scents of dinner—chicken with pasta and some sort of tomato sauce—could be made out drifting into the hall. The kitchen staff were the only others that stayed as late as Russo, Sundays the same as every day.

He walked gingerly through the beds to a small nurses' station situated midway through the room and leaned down over the military green metal surface, scanning through the day nurse's shift notes. Nothing unusual. A few scraped knees, a few falls, three cases of recurring daytime terrors. Only to be expected. The children here were orphans, unlike the 127 other youngsters in his study who lived at home with their families. Their blindness was the least frightening thing many of them had experienced, and sudden panic attacks were commonplace.

Dr. Russo opened his clipboard, switching his attention to his own notes.

He heard a cough behind him, the unremarkable noise followed by a shuffling in the sheets. Russo didn't look up, but when the jostling of the wire-framed bed didn't cease, he muttered from his notes, "It's not time to be up. The bell hasn't rung yet. Go back to your nap."

A slight hesitation. "Dr. Russo?" The words came with a soft, timid girl's timbre.

"Yes, Alina," he answered, recognizing the voice and immediately softening, "it's me. Go back to sleep. We'll visit later."

"Dr. Russo," she repeated, "I don't want to sleep."

He scratched a few lines into his notes with a pencil and was about to answer. But the girl's next words came first.

"Dr. Russo, what's that?"

He lifted his head. A strange question, given the circumstances. Slowly he turned to face young Alina. Aged seven, blond-haired, with round cheeks and the beginnings of a dimple at her chin. "Princess Alina" he often called her, her hair flowing in curls that fitted every childhood vision of feminine royalty.

She sat upright in her bed, cross-legged, pointing toward the coffee-stained patch on his white coat.

Her eyes were open. And focused.

Alina could see.

"What's that on your coat, Dr. Russo? Did you have an accident?"

Russo gaped into her bright eyes, too stunned to speak. A second later, his metal clipboard crashed to the floor.

12

The expired body of the young Professor Marcus Crossler had been brutalized.

Alexander Trecchio had never before been confronted with a mutilated body. He'd buried a handful of parishio ners during his years as a priest, but that kind of organized, ritualized death was something else entirely. Even as his faith had faltered, he'd always taken comfort in the admittedly fabricated peacefulness of a good Christian funeral. Yes, the coffins looked too much like comfortable beds, and the embalming and preparations made the bodies appear more lifelike and serene than even the most well-tempered among them had been before their passing, but that was as it should be. Hopeful signs of the peace of the afterlife. *That they might rest in the heavenly places, where there is neither death, nor sorrow* . . . The words of the funeral rite still rolled automatically off his lips.

But what he was confronted with now was death without the slightest trace of hope or comfort. Crossler's eyes were swollen and red, surrounded by raw blues and blacks. His jaw was horribly contorted. There was a slash through his neck, propped open by the horrible angle at which the man's head had come to rest. Alexander could see the bone of his spine through the mess of red flesh and blood. The severing of the throat had been so severe it was nearly a decapitation.

And the blood. Alexander stood frozen in place, suddenly aware that his small plot of carpet was one of the few places in the room not spattered with Crossler's blood. Such quantities, such spread—he had never witnessed anything like it. It seemed intended to make the worst horror-flick scenes seem tame and gentle.

He was suddenly conscious of a pounding in his chest, of the intense clamminess to his own skin. Instinctively he spun around as the shock of observation gave way to the panic of analysis. Crossler had been killed, and Alexander didn't know by whom. Or why. *Or if the killers were still here.*

Panic immediately became horror. The physical responses to such a level of fear came all at once: sweat formed on his brow as if from a tap that had suddenly been opened. The urge to cough coursed through his chest as his throat constricted, while the pace of his breath increased and every muscle in his body seemed to tighten and knot. His movements became frantic. He scanned the sitting room with racing speed, looking from one corner to the next. But the room was small, and it was obviously vacant except for Crossler's body.

Alexander tried to listen for sounds elsewhere in the house. All he could hear was the beating of his own heart, which seemed amplified in his ears.

You're alone, there's no one else here. But he needed to be sure. Stepping backward out of the room, avoiding the blood on the floor, he tiptoed through the corridor to the room at the back. A small kitchenette, messy and looking more like it was owned by a college freshman than a professor, but otherwise empty. A little more relief from his fear.

A few minutes later, Alexander had completed a quick survey of the whole two-story house. Whoever had been here was gone. It was only him and the corpse. Finally his heartbeat started to slow.

He extracted his LG mobile from his coat pocket and hit 112 with trembling fingers. The line to the emergency services connected seconds later.

"There's been a murder," he announced without introduction. He was back in the main room, staring down at Marcus Crossler's tragic frame.

"And it looks like it's not even a few hours old."

The Polizia di Stato arrived twenty minutes later. Within an hour the late Marcus Crossler's small rented house was filled with inspectors, forensics officers and the other forces that assembled en masse to deal with an urban homicide. Alexander was directed into an alcove out of the way and told to wait for a statement to be taken. He stood and watched as crews of men, who seemed only too familiar with the ritual of responding to brutal death, worked through their routines.

While his stomach turned at the mere thought of Crossler's nearly decapitated head and he averted his glance every time it risked falling upon the scene, the men in the room seemed disturbingly unfazed by it. They worked over the body, the pools of blood and the other evidence of the crime with the same dispassionate concentration a baker might have as he worked over a cake.

In his corner, Alexander could feel the effects of trauma in himself. His pulse had finally slowed to slightly above normal, but that left the adrenalin in his blood like an agonizing, cramping poison. His joints ached, his chest throbbed and his headache was beyond description. As the threat of danger had evaporated with the arrival of the police, shock had stopped having its dulling effect on his pain receptors and he had been suffering all the more.

When the time for his interview had come, he had relayed everything he knew to the investigating officer—a man whose behavior suggested he ranked particularly high up the police food chain. He wore a wrinkled suit and a five o'clock shadow, with the bleary look in his eyes of a man who'd been on the job far too long.

"You knew the victim?" the officer asked, the question sounding routine, teleprompted.

"Only by telephone. He was a source."

"A source. You're a reporter?"

"With *La Repubblica*. Professor Crossler agreed to meet me this evening for a story I'm writing." Alexander eyed the officer, his own mind quickly cataloging the subject that stood before him in a series of bullet points. *Fat. Sweaty. Combover. Body odor. Seems smugness comes with rank.*

"What's the story?" The question came without any real show of interest. The next page of a prefabricated, well-rehashed script.

"I'm writing about the man who appeared in the Vatican this morning," Alexander answered, feeling that should probably be enough. The officer peered up from his notes, a brow half raised.

"The one who healed the Pope?"

"The one who's getting the credit." Alexander looked curiously at the officer. Instinctively he didn't like this man, but that was probably just the overly abrupt judgment of fear and adrenalin. "You've heard about him?"

"Course I have. To say it's the talk of the day would be putting it mildly." The officer let out a sigh, his eyes falling back to his scrawls. His temporary interest passed as fast as it had come.

"When did you last speak to the victim?"

"We spoke by phone a little after lunch. Maybe two thirty or three o'clock. It was our one and only phone call."

"He tell you anything useful?"

"Only that he thought today's hype was something more. He didn't get a chance to say what."

"He instructed you to meet him here for the details?"

"At five. I showed up about ten minutes late. The door was open, and I found him like . . . that." Alexander swallowed.

"Anyone else in the house?"

"No one. I checked."

That seemed to surprise the officer, whose shoulders tensed slightly. "Did you find anything?"

"What do you mean?"

The inspector gazed up at him. "Anything suspicious. Anything that might be relevant to our investigation."

Alexander shook his head. He'd only wanted to know he was alone and that the crazed murderer who had slaughtered his source wasn't still hiding behind some door, like he'd seen in too many films.

The officer paused, back at his notes. His shoulders still seemed to be a little more tense than before. Then, with a dismissive sigh, he said, "Well I guess that's about all."

And that had been it: the interview in its fullness. The inspector took down a few more notes. then shoved his small notebook into a pocket with a grunt.

"I don't know what to tell you," he'd said in summation. "Looks like a routine homicide. Sorry you had to stumble into it."

With those words, Alexander's stomach had rolled all the more. *A routine homicide.* As he'd stood waiting in his corner, the phrase had echoed over and over in his head. There was a man on the floor who had agreed to talk to the press about the story of the day and who'd been violently killed before he'd had the chance to open his mouth. *A routine homicide.*

Who'd nearly been decapitated. *A routine homicide.* Whose death was *obviously* connected, somehow, to whatever information he had. *A routine homi—*

The echoing phrase became too much. Alexander stepped up to the investigator when the moment looked opportune.

"I'm sorry to interrupt," he said, tapping the man's arm. It was the same officer who'd spoken to him before, and he looked mildly surprised—and annoyed—to see Alexander was still there.

"What is it, Mr. Trecchio?"

"I've been . . . been thinking. Despite what you said, Crossler's death isn't routine. It can't be. I have a theory that it might be connected to—"

The inspector waved a rough, calloused hand, abruptly cutting him off.

"Thanks, but no thanks."

Alexander's face became a question. "What's that supposed to mean?"

"It means we don't need you or anyone else jumping to conclusions, or formulating theories. There are a hundred reasons why this could have happened. We're the investigators. We'll figure it out." He reached into a chest pocket and flicked a business card at Alexander in a manner that suggested he desired nothing less than the idea of ever being contacted by him again. The name on the card read *Sostituto Commissario Enzo D'Antonio*. A deputy commissioner. Turned out he was precisely the high-ranking figure Alexander had presumed from his demeanor.

"But the timing is suspicious," he persisted. "Crossler had only just agreed to speak with me."

"Everything is suspicious in a murder." D'Antonio's gaze hung steadily on Alexander's face, unmoved.

"But you'll look into it?" Alexander finally asked, realizing this new thread of conversation was going nowhere.

The deputy commissioner sighed, scratching a fringe of salt-and-pepper hair that clung awkwardly to his brow.

"What do you think they pay us for? We'll look into everything."

Alexander had never been less convinced of anything in his life.

13

Vatican City: 8:18 p.m.

The meeting of the Fraternitas Christi Salvatoris, the Fraternity of Christ the Savior, was held in utmost secrecy, as always. The usual meeting place of Castel Sant'Angelo was not a possibility, given the unique circumstances that had befallen them, and arrangements had had to be rushed. But the membership were all here and there was no way they could forestall the meeting.

"We're all gathered, just get on with it." The disgruntled nudge came from one of the fattest men in the dimly lit room. Most of the members had known him for years—he was like old furniture at their meetings, tired and traditional. Nevertheless, they had all long since grown accustomed to not saying his name, or anyone else's, during their gatherings, a rule that seemed especially pertinent today. A group with their aims had to maintain secrecy at all costs. One never knew who might be listening from the woodwork.

"This is terrible," a lankier figure blurted out. Fidgeting with his collar was a nervous habit in which the man indulged with almost fetishistic determination as he spoke. "All our work, everything we are, is jeopardized by this outrage."

"Keep your voice down," another brother answered. Of the thirteen men in the small room, he was the most visually striking, his face perfectly proportioned and the silver streaks in his otherwise dark hair giving him a professional, surprisingly handsome look. "And don't overreact. The Church has had to deal with pretenders before. Those moments passed. So will this."

"The Guard down on their knees in St. Peter's!" spat out the lanky brother, his face reddening. "The Pope weeping at the presence of a man who interrupts his Mass and claims to be the second coming."

"In front of the world!" came another voice, just as repulsed.

"And then he kisses his fucking hand, on live television!"

A fourth man, far younger than the first three, leaned forward from his perch at the corner of the rosewood table. He couldn't have been more than forty, but his eyes wore the severity of an older life. When he spoke, the words slithered out smooth and snake-like, deliberately slowed for emphasis.

"You need to lower your voices, brothers. Don't make us say it again."

"Then tell us what the fuck we are supposed to do with . . . with this *fiasco!*"

"I'm afraid you are not seeing things clearly." The voice of the leader of the Fraternitas Christi Salvatoris was calm and measured, his words spoken, as always, as if every phrase had been planned long ago and bore with it the authority of that preparation. Though he talked in little more than a whisper, the twelve other men heard every syllable. They were accustomed to listening closely to his words.

The Fraternity had come into existence over forty years ago, in the months that followed the Second Vatican Council and its ridiculous "reforms." A collaboration of brethren who knew that not all change was good, and that sometimes the rights and powers of antiquity had to be protected by force. Its current leader knew that never in all its decades of existence had its membership been more nervous than they were now. The very *raison d'être* of the individually selected group of clerics—to preserve the customs, privileges and rights of the Church's magisterium in the face of the liberalizing tendencies of the modern world—had known no greater foe since its creation than the current pope. Since his election, fewer than twelve months ago, the Fraternity had been meeting far more frequently than ever before, planning a way forward through the "Vatican clean-up work" the pontiff had declared would be a central part of his mission.

Some messes, the members of this Fraternity believed, did not benefit from cleaning.

They had tried to prevent this. Tried to sway the movement of the conclave before the previous papal incumbent had even died. But not every plan meets with success. A sorely felt loss, to be sure, but not one they were prepared to take as spelling ultimate defeat.

"Your perspective is short-sighted," the Fraternity's leader continued, chastising the group's most visibly worried member, "though that can be forgiven." He held his eyes a long while upon the man, who was still twisting his fingers around his collar. "But I assure you, there is another way to look at our situation."

"Tell us," came a new voice from the corner of the room. It sounded skeptical, and emerged from a man for whom two words generally constituted complete sentences. When he spoke more, eyebrows around the room rose in surprise. "If you believe there is another way for us to look at this 'situation,' explain it, so that the rest of us might understand."

"Do none of you see how this strange man and his actions might work in our favor?" the leader continued.

Murmurs emanated from all sides.

"Our *favor?*" the fat brother asked. "I agree with—" He bit his lip before the name of the twitching man beside him came out. "I agree with our brother that this is cause for scandal and the general disrepute of the Church. I am told it's already the talk of Italy, and most of the world."

"That is precisely how it might promote our agenda."

"Brother, all of us here wear black, or purple, or red. We're not here to destroy the Church!"

"Of course we aren't. We're here to defend it, even from those who would feign to lead it. But this man who's arrived on our doorstep will not destroy the Church. God's house is stronger than that."

"Then what, precisely, are you suggesting?"

"Look at the effect our stranger has had on the Holy Father," the leader of the Fraternity continued. "And I don't mean physically. The Lord only knows why or how the Pope now stands unaided. It clearly has nothing to do with this man." Grunts of agreement. God didn't send vagrants to heal prelates. "Yet the Holy Father seems convinced, at least if his reactions so far are any sign. The stranger has captivated him. And that, my dear brothers, is something we can use."

"But his degree of influence on the Pope is unhealthy," the third man interjected. "We know nothing of this man's pedigree, his background. He could be anybody!"

"Precisely so, my friend." The group's leader leaned forward. "We do not know, nor does anybody else. And that is exactly what we will play to our advantage."

The leader's interlocutor clearly didn't understand the advantage being spoken of, or the ultimate purposes to which the Fraternity's head was referring. He blurted out simply, "He could be a charlatan! An idiot!"

"It is not that he could be," the leader answered, more sharply now, "but that he almost certainly is. Don't you see it? Whether this man is malicious or simply inept, his background is going to be the cause of scandal when it's finally discovered. I've already spoken with our friend outside. She's—" He caught himself. "They're as interested as we are."

There was a moment of new tension in the musky room at the leader's slip of the tongue. Mention of *her* was as unwelcome as any subject that could be broached in their company. No man liked to be reminded of the fact that his safety, his reputation and his future resided in the controlling hands of another. Yet for almost every soul in the room, that was the case.

That particular shiver passed—unwanted but familiar. The present circumstances still demanded a response. Fidgety collar seemed only more confused by the leader's words, but not everyone was lingering without comprehension.

"Christ, you think like a prophet!" The fat man's voice broke the silence with sudden emphasis. He leaned forward as far as his body mass would allow, one chin folding over the next as he craned his neck toward the leader, a look close to admiration in his eyes.

"What the fuck are you talking about?" the skinny man with the collar demanded.

"He's talking about using this stranger to allow us to do what we could never do ourselves," the fat man answered. "No more attempts to limit the Pope's power. No more efforts at influencing conclaves and eliminating opposing voices. He's talking about taking our fraternity's aims to their highest level."

The fat man turned until he was staring straight into the skinny man's confused eyes.

"He's talking about dethroning a Vicar of Christ."

14

Rome: 8:14 p.m.

Alexander left Marcus Crossler's house a little over two hours after he'd first discovered the professor's body, stepping into the dusk of an early Roman evening as the first street lamps started to flicker into life. He'd debated staying longer, but there was little he could contribute to the officers' labors, and the subtle clues that they'd rather be without him had been growing less and less refined as the evening wore on. When he'd finally notified them that he'd be leaving, he was shown the front door with more energy than he would have liked.

An hour later, he was at his kitchen table, cigarette in hand and a reheated plate of two-day-old pasta steaming on the Formica top, waiting for him to finish his low-brow aperitif. The small apartment block on Via Varese, his home since he had left the priesthood four years ago, was situated conveniently close to the paper's offices in a pleasant enough quarter of Rome. The redbrick structure was modern, going back no further than the 1960s, which for Rome was essentially yesterday. It wasn't as quaint as a parish vicarage or as grandiose as a curial apartment, but when faith dies, certain perks go with it.

Alexander swallowed hard. He'd been through enough trauma today. He didn't need to reminisce about the most difficult choice of his life.

The pasta steamed beneath a blanket of melted cheese. Alexander was not a man without a healthy appetite, and as far as he was concerned, the more cholesterol there was dripping over a dish, the better. But this evening he realized as he stared at the plate of food, its vapors swirling into interlocking folds with the plumes from his cigarette, that he had no appetite. The lifeless expression on Professor Crossler's face stared back at him from every surface. It was there on the countertops, on the table, in the bubbling lumps of browned cheese.

He stubbed out his cigarette and walked to the refrigerator, pulled open the door and retrieved a beer. Whether a drink was any more suitable a post-trauma option he didn't know, but it was worth a try.

He moved back to the table, uncapped bottle in hand. As he took a long first sip, the icy draft bubbled its way down his throat, soothing more than just his tongue. He closed his eyes, praying that Crossler's face wouldn't be there behind his eyelids, looking back at him. But even the thought evoked the memory, the scents, the bile . . .

He forced open his eyes before the sensations could grow stronger. He needed distraction—to put his mind to work. He leaned forward and set down the bottle, plotting a way to begin. *Facts. Data. The skeleton of a story yet to be written.* These were the things to battle his preoccupation.

He reached into his leather satchel and withdrew his laptop. Cracking it open, he shoved his dinner plate out of the way as it powered up. Front and center of the screen was his Twitter timeline, the means by which he'd discovered

Crossler, hovering where he'd left it as he'd departed the office before heading to the man's home. He'd been monitoring the main hashtags for gossip over the stranger's appearance in the Vatican, and as the wireless connection in his flat now came online anew, the status bar at the top of the refreshing window switched from "15 unread messages" to "2,340 unread messages."

So it hasn't been a slow evening for the hype.

The messages on display were the last he'd read before powering down: a series of exchanges between hundreds of concerned citizens, faithful believers and honest skeptics. In the midst, @DrMCrossler292 had interjected his thoughts at routine intervals—always sounding authoritative and keen to insist that any hype about a divine origin to the visitor was "a traditional religious response to the unknown." The responses he'd received had varied from those who believed him to those who had reacted with anger and vitriol. But it was Crossler's calm insistence that he could prove his claims, despite the heated responses of others, that had made him stand out.

Suddenly Alexander leaned forward, an idea ticking to life in his mind. Twitter called its display a timeline, and there might be something useful in that fact.

He clicked the bar to reveal the thousands of newer messages above, and started to read forward in the chronology. He was less interested in what was being said and more interested in the time stamps that headed each comment. He scrolled speedily upward until he reached the times that mattered, slowing as he reached the messages—hundreds of them—stamped with 2:40 p.m., about the time he'd phoned Crossler. He took note of their flow more closely. @DrMCrossler292's contributions became less frequent, then stopped for a span of nearly fifteen minutes. *That's it, a definitive connection to our exchange.* The lapse in contributions indicated, so far as he could tell, that the professor had kept on tweeting, a little less fervently, as their phone conversation had begun, but then had stopped altogether as that conversation deepened. Alexander remembered the energy the other man had exuded over the line, suddenly feeling the grotesquery of his death in his stomach again.

He slid his fingers over the computer's trackpad and advanced through the timeline yet further. Precisely seventeen minutes after Crossler's account had gone silent, about the time their call would have concluded, he re-emerged online with a new vigor, tweeting at almost five-minute intervals for the next forty-five. *Have made contact with the press; will show you all what I mean!* at 3:22 p.m., followed by a long string of exchanges with individuals who alternately believed he was full of hot air, or a voice of reason about to enter into a fraudulent and overly hyped debate.

Then, at 4:06 p.m., Marcus Crossler had posted his last tweet: *Someone at the door. A bit early. Hold tight, my friends. The truth will come out. Back soon.*

He'd never come back. That was the last activity on the Twitter account of Dr. Marcus Crossler of the Sapienza University of Rome.

It had been posted precisely sixty-five minutes before Alexander had arrived at his house.

Over the next half-hour, Alexander continued to scrutinize his timeline. There was something here, he knew it. Evidence mixed into the time stamps of Crossler's messages— evidence of a connection between the man's agreeing to talk to him and his death a few hours later.

But he knew he needed much more than vague 140-character implications. "Circumstantial" was the title given to this kind of evidence, for a reason. There could, in theory, be any number of reasons for Crossler's silence.

He scrolled backward through the screen. He'd already found the terminus of Crosser's online activity, but it suddenly struck him that he hadn't yet looked in the other direction. He now scrolled toward earlier time stamps, seeking the moment that Crossler had begun his activity. The chronology went back for hours, to midday and then late morning, the professor active throughout. It was becoming clear that Crossler had gone to the internet almost as soon as he'd heard of the event at the basilica, which couldn't have been much after it had taken place.

Finally Alexander located the man's first post of the morning, at 8:49 a.m.: *Have just heard about something going on at St. Peter's. Any news?*

A series of responses passed along links to newly emerging video clips, and Alexander watched the phrase-burst history of the beginning of the hype.

In the midst of it, something caught his eye. Dr. Crossler had entered into the public debate with a flare, but he'd not in fact been the lone credentialed voice Alexander had previously thought him to be. He'd had a counterpart. Alexander grabbed a pencil and paper and wrote down the second man's name from his Twitter profile: Professor Salvatore Tosi. It wasn't a name he'd heard before, but that hardly surprised him. Rome was full of universities, each full of professors. Academics were like snow from heaven: they came in droves and required a hell of a lot of shoveling to get them out of your way.

But this interlocutor spoke with the same kind of conviction as Crossler, and he'd started in just as fast. What the public was seeing, he announced, was a fraud. And not a peaceful, innocent scam. People would be hurt by this, there would be ramifications, and so on. Tosi posted fervently and quickly, though, like Crossler, he never said specifically what it was that stood behind his claims that he could prove all that he was saying. *I need to speak to the relevant officials*, he tweeted at 9:18 a.m., while the stranger would still have been seated in St. Peter's.

Alexander advanced forward through the timeline, straining to see what Tosi's next contribution had been. Perhaps the man had noted whom he'd spoken to, or what response he'd received.

But there was no follow-up to the comment. In fact there were no further posts at all by Salvatore Tosi. At 9:18 a.m., the first man claiming to have proof that the morning's happenings in the Vatican were a fraud had gone silent.

Later, at 4:06 p.m., the second, Marcus Crossler, had fallen just as silent.

Suddenly Alexander's stomach tightened into a knot. He was willing to stake his journalistic nose on the disturbing suspicion that spun its way out of these facts. Salvatore Tosi, whoever he was and wherever he lived, was just as dead as Marcus Crossler.

He stood up abruptly and walked to the wireless phone that sat on his kitchen counter. The temptation to dial the police station was almost overwhelming—it was the normal, obvious thing to do. But the shove-off he'd been given earlier in the evening was firm: no theories, no help, thank you very much. The man in charge had dismissed Alexander's immediate observations outright, and those had the benefit of being based on a direct, physical connection. How much more spitefully was he likely to reject a theory built off social media references on the internet?

But Alexander had discovered something that his gut felt was concrete. Real.

The story had managed to attract his attention when it had just been about a man appearing at the Vatican and the strange effect he'd had on the pontiff. But if his only contact was dead, another quite possibly just as coldly murdered and the police persistent in calling it 'routine,' he wasn't going to be put off that easily.

He would simply have to go about things another way.

As uncomfortable as it was going to be, he had to make a different call.

He clutched the phone in his hands, took another swill of his beer and swallowed hard. By the time the bottle was back on the table, he was already dialing. He lit a new cigarette as the line began to ring. He was going to need it.

15

The Apostolic Palace: 8:30 p.m.

Pope Gregory XVII sat quietly in his study. This was not the official private office of the pontiff, which ironically was only marginally less public a working space than his ceremonial cabinet. This was his true, personal sanctuary at the edge of the upper floor of the Apostolic Palace. It had formerly been a sitting room in the pontifical residence, light and airy despite being paneled in cherry and frescoed overhead by one of the great masters. Gregory had taken to it immediately. He'd had the room repurposed only a few weeks into his pontificate, and it had fast become his favored private retreat.

And the man who sat on the far side of the room, gazing serenely out over the manicured gardens beyond, had needed no invitation. The Pope was intent on making the stranger feel as at home here as he possibly could. Because his being here was a sign. And the Pope had needed a sign.

The work of Catholicism's senior bishop was unlike any other he could have imagined in his life. Not in its scope or responsibilities, all of which he'd been aware of for years, long before he was ever handed the fisherman's ring or invested in the pallium. These had not surprised him, though he'd dreaded them—especially the spiritual weight of the authority that came with them. Gone were the days when he had superiors who could help carry the burden of his cross. Gone, too, were the days even of having peers in any real sense. With the pontificate came a deep isolation: the sense of being profoundly, inconsolably alone.

But sorrowful as it might be, this had not been a surprise. The higher Gregory had ascended in office, the lonelier his work had become. It was the way of things. He was used to it.

What he hadn't expected, what he could never have foreseen back in the days of his youth, as an eager seminarian or a first-year assistant priest sent out to serve the flock, was the degree of corruption that existed in what was now his institution. How could he have supposed, a man of faith and sincere belief, that there would be so much darkness in the palace of light? Or so much within the bosom of Mother Church that reminded him more of a fussy, fighting sibling than the sturdy arms of a parent?

It had been a surprise, but even this had come long before his pontificate. He had spent his ministry fighting that corruption, pouring his soul into the righteousness of the work. He'd first targeted the sex scandals exposed when he was bishop of the diocese of Novara in the far north of Italy. He'd not responded with the gentle moving-priests-around or retiring-them-into-silence tactics that had been exercised elsewhere in the Church. Those tainted with this corruption had been sacked, and Gregory had pushed for criminal convictions as well as spiritual sanctions. The sword of excommunication was meant to be wielded at times like these, and he'd wielded it aggressively.

It was then that he had begun to ascend the ranks. In a world tired of evil, his aggressive work to battle the darkness within the Church had pushed him ever more into the public eye. He had come to be known as "the purifying prelate" long before he was styled "the purifying pontiff."

But somehow, pontiff he had become, and the only way Gregory was able to come to terms with this was to see in it God's affirmation of this necessary work. So he'd redoubled his efforts since he'd taken the white cassock. In the past months, he'd managed to introduce wide-ranging investigations of almost every major institution of the Church in every territory around the world. He'd even managed to sack two corrupt bishops and a cardinal from their positions in the curia—no small feat, even for a pope. The curia was a force to be reckoned with, never in any pontiff's pocket. But holy work had to be done.

All of which had made Pope Gregory enemies as well as friends. Perhaps that was as it should be. If everyone hated him, it might be a sign that he was ill suited to the Church's highest ministry. On the other hand, if everyone loved him, he would surely fall prey to pride and arrogance. In the middle, perhaps there was the possibility of doing good, even attaining salvation himself.

And then, amongst all this, the stranger had come.

Gregory had every reason to be suspicious, he was well aware of that. He knew nothing, absolutely nothing, of this man. Advisers were whispering in his ear that "a traitor in blue jeans" had infiltrated the Vatican. Members of his security retinue were concerned the man could be a terrorist. One of the older archbishops was positively certain he was the Antichrist. And why couldn't any one of these men— men the Pope had always trusted—be right? There could be fraud taking place right under his nose. Deception of a sort he couldn't even imagine.

And yet, and yet . . .

Were not the events of the past twenty-four hours a sign of comfort? Was not the Lord deigning to provide solace to his weary vicar in the midst of his trials? Pope Gregory gazed across his desk at the man who sat so serenely at the far side of his office. In his presence, questions seemed to slip away, and all that was left was a profound peace, a certainty of good and holiness. It was as if the Pope's heart, so trauma-tized by the sinfulness of the world and his own flock, was made whole in this man's presence, just as miraculously as his back had been made straight.

Headquarters of Global Capital Italia: 8:32 p.m.

In her office on the top floor of the Global Capital Italia head-quarters, Caterina Amato felt a tingle of anticipation shud-der down her spine as she reached for the intercom button at the corner of her desk telephone.

The plan she'd concocted the moment a contact within the Vatican had live-streamed the arrival of the stranger to her across a FaceTime connection had been thrust into motion immediately. All day, her men had been putting its various elements into play. Some of those elements were long in the works—resources her firm had built up over years, secretively and with unclear intention, which would be used today in ways she'd never before conceived. One of those was already out in the open, stirring the public imagination. Yet other elements were responses, worked out on the spot as the day's possibilities had started to unfold.

Life, healing and death, mingling together. It was almost like a symphony. A symphony of her conducting. For the spark that had started this day might not have been of Caterina Amato's devising, but she was sure as hell going to make the flame it created her own.

She pressed the intercom button and her secretary's voice clipped to life almost instantly.

"Yes, Ms. Amato?"

"Gather the board," she instructed. "An emergency meeting. Tell them to be here in two hours, no exceptions." A project as big as the deception Caterina was crafting was going
to take her whole inner circle. Most of the board of directors
had already been called into action individually throughout
the day, but it was time to bring them all together. To circle the
wagons and make sure that every element of a plan that was
still taking its final shape in Caterina's mind was worked out
and timed to perfection.

"Yes, Ms. Amato. I'll see that they're here."

Caterina tapped her finger on the intercom button again,
ending the brief conversation. Two hours. By that time,
the next piece of earth-shattering news would already be
in the public domain. The whole country would be singing
the song she was writing.

And the Pope would only dig himself more deeply into the
pit she was preparing.

16

Rome: 8:50 p.m.

Alexander began his phone call professionally, unsure how Ispettore Gabriella Fierro would take to hearing from him like this. Or hearing from him at all. That was the question that always hung over a relationship that had a past, and he was inexperienced enough with those to recognize that he simply didn't know what to make of his own lingering feelings. They registered somewhere between embarrassment and shame, with an ample dose of disappointment. The easiest way to deal with them before had been to run away, which was essentially what Alexander had done when their short-lived relationship had come to its abrupt end. The question was whether he'd done so without burning his proverbial bridges behind him.

"Inspector, it's Alexander Trecchio." Everything completely formal. He paused, waiting for a reaction, but nothing came. He opened his mouth again, his tongue noticeably drier and textured a bit more like sandpaper than it had been a moment ago. "I hope you don't mind my ringing your mobile." He hesitated at the end of the sentence. It wouldn't be out of line if the first words he heard back were harsh, instructing him to call the station switchboard if he wanted to speak with the police.

"Alex, my God." Gabriella's tone was surprised, but she didn't sound angry. That was a good start.

"I hope it's okay that I'm calling."

"It's been a long time," she continued, and he noticed she hadn't answered the question.

"The whole affair at San Sebastiano. Two years ago." They'd been assigned to a common case then, she to investigate and he to report, and it had been the only thing to bring them together since the strange whirlwind of a relationship they'd had almost two years before.

Alexander hadn't seen her since.

"That seems like such a long while ago," she said, her tone unreadable. Yet she referred to the case as a stand-alone item without any hint at the backstory they both knew it had. A slight pause. "Why are you calling me, Alex?"

Traffic and the sounds of social life emerged behind Gabriella's voice. Perhaps Alexander had caught her off duty. Suddenly he felt he was invading the woman's privacy. He'd promised himself he would never do that. Not after she'd told him, her hand resting tenderly on his, that there could never be a return to what they'd had before.

He abruptly exhaled a lungful of smoke.

"I'm sorry, I've caught you at a bad time. We could speak in the morning."

"Don't worry about the time, Alexander. Tell me why you're calling."

He realized his eyes were closed. Funny how a man could lose his faith yet the old habit of prayer still rise automatically in him. And that was what he needed now: a prayer. A prayer that their past wouldn't stop Gabriella from listening to him.

"I need your help."

"My help with what?"

The question was an opening. Alexander decided to get to the meat, fast. "I was witness to a murder this afternoon. Not to the murder, actually, but I discovered the body."

A lull, but no immediate reaction. He could hear a bus pass by Gabriella's phone.

"Did you report this to the police?" she finally asked.

"Of course I did. They came out to investigate immediately."

"Were you involved in any way?" Gabriella's questioning suddenly had an unmistakably professional intensity.

"Only in finding the body. I walked into the man's house and found him dead in the front room. Throat cut, almost decapitated."

She didn't respond to the details. "What were you doing there?"

"I was there to talk to him about a story. He was my sole source, and he'd asked me to come by this evening." He relayed the events of his day in potted form, almost able to see the change in demeanor that he was sure came over Gabriella as he mentioned the stranger and the apparent healing of the Pope—events about which she'd clearly already heard. Alexander knew she was a woman of deep piety and that what had happened today would not affect her dispassionately.

"I don't know what to make of the Pope angle," he added quickly, "but there's definitely something questionable about the appearance of this stranger. The man I found dead, Marcus Crossler, was the only individual willing to give me some insight into what, and why."

Gabriella's tone remained unaffected and professional. "Alex, there's no obvious reason that his willingness to speak with you should have placed his life in danger. You said yourself, the whole internet is buzzing about it."

"That's what I thought at first, too. But from the little he told me on the phone, Crossler was convinced there was more going on than people realize. Then, a few hours later, the man is killed in his home—before I can meet him and take down the details. Now I discover that he's not the first voice suddenly to have gone silent."

Gabriella seemed quietly to consider the material before her voice crackled back across the line.

"I'm not sure what I can do for you, Alexander. This all sounds pretty tenuous. I'm sure the investigating team will look through the details and pursue all the possibilities."

"They won't," Alexander answered flatly.

"Excuse me?"

"They won't even hear me out. I tried to talk to them, but I was dismissed out of hand. The man in charge was a right ass about it. Someone called D'Amorio, or D'Ambrogio . . . I can't quite remember. I've got his card somewhere. Maybe you've heard of him."

Alexander could hear the sudden intake of breath from Gabriella's end of the line.

"I know him well," she answered. "The name you're looking for is D'Antonio, and he's my supervisor."

Alexander brightened. "Then maybe you can talk to him. Get him to listen to you, because he sure as hell won't listen to me. You've got to admit, from everything I've told you, something untoward is going on."

There was another pause. Gabriella's voice was hesitant when it came. "It sounds . . . unusual. But I don't know any of the details. There may be a good explanation for it."

"I was given a pretty cold shoulder, Gabby."

Ignoring the familiarity, she simply answered, "That's the only kind D'Antonio has to give."

A long silence overtook their conversation, and in the midst of it Alexander realized that that was it. He'd said his piece, there was nothing more to add. If Gabriella wasn't willing to push further, there was little place else he could think of to go.

It was long in coming, but finally she spoke.

"Alexander, I'll have a word with some people downtown, but I need you to know I'm doing this as a professional courtesy."

"Of course, I'm not—"

"Anything else that might have happened between us . . ." She cut him off, then hesitated. "The only way I can go forward with this is if we agree that nothing ever happened."

He paused. Suddenly there were more emotions in his chest than he'd remembered feeling there for a long time. But Gabriella was right. It was the only way.

"Agreed," he said. "Nothing ever happened."

Inspector Fierro sighed her relief. "In that case, give me until the morning."

17

Central Rome: 8:53 p.m.

There is no cure for mantle cell lymphoma.

Of many things in Dr. Marcello Tedesco's life and career he was uncertain, but this was not one. It was a fact, and it had propelled him into his field. He had watched his sister, when they were both still teens, begin to wither, the life disappear from within her as if sapped from some unknown, hidden tap. Lisa had been diagnosed when she was only eleven—an extraordinary phenomenon in its own right, given that the cancer normally struck those in their fifties and sixties. He, the fifteen-year-old elder brother, had watched as her spirit simply ebbed away. First her play and then her singing had become less spirited. Soon she had become housebound, then bedridden. Finally they'd moved her to the hospital.

The last memories Dr. Tedesco had of his beloved sister were stained with the antiseptic teal colors of hospital sheets and slick-painted walls, with the pinching smell of floor cleaner and the ashen, drawn face of the little girl he'd once

raced up trees, with whom he'd gleefully arranged the pil-
lows of their parents' bed into a palatial fort. All the joy and
sunshine of her features had been stolen by the disease. At
the end, her eyes had barely moved. She'd looked frozen,
like some mournful porcelain doll.

They had done everything they could for her—the doctors, his parents. Lisa had been given every treatment, she
had undergone every therapy. But there is no cure for mantle
cell lymphoma.

That statement, coupled with the forceful evidence of his
sister's death, had changed Marcello's life. A zeal for medicine had developed before he'd left secondary school, and
he'd gone on to degrees at one university, then another, then
specialist studies in oncology and research protocols for MCL.
He'd poured his whole life into his work—all his training, his
emotion, his heart, his loss. He'd attracted funding for his
research, and after sixteen years at the helm of what he'd
named the Lisa Tedesco MCL Research Unit had become one
of Europe's most notable authorities in the field. They had
developed new chemotherapy regimens that were sixty percent more effective than their predecessors while being half
as destructive to the body's other organs. They had worked
to refine robotic radioimmunotherapy deliveries that allowed
for higher-intensity aggression against certain tumor types.
They were working on some of the newest biologic agents
and therapies.

But there was still no cure, and he had sixty-three patients
in his core test group, and over two hundred in the secondary phase group, to prove it. All were living a little better, but
still on their way to certain death.

Which was what made the CT scan image results he held
in his hands an utter impossibility.

It was the third image he'd been passed since being called
into the imaging center, each as incomprehensible as the
last. Each showed a lymph node under a focused exposure,

highlighting the traditional regions of mantle cell expression. Each was earmarked with the name of one of his patients. Patients who had advanced-stage MCL.

And each CT scan was clean.

The signs of the aggressive systemic disease that had plagued them in the previous months were entirely absent. There were no signs of . . . anything.

"I called you as soon as I processed the first scan," Dr. Tedesco's assistant said anxiously, "but I couldn't wait. I called in these other two patients for imaging immediately. They live close by and didn't mind being disturbed on a day of rest."

"You did well," Marcello answered. His assistant, he'd long ago learned, had no comprehension of a day off.

"Not a trace in any of them." The assistant said the words with genuine awe.

The observation was now being confirmed by a fuller PET scan, the digital images of the second patient scaling on to the hi-res display as they spoke. They were as pristine as the CT results, leaving only one possible interpretation. Whatever the causes or indications, all signs of the cancer were gone.

"We need to get everyone in for complete scans and work-ups," Marcello instructed. "Today, if possible. Those who are well enough."

"All sixty-three?"

"Each of them. We have to see how widespread this—" He bit his lip before he could say "cure." "We need to see how many others are showing these indications."

The assistant nodded and Dr. Tedesco retreated from the PET facility control room, clutching the original CT scan images to his chest. He navigated his way down the hallway silently, his mind in disarray. A few moments later, he was in his office. He closed the door behind him and threw the bolt. For a few minutes he needed to be alone.

Marcello Tedesco was a deeply religious man whose faith had grown firmer through the fires that had refined it over the years. Trials, sorrows, challenges—these were the things that broke the fervor of some men. But Marcello had seen every one as a challenge God would use to see him through to new heights. And he had.

And he was clearly doing so today.

Marcello walked to the corner of his office, where a votive candle was kept burning constantly before a small statue to the Blessed Virgin he'd picked up years before on a pilgrimage to Lourdes. He took down his rosary and impulsively wrapped it through his fingers. Next to the statue was a small copy of William Holman Hunt's famous painting of Christ knocking on a lamplit door, *The Light of the World*, and Marcello moved the image closer to the center.

He glanced toward his desk. On his monitor was the frozen face of the stranger who'd visited the Vatican that morning. Before his assistant's call had come through, Marcello had been reading about the man's arrival. He'd watched the video of the Pope's astonishing healing.

And now . . .

He turned back toward the image of Christ, then closed his eyes, clutching his hands and beginning his prayer.

"O Lord, I know you have come again, and are here, working your miracles . . ."

A few moments later, his prayer of thanksgiving complete, Dr. Tedesco reached for his phone. What he was witnessing was something about which the world needed to know.

Headquarters of the Swiss Guard, Vatican City: 8:57 p.m.

In the depths of the Swiss Guard's operational headquarters, tucked a full two stories beneath the ground level of the Apostolic Palace, there were no ceremonial gowns decorating the officers or Renaissance frescos adorning the walls. Those embellishments were a required part of the ceremony above, ancient and worthy, but in the network of rooms that surrounded Oberst Christoph Raber's office, such things were far from anyone's mind. The walls were stained wood and glass, the desk surfaces a black sheen and the technology on tabletops and wall mounts as modern and advanced as anywhere on the globe. The force that Raber commanded might be perceived by the world as little more than a ceremonial guard paying homage to antiquated customs and heritage, but in reality it was one of the most highly trained, best equipped and fiercely loyal security forces the world had ever known, with a reputation well earned over the centuries.

Raber sat in plain clothes, his eyes transfixed on the right-hand display of a set of interlinked plasma-screen monitors on his desk. No fewer than fifteen camera feeds were thumbnailed on the left display, and as the playback from the morning's Mass progressed, he clicked from one to the next, drawing the best angles on to the full-screen window to his right.

He'd watched the recordings three times already and still couldn't explain what he was seeing. And that made Christoph Raber intensely uncomfortable.

Who is this man? Where did he come from? The stranger's face was uniquely calm, almost serene, despite the opulence of the capital of Christendom and the awe of the people surrounding him. The cameras had caught the man entering into the basilica, walking through the central doors with the same resolved and dispassionate look upon his face. Raber had already checked the external recordings, looking for any sign of his approach, but the man was not to be found on any of the feeds from the Piazza San Pietro—a strange fact that he would need to explore more closely. That a man could hide himself within a crowd was not in itself unique. That he could do so well enough to avoid being picked up on any of the twenty-seven cameras that covered every square meter of the piazza was something rather more disconcerting.

Raber watched the videos of the stranger's progression down the aisle, toward the high altar. He was arriving at the point of the incident that perplexed him the most, and it wasn't the healing of the Holy Father.

He watched, silent, as the man approached his ring of guards. He watched as they looked into the man's eyes, and he watched as they then fell in almost perfect synchronicity to their knees, necks bowed and faces reverent.

Raber couldn't explain his men's behavior. There was no way they could have all been turned away from their duty. All men were corruptible, of course, but his were the most loyal in the world, vetted and picked by him personally. And they certainly couldn't have been turned en masse. They wouldn't be bribed or pushed into behavior that risked the safety of the Pope.

He knew this with absolute certainty, not because of a naïve overestimation of his men's loyalty, but because of the actions of one man at the side of the ring of guards. On his screen was the image of an individual whom he knew could not possibly have sold out or been influenced toward such behavior.

There, only meters away from the Holy Father, was the crisp image of Commandant Raber himself, kneeling on the marble floor.

Christoph had been a man of devotion his whole life. He'd longed to be in the Guard since his youth; he'd trained every day in his teens. He'd obtained his parents' blessing and signed up as soon as age permitted, and he'd served all the years since with an absolute dedication to his cause. It was the perfect marriage of honor, duty and the sacred. Something to which he was willing to give every fiber of his being. Raber was not a man of flowery piety or emotion—those elements of the Church weren't his. But he was a man of steadfast loyalty and a love of duty, and that had served him well for many, many years.

But in all those years, through all that conviction, nothing like this had ever happened to him.

He clicked the space bar on his computer to freeze the image just as the recording caught his face rising from its reverent declension. It was like staring into the face of another man. *That expression, that look.* It was spellbound, reverent, captivated. He didn't recognize these attributes in himself. *That . . . awe. Where did it come from?*

And where had it been his whole life?

Raber had no more explanation for his own behavior than he had for any of his men's. He only recollected how in that moment he had not thought, had not deliberated—he had simply felt overcome and his knees had seemed the only place for him to be. And so he had knelt of his own will. He hadn't looked to his men in either instruction or confirmation; he couldn't even recall taking any notice of them. And yet they had all acted in the same manner, together.

Raber desperately needed to know what had caused this. The Vatican was in shutdown. The city outside working itself into a frenzy over the event to a degree that surprised even him. And yet Raber still didn't have any idea what had happened. *What is still happening*, he reminded himself. *The stranger is still here, within these walls.* The Pope had taken him into the residence and the two hadn't emerged since.

And I do not know who this man is who sits with the Holy Father.

He scratched at the slight stubble sandpapering his chin and clicked to a different camera angle, this time reaching out over the mass of faithful who'd gathered for divine worship but who instead stood transfixed on the strange events happening at the front of the church. Camera nine automatically panned slowly from left to right over a ten-meter-wide span of floor space on the southern side of the central nave, closest to the entrance to St. Peter's crypt.

And then Raber's breath stopped. He snapped forward, slamming his palm down on the keyboard and pausing the feed. The frame was blurred, and he frantically pushed at the keys to reverse the play frame by frame until it was back on the image he'd spotted.

There, in the midst of the crowd, was a face he knew. The face of a man he'd met before. The face of a man he would never, in a million years, have expected to see in a church.

18

Polizia di Stato, Monteverde XVI Station: 9:17 p.m.

"I wasn't aware you'd been assigned to this case, Inspector Fierro."

Gabriella always hated coming directly before her superior, especially on his own turf. Sostituto Commissario Enzo D'Antonio was an unpleasant man, rarely helpful, perched on his pedestal of power from long years of service and an adeptness at the art of political sycophancy. He'd been in charge of Gabriella's unit since she started with the Polizia di Stato, and in all that time he'd always appeared to be covered in a thin sheen of disgusting sweat. He had the kind of hair that looked pitifully disheveled even on the days he bothered to comb what little of it remained, and in general bore the appearance of what Gabriella considered a thoroughly disgusting individual. He peered up from his desk with one of his unreadable, yet customarily displeased, glowers.

"I'm not on the case," she answered.

"That's right, you're not. And the reason I know this with such perfect clarity," Deputy Commissioner D'Antonio continued, "is because I, in fact, am. Not just on the case, but heading it."

"You?" Gabriella's surprise was palpable. It was unusual for a deputy commissioner to take hands-on control of an investigation in its first stages. But it did make sense of why Alexander had encountered him at the crime scene.

"I was here when the call came in and went out with our homicide team earlier this evening," D'Antonio continued, pre-empting her obvious question. He flicked closed a red file folder on his desk, tapping it with a fat thumb. "I was there for the whole process of discovery and cataloging of the crime scene."

"Including discussions with the man who found the body?"

"Yes, including . . . him." The commissioner peered up suspiciously at Gabriella. "I trust by now you've been made aware of his identity."

Gabriella tried to will a redness not to rise in her cheeks. "Yes." She nodded curtly. "The reporter."

D'Antonio huffed a laugh. "The reporter. Hell, you say it like he's just one out of the shit-heap." His eyes were accusing. "Don't think I'm not aware of your past."

Gabriella bit back a swirling mixture of embarrassment and anger and looked directly into his eyes. This was not the first occasion in her professional career she'd felt her body surge with an overwhelming desire to belt her senior officer out of his smug, arrogant superiority. But that career had gone as far as it had because she'd always been able to fend off the urge.

Even if only barely.

"Our past is irrelevant." She attempted to imbue her words with warning. This was territory in which her superior had no business trespassing, and the pungent man knew it. "Did you interview Trecchio? Find out anything useful?"

"Something about him working on a story, intending to meet up with the victim as a potential source." The commissioner's tone lost intensity and retreated to a familiar sonority of disinterest. "Stumbled upon the murder scene instead."

"You're sure it was a stumble?"

"There's no sign of him being the killer, if that's what you're asking."

Gabriella shook her head. "It isn't. Are you sure the murder wasn't connected to his investigation?"

D'Antonio's expression became momentarily curious. "Investigation? Far as I know, he's only working on a story. For the *religion column*." He emphasized the final words as if they clarified that anything published in the religious section had all the consequence of material written for a children's storybook hour.

Gabriella persisted. "I'm curious about the possibility that his going as a reporter to meet this particular individual might have been a motivating factor in the victim being killed. It wouldn't be the first time sources have been silenced before they could talk to the press."

Silence, and then D'Antonio's tone turned hard.

"Fuck me, you've been talking to him, haven't you!" he snapped. "You sound like a recording of his babbles at the scene."

The urge to lean forward and punch the senior officer squarely across the jaw was now almost overpowering. Instead, Gabriella breathed deeply, fingering the purple plastic rosary she always kept in her left pocket. It had been a gift from her grandmother more years ago than she could remember: a "little nothing" picked up at a thrift sale, but which Gabriella treasured. Its presence in her pocket usually brought a reassuring comfort.

In this instant, she wondered if it was strong enough to be used to throttle her boss.

"Alexander Trecchio contacted me," she finally said. "He wanted to make sure the connection between his work and the murder gets examined."

"And I told him we always explore every lead."

"So you're following up on the second disappearance? The other professor he monitored online?"

For an instant D'Antonio looked surprised, as if the existence of a second professor was news to him. But his annoyance quickly overcame any questions he might have had.

"I wasn't born yesterday morning, Ispettore Fierro." He leaned forward, stressing her lower rank. "There's nothing to this case. If Alexander Trecchio were a headline reporter and our victim was about to turn over details on Mafia activities or terrorist plots, maybe he got offed before he could talk. But Crossler's a bottom-rung university professor talking to a second-career page-eleven journalist about whether or not a hillbilly in jeans who's walked into a church is actually an angel. Fuck sakes, Fierro, who in their right mind would care enough about this to kill a man?"

Gabriella wasn't ready to let the deputy commissioner off the hook. D'Antonio's smug dismissiveness was grating her the wrong way.

"There's no way you can be so definitive. Not this early on."

Her words came out as an angry accusation. She hadn't really bought into Alexander Trecchio's suspicions before this discussion—she'd agreed to take a look more to get him off the phone than from any belief in his theory. But suddenly an interest was emerging, if only due to the fact that D'Antonio was treating the case with such obvious disdain and unprofessionalism. That, and he was being a rank jackass.

"File a complaint with Internal Affairs if you want," he said dismissively, waving a fat forearm in front of his face. "I make my own decisions around here, and I sure as hell don't run them by you."

"We need to be looking at all this much more closely," Gabriella insisted. "I can help with that." If nothing else, she could get her foot into the investigation.

"You can stay the hell out of it." D'Antonio was suddenly leaning forward in his chair, both hands on his desk. "You aren't assigned to this case, now or at any time in the future. Is that absolutely clear?"

She nodded, knowing that if she spoke, her anger would betray the lie in her answer. For in that moment, Gabriella had made a decision. She was going to look into this, no matter what instructions her commanding officer gave her.

D'Antonio raised a finger and pointed it at her face. When he spoke, his words were suddenly quiet and cold.

"I am going to warn you once, and only once, Inspector Fierro. Stay away from this case."

Alexander's apartment: 9:41 p.m.

Alexander was still sitting in his kitchen, a half-drunk beer in his grasp and the open frame of his laptop perched before him on the yellow Formica of the table. He hadn't intended to stay engrossed in his research so late into the night, but something about the details he'd uncovered had captured his attention and wouldn't let go. There was a gentle haze of smoke filling the kitchen from the near-constant stream of cigarettes he'd been smoking for hours. He'd only stopped when the pack was empty.

When the doorbell rang, he felt a jolt of surprise. He'd lived in this flat for four years, but he'd only heard the buzzer ring twice, maybe three times. He'd almost forgotten it existed at all.

He stepped heavily through the kitchen to the front room, and finally to the oak door that opened out into the main corridor of the apartment block's third floor. As he swung it open, he was confronted by the unexpected figure of

Inspector Gabriella Fierro. Her shoulder-length hair, the same light straw color as he remembered it, was slightly windswept and her jaw, normally elegantly sloping and soft, was hard-set.

"Mr. Trecchio, I'm sorry to disturb you at home." There was a hint of apologetic embarrassment on her features, but it could barely be spotted beneath the intensity that gleamed in her hazel eyes.

Her language was curtly professional. Alexander fumbled to reply in kind.

"Inspector, this is a . . . surprise." He immediately felt self-conscious, realizing in an instant that he hadn't set eyes on her in almost two years, that his stubble from the long day was at full growth and that the suit he'd been wearing since morning desperately needed a clean.

Gabriella paid no heed to his discomfort. Instead she stepped past him, through his door and into the flat's comfortably appointed front room.

Her professional tone evaporated.

"Alexander, we need to talk."

19

9:49 p.m.

"What are you doing here?" Alexander asked, startled by Gabriella's unannounced presence. "I wasn't expecting to hear from you until the morning." If he was truthful, he hadn't entirely expected to hear back from her at all. He ran his fingers self-consciously through the short, gentle waves of light-brown hair atop his head, wondering whether he looked as disheveled and unkempt as he suddenly felt.

"Our schedule got bumped up a little." Gabriella entered fully into the front room of his flat. She'd been here several times before, though almost four years ago, and looked about as though she might be able to elicit the details of Alexander's life in the intervening period from the decor. Her nose scrunched slightly. She had never liked the scent of stale smoke.

"Your story," she said, coming quickly to business as he closed the door and switched on more lights, "it's already causing problems."

"Not bad considering I haven't written a word of it," he replied, trying to inject some levity into the moment.

"Sometimes asking questions is enough." Gabriella made to sit down in the blue twin-seater sofa with a kind of automatic familiarity, then caught herself mid-bend and rose back to a normal posture. She motioned toward the sofa.

"May I?"

"Make yourself at home." Alexander waved a hand toward the seat. "Can I offer you a drink?"

"No drinks, Mr. Trecchio." Her tone was again conspicuously businesslike. "The circumstances may have changed, but this is still a professional visit."

"I understand." So the going would not be entirely smooth. But it didn't have to be entirely uncomfortable, either. *We never did anything wrong*, he reminded himself. *I have nothing to be embarrassed about, except the way I ended it.*

"Well I'm halfway through a beer," he said, walking toward the kitchen, "if you don't mind."

There was a slight pause. Then, from the front room, "All right, then, bring me one as well."

Alexander smiled, his nose in the refrigerator. "You're not on duty?"

"My shift was up twenty minutes ago."

Alexander handed her the beer and dropped himself into a tired brown leather recliner facing the sofa from the side of the room. He took a long swill from his own half-empty bottle. He let his teeth rattle against the glass lip, an old habit.

"What's brought you all the way over here this late at night?"

Gabriella paused to reflect before answering, and Alexander took advantage of the moment to pass his eyes over her for the first time in what suddenly felt like far too long. Her light hair and porcelain skin were just as he remembered them, her figure slender, well-toned and hardly concealed beneath the smart professional suit she always wore.

But there was something different about her now. She had
gained a confidence that showed through in her demeanor.
Her back was a little straighter, her shoulders pulled at just
that much more authoritative an angle. She was a woman
who had taken possession of herself. Something in that realization brought Alexander a sense of satisfaction. Or at least
an ease of conscience. He was glad things had gone well for
Gabriella Fierro.

Their introduction, four years ago, had been purely professional. He was still a priest, still in post with the Vatican
curia. There had been a string of thefts of church property
in local parishes in Rome, and Alexander had been asked to
liaise with the police in the investigation. There he'd met
her, as junior an officer in the State Police as a woman could
be, and yet something had immediately flared up inside him.
It wasn't lust; it wasn't really carnal at all. He had met this
woman, he'd walked with her and talked and worked with
her, and he'd experienced the most overwhelming desire
for *closeness*.

Gabriella certainly couldn't be blamed for enticing him
away from the clergy. He'd had been on that outward path
for quite some time before he'd met her. That loss of faith
had been something deeply interior, private—something
he'd only been able to share with his uncle, whose vocation
as a cardinal of the Church never overpowered the closeness
of their family bond. Alexander had been faltering, falling
under the weight of the corruption he encountered in the
institution he had been raised to love. In the end, he hadn't
been strong enough to resist that sorrow.

But even if she hadn't drawn him away from the Church,
something about Gabriella had captured him from that first
encounter. She was beautiful, with her straw-like golden hair
that batted at her shoulders. With eyes that always seemed to
radiate warmth. But what really struck him was something
far deeper. Unlike so many other people he'd met, Gabriella

seemed genuinely to care. To believe. To broadcast sincerity and stability long before she ever opened her mouth.

Alexander had been captivated. He'd clumsily ensured their interactions continued as long as possible, expressing his interest with all the grace and tact of a fumbling teenager. There had been an initial phone call, the first not related to work, and then another. They'd grown longer and more personal. Then there had been a café, a restaurant, walks in parks and drives outside the city.

And then, one day, there had been Alexander's apartment. Gabriella had looked so beautiful, arriving in a sky-blue dress, silky and form-fitting, her hair drawn back and her neck sloping beautifully. Alexander had prepared pasta, the only dish he knew how to cook, together with a decanted bottle of the finest Chianti he could afford. He'd dressed, too, for the first time, without the dog collar.

The next morning he'd awoken, his body next to hers atop his narrow single bed. They had stopped themselves. Or perhaps it was more correct to say that Gabriella had stopped them. Alexander wasn't sure how far he'd have gone if she hadn't checked what was for him a new and overwhelming desire. As it was, the night had been spent simply in a locked embrace as they drifted off to sleep. But Alexander's decision was made. His life in the priesthood was over. He'd notified his uncle the following day. The collar he'd taken off for that meal had never gone back on.

Their relationship had carried on for two months, though it had never approached anything close to normal. His announcement that he was leaving the priesthood hadn't surprised Gabriella, but even after it had been made formal, there was a barrier imposed by his past that wouldn't disappear. Outright romance never felt any more right than it had that night, which, slight as it had been, had been the only one of any physicality between them. Alexander didn't deny he felt something true and real for Gabriella, but he'd gradually begun to fear that it was simply a rebound. A rebound from a life with which he'd been struggling for too long, for other reasons. He was able to go no further. And so he'd called it off, suddenly and dramatically. Gabriella's shock had led to heated words and an exchange he'd regretted for the four years since. Alexander had gone so far as to accuse her of being his Eve, leading him into temptation—at which point Gabriella had grown red-faced with anger and stormed from the room. Such a stupid comment, but he had been as unprepared to end a relationship as he'd been prepared to begin it.

Their only interaction since that last afternoon had been two years ago, when once again their jobs had brought them to the same place, the same story, at the same time. The case at San Sebastiano had been dramatic for both of them. For Gabriella the long-sought-after beginning to a real career in the force. For Alexander another encounter with corruption in holy places, but one which he was able to write about to a degree of success that had secured his place at the paper for at least a few years to follow. Yet the tension of that encounter had not healed the wounds between them. Gabriella had called him aside at the end, on the last day they'd spoken, and been tragically honest with him.

"I know you, Alex. Too well. I can still see it in your eyes."

He'd not really needed to question what it was she'd seen, but he'd asked anyway.

"Discontentment. The same unsettled discontentment I saw when we were together." She'd reached out to touch his wrist as she spoke. "You didn't know then who you were becoming. Who you were. That's why it didn't work out between us. And it's why it wouldn't work now."

And that had been it. She'd smiled kindly, even warmly. She'd looked forgiving, though still hurt. And then she'd simply walked away.

At this moment, however, she looked worried. She arced her head and downed more than half her beer in a single swallow, then reached forward and set the bottle on the squat faux-antique coffee table positioned between the two of them.

"I want you to tell me everything you know about Marcus Crossler, Alex. Everything."

"I've told you everything I know," he answered honestly.

"What you've told me is almost nothing."

"That's because I know almost nothing. I'd never met him before this evening, if that counts as a meeting." He hesitated as shivers came with the memory. "Everything I know about him I gained from the internet—his bio on the Sapienza university website, his interactions on social media and a few online articles here and there that referenced him."

"You'd never spoken?"

"Only the one phone call, this afternoon, to arrange our meeting."

"Did you tell anyone about that call?"

"No, but he did. On his Twitter account. Didn't say it was with me, but he posted about having arranged a meeting with someone from the press."

Gabriella shook her head, clearly dissatisfied by the scant level of background detail. "That's all, Alex? You can't think of anything else?"

"If I could, you'd have it."

"Then tell me everything you know about the other man you mentioned, Salvatore Tosi."

Alexander sighed. "I know even less about him. My first encounter with his name was this afternoon online, when I noticed his interactions with Crossler. His profile said 'Assistant Professor, Pontifical Gregorian University.' That's the full extent of what I know."

"You're a reporter. You didn't make a few calls?"

"By the time Tosi had come to my attention, it was already evening. I phoned the university switchboard and asked for his office, but it went straight to voicemail."

"Did you leave a message?"

He shook his head. Gabriella didn't say anything more.

It was Alexander's turn to press for information. "What did you find out at the station? Something's brought you here. You could have asked me these questions over the phone. Come to think of it, you did."

Yes, Alexander, be sarcastic. That's the way to go, he chided himself silently.

Gabriella reached forward, grabbed her beer and downed the remainder.

"I looked into things, Alex, as I said I would. And that's exactly why I'm here." Her eyes caught his, holding them a split second longer than normal before darting across the room.

"I went straight to my chief, Deputy Commissioner D'Antonio. The same man you spoke to. Told him everything you'd relayed to me: the link to your story, the online disappearance of a second source earlier in the day."

Alexander recollected D'Antonio's behavior toward him at the crime scene. "Hopefully he was willing to listen. I can't say your boss made the best of impressions on me."

Gabriella rolled her eyes. "You and the rest of the world." For a flicker of a moment, she smiled. In the mutual dislike of her superior, they again had something in common.

"What did he say?" Alexander asked.

Her face suddenly turned red. The smile was gone and she looked angrily at him. "He said I shouldn't put much stock in the stories told to me by an ex-lover."

"Gabriella, our past was—"

"No," she cut him off, a hand in the air, "it's not important. If D'Antonio was just harping over my personal life, that would be one thing. But the manner in which he was acting . . . it was something more."

Alexander sat silently with the new information.

"He told me in no uncertain terms," Gabriella continued, "that these leads were non-leads, and that it would be professional suicide for me to look into them any further."

"I'm sorry I brought you into this." Alexander leaned slightly forward in his recliner. "I shouldn't have called you." He wanted to reach across the coffee table and place a hand on hers. He knew he couldn't.

"The bastard all but threatened me," Gabriella blurted out, her eyes angry. Then, recognizing the profanity uttered in company, she instinctively looked embarrassed, crossed herself, then proceeded to look more self-conscious still at the overt show of piety. Alexander knew it was a habit she'd borne since her childhood: every time a swear word escaped her lips, her right hand immediately flung into the motions of the sign of the cross. A swift purification for a poor show of piety. He'd always thought it endearing, the way she seemed to believe it almost physically counteracted the bad language.

"The former nun is embarrassed about her piety in the presence of a former priest?" Alexander asked, a new smile crossing his features.

"Alex, you know I was never a nun." Gabriella tried to shake off the whole conversation.

"Okay, a novice. But it's not a far cry."

"It was a long time ago. I was a girl." She looked as if she was about to recite a well-worn explanation for the thousandth time in her life, but bit her lip, exhaled deeply through her nose then turned to stare straight into Alexander's eyes.

"I'm not used to being threatened by my boss for doing my job. And I'm not used to an investigation being mismanaged by a deputy commissioner of the State Police."

Alexander could feel the sudden intensity in the air.

"What do you intend to do about it?"

She gave him a pointed look.

He smiled. "Okay, what do you intend that *we* do about it?"

Gabriella's intensity only increased.

"We're going to find out everything there is to know about your other man, Salvatore Tosi. We need to—"

She was cut off as Alexander's doorbell rang.
A moment later his landline began to ring.
Then his mobile.
Then Gabriella's.
And then, simultaneously, they all stopped.

20

10:22 p.m.

"They're together, inside the flat." The voice of Umberto's younger brother was suffused with an enthusiasm that came only in these moments before the kill, when what Maso regarded as sacred work was about to be accomplished. When he could wet his hands with unrighteous blood. He looked all but giddy.

"You're certain? Both of them?"

"Both cellular signals are pinging to the same location. They're within feet of each other."

They'd tracked down the name of Alexander Trecchio from the online exchange that had led them to their kills earlier in the day. He was a man who'd clearly made too many inroads, who more than likely knew too much. And the woman's snooping around since he'd made contact with her put her in the same category. As if her being a police officer itself wouldn't have done so on its own.

Two more targets to be eliminated. As they'd been ordered.

"You're sure it's his apartment?"

The words were still in Umberto's mouth when the crackle of the entrance intercom sounded from behind its slitted gray metal panel.

"Hello?" The voice was tinny, barely audible over the gentle street noise around them. But it was a man's, and it came directly after Maso had pushed the buzzer marked "A. Trecchio."

"I'm sure now," he answered, smiling. The yellow edges of his teeth made the smile look as menacing as he intended.

Umberto needed only a moment to consider their position. They were at a logistical advantage, their targets together in a closed environment with neither aware they were being pursued. There was no reason not to move forward.

Umberto ignored the sound of Trecchio's voice from the intercom and gave a nod to Maso, who extracted a heavy iron bar from his haversack. Without a second's hesitation he slammed its flat edge into the lock of the double doors, huge muscles flexing at his shoulders. He accompanied the action with the grunt of a satisfied child at play. A moment later, the two men were inside the apartment block. Maso returned the bar to his sack and extracted a three-foot length of heavy chain with an iron padlock. He wrapped the chain around the handles of the two doors, binding them together with less than an inch of give, then clicked the lock into place.

His yellowed teeth beamed a broad, happy grin. The man's IQ might not place him amongst the cleverest villains in Rome, but he was good at what he did.

No one was leaving this building until he and Umberto had done what they came to do.

Gabriella looked up from her mobile phone, where "Missed Call: Unknown Caller" continued to display on the glowing screen. Alexander stood near the flat's entrance, the plastic receiver of the building's intercom system still in his hand.

"Were you expecting anyone else, this late at night?"

"No one." Alexander swallowed, listening for voices from the street, but the intercom had gone silent.

He turned to face Gabriella. For the briefest instant there was the temptation of male machismo and a drive to show no fear, but it passed in favor of straightforward honesty. "I've a bad feeling about this," he said abruptly.

Gabriella was already rising. "Unexpected callers aren't a usual thing for you?" Her tone sounded strangely as if it represented both a professional and personal interest.

Alexander pulled out his mobile phone, shaking his head. Not that he didn't want to pursue her quizzical forthrightness further, but the situation wasn't just unusual. It was unheard of. Prior to Gabriella's arrival here this evening, the last time he'd had a visitor had been . . . Gabriella, four years ago.

He turned his attention to his phone. The screen showed a single missed call with no available caller ID. The suspicious tension in Alexander's shoulders tightened. His phone, Gabriella's, at the same moment . . .

"Let me guess," he said, looking up. "Your call record from a second ago looks the same as mine?" He held up the phone so Gabriella could read the display. She nodded.

"Two calls, to the two of us, at the same time." Alexander walked instinctively toward the kitchen as he spoke. "And my landline, and my door buzzer."

"Alex, what's got you so—"

"Someone knows we're here, Gabriella." His gaze locked with hers. "You and me, in this flat, right now."

"Who are you talking about, Alex?" Gabriella looked surprised by the manner in which he was acting, but Alexander's rising intensity was stirring up her emotions as well.

"I'm not sure who," he answered, shaking his head. By now he was at the table, folding closed his laptop and tucking it into the crook of his arm. Then, on second thoughts, he realized this was impractical and moved toward the bedroom for a rucksack from his closet. "But after what I saw this afternoon, I'm in no mood to find out."

He reached his bedroom, shoved open the door and headed straight for the narrow closet. Gabriella was at his heels as he pushed aside hanging clothes—blues and beiges, and still a few residual blacks—and yanked out a drawer from the back. An old navy-blue rucksack was compressed into the drawer and he shook it open roughly.

"Alex, you're overreacting," Gabriella held out a hand and grasped his shoulder as he shoved his laptop into the sack. Human contact, comforting . . .

"Take a moment. Breathe."

Alexander spun to face her. He could only imagine what his visage must look like: he'd been tired and wearied before this sudden development, his face painted in the dreary end-of-day colors of dark stubble and greying rings at the eyes. And that was then. If his features now expressed even half the worry in his chest, it would be a disconcerting sight. But it didn't compare to the image of the disfigured Crossler stuck in his mind, vivid every time he blinked his eyelids.

"Gabriella, I've seen things today . . ." He could feel his own throat catch.

"I understand, but you're being irrational—"

He stopped her, his words cutting across hers. There was a knot in his gut that was getting tighter, harder, and he had to make her understand how the dots of his day were connected in a way that was causing it.

"Salvatore Tosi asks questions, and he disappears," he said abruptly.

"I know, Alex—"

He held up a hand, a single finger extended. His first point. It lingered a moment and he held up a second finger.

"Marcus Crossler says he'll speak, and a few hours later he's killed in his home." A third finger. "I ask questions, I'm shot down by the investigating officer. Your boss." Another.

"You ask questions, and you're threatened by the same man." A fifth. "And now we're here, and someone's using our phones to make sure we're together."

Alexander's eyes were wide. His anxiety was spiked, certain of impending danger.

Gabriella hadn't broken his stare since he'd begun. Her expression, however, had begun to change.

"When you put the pieces together, it's not a good list," she finally acknowledged. "But paranoia's common after witnessing a tragedy. You need to keep your reactions measured."

Alexander opened his mouth to speak, but before he could, the sound of a strong fist beating against his door burst through their tense exchange.

Outside the wooden entrance to apartment 34A, the two hit men stood with guns drawn. The Glock 19s, both with suppressors affixed, were loaded with high-power hollow-point ammunition, and in Maso's haversack was a Heckler & Koch MP7 with hard-tipped 30mm rounds that could eat through concrete as easily as wood. If necessary, they could vaporize Alexander Trecchio's flat and both its inhabitants. But Umberto liked to keep their work more nuanced and subtle whenever possible.

"Mr. Trecchio, will you please open the door. We'd very much like to speak with you."

He didn't bother to concoct a false identity or fabricate a reason for their being at the door. The little on-the-fly research he'd been able to assemble on Trecchio suggested he was a bright man, and he was in there with the police inspector—a woman whose file indicated she had brains to match her obvious beauty. By this stage, they would both know that the encounter they were about to have was not . . . what was his boss's favorite word? *Legitimate.*

Silence answered Umberto's appeal. Not unexpected, but disappointing.

"Mr. Trecchio, Inspector Fierro, we need to speak with you, urgently." He allowed a slight pause. "We *will* speak with you."

Ten seconds passed. Twenty. He looked down at his watch.

It was late. There was no reason to delay.

He turned to Tommaso.

"Open the door."

Gabriella's doubts about Alexander's suspicions were swept away the moment the first knock came on the front door. Moving on instinct, she slid her right hand beneath her jacket, unclipped the holster that hung concealed at her side and released the Beretta 92FS—the standard-issue sidearm of the Polizia di Stato. A second later, the safety was off and the muzzle pointed at the door.

"Alex, stay in the bedroom," she ordered quietly, taking a step forward. Her training kicked in and she moved with a practiced and confident ease. "Let me deal with this."

Alexander appeared startled by the sight of the weapon. He started to withdraw at her instruction—a man trained in religious obedience, reacting instinctively, Gabriella quickly assessed. But a millisecond later he stopped and stood tall.

"We're not splitting up. I'm not standing to the side and leaving you to handle this alone."

Gabriella swung her head toward him. *Of all the moments for machismo . . .* This wasn't the time for protests.

"You're a reporter, I'm a police officer. You'll do what I tell you." She spun her gaze forward. "Stay behind me, out of the line of fire. Close the door."

But Alexander moved up, sidestepped her position and stood in front of her. Suddenly his tall frame and athletic build seemed like a wall.

"Listen, Gabriella, I'm not just being noble. That man wasn't speaking in the singular. That means there's at least two of them outside."

Gabriella looked annoyed at his interjection but recognized he wasn't wrong. "What would you have us do instead? Stand here and hope they go away?"

Alexander shook his head. "I vote we leave."

"You know another way out of your third-floor flat?"

He pointed behind her, toward a wide window that opened out on to the cityscape beyond.

"As a matter of fact, I do."

Thirty seconds later, the window was open and Alexander was standing on the metal fire escape landing outside, lowering the extendable ladder to the second-floor platform below. Gabriella had insisted he pass through the window first so she could keep cover. Only when the ladder clicked into position and Alexander had his foot on the first rung did she saddle herself over the jamb and swing a leg out into the cool air.

As she did so, the door to the apartment exploded in a spray of wood chips and dust.

21

10:28 p.m.

The door in front of them at first seemed to split apart in violent, thrashing chunks. Then, as Maso held his finger down over the automatic firing trigger, 950 rounds per minute quickly turned the chunks to fragments and the fragments to dust. The door appeared to dissolve, and the deafening report of the MP7 cut out all other sound.

It took only three seconds. When Umberto motioned for his partner to cease his firing, there simply was no door left to prevent their entry.

In an instant the two brothers were in motion. Their sidearms were raised to eye level as they partnered their way into the flat, filled with haze and dust from the destruction. The suppressors at the end of their barrels seemed entirely pointless now and they detached them with a quick twist. *When plans change, accept the change.* The firearms were more accurate without them anyway.

The flat was a scene of chaos. Splinters of wood still soared through the air and the impact of the bullets had shredded a blue sofa and nearby chair, whose linings and synthetic fluff filling now floated through the room's interior in a frenetic cloud.

Umberto was on highest alert. He swung his arms steadily from the center of the room to the right, allowing Maso to take the left half of the flat. His forearms never left their solid pose, the gun sighted directly forward of his eyes. The moment something, anything, came into his line of vision, it would be dead center in his firing line.

It came less than a second later.

On the far side of the room, beyond the haze, Umberto caught a flicker of motion. It was tall, nearly six feet—the height of a man. He spun toward it, and at the same time the shape spun toward him.

His skin prickled. *The hunt, running in both directions.* He would have to give Alexander Trecchio credit for fighting back, for taking a stand. But Umberto was too well trained, and he was too fast.

He pulled his finger back on the trigger, the smooth shape of the metal sliding beneath the pad of his fingertip until he felt the familiar click of the pressure threshold giving way. The gun fired. Before the muzzle flash had died, he'd fired again. Twin shots blasted through the room, their loud report crashing from the walls.

Umberto instinctively crouched aside as his finger came off the trigger, making himself a moving target in case the other man happened to get off a shot in return. But that shot never came. The man simply exploded before Umberto's gaze.

Exploded.

It was so surreal it took his mind a moment to register. The man with the gun aimed at him through the dust and swirling debris fragmented into a thousand pieces, accompanied by the sound of glass shattering as he fluttered out of existence.

"Fuck!" Umberto cried a second later, his senses grasping what had just taken place. On the far side of the sitting room the shattered fragments of a full-length mirror fell to the floor. He had skillfully assassinated his own reflection.

"Boss, look here!" Maso's voice burst through his angry self-reproach. His younger brother had called him "boss" since they'd started working together, a habit he couldn't break and which Umberto didn't mind. He looked across the room to the younger man.

Maso was pointing toward his left. Just beyond the edge of the room, a few steps into a small corridor, the door to a bedroom stood open. On its far wall was a window, open to the night air of the city beyond.

Alexander had never descended a fire escape in his life, and the absurdly inappropriate thought that raced through his mind as he took the last steps down to ground level was that it was far harder going than it appeared to be in films. The quick escape out of the side of a building always seemed to show people racing downward as if they were taking a set of stairs. The reality was that the escape was an extraordinarily steep series of ladders woven through tightly spaced iron framing, all of which was constricting, difficult to manage and made for slow going. They had started only three flights up, but it seemed like minutes later when Alexander finally landed on solid ground.

Gabriella was a few feet above him and he held out his arms to help her with the final drop—an act of bravado that felt comical a moment later as she reached back under her jacket and reclaimed her firearm from its holster. *Hardly a woman who needs help off a ladder*. But he also noticed she hadn't resisted the hand.

"Get moving," Gabriella commanded. She motioned toward the corner of the building, redbrick and sleek, then raised her eyes and her handgun back up the fire escape.

Alexander followed the motion. On the third landing, a head poked its way out of his bedroom window.

Alexander froze as he caught the man's eyes staring down at them. Cold didn't begin to describe the complete lack of emotion there, and that dispassion was far more terrifying than any expression of rage or hatred could have been. He knew in that instant that this was a man who would extinguish his life without emotion or remorse.

A moment later, beneath the man's shoulder and head, an arm emerged from the window.

"Run, now!" Gabriella commanded. Her voice jolted Alexander into action. He forced his legs to move, glancing back to ensure Gabriella was doing the same.

Her arm was raised to the man at the window, and Alexander saw her hand clench as she fired the gun. Sparks flew from the metalwork of the fire escape and she darted to the side, aiming high and firing again.

Alexander rounded the corner as the sounds of more gunshots and impact ricochets filled the air.

He could only pray they were coming from Gabriella's weapon.

22

10:34 p.m.

Umberto waited a few seconds after the sound of the last shot had faded before he darted another glance outside. The woman was gone, as he expected, but at least he could now start his descent.

Inspector Gabriella Fierro was clearly well trained. She'd missed him in the exchange of gunfire, but not with the accidental spread of an amateur. If there hadn't been the metal grating of the fire escape between them, Umberto would be dead.

The forces of evil are cunning, he reminded himself as he moved, the quasi-sacred nature of his approach to his work showing through as it so often did. *There is skill in the heart of our enemies*. It was a lesson he would have to keep in mind.

In under a minute both assassins were on the street. Their motion never slowed.

"Go around the other side of the building," Umberto shouted to Maso. His brother swerved to the left as Umberto continued forward, following the path of their soon-to-be victims.

It was only as the night air, rich and heavy with the diesel fumes that marked out the urban Roman ethos, began to sting the wound that Alexander realized he'd torn the skin of his right hand in descending the fire escape. As he ran, pain shot through his wrist and up his arm—a too-sudden reminder that this situation had just changed dramatically.

There was no longer any doubt that Crossler's death and Alexander's story were connected: that the professor had spotted fraud in the works and had been executed for it. And the men who had killed him were only a few hundred meters behind them.

Gabriella rounded the corner a few seconds after Alexander, the exchange of gunfire still echoing off the stone and brick buildings. She made up the distance between them in only a few bounds.

"Do you have a car?" She asked the question through tense breaths and glances darted behind them. She clearly expected the gunman to reappear at any moment.

"In the garage, under the building." Alexander sucked in a quick breath, keeping in motion. "The entrance is out front. Back the way we came."

Gabriella shook her head. "No good. We'll go for mine. I parked four streets away."

Parking congestion, Alexander thought, glancing over his own shoulder. In the neighborhood it was next to impossible, forcing people to park streets and even blocks away. *Tonight, that fact might just be our salvation.*

Gabriella reached out and grabbed Alexander's arm, pulling him to the right. Then, looking back to ensure the gunman hadn't emerged from the front corner of the building, she yanked him across the street.

*

Umberto stuck close to the side of the apartment block, his left shoulder scraping the brickwork as he pushed forward to the corner. He took a deep breath, counted to three and turned, his gun forward.

Nothing. He scanned the side street quickly, but darkness merged shape and shadow and made it hard to know what he was seeing. A car. A hedgerow, perhaps. A fire hydrant. He stood perfectly still, waiting for any signs of movement, but nothing hustled its way into his vision.

Shit, he muttered, moving forward along the street. Had he lost them so quickly? Fierro and Trecchio must be running behind the building, heading for the interior of the residential neighborhood. A smart move: fewer streetlights, a more broken structure of separate buildings.

But this chase was far from over. Maso would round the building from the other side soon enough and they would pincer the pair between them. They might run for a bit, but they wouldn't escape.

Then, out of nowhere, motion.

Six hundred meters down the road, give or take, two shapes emerged from the left, from behind a blocky shadow in the darkness that must be a parked transit van. They moved swiftly to the right—two people running from one side of the street to the other.

Umberto had them.

Without hesitation, he aimed his gun at the two figures and squeezed the trigger.

The bullets came fast, the pavement exploding beneath Gabriella's feet. She didn't bother to look for the source of the gunfire, knowing that in the darkness aim was only an approximation. And despite a powerful urge to return fire, she resisted the impulse. They were in the middle of a residential area. There could be people around. Children.

"Alex, get in the car!" she shouted.

"Which one?" he yelled back over another explosive report.

"Red Fiat. There." She pointed to her minuscule car, parked three spaces further down the street.

"A *Fiat*! Christ, it'll be as dangerous inside as out!" The sarcastic eruption was an automatic reaction, as another gunshot planted itself inches from Alexander's feet.

A second later, the rear light of the car parked in front of Gabriella's exploded and Alexander's wit vanished. Gabriella chirped open the lock and they both made for the doors. Alexander was nearest the driver's seat and he dived in without thinking.

"Give me the keys!"

Gabriella's hand was already extended. As he took the keys and thrust them into the ignition, she turned toward the rear windscreen, extending her arm and her gun in case their attacker came into view.

Instead, the rear windscreen exploded in an eruption of glass. Gabriella screamed.

"Drive!"

23

Headquarters of Global Capital Italia: 10:37 p.m.

Within the walls of Caterina Amato's Global Capital Italia, the news coming in from the outside could not have been more encouraging. Her aims were always power—power and money—and such aims almost always involved managing and manipulating affairs in the world around her. But her present project was more personal, and far grander than any other she'd ever attempted.

Before she was done, the man at the head of the church that had so scarred her family was going to be obliterated. And the church he ran would have its reputation as scarred as she had been. With all else that Caterina Amato had accomplished in life, it would be one of her greatest achievements.

And the news flow of the day seemed almost custom-suited to her interests. All her planning, rushed as it had been once the scenario had seemed to set itself, was paying higher early dividends than anticipated.

"Press attention is flourishing, just as we foresaw," one of the members of her board of directors said, pleasure brightening his vowels. They'd come together on short notice at a summons from Amato's secretary, though most had been active in the plot in one way or another since the morning. "The medical events have captured public attention. We managed the timing perfectly."

The board meeting was run like any other. Its membership preferred that the veneer of professionalism never be dropped, even if the board of directors was the one entity within Global Capital Italia entirely composed of those involved in the firm's more secretive interests. This was a group of men—Caterina the only woman in the mix, and firmly at the helm—that fought against any law that stood in the way of their personal wealth, who manipulated markets and destroyed lives without a second thought if it meant their interests would be better served. *And fuck it if people think that's cruel*, one board member had stated years ago. *It's life and it's finance and I don't have a single goddam problem with it. Survival of the fittest is a law of nature, and it's just as much a law here.* When, years ago, Caterina had for the first time flatly ordered the murder of a man who'd been standing in the way of their work, the board member had merely shrugged. *Needs to be done. Do it.*

But despite their intensity, they were men who appreciated corporate civility. There was coffee in a silver thermos pot at a side station in the meeting room. A ring of perfectly polished glasses surrounded a jug of Fiji water at the center of the table. Their embossed dossiers included charts with full-color graphs on high-gloss paper. And their CEO sat at the head of the table in a cream business suit, looking as she always did: the picture-perfect image of professional elegance. Her hair was brushed simply, its mostly auburn locks falling straight to her shoulders with a slight inward curl at the ends; none of her board members had failed to notice that over recent years Caterina had not fought but fostered the advent of streaks of gray that had begun to flow down around her ears. In some people's minds gray meant age and decrepitude. In the CEO of Global Capital Italia's it meant wisdom and the power of experience.

"Is the timing of the medical events generating the results we want?" another board member asked.

"Do you mean are people piecing A and B together?" The man who'd spoken first was called Regio, and looked as if nothing could dampen his positive spirits. "Of course! How could they not? It's called playing the advantage, and we've done it perfectly. One little event in the Vatican, and we become limitless beneficiaries. Everything we stage after it is endorsed as a miracle. Just as Caterina predicted."

"'Endorsed' is hardly the right word, Regio." The man who answered was slick, immaculately groomed and could easily have played the poster child for a campaign on beauty in the workplace. His navy-blue, pinstriped suit was fronted by three mother-of-pearl buttons in the old style, the perfectly tailored sleeves coming to an end with plenty of room to accentuate the folded cuffs of the cream shirt beneath, their clamshells clasped with matching cufflinks set in gold. But his words were less glowing. "These people aren't recommending some product we're selling. You heal their sick and they're going to rejoice. These are real people, expressing real emotions."

The call toward sincerity sounded duplicitous coming from such a plastic man, but behind his high cheekbones his expression was genuine.

Two televisions on the walls continued to broadcast the images they'd watched earlier, though the board had muted the sound after fifteen minutes of reports. All the stations were focused on the same thing. Two Italian hospitals, dealing with two very different types of incurable medical conditions—genetic blindness and terminal cancer—had announced unexplained mass healings. The newsreels were non-stop with interviews of tear-laden family members rejoicing in the good news, the testimonies of little blind children who could now see, of medical professionals as baffled as they were delighted. And through it all the word "miracle," dancing off the tongues of religiously pious and secular alike.

"Don't be so damned sentimental," one of pinstripe's colleagues answered. The man had just as much personal wealth and corporate experience but didn't share the interest in fashion or personal decor. He sat in simple trousers and a shirt he'd purchased in 1983. His face was wrinkled like a walnut and bore the marks of long years of experience. "The more real, the more effective," he continued. "And you're a fool if you think this isn't a product," he waved toward the televisions, then down at their files, "or that this isn't marketing. An opportunity arises, the right atmosphere is set, and we go in and control that market to get what we want. Guns, news, miracles—what does it matter what we're offering?"

There was no answer. The dossiers outlined public approaches and strategies for managing both mass-market appeal as well as consumer rejection and public negativity—just as they'd done for every major product launch in their history. The only difference was that this time, their purpose in utilizing public interest wasn't to sell a product but to destroy an enemy. Though that wasn't really all that new either. They'd done it before, countless times, just perhaps not on quite this scale or with such a high-profile target.

"Things are going to move forward quickly from this point." The CEO spoke matter-of-factly, fingers rapping lightly over the thick pages, printed as always on the highest-quality paper. Nothing was ever done on the cheap, Caterina insisted upon that. "The medical reports are now in the media. I'd thought we'd have a day or two before they got out, but one of the doctors was a little more pious than we'd anticipated."

On one of the television screens, the face of Dr. Marcello Tedesco moved in muted display. His revelation of the inexplicable healing of his entire study of terminal cancer patients was making the rounds of evening news coverage, adding to the sensationalism of the mass healing at a residential ward for the blind in Pescara.

"This means the financial phases of the deception need to be firmly in place, and soon," Caterina Amato continued. "Investigations are going to begin—they may be starting already. And what they find will decide whether our endeavor fails or succeeds."

The senior staff nodded their agreement. But the plastic man's unease was showing through.

"We should take more time. Think this through." He was obviously the most hesitant of the group. "The consequences of what we're doing need to be weighed carefully before we take any further steps. It's time to pull back on the reins."

A heavy silence descended quickly upon the assembly. Everyone recognized that their colleague had gone too far. He had dissented, and dissension was never met well at this table. Even he recognized the gravity of his words, and his face blanched.

Only Caterina Amato moved. She rose from her seat, straightened her blouse, and walked slowly toward the well-dressed man. The tension in the air increased tenfold.

"Delays, delays," she muttered as she approached him, "that's all you're good for, Alfonso." She walked to his side, her air laissez-faire and almost preternaturally calm. Yet as Alfonso swiveled his leather chair to meet her, she suddenly wrapped her knuckles together and slammed a powerful fist into his jaw. The blow was forceful, yet the man didn't react, except to wince in obvious pain. Then he drew in a breath as Caterina swung again, her second blow crunching against his nose. Blood immediately began to drip down on to the pinstripes of his suit. But still he didn't react.

He knew better.

The rest of the board waited. They had been in these situations before. For the man to end this encounter dead would be perfectly in keeping with what they'd termed "past practices" on the part of their director. Board membership came with an accepted set of risks and responsibilities. One responsibility was never balking at difficult situations. The risk for dissenting was usually dismissal of a very final sort.

But after her second blow, Caterina rubbed her fingers, wiped the blood off her right hand on the beaten man's shoulder and silently walked back to her seat.

"I am not interested in delays," she announced calmly.

"We can move the necessary funds between the companies and individuals within the next few hours," another board member said, professionally, as if nothing had just happened. The beaten man whimpered quietly in his seat, sopping up the blood from his nose with his sleeve.

"Not the next few hours, *now*." Caterina's left hand went up, signaling toward the televised reports. It bore a single gold band on her ring finger. Though she had never married, and had no intention of doing so, the image seemed to reinforce a certain authority. "People are already linking A and B: the arrival of this visitor in the Vatican and our subsequent miracles. But the plan works only if B is *connected* to A. The money has to be seen to move simultaneously. Visibly. Immediately. Without that, we gain nothing."

A finger-tap from the fashionless member confirmed the strategy. "We can have things in motion in a few minutes."

Caterina nodded. "Do it. Just be sure to keep the board out of the equation. There can be no association. And keep the rest of the firm in the dark. Best if they remain innocent as doves."

Her words were met only with a nod.

"No one will ever know we were involved."

24

Central Rome: 10:41 p.m.

The tiny red Fiat 500 hatchback sped down the street with all the muscle its 101 brake horsepower could produce, the engine whining at the strain and the bodywork creaking with the sudden acceleration. Alexander pressed his foot all the way to the floor as he dropped the clutch, and the screech of tires burning against tarmac announced their departure to more than just their two pursuers.

"Which way?" he asked, the noise of the engine magnified through the absence of a rear windscreen.

"Turn down the first side street you can, then straight on to get us out of here."

The words were barely out of Gabriella's mouth before another gunshot fired through the night, its round landing in the back bumper with a great thud. It was only a few inches above the rear tires.

"There, Alex." She pointed to a side street.

Alexander wrenched the wheel to the left and pushed his foot down again. They were headed toward the Viale Castro Pretorio, which meant that in a few seconds they would be on a main road with plenty of traffic and the chance to put distance between them and their pursuers.

"Are you all right?" Alexander finally asked, not taking his eyes from the road as he pulled around another corner and headed toward the main thoroughfare.

Recognizing that they were out of range of the two attackers, Gabriella finally turned forward and sat down properly in the passenger seat. "I'm fine. You?"

He shot her a quick glance. "Fine." But there was sweat on his face and a haggard look to his features.

"Who were they?" Gabriella asked, but she was already en route to answering her own question. "From their marksmanship and movement I'd say they're professionals." She glanced backward to see if they were being followed, but there were no headlamps behind them or signs of other movement on the road.

Alexander nodded. "I suspect they were responsible for Crossler's death."

"No further argument from me," Gabriella answered. "I'm sold on the connection. But that doesn't tell us who they are or what their interest is in all this." She forced deep breaths. The speed with which she'd regained her composure was a by-product of training and experience, and her face swiftly attained a hard resolve.

Alexander kept the car at as close to full speed as he could manage as he navigated his way toward the Sottovia Ignazio Guidi and started to put considerable distance between them and his flat.

Suddenly Gabriella lurched toward her handbag. "Our phones," she said. "We have to get rid of them."

"Excuse me?"

"The way they rang before . . . you said it yourself," she answered. "They're how they tracked us to your flat. They must have done a little research, found our phone numbers, and hacked their way to our GPS coordinates. Or good old-fashioned triangulation. In either case it means they're good, and hanging on to these phones is a very bad idea." She was already rolling down her side window and a second later had tossed her mobile out on to the street. "Give me yours. Now."

Alexander could hardly protest and forced a hand into his pocket as he drove. He passed his phone to Gabriella, and without giving him a moment to react she tossed it out as well.

"They'll have seen this car too," she added as she rolled her window back up, "and if they were good enough to track our mobiles to your apartment they'll have no trouble tracing number plates. We need to abandon Emilia as soon as we can."

"Emilia?"

Gabriella gave a slightly embarrassed smile, but then tapped on the plastic dash with all her official seriousness. "Emilia."

"You named your car?"

She shot him a look. "She's cute, she's reliable, and until this evening she was in tip-top condition. She deserved a name."

Her look was complete seriousness for all of a few seconds, before both she and Alexander burst into laughter. The tension of the chase, of the near-death encounter, finally broke in a flood of relief and smiles. And for an instant, the relief Alexander felt was more than just at having escaped a barrage of gunfire. He felt a relief at being back with Gabriella—the old Gabriella with her quirks and her ridiculously energetic laugh. Even if he knew that connection would only last a moment.

"Fine," he finally said, "we'll ditch Emilia. But then we'll not only not know where we're going, but we'll have no way to get there."

"Take the exit for Regina Elena, a few bends up this road. It's only a couple of streets to the Policlinico metro station." Gabriella gazed forward as the traffic moved in its flow with them. "I know a place we can go."

25

The next morning
Headquarters of the Swiss Guard: Monday, 6:44 a.m.

Morning came too slowly for Oberst Christoph Raber's lik-
ing. Work could be done during the night, of course, but the
interrogations his investigation required demanded the light
of day.

There was no question about the identity of the man the
commandant of the Swiss Guard had spotted in the video
feeds from yesterday's Mass. But the certainty of that identity
provoked an almost endless series of new unknowns.

The man in the feeds was Arseniy Kopulov, a Russian-
born businessman who had made his home in Italy after
escaping the Soviet imposition of "unfavorable hardships for
capitalist-minded men," as he'd famously called them in a
television interview years ago. He had gone on to become
one of the great and the good in the advancing field of medical enterprise in Italy. For the past few years he had been the
head of Alventix Ltd., one of the two largest pharmaceutical

manufacturers in the country and one of the top ten in Europe.

All of which Christoph Raber knew, because Kopulov was notoriously anti-Church, and anti-Catholic in particular. Raber made it his business to know everything there was to know about anyone with that level of power and those opinions. Anyone who might be a threat to the Vatican, no matter where they were in the world.

Arseniy Kopulov loved the press. Though his company spent millions of euros on media campaigns designed to boost consumer demand for the drugs it produced and investor interest in the research it constantly undertook, the head of Alventix seemed to cherish most of all the free press that came through creating controversy. He was always the first to volunteer for radio interviews or appearances on the panel shows that crowded Italian evening television. They were a pulpit to preach his pro-research positions in loud antithesis to the activities of "ethical protesters," whatever form they took—whether they came in the shape of animal rights activists lobbying against his company's proven research methods or anti-poverty campaigners claiming he had no right to sell a pill at twelve euros a pop, even after it had cost him 350 million to create.

Or if the protests came from the Church. Kopulov's disdain for religion was never hidden. Raber had watched at least two dozen recorded interviews in which the man had vehemently blasted the Roman Catholic Church—clearly his pet hate when it came to religious bodies—for its stance on contraception, the right to life, euthanasia, or as far as Raber could tell, anything and everything that the Church had a stand on. If the Church was for it, Kopulov was against it.

Even when "it" had little or nothing to do with the realms of medicine or science in general. One particularly aggressive video recorded him lambasting, in traditionally animated terms, the Church's Mass as "a ritual of ignorance to inspire the ignorant." The words he had for the Pope were only mildly less offensive, though his characterization of the pontiff as "the lead alpha in a pack of blind, angry wolves" had garnered tremendous media play.

Which led Raber back to the central question weighing on his mind. What was Arseniy Kopulov doing attending the papal Mass at St. Peter's yesterday morning?

And not only attending. The CCTV footage showed more than merely his presence: his demeanor had been . . . hell, the only word for it was pious. He'd crossed himself at various points throughout the service. He'd folded his hands, lowered his head and closed his eyes, as if in the depths of fervent prayer.

Why was an avowed atheist and open enemy of the Church kneeling in its most sacred shrine and praying to the God he'd called "the greatest lie of all," at the very moment St. Peter's was being invaded by a man whose presence no one could explain?

A knocking on his office door snapped Oberst Raber from his thoughts. A head was already poking through as he looked up and called out his usual *"Ja, bitte."*

The face of Hauptmann Heinrich Klefft looked pale.

"What is it, Captain?"

The younger officer was in his standard duty uniform of plain blue garb fixed with an unadorned brown leather belt, a broad white collar laid flat over his shoulders. The black beret he would normally have propped at an angle on his head was instead tucked under his arm.

"You did not answer your telephone, sir," he said, pulling the door closed behind him. "I thought to bring the news to you myself."

Raber looked down at the phone on his desk. The small LCD panel showed four missed calls, all within the past two minutes. *I didn't even hear them.*

"What news?" he asked, bringing his attention back to the captain.

"The Holy Father," the man answered, his throat seeming to tighten around the words, his body immediately in the stiff pose of formality. "He's ordered the media to be assembled in the Sala di Constantino."

"The media?"

"An invited group, with television cameras," the young officer answered. "The Pope wishes to address the world."

Headquarters of La Repubblica newspaper: 7:02 a.m.

In his editor's office at *La Repubblica*, Antonio Laterza stared angrily at the twin television sets perched on a table opposite his desk. The damned television news media were like vultures. They circled over the city with budgets far in excess of anything a newspaper could pray for, and the moment a story fell to earth they swooped down and claimed it as their own, never mind who had actually done the work. They'd taken the story of the stranger's arrival in the Vatican, of the Pope's healing, as theirs from the moment it became interesting and hadn't stopped running it since. Sixty minutes an hour, every hour of the day. There were cameras pointed at every gate, wall and window that led into Vatican City. They had whole troops of reporters standing in front of lenses reporting ad nauseam that there was nothing new to report, but that they'd keep on it until there was.

And where the fuck was Alexander Trecchio, chief reporter for Church Life? Laterza had given him the assignment—one of the few real stories ever to come Alexander's way, the man having built his farcical journalistic reputation on a single, accidental story a couple of years back—and he had simply disappeared. Vanished. Laterza had phoned him on every number he had. He'd sent emails. Hell, he'd even gone on Twitter and messaged him there, out of sheer desperation. But nothing. Alexander Trecchio had gone dark.

Bastardo.

And yet . . . Laterza let a smile play across his face. He'd already reassigned the story, of course. What had been page eleven news was now page one, top of the fold, and Trecchio wasn't in that league even on his best days. The paper was covering the story, despite the attempts of the television media to claim ownership.

What made Laterza smile was the fact that this, at last, was an inch too far. No matter how close Alexander's relationship with Niccolò Marre, even the paper's owner wouldn't keep him on staff after a fumble like this. He would be out. Laterza would have the joy of firing him himself. Maybe he'd do it by tweet, just to add insult. But however he did it, Trecchio would go.

And that, more than anything else, threatened to make Antonio Laterza believe in miracles.

26

Alexander awoke with a start. His senses expected familiar sights: his minimalist bedroom decor, or the homey, masculine warmth of his sitting room. They didn't expect the kitsch-and-doily wonderworld that was Isabella Fierro's living room. The furniture pieces owned by Gabriella's aunt were the kind of living antiques that screamed that the last time the owner of this house had gone shopping was in 1965, and there wasn't a surface in the room that wasn't covered in either scraps of lace or the floral drippings of daisy wallpaper and poinsettia lampshades. It was a brutally floral assault on his disorientated mind.

But his memory quickly pieced together the surroundings, the chase of the night before, the 1:30 a.m. arrival at Gabriella's aunt's home after abandoning her abused Fiat and making their way to the northeastern edge of the city by metro. Isabella Fierro was away visiting her even more elderly sister, and as honorary caretaker and plant-waterer during her absence, Gabriella had full access to her house. Grannyland was their haven, and as the memories resurfaced with alarming speed, the antithesis of fashionable decor began to feel warm and reassuring.

And so did the thought of action.

Alexander plucked his laptop out of his rucksack, slid in the dongle and set himself to work. The image of their chief pursuer's face wouldn't leave him—haunting, calm, cold, unyielding. But Alexander knew he didn't have anything to go on in terms of finding out who the man was. He'd only seen his face, and that on the run. Of the second man he'd barely caught sight at all. He had no place to begin.

With those men. But there were two other men he now wanted to know a whole lot more about.

Steam whistled from the old yellow kettle as Gabriella switched off the hob and lifted it from the burner. She flipped open the whistler and poured the boiling liquid over the grounds at the bottom of the cafetière. Its scents rose up and wafted at her nose like the familiar caresses of a lover.

Like the familiar caresses of a lover? Why was everything reminding her of romance this morning? Since she'd woken in the guest room and had her first thought of the new day— the inexcusably unhappy observation that she was alone in the bed—her mind had been possessed. Was she really so love-starved that merely being around a man with whom she'd once had a brief fling could turn her mind in such a way? And shouldn't the fact that they'd been shot at and chased mitigate at least a little of the emotion she was feeling?

Of course, it wasn't the first time she'd been shot at in Alexander's presence. Last night marked the second exchange of gunfire they'd shared since their break-up four years ago. Maybe they were still in some kind of a relationship after all.

Gabriella chuckled at the thought. In the light of day there was nothing between her and Alexander Trecchio. He was handsome and sensitive, but he was . . . she didn't know the right word. Unsettled? Ungrounded? In any case, he'd left her. She said it to herself again. *He. Left. Me.* And the words he'd used to do it had made things worse. The gall of calling her his Eve, the biblical image of temptation who led men astray. It tightened her throat even now to think of it.

She stirred a spoon through the coffee pot then fixed the lid and pressed down the plunger. She'd already prepared a small tray with two cups and toast.

Was she bringing him breakfast in bed? How would *that* be read?

She caught herself. Even thinking these thoughts gave substance to the memories as something more than remnants of the past. Let Alex think whatever he wanted. This was her aunt's place, she'd rescued him, and damn it, she liked coffee in the morning.

Alexander was still sitting in nothing more than his T-shirt and shorts when Gabriella walked into the room, a tray of coffee in hand. For an instant, all his interest in the materials on his computer screen vanished, displaced by discomfort. To be alone with her, not fully dressed. This was something new, despite the circumstances. He wasn't entirely sure how he, or she, would react.

"I'm sorry," he said, pulling the quilted, flower-laden blanket toward himself. "I've only got the one set of clothes with me. Thought it best not to sleep in them."

Gabriella set down the tray on the coffee table next to his laptop. "At least you don't sleep in the buff. I think I can handle the sight of a man in a T-shirt."

He forced a laugh, then reached forward, poured half the contents of the cafetière into the two mugs and handed one to Gabriella. He tried desperately not to think of being in the buff, an almost impossible feat after a woman of such evident beauty had brought it up.

"Thanks for this," he said, raising his own mug and shaking the thoughts from his mind. "I definitely need it." He took a long, slow sip of the steaming liquid. It was black and oily and the perfect consolation to a restless night.

"You're already at work," Gabriella observed, motioning toward his laptop. "I should have guessed as much." She sat down on the sofa next to him, and he could smell that strange scent that only women had in the morning—a scent that for most of his life he'd thought he'd never know.

He forced himself to turn to his computer.

"I've been doing some further background research on Marcus Crossler and Salvatore Tosi."

"Our two professors."

"Both men were academics, though not in the same field. Crossler was a professor of religion, while Tosi was senior research fellow in . . ." he leaned forward and scanned over his monitor, "in Italian social politics."

"So their connection probably wasn't related to their research."

"That's what I thought too. At first."

Gabriella's eyebrows rose. She let the question ask itself.

"As I started to look at their professional lives a little further," Alexander continued, "examining their CVs and publishing records, I could find only one thing that the two men had in common."

"You're going to keep me in suspense?"

He smiled. "They both published papers on the Istituto per le Opere di Religione."

Gabriella's posture tightened. "The Institute for the Works of Religion—the IOR."

"Better known as the Vatican Bank."

Her back straightened. The police officer in her was instinctively emerging. "Crossler and Tosi worked together on these papers?"

"Not from what I can tell. I was able to gain access to electronic versions of each of them for nothing more than an extraordinarily expensive subscription to two journals I can promise you I'll never read again. But it allowed me to compare their notes and references, and neither of them cites the other."

"So they were each studying the bank on their own terms, independently."

"Salvatore's paper is chiefly concerned with the IOR's interaction with public business and political capital, while Crossler was looking at the sociological question of a sacred institution being involved in economic affairs."

"Sounds like both men were suspicious."

"That's putting it mildly. Both articles are critical of the IOR and of the Church, and they both raise some pretty substantial questions about the links it maintains with outside organizations and institutions."

"What sorts of links?"

"The IOR is a bank, privately held by the Church. But just because it's ecclesiastical doesn't mean it doesn't work like any other major bank. It deals in astronomical sums of money in just about every currency on the planet, and interacts with other banks, financial markets and investors. Everything you'd expect from big banking."

"Except that it's all linked to the Church."

"Right, the moral guardians of virtue at the helm of an institution that deals in the root of all evil. I thought Christ said one or two things about not serving God and Mammon."

Gabriella sighed. There was exasperation in her breath and Alexander immediately regretted the sarcasm. He remembered how much she disliked his jabs against religion and the Church. *You may have lost your faith, Alex*, she'd said to him in one of those intimate moments four years ago, *but I haven't. You can keep your cynicism to yourself.*

"What's most frustrating," he said, drawing them back into the facts, "is how little is actually known about the inner workings of the IOR. Though it was founded back in 1942, it didn't make its first public statement on its operations until 2012. Its first annual report was issued in October of 2013, and then apparently only under pressure from the new pope, then a cardinal. He'd been asking for greater transparency at the IOR for years. He finally pushed through a mandate for a public report."

"How does that tie in to our scholars?"

Alexander turned back to his computer. "Tosi published two articles on his theories about internal corruption at the IOR, in each of the two years prior to that first report. He published a third article in November 2013, just after the report went public, accusing the bank's Board of Superintendence of fraudulent accounting."

"Not making any friends."

"Crossler's article on the bank came out just a month later. It's a scathing attack on the moral turpitude of an institution headed by five cardinals and a prelate that has been involved in what he calls 'some of the shadiest dealings in modern financial history.'"

Gabriella was now leaning forward. She set down her coffee, her eyes fixed on Alexander's computer.

"What is it?" he asked, noticing her intensity.

"I think we need to arrange a meeting with the bank's president," she answered bluntly.

"The president? Talk about jumping to the head of the wagon."

"In my experience, it's generally where the direction is coming from," she answered, turning toward him. "And for the first time since you rang yesterday, this is starting to make sense to me. The deaths, the pursuit, everything."

"How's that?"

"A man pretending to be Christ is interesting, Alex, but not enough to kill for. Even healing the Pope . . . it's sensational, but hardly the stuff to motivate murder. Money, on the other hand, is a different story. Especially the kind of money we're talking about with the IOR. There are billions at stake there, and that's motive enough for most men."

Thirty minutes later, Alexander had shaved and bandaged the scrape on his hand, they'd both taken quick show- ers, and Gabriella had made a series of phone calls to col- leagues at central office. Relations between Rome's police forces and Vatican City were not always easy, but neither were they always tense, and Gabriella knew a few officers who had close working relationships with the ecclesiastical authorities.

To her relief, they'd been able to determine that the IOR's office had not been closed down with the rest of Vatican City. Financial markets don't switch off internationally for any man's whim, even the Pope's. The bank couldn't afford not to engage in Monday-morning trading.

And to Gabriella's surprise, her contact had another bit of good news for her and Alexander—news that had them rushing, even now, toward her aunt's garage with keys from the kitchen drawer in hand, plotting the best route into the city center.

Despite every expectation, the head of the IOR was willing to see them.

27

Headquarters of Global Capital Italia: 7:18 a.m.

The instructions from the CEO demanding immediate action had been clear, but not everything could truly be immediate. Not if the desired end-result was something that would hold up to scrutiny. The first rule of a good cover-up is that your target has to be able to look squarely at it and see only the truth that you want them to.

And that sort of thing wasn't easy when your target was the public, and when what you were manipulating was money. People were used to suspecting the evils of money, so systems everywhere were designed to safeguard against precisely the kinds of things Caterina Amato's specialists needed to do if they were going to make the world believe what she wanted them to believe. This kind of manipulation required skill, means, and enough time to do the job right. The fact that they didn't have the latter would not be accepted as an excuse for failure.

This duo of men, whom Global Capital Italia employed as "financial technologies specialists," had therefore been working for hours in the enclosed, windowless space that constituted their basement office. Their surroundings looked less futuristic than some might expect of talented hackers at their pay grade, but nonetheless represented some of the most powerful computing technology in their field.

They'd been given their list of targets: a few firms, a few companies, a few individuals. On paper it looked innocuous; in reality, the work required was far more complicated.

They'd already completed their tasks on the first target institution and its associated agencies. They'd look guilty as sin when they were discovered. Now they were at work on the second, which in the newscasts of the previous day had become by far the most visible.

The bank accounts of the Lisa Tedesco MCL Research Unit were listed on one of the LCD displays in the room, a slightly longer listing of source investor accounts on another. They went through the lists, moving funds at the prescribed rates from the assigned sources. Two million euros here, ten there, half a million there. It was the backdating that was the hardest part. Banks and financial institutions had systems designed precisely to prevent this sort of fraudulent activity, and ensuring that the transactions they were effecting wouldn't raise any red flags, that they would look entirely legitimate and register back as assigned—this one a day before, that one three days, the next two months—was critical.

But they'd done it. The work was pure showmanship, of course. Amato and the massive reach of her firm all but owned these companies, although this ownership was hidden behind layers of corporate distancing that would deceive even the most industrious of tax assessors. Through those walls Global Capital Italia had complete access to their resources. Invest billions behind the scenes, and you can buy a lot of power.

But tonight's work wasn't about control and it wasn't about secrecy. It was about placing companies in such a position that they would be unable to deny their involvement in something they had known nothing about. It was, both of the computer specialists thought, brilliant.

All that remained now was the personal touch.

One of the specialists called up the private banking details of Dr. Marcello Tedesco, the "pious dupe" as they'd come to dub him. The tech had already created a second current account in the scientist's name to go alongside the account the doctor had used for more than a decade. It looked far better to have another account, with its whiff of illegitimacy and intended secrecy.

With a few keystrokes, he transferred 25,000 euros from one of their client corporations to the account, backdating the transaction three days. Then a second, equal amount, dated to this morning.

Half then, half now. Wasn't that the traditional way payoffs worked?

28

Office of the Institute for the Works of Religion, Vatican City: 8:30 a.m.

"This is a threshold I never thought I'd cross," Alexander whispered to Gabriella as he stepped up to the door that led into the lobby of the Vatican Bank.

Nothing about the central offices of the Institute for the Works of Religion inspired sentiments of openness or warmth. The round tower, situated at the edge of the Apostolic Palace, was one of the only places in Vatican City that hadn't been completely isolated from public interaction since the arrival of the stranger at St. Peter's yesterday morning. Protruding like a circular butt from the side of the palace on to the outer edge of the city state, it was accessible from beyond Vatican territory by a small black door that opened on to Via di Porta Angelica—that is, if one had the access to get it to open at all. Most of the tourists who passed within a stone's throw of the building in their thousands every day on their way into the Piazza San Pietro never knew what lay within it.

But knowledge, Alexander mused, did not always do away with fear. He'd noted the forbidding uninterrupted stonework that rose well over three stories from street level, its first row of inset barred windows ringing the tower well above a height that would allow anyone to peer inside. Everything about the structure was impenetrable, which was essentially what the Vatican had made it for the past few decades.

And yet here he was. They'd driven directly here from Gabriella's aunt's, stopping along the way only to buy two new phones. Gabriella purchased a simple flip-top model. Alexander opted for a fancier LG G2—the same phone he'd had before. He'd grown accustomed to it as a portable research tool, however much he enjoyed grumbling about new-fangled technology. This time, however, they both bought pay-as-you-go versions and provided false names to the none-too-interested retailer. Better safe than sorry.

"As mysterious as you thought it would be?" Gabriella asked, pointing at the round building before them. They'd taken her aunt's tired but pristinely cared for Opel on as direct a route as they could manage toward the Apostolic Palace.

"Quite," Alexander answered. "Its reputation appears well earned."

"If it sets your mind at ease," Gabriella said, "they didn't hesitate in granting us this appointment, even with every-thing else going on inside."

"The influence of your warrant card and police identity. It's not like that in the world of mere mortals."

"Not even when you were one of them?"

Alexander nodded as they stepped through the cramped entrance into the reception room proper. "As priests we were never allowed anywhere near the IOR. In my short stint working in the curia with my uncle, I think I only heard mention of it twice. It was as if the place didn't exist."

As they entered, Alexander and Gabriella were confronted with a reception area unlike that of any bank either of them had experienced. The small space was surrounded by plain whitewashed walls. Monotone beige carpeting lined the floor. Three plain chairs sat along one wall, upholstered in cream fabric that could easily have passed for standard fare in any hotel lobby. Opposite them was a single small wooden desk. The only adornment was a crucifix above a white door that led deeper into the building, and a photo of the Pope that hung above the desk. On its surface a violet lily stood in a glass vase, providing the only sparkle of color in the bland room.

"Not exactly the opulence I was expecting," Gabriella muttered. There was no extraneous decoration anywhere. Nor, for that matter, were there any computers on the desk nor video cameras on the walls. The only technology in the room appeared to be an older-looking telephone, detailed in brass, next to a spiral-bound notebook on the desk.

"Don't be fooled," Alexander answered. "Power doesn't always sparkle."

A second later, the white door on the far side of the room opened and Gabriella received her second surprise of the morning. Into the foyer of one of the most concentrated realms of power in the famously male-centric world of the Vatican walked a woman. She was thirty-something, professional-looking. She stepped up to meet them with an air of corporate confidence.

"I'm Beatrice Pinard," she said in a strongly French accent. She extended her hand as she approached. "I'm the public liaison for the Istituto per le Opere di Religione. A pleasure to meet you."

Alexander shook her hand and Gabriella followed in turn.

"I was under the impression we had a meeting with the IOR's president," he said, annoyance immediately showing through in his voice.

The woman smiled. "You do. Don't worry, you haven't been fobbed off with a lowly subordinate. But with the Vatican closure, our staff have been restricted from regular duty." She stared into Alexander's eyes, then continued with a softly concealed pride. "I'm not normally the one who answers the front door."

"We're grateful for your help." Gabriella stepped in, covering for Alexander's gaffe. "And for your willingness to arrange a meeting on such short notice."

"Mr. Holtzmann, the president of the Board of Superintendence, is looking forward to speaking with you. He confirmed the meeting himself."

Alexander balked. The idea of the Vatican Bank's senior executive officer being eager to meet with a reporter and a police officer was hard to fathom.

Their host noticed his expression. "You were expecting something else, Mr. Trecchio? Perhaps I should make my entrance again, come in a little more furtively and suggest you'd better not ask any questions, then send you demonstratively on your way? Perhaps I could wear dark glasses and quietly whisper that some things are never discussed or mentioned?"

Gabriella couldn't stifle a laugh at the other woman's self-deprecating humor. Alexander shifted to another shade of red.

"Don't worry," Beatrice Pinard said. "It's not the first time I've encountered your reaction. But the IOR isn't obligated to live up to the preconceived notions that others have of our work." She smiled gently, then motioned toward the chairs along the wall. "Please, take a seat. I'll inform the president you're here and be back in just a moment to collect you."

Alexander and Gabriella sat, and a moment later Ms. Pinard had slipped back through the white door and left them in solitude.

"That certainly went well," Gabriella said, edging an elbow at Alexander's ribs. "You want to do anything else to make us unwelcome before we've even told them why we're here?"

Alexander opened his mouth but bit back his answer. What he was feeling was something Gabriella wouldn't understand, and that Pinard's humor didn't alleviate. It was the twinge of experience. Of knowing how the Church and its institutions worked. And knowing that this wasn't it.

He pulled out his new phone, opened the messaging app and entered a number he knew by memory. His uncle was the man he trusted most in the whole world.

He typed only a single line.

You won't believe where I am.

29

The Apostolic Palace: 8:40 a.m.

Pope Gregory turned to the stranger, who sat silently opposite his desk. They had spoken together, they had been quiet together. There had been long spans of reflection and prayer. But now, as the progress of a new day pushed forward, the Pope was filled with resolve.

"I will speak to the people," he said softly. "I've already conveyed my intentions to my staff. They will make the arrangements for a small press conference here in the palace. I'm certain, given the climate outside, that my words will be broadcast live."

"And what will you say?" The man's question was smooth and unrushed.

"I will tell the world of the good works we are witnessing." The Pope's answer was direct, though behind it there were concerns that wouldn't fully leave his mind. The miracles that he'd learned had taken place outside the Vatican's walls were extraordinary. But they were also just as unexplained as his own healing.

Yet that healing was real. That much he knew as an absolute fact. And as to the rest . . . he was, after all, a man of faith.

Besides, even a pope could speak in veiled terms.

"More importantly," he continued, "I will urge them to make the witness of these things a beginning. To undertake good works of their own."

The Pope looked into the face of the stranger. For the thousandth time he felt the pinch of curiosity. He considered asking the man his name—asking where he'd come from, *why* he'd come. But just like each instance in the past, the temptation fled as quickly as it had come. What remained was the feeling of serenity, of otherness, of timelessness that had been with the pontiff since he'd first met the stranger the previous day.

The feeling of hope. It was a feeling that, for the moment, was enough for Gregory.

"These are noble sentiments," the stranger answered. There was a comforting smile in his eyes. "The goodness we see in the world should always spur us to a deeper virtue. What miracle has ever been an end in itself?"

The Pope sighed deeply and with gratitude. He reflected on the millions of faithful outside these walls who so desperately needed hope. The reassurance of love and grace. If he could offer them words that would inspire this, in the face of the wondrous things being done in their midst, his own heart would rejoice. Surely this was the great work to which the descendants of the Fisherman were called.

"There is only one thing I ask of you, if you are willing." The stranger spoke after a few moments' pause. A request. The first the man had made. Pope Gregory leaned forward in his chair.

"Of course."

"I ask only that you say what is truly in your heart." The stranger kept his eyes on the Pope's as he slid a hand into the breast pocket of his shirt. He extracted a small slip of paper, folded once down the middle.

"Say what you feel, say what your heart whispers into your mouth," he repeated, sliding the paper across the Pope's desk.

"And then say this."

30

Office of the Institute for the Works of Religion: 8:51 a.m.

"Am I to assume that you're here to determine whether we're corrupt?"

The question, delivered with a smile and absolute charm from the pudgy, rose-colored German face of Ernst Holtzmann, President of the IOR, was immediately disarming. Nothing about the man spoke of the kind of deception-laden, corporate criminal that popular belief asserted ran the Vatican Bank. Instead, Holtzmann was the spitting image of a fairy-tale village baker: rosy-cheeked, cheerful, rotund. He smiled warmly through perfectly round glasses, thinning hair mopping his forehead in a manner that was more comical than off-putting.

"No, that's not why we're here," Gabriella replied apologetically. It was clear that the public-liaison-cum-receptionist had relayed her experiences from the lobby. "We're sorry if you were given that impression." She shot Alexander a furtive look. "We're here to see whether you might be able to assist us with a police investigation currently under way."

The man seemed to notice Gabriella's embarrassment. "Please, don't worry. I'll be pleased to help you however I can, though I didn't realize there were any police matters currently pending with our office." He motioned for them to take the two leather seats opposite his small desk. "A drink?" Both Alexander and Gabriella declined, but the man poured himself a dram of what looked like Scotch. The morning hour seemed to pose no stumbling block to his habit.

"The accusation of corruption is one I hear often," he said, taking a seat and following it with a sip, "and you probably wouldn't be surprised at how many people end up here thinking they've landed in the heart of some grand criminal enterprise." He smiled, his teeth clean but crooked. His lips were naturally a bright red, the color of a hearty lipstick, giving him a comical aspect perfectly fitted to his personality.

"They're wrong?" Alexander asked, too confrontationally.

"But not for inexcusable reasons," Holtzmann answered. The man wasn't thrown for an instant. "It comes with the territory. I knew it would, the day the Pope appointed me to the office. We're the financial arm of the Church, and the Church is an institution of great power and significant wealth. Both of those breed suspicion."

He spoke in erudite tones that suggested more than an education only in finance. His words were to the point and delivered with a compelling openness.

"It seems there's been plenty to be suspicious over in the bank's past," Alexander countered.

Holtzmann sighed. "Everyone has a past, including us. But unlike the majority of institutions, ours is heavily scrutinized. We've never been more transparent than we are now. And isn't the most important question not what we've done in the past, but what we're doing today?"

"Sounds right to me," Gabriella answered. Alexander grunted softly.

"We've opened our doors to unparalleled levels of public scrutiny over the past few years," Holtzmann added. "His Holiness Pope Gregory is well known for his desire to shed light into some of the darker corners of the Church's extensive attic. And there's no place more prone to darkness and back-room dealings than finance."

"You're sure you're a banker?" Gabriella asked, only half sarcastically. Holtzmann smiled.

"I like to think that I'm a servant of the Church, helping support her good works in the world. But yes, I'm a banker and the former chairman of Holtzmann Financial, begun by my great-grandfather. I don't see any reason why honesty and transparency shouldn't reign in financial dealings."

The IOR president took another drink of his Scotch, drawing it back the way most people drank coffee at this hour. "But you said you were here about a police investigation?" He looked toward Gabriella.

"We're following up on the deaths of two scholars who perished under suspicious circumstances."

"Deaths? Oh, I'm sorry to hear that," Holtzmann answered, making the sign of the cross over his chest. He paused and closed his eyes, uttering a silent prayer. When he opened them, he looked directly at Alexander.

"Since you're here, I gather you're wondering whether these two professors have some connection to the bank?"

Again, Alexander noted, the man was strangely open. Given the circumstances, he would normally have expected to have to drag such an observation out of one of the Church's employees.

"They'd both written journal articles on corruption in the IOR," he answered, leaning slightly forward in his chair. "Neither seemed to make much of a stir at the time, but the murder of both men in the past twenty-four hours suggests that someone was not pleased with their conclusions."

Holtzmann released a long sigh. "Terrible, just terrible. Though I can't see how academic work on the bank's affairs could kindle such a reaction."

"Do the names Marcus Crossler or Salvatore Tosi mean anything to you?" Gabriella asked. Alexander closely monitored Holtzmann's features, but he saw there only the genuine signs of a lack of recognition. At least so far as he could read them.

"No, I don't think I've heard either of those names before." The bank's president paused. "These are the names of the two men who were . . . killed?"

Gabriella nodded and Holtzmann crossed himself again. He looked paled by the attachment of actual names to what had formerly been the abstract concept of murder.

"Crossler's paper suggests you're still keeping secrets," Alexander persisted. He could see Gabriella eyeing him at his side, her glance an exasperated, silent *Alexander, shut up.*

"Of course we keep secrets," Holtzmann replied. He seemed undeterred by the question. "Every institution does. Confidentiality is an important ingredient in effective business. It's all the more so in church affairs. We help the poor and the repressed, and this often means acting in direct violation of the wishes of the governments doing the oppressing. Look at the work undertaken in the days of John Paul II. The Church's activities, many of them financed through this office, were a significant ingredient in toppling communism in many parts of the Eastern Bloc. We couldn't just allow those governments to know what we were up to."

The response gave Alexander pause. "Still," he said, "in little more than half a century of existence, the IOR has had its fair share of scandals. Corrupt officers, illegitimate business dealings—"

"Alleged, on all counts," Holtzmann interrupted. "With all respect, a thing is not true simply because it's reported in the media." He smiled again, and the ice clinked in his glass.

"Alleged," Alexander allowed. "But ongoing secrecy doesn't help alleviate suspicion. Crossler's paper said he was unable to get concrete information from your office. Detailed materials on interactions with other agencies, that sort of thing."

At first, the comment seemed finally to have thrown Holtzmann. He did not answer. He set down his drink. A moment later he was standing, turning away from Alexander and Gabriella, yet he did not head for the door. He arrived at a filing cabinet and drew open a metal drawer. Flipping through folders for a few seconds, he located a stapled collection of papers and drew it out from a stack of others like it.

"Do you mean this kind of information, Mr. Trecchio?"

Holtzmann returned to his desk with a satisfied smile on his face. He dropped the papers before them.

"A full listing of the IOR's current financial and business partnerships." He plopped himself back into his chair, looking eminently satisfied at the disbelieving expressions on both Alexander and Gabriella's faces.

"Call it a little gift," he added, "from your good friend the sinister keeper of secrets."

Eleven minutes later
Vatican City: 9:01 a.m.

A black telephone rang, deep within the corridors of Vatican City. It was answered by a man who kept his words soft and brief.

"Yes?"

"There's been activity."

"Where?"

"The IOR head office. Holtzmann's been talking."

"To whom?"

"The registry book lists a male and a female." The informant gave the names: Alexander Trecchio and Gabriella Fierro.

"You can get me a recording of the meeting in Holtzmann's office?"

"Of course. You'll have it in a few minutes."

The man in the Vatican sighed, relieved. Ernst Holtzmann was an honest man, cooperative and fully above board in all things. Which was why he had never been privy to the true nature of what went on with the funds he nominally controlled.

The relief vanished entirely after the informant's next words.

"There's more. When the visitors were present, Holtzmann gave them the full IOR partnership listing."

"They have the list?"

"They took it with them when they left."

The informant started to say more, but never got the chance to finish. The voice in the Vatican was already gone and the line was dead.

31

Near the Tiber River, central Rome: 9:22 a.m.

The call had come in to central dispatch at 8:40 a.m., only twenty minutes before beat officers Enzo Juliano and Ivo Turci were due to go off shift. But that was how intriguing calls often came—in the last moments, unexpected.

They arrived at the appointed spot on the Viadotto della Magliana nine minutes later, pulling their patrol-issue Alfa Romeo 159 alongside the road that twisted beside the south bank of the Tiber. Juliano always hated these calls. Despite its romantic past in bygone Roman days, the modern Tiber was little more than a stinking open sewer traversing the city. But it was generally what was found on these occasions that really made his stomach turn.

A middle-aged woman with disheveled gray hair stood statuesque along the embankment, her face too ashen and white for the sunny weather. Juliano's suspicion that she was the individual who had called the station was confirmed as he and Turci approached and she simply pointed downward toward the waterline.

"Wait here," Turci instructed her as they passed. A moment later, both officers were descending the brick steps that led down to water level, then walking nimbly over the large rocks that bordered the ancient Tiber.

Juliano could already see it.

"Just there," he said, pointing ahead to his eleven o'clock. Lapping in the water, just breaking the surface, were two legs. They were covered in jeans, indeterminate brown shoes on the feet, something wrapped around them. As the officers approached, more of the body became visible. It was lying face down in the water, a flannel shirt covering the torso. Hair that looked to be a light brown and about three inches in length flowed about the back of the head, its motions strangely beautiful in the midst of the macabre scene.

"Careful," Juliano sputtered, reaching out to offer his partner a hand as the latter lost his footing. The rocks that banked the river were rounded, algae-covered and slippery.

"I got it." They were only steps away. Within a few seconds the two officers were standing to either side of the body.

"No obvious signs of trauma," Turci noted, looking over the dead man's corpse—though it was a largely useless comment. With his body covered in clothing, there could be any manner of trauma they couldn't see. Knife strikes, gunshot wounds, the bruises of a fall. All that could be seen clearly was a heavy set of chains wrapped around his lower legs.

"Let's get him turned over, see what we're dealing with."

Officer Juliano reached down and the two of them together grabbed the body by the torso.

"On three," he instructed. Then the short countdown and the two officers together flipped over the body of the unknown victim.

The water splashed against Juliano's legs as the body turned, and he stepped back on instinct as it came to rest in its new position. Golden-brown hair was matted against its face.

He reached down, grabbed the locks of hair around the eyes and nose, and pushed them aside.

It was then that they both saw the man's face.

Only Turci found words to speak.

"Oh Christ."

32

Salita ai Giardini Street, bordering Vatican City: 9:31 a.m.

"I'm not entirely sure I understand what just happened," Alexander confessed as he and Gabriella left the round tower at the edge of the Apostolic Palace.

Gabriella made no attempt to keep the smile from her face. "Admit it, Alex, you walked in there expecting to be stonewalled and dismissed at every turn. Cynic!"

Alexander raised his hands in mock surrender. "Guilty." He reached into his pocket, pulled out a new pack of MS Filtros bought at the same time they'd purchased their new phones, and lit up. "That went nothing at all like I was expecting."

"Later, you and I are going to have a conversation about your attitude toward the Church, Mr. Trecchio," Gabriella said. "Enough experiences like this and I have hopes of bringing you back into the fold."

Alexander smiled as they approached the mid-sized, wretchedly orange Opel. The locks clicked open. She was talking about a future.

"That being said," Gabriella continued as she sat, "the bank's openness was a little worrying."

"Good to know there's some suspicion left in you."

She shook her head. "Only a suspicion that we might be on the wrong track entirely."

"Why's that?"

"Precisely because of the president's candor. Crossler and Tosi thought they were exposing secrets, and we're following their path on that assumption. But Holtzmann apparently had nothing to hide. He produced the bank's bloody liaison list without a moment's hesitation!" The sign of the cross was again in motion.

Alex raised a brow. The prim and professional facade of Gabriella Fierro occasionally slipped enough to let some of her police gruffness through, together with her personal quirks, and he liked it.

"Don't be so sure," he answered. "That list means nothing until we check it out and confirm what it is we've really been given."

"I'll manage that," Gabriella answered, nodding. "You just drive us by a coffee shop. Holtzmann may take whisky before ten, but I could go with a latte. And put out that cigarette. My aunt will complain about the insult to her car's upholstery for months."

Alexander smiled, flicked the half-smoked cigarette out the window and started the engine. But before he could put the car into gear, his new mobile began to ring. He fished it out of his pocket, and when he saw the number on the display, his face contorted in surprise.

The series of digits were those he'd texted earlier. He and his uncle had kept a kind of running dialogue on their lives by SMS since text messages had become commonplace, and he'd texted him earlier chiefly out of habit. Since they'd discussed the absence of access to the IOR in the past, Alexander had thought that news of his being there would interest his uncle.

But given the current situation in the Vatican, and his uncle's status there, he hadn't expected a reply. In the circumstances, the call shouldn't even be possible.

He clicked answer with an unusual hesitation. "Hello?"

"Alexander, is that you?"

"Uncle Rinaldo, I almost didn't believe my screen. I thought you were all cloistered. How are you calling me?"

"The cloister has been in effect since the call went out to all the Cardinals yesterday afternoon. I was already here, so the trip was quick. Others have been flying in from all over the world."

"We were told you were completely isolated. No calls taken, none going out."

"That's true, Alexander. But please, stop asking questions."

The nervousness in his uncle's voice was throwing Alexander. It wasn't an emotion he was used to hearing there.

Rinaldo Trecchio had been a cardinal for sixteen years, a loyal and dedicated prince of the Church. He'd also been a caring and compassionate uncle as long as Alexander could remember.

As Alexander's own faith had weakened, bit by bit, until his conscience finally approached a threshold he'd never anticipated nearing—the realization that he could not continue as a priest—his uncle had stayed by his side. By the time Gabriella had entered the scene, Alexander's decision was all but taken, but even then Rinaldo had continued to show him love and kindness, while the rest of his deeply Catholic family had reacted with anger and disappointment. He was sure his uncle had felt those same sentiments, but to his credit he had never let them interrupt the care he showed his nephew.

"Where are you right now?" Rinaldo's voice pressed through the phone.

"I'm in a car, not far from Vatican City."

"And why have you changed your phone number?" The question sounded anxious, not curious.

Alexander wasn't sure how to answer. "I've been involved in a bit of an . . . incident. The change was prudent."

Suddenly his uncle's tone was chilled with warning. "Alexander, listen to me closely. You have to be careful. Very careful."

A rock formed in Alexander's stomach. "What are you talking about?"

"I know you're investigating the healing of the Pope and the arrival of this man at St. Peter's," Rinaldo answered. "I also know you're looking into the deaths of two professors."

Alexander blanched, his grip tightening simultaneously around the mobile phone and the steering wheel.

"How do you know that? Are you having me monitored?"

"It's not important how I know, Alex. It's better that you don't. It's only important that you listen to me when I tell you that there is far more going on than you can possibly understand."

"Am I being followed?" Alex demanded, confused. "Watched, by the Vatican?" Was this what the magisterium did with priests who resigned? With the press?

"Alex, please. There's no time to go into details," his uncle answered, pleading. "But the further you step into this, the more of a threat you become to, to . . ."

"To who, Uncle?"

Rinaldo hesitated, then spat out the words: "To men who will have little hesitation in eliminating those they view as threats."

Alexander swallowed hard. He glanced at Gabriella, who by this stage was looking up from the paperwork they'd received at the IOR. She was aware that something strange was taking place in Alexander's conversation but was only able to hear his half of it.

"You've got to tell me more than that," Alexander demanded of his uncle. "Who are we dealing with?"

He waited for an answer, but none came.

"Uncle Rinaldo?"

He glanced at the phone. The line was dead.

33

Central Rome: 9:51 a.m.

"What was that about?" Gabriella asked impatiently. Alexander had sat silently for several long seconds since the call with his uncle ended. Something obviously wasn't right.

Suddenly he reached forward and switched on the car's radio. He scrolled through the stations disinterestedly, landing on the first with solid reception, as if he craved nothing more than background noise to distract him from his thoughts.

"Alex," Gabriella persisted, "talk to me." She reached out a hand and laid her soft fingers across his knuckles. The sudden human contact seemed to calm him.

"You know my uncle's a cardinal," he finally said, "so you know where he is right now, and what he's privy to."

"Has he met the man, the stranger? Did he share anything with you about him?"

"Nothing. He barely mentioned him. He only warned me about our investigation."

Now it was Gabriella who paused. "How does your uncle know what you're investigating?"

Alexander's head was shaking. "I don't know and he wouldn't say. He only warned me that there are people out there who know what we're looking for. People we don't want to get on the wrong side of."

"It's a bit late for that. I'd take last night's gunfight as a pretty solid sign that we're already on their bad side."

Alexander stilled at Gabriella's words. As she'd often found she was able to do before, Gabriella could read the thoughts on his emotive face as if they were words printed on a page. *Someone is obviously after us, but how could my uncle possibly know that? Was his warning just a hunch—a voice of general concern that happened to coincide with the most traumatic experience of my life?* But she knew that Alexander didn't like coincidences. Certainly not of this magnitude. *How could he know what we've been investigating? How could he know who was after us? And more than that,* why *would anyone be after us at all?*

Gabriella broke through his thoughts. "Did your uncle say who these people were?"

"I don't think he could. It sounded like he was taking a risk to make the call at all. He wanted to keep it short."

Gabriella peered down at the papers on her lap. "Then urgent or not, his warning isn't a lot of help." She glanced up again and saw the disconcerted expression on Alexander's face. She was suddenly keen to divert him from a train-wreck of increasingly convoluted, speculative thoughts that would lead nowhere. Diverting the topic seemed her best option.

"Why don't you drive, Alex? I've glanced through the list of institutional affiliations from the IOR. If it's meant to provide us with anything, I'm not seeing it."

Alexander put the car into gear and pulled forward, but his head was shaking again. "There's got to be something in there."

"Since I'm not sure what we're looking for, it's hard to know. On the surface it's just a listing of client and partner corporations. I'd expect to see the same thing from any bank."

"Marcus Crossler wouldn't have had more insider information than this," Alexander insisted, "but he was able to convince himself of illegitimate activity. Activity he linked to the stranger."

"He also had more time and more of a background than I do," Gabriella answered. "On first reading, the only thing these companies appear to have in common is that they're big names."

"Private clients aren't in the IOR's charter. The only individuals who can open accounts are members of the curia and high-ranking church officials. Otherwise, it deals only in the financial ventures of the state."

"Well, when it comes to those ventures, the list of the Vatican's investment partners looks like what you'd expect. Big corporations. Eurobank, the IMF, Celentis, Alventix, Cygna-Gen, Financia Italia, that sort of thing."

Gabriella concluded her listing, rattling off the names. But when she looked up, Alexander was staring at her from the driver's seat. His eyes lingered with a strange intensity before he switched them back to the road. She wondered, for a moment, whether her touch a few moments before had evoked memories in him that she shouldn't have teased. But an instant later he swerved the car to the shoulder and pulled to a stop.

The look on his face wasn't longing.

"Read those names again, the ones you just listed." His expression was curious, and Gabriella turned back to the printouts without asking for an explanation.

"Eurobank, the International Monetary Fund, Celentis, Alventix, CygnaGen, Finan—"

"Stop there," Alexander interrupted. He struggled beneath the safety belt but managed to turn more fully toward her.

"Does that list explain the type of relationship the Vatican Bank had with each of the companies?"

"There's no indication of euro or dollar amounts. Just the fact of institutional connections." She gazed into his determined stare. "Alex, what are you on to?"

"There's something that at least three of those firms have in common that goes beyond simply being large, rich companies." His fingers rattled along the gray plastic of the steering column, then suddenly stopped.

"Let's start with Celentis. You've heard of them?"

"Of course," Gabriella answered. "They make the vitamin supplements I see in every supermarket." *See, and buy.* Gabriella was a sucker for supplements, to a degree that even she found embarrassing to admit.

"Vitamin supplements, together with a lot of other things," Alexander nodded in agreement. "The next was what . . . Alventix?"

"I don't know anything about them."

"Sure you do. They're the company headed by the Russian tycoon. The one the protesters are always out to crucify, who fights back on primetime at every opportunity."

"Kopulov," Gabriella suddenly remembered. "I didn't know the company, but I know the man."

"And what was the next one?"

"CygnaGen. From the name, I'm going to guess it's involved in some kind of genetic research."

"I've never heard of them before," Alexander said, "but I'd assume the same. Which means we've got three companies involved in medical research and pharmaceutical production."

Gabriella considered the connection.

"Are there others?" Alexander asked.

Gabriella dragged a finger down the list of company names. "Europa MediTech . . . GenCore . . ."

Alexander's head was nodding as if he'd predicted the answer. As the white noise of the car radio mumbled beneath them, Gabriella took note of the ongoing change in his expression. Where there had been curiosity a few moments before, there was now a mixture of resolve that seemed to merge with worry. His eyes danced a back-and-forth pattern between unknown targets somewhere between his knees. She remembered that expression. Something had him hooked.

"Alex, at some point you're going to have to tell me what you're thinking."

He didn't look up. "I'm not thinking, I'm listening." He motioned toward the car's minuscule stereo. At this point Gabriella no longer tried to conceal her confusion. His behavior was becoming bizarre.

"Alex, this isn't the time to—"

"What have we just learned?" He cut her off. When Gabriella gave him only a wide-eyed shake of her head, he answered for himself. "We've learned that the IOR maintains ongoing financial connections with a whole suite of medical research firms. We've learned that this list of connections was at least in part what lay behind Crossler's conviction that the events of yesterday are fraudulent and criminal."

"And?"

"So *listen*," Alexander said, waving again at the car's speakers. A male newsreader's voice tinned its way out of the low-grade equipment.

". . . the sudden recovery of the sixty-three terminal cancer patients in Dr. Tedesco's ongoing study marks the second mass healing, as they've come to be known, to make the news in the past twenty-four hours, following swiftly upon the recovery of the sight of over one hundred permanently blind children in a Pescara hospital ward suffering from a genetic condition for which there is no known cure."

Gabriella was suddenly aware of the goose pimples standing at full rise on her arms.

The voice of the newsreader returned.

"These events follow the as-yet-unexplained occurrence at St. Peter's yesterday morning, during which the crippled Pope suddenly stood upright, his lifelong condition apparently healed. Needless to say, in a nation of Catholics, the word 'miracle' is floating through the Italian vocabulary today with an unusual intensity."

Gabriella peered up at Alexander. Suddenly her face was as white as his.

34

The Apostolic Palace: 10:02 a.m.

"I wish to speak to the world, and I have both the ability and the right to do so." The words came from Pope Gregory's thin lips with an air of firm insistence, as if he were anticipating the fervent protests of his Secretary of State. On that front the supreme pontiff was not disappointed.

"Your Holiness," Cardinal Viteri appealed, "are you sure this is the wisest course of action?" His aged features were a picture of distress and concern.

"I am."

Viteri looked uncomfortable with the short response, especially when the Pope did not follow it with any explanation.

"But what could you possibly say to them at this moment?" His face broadcast his increasing anxiety. "Your Holiness has been healed," he motioned to the Pope's erect figure standing regally before him, "for which we all stand in immense gratitude before our Lord. But we know not the how, nor the reason." He hesitated. "You cannot be intending to speak to the people about . . . him."

Gregory peered down at the cardinal, a new position given his change in stature. Prior to yesterday morning, he'd always stood a good three centimeters shorter than Viteri. Today he was the taller man.

When he spoke, the Pope's expression was unreadable. "I haven't yet decided whether to mention anything about our guest. But there are wonderful things afoot, Viteri." The Secretary of State needn't know about Gregory's ongoing questions—the fact that he still had concerns over the identity of this man. The peace that was in the Pope's heart was strong enough to outweigh his concerns, but since he knew it would be unlikely to have the same effect on Viteri, it was best simply to speak without qualification. "We must not hide the mercies of God."

Cardinal Viteri flinched. His body language made clear that "guest" was not the word he would have chosen for their visitor, and that "mercies" were not how he was interpreting the events of the day.

"If you don't intend to speak of him, then I ask again, of what?"

"Am I now to understand that the Pope is to filter his remarks through your office, Donato?" Gregory asked.

Viteri blanched. "Of course not, Your Holiness. I am simply trying to bring measure and calm to a situation that, beyond these walls, is greatly exciting the masses."

The pontiff nodded, understanding. "Do not be afraid, Donato. I will tell the people what they need to hear."

Five minutes later, Cardinal Viteri was alone under the small portico, the Holy Father having returned to his study to make ready his remarks for the press.

Viteri's expressions of concern and reticence had departed with the Pope. Standing solitary beneath the arched roof, relief now covered his face.

Had he been adequately convincing? It was hard to say, and he'd had to navigate a fairly tender line. But the

antagonism between Gregory and himself had been strong
before the new pope's election, and stronger since. The
two men had never liked each other—what a godsend that
was today proving to be. He knew Gregory would naturally react against the inclinations of his Secretary of State.
Showing concern over any mention of miracles or the presence of the stranger was the best way Viteri could think of
to cause the pontiff to react with deeper resolve.

Now he could only hope that Gregory would mention
both.

35

Vatican City: 10:20 a.m.

"Is it right for us to meet without the rest of the brethren?" In the four years he had been a member, Monsignor Farro had never known the Fraternity to meet *ex parte*, without the whole membership assembled. There were, after all, only thirteen of them. And they always met in secret. It was not as if a full gathering required elaborate preparation.

"It's right if I say it's right," their leader answered curtly. "Several of our brothers are occupied in other matters, but Father Taylor has urgent news that requires immediate attention."

The Reverend Taylor Abbate was Brooklyn born and raised, and, though he came from several generations of Paduan stock, was the only member of the Fraternitas Christi Salvatoris not to be Italian by nationality. He was known universally as "the American" as a constant reminder, and he wore the title with pride. He was a young man who stood out for his ruthlessness, and he didn't mind having a title that marked him uniquely as well.

At this moment, he looked concerned.

"We might have a problem," he blurted out, not particularly worried whether it was rightly his moment to speak. There were only five of them in the office and they were here to receive his intelligence.

"What sort of problem?" Farro asked, his previous concerns over questions of protocol and quorums forgotten.

Father Taylor's worry was accentuated by the features of a face not accustomed to expressing this particular emotion. Through college and seminary he had been an avid sportsman, playing football of both the American and European varieties. He'd kept up a demanding physical regimen over the years since, as he'd worked his way through various positions in the USA before being called to serve in the curia two years ago. His body was fit beneath his black shirt and dog collar, and his face was much more experienced in expressing confidence and control than concern. It was a face that, when most people first saw it, struck an immediate note of fear, despite it being poised above a priestly collar.

"You've been told of the call I received from the IOR about Holtzmann's visitors."

The four other necks in the room immediately tensed. They'd all been passed word of the last-minute additions to the agenda of the figurehead president of the IOR.

Father Taylor's normally controlled face lost a shade before he continued. "Our listeners recorded their conversation. They contacted me because two red-flag words came up in the discussion."

"Which?" the leader of the Fraternity asked, his voice measured and calm.

"Names, both of them."

"Chrissakes, man," one of the members, a bishop, pressed. "Which names?"

Another shade of color melted from Taylor's features. "Tosi, and Crossler."

"The professors?" the group's leader asked, his recognition immediate. "The ones who wrote articles on financial scandals at the bank?" He obviously knew the men, but his reaction hardly matched the discomfort in Father Taylor's expression. The priest nodded.

"They're renewing their research now, of all times?"

"No," Taylor answered. "They're dead. And someone else is asking questions about them."

"Do I have to fucking ask you who?" the bishop said angrily. No one seemed especially surprised by the episcopal minister's foul tongue. The myth of puritanical virtue plaguing the higher rungs of the clergy held no stock in this circle.

Father Taylor spat out the words. "A reporter," he announced, "and a cop."

Suddenly the air in the room was different. All five men were silent, Taylor waiting to see the reactions of the rest, the other four trying to figure out how to react.

The leader of the Fraternity sat motionless, as was his wont. But then, with shocking immediacy, his stoic stillness fled and the man exploded in furious, unrestrained anger. Two fists rose together from the wooden desk and slammed down on its surface, the red in his neck and cheeks instantaneously of the same intensity as the piping of his garments. Everyone else froze.

The Cardinal Secretary of State swore aloud, spitting out his words.

"Damn it all! A reporter, asking about Tosi and Crossler. With a police officer?"

His fists smashed down on the desk a second time, papers taking flight at the jolt and a reading lamp jostling dangerously close to falling.

Cardinal Viteri was breathing heavily, his nostrils flared.

"This changes everything! The whole point of this venture is that materials get released when *we* want them to. They could ruin everything! It will be San Sebastiano two years ago all over again. Only this time, the stakes are substantially higher. We cannot afford to be exposed!"

Few had ever seen the Fraternity's leader this angry, or this concerned. The appearance of both traits was worrying.

"Any threats were already supposed to have been taken care of," Viteri added a moment later. He clenched his fists. "Presumably the two professors were deemed such threats. They were dealt with. Now the reporter and the police officer will have to be handled the same way."

The statement frosted the air in the already frozen room. Given the stakes, there was no question as to what the words meant.

"We can't be involved in, in . . . that," one of the membership said timidly, his voice at a whisper. "Such action," he stumbled around the clumsy words, "it's not in our character to dirty our hands directly."

"Our character, in these situations, is to do as we're told," Viteri spat back. He shook his head angrily, though he agreed in principle with the other man's hesitation. Few things troubled Viteri's conscience, but killing was one of them. "I'll contact the firm myself. It'll be their men, not us, who do what needs to be done. Just as it always is."

He peered up at the other men, his face suddenly hard.

"Bear up, brothers. We all accepted long ago that sometimes even men of God have to play with the devil."

36

Central Rome: 10:24 a.m.

When revelations come, they tend to come fast. Gabriella felt the truth of that maxim as a ringing emerged from her mobile phone only minutes after Alexander had made the connection between the IOR records, medical research and the miracles consuming the public interest.

"Yours?" he asked, the ringtone indistinct in the car's interior.

Gabriella was already reaching into her pocket. "I haven't shared this number." Her face was concerned. "I'll take it while you drive. Let's skip the coffee. Take us to your office. We can do a bit more digging there."

Alexander nodded his agreement. Performing a quick, illegal U-turn, he began heading toward the city center.

Gabriella opened the phone and held it to her ear. Habit almost made her announce her name by way of introduction, but she caught herself and spoke only a guarded question.

"Who is this?"

"Is this Inspector Fierro?" a male voice questioned back. Young. It didn't sound menacing, but that meant nothing.

"Who is this?" she asked again, refusing to answer.

"Inspector, this is Assistente Tito Tonti. From the central station."

Gabriella tried to place the ridiculous-sounding name. There was something vaguely familiar about its absurd alliteration, but she couldn't put a face to it.

"You have the wrong number," she said. "I'm sorry, but—"

"I don't have the wrong number, Inspector Fierro," the man cut her off. "I've just spent the past half-hour trying to figure out how to contact you. Your registered mobile is going straight to voicemail."

Gabriella remained silent.

"I'm a friend," the man called Tonti continued. He sounded keen to gain her trust. "And a colleague. We met a few months ago at the officers' banquet at Tre Scalini."

"Ah, Tito," Gabriella answered, the memory triggering. *Kiss-ass boy who looked like he graduated from the academy before he hit puberty*. The thought was followed by an internal sign of the cross. Profanity was profanity, even if unspoken.

"How did you get this number?" She might recognize the man, but that still didn't explain his calling her on a phone she'd owned for only a few hours and which she'd registered under a false name.

"I may be young, but I'm good at my job," Tito answered. "You can call yourself Anabelle Cross on your new phone's record if you want, but you paid for it by card, Inspector Fierro. Amateur hour. It didn't take me long to track it."

Gabriella shook her head, annoyed at her own stupidity. She represented the law; she wasn't used to living in the avoidance of it.

"Okay," she finally admitted, "you found me. What's so important for you to track me down like this?"

"There's something I think I can do for you." The boy was rekindling the kiss-ass reputation she remembered from their previous encounter. "Something's come in down here that I think will be of interest to you."

"Is there some reason you would know what's of interest to me? I didn't realize we'd become that close at the banquet."

Alexander eyed her from the driver's seat. She peered back at him awkwardly, realizing how curious that phrase must have sounded on its own. His expression beamed the slightest hint of jealousy, and for an instant it pleased Gabriella to see it.

But Assistente Tonti was eager to bring her to his point. "I'm assuming it will interest you because of the case you're working on. Or not working on, as the situation might be."

Gabriella's focus suddenly intensified. How would a junior officer know that she'd been asked not to participate in a case?

"You've got something connected to the Crossler murder?"

"Something bigger. Much bigger. Something to do with the story you were blacklisted for pushing."

"Blacklisted?" Gabriella exclaimed without restraint. "What are you talking about?"

"You haven't heard? Deputy Commissioner D'Antonio sent round the calls this morning. You're suspended from duty for insubordination. The whole force has been instructed to maintain no contact with you unless it's through him."

"Un-fucking-believable," she answered. The cross was getting its workout today. "He hasn't even told me!"

"Whatever you've done, Inspector, you're not on his good side."

Gabriella's suspicion was suddenly back. "If that's the case, you're putting your neck on the line tracing my new number and ringing me."

"D'Antonio's been a hard-ass with me since the day I arrived," Tonti answered. "Call this a favor."

"A favor it is." Gabriella suddenly liked the kid a lot more than she had a few minutes ago.

"Does your new phone receive picture messages?" Tonti asked.

"No, but I'm with someone whose mobile does. Can I give you that number?"

A moment later she was reciting Alexander's number from memory. Only when it was complete did she remember that his old phone was gone, tossed out the window with her own. She blushed as she looked over to him, but the look on his face suggested that he was not unhappy that his private number was still in her mind.

"Scratch that," she said, shaking her head, her blushing deepening. "Give me a second." She signaled for Alexander to pass her his new phone and a moment later read his new digits off the set-up screen and handed it back to him.

"Great," Tito answered. "I'll send the picture over now. It's of a body found in the river earlier today."

"What's that got to do with me?"

"Inspector Fierro, just look at the picture." Young Tito Tonti paused. "Don't say I never did anything for you."

Before Gabriella could thank him, the young man was speaking again.

"And Inspector, if for whatever reason you're trying to play hard-to-find, just remember . . . if I could track you down, others can too."

She prepared a reply, but before she could speak, Tito had hung up.

A few seconds later, Alexander's new mobile pinged the arrival of a message and he passed the phone back to Gabriella.

"You want to tell me what this is about?"

"I've no idea. A junior sergeant at Rome Centrale said he was sending me a photo of a body found in the river. His voice suggested I'd understand the relevance when I saw it."

"Not the traditional way to impress a good-looking superior," Alexander teased. Gabriella merely rolled her eyes, sliding her finger across the screen to unlock the phone and opening up his messaging app. There was one new message from a number in the central Roman dialing code. It had to be Tito.

A second later and the message opened. There was no text, only a photo downloading at an excruciatingly slow rate. It took a few seconds to complete, then Gabriella clicked the thumbnail to view it.

"Oh, hell." The words came from her mouth on impulse, before thought.

"What is it?"

She held up the phone, angling it toward Alexander. He tried to look, but the motion of the car made it hard to focus on the image. He snatched the phone from her hand and held it directly in front of him.

"What is this?"

On the small screen was a male face, whitened and blued from the lack of life. The skin was wilted with the after-effects of long submersion in water, but the features were still immediately recognizable.

It was the face Alexander had watched on the video feeds that had started his investigation. The face that millions all across the world had become familiar with over the past twenty-four hours.

It was the face of the stranger.

37

"The Pope intends to speak to the media?" Caterina Amato couldn't hide her surprise. "Do we have any idea what he's going to say?"

"Our men inside the Vatican have only been able to determine that he's set on speaking, and that the press event will take place soon. The Pope's not told anyone what he intends to say."

Caterina's mind churned through the potential outcomes of this news, annoyed that the Fraternity hadn't provided more concrete information. She was constantly exasperated by the group, furtive and secretive as they were, and utterly consumed with a project that was of the least possible interest to her. A fraternity of the Roman Catholic Church's old guard, dedicated to rooting out the influences of modernity and reform on their beloved magisterium. Christ, could there be a more loathsome, pointless undertaking? Or one that less convincingly masked these men's real character? They were individuals driven by their lusts and desires, just like everyone else.

Lusts and desires. Old memories flashed back. Caterina was eleven, her brother Davide was fifteen and her mother had only recently sent them both off to the Sisters of Perpetual Mercy boarding school near San Vittorino. Caterina could still smell the stench of that place: stone and wood and pine cleaner lingering in the air of dark, seemingly endless corridors. But what she truly remembered was what had taken place there—not to her, but to her brother.

Caterina had been treated like every other young girl in the school: harshly, lovelessly, indiscriminately. But the boys experienced the place very differently. She remembered Davide being taken off to see the school's ecclesiastical supervisor, a twenty-eight-year-old priest who would come to the institution intermittently to make his inspections. Those invariably included special meetings with hand-selected students, always boys.

She remembered how Davide trembled each time he was called to those encounters. How he came back from the distant inspector's office pale, unable to speak, faltering in his walk. She never asked, but she knew what happened to him there, and to others like him, at the hands of "our reverend father."

And she never forgot the abusive priest's name: Father Donato Viteri. It burned its way into her mind as she watched her brother grow wearier and wearier, his love of life stolen from him. When, three months after Davide had graduated from the school and departed into the world, news reached her that he had committed suicide, her world changed permanently. Davide had bled out, alone in an alley, his wrists slashed by the fragments of a beer bottle that was found still clutched in his grip. Caterina had been fourteen.

She had run away from school within a week, making her way to the capital. She found work in Rome at a bare wage until she'd earned enough to buy a cheap camera and a few rolls of film, then she'd put the first career plan of her life into action. She'd returned to the Sisters of Perpetual Mercy. She'd broken into the grounds undetected and hid herself away in the garden outside the inspector's quarters. She'd lain in wait for two days before Father Viteri arrived, and when, a few hours later, he called a boy into his office for the kind of meeting that had driven her brother to his death, Caterina caught it on film. Every repulsive, horrible dimension of it.

From that moment on, she knew she had something of which she could never be deprived. Power. Father Donato Viteri was elevated to the rank of monsignor on his thirty-fifth birthday, and a few days later, a young woman he didn't know from Eve had appeared in his office. She'd laid a series of photographs on his desk in silence. Within that silence the monsignor had come under her complete control, a control that remained as he rose through the ranks—becoming bishop, archbishop, cardinal, even Secretary of State. And through it all, a member and then leader of the Fraternitas Christi Salvatoris.

Deep breaths. Calm. Caterina forced herself back into the present and the new unknowns facing her. Of the possibilities emerging from news of a papal speech, almost all were good.

"All the financial preparations are in place?" she asked her assistant.

"I'm assured that the transfers have been managed in the manner that will have the most effect, once further discoveries are made."

This was positive. Nothing spelled out conspiracy and fraud like cash. It often only took a few surreptitious transactions to make the innocent appear guilty. Caterina had destroyed enough of her competitors in the past in this manner.

Though some enemies she kept close. She'd never exposed Viteri, because she had realized early on that he was much better used than eliminated. His Fraternity in particular gave her opportunities for control within the Church. Bishops, priests and cardinals its membership might be, but these men were just as power-hungry as Caterina and just as little interested in the behavioral confines of an imposed morality. Get behind their white collars and they smoked and swore and dealt under the table with the best of them. They did whatever they perceived they had to do to get what they wanted. And as she'd used Viteri to find dirt on each of them, so she had gained what only the risk of damning exposure could ever truly ensure: their absolute obedience. It had developed into a working relationship that functioned well, and that she was happy to use until the moment came when she would destroy them all.

But at this moment they remained useful, though they'd provided only scant details about the newly announced press conference. Caterina felt confident in the knowledge that the pontiff wouldn't be appearing to speak out against the miracles of the day—not after he'd been affected himself. The healed don't usually lambast their healing. That meant there was a more limited number of potential avenues his messages might take.

Yet there were still reasons for concern. They needed time—time for the world to grow in its belief that the pontiff was standing in solid adoration of his guest, in affirmation of the miracles. It needed to be clear to everyone that he was a believer. That he had something at stake in what was disclosed. Only then could the culminating phases of their plan be unleashed.

But the Pope was planning to speak. To this degree, at least, the timing was out of their hands.

Caterina nearly smirked at the irony that, just at this moment, what was required of her was faith.

38

The dead man on Alexander's mobile screen was identical to the man who had arrived at the Vatican the morning before. He had the same captivating eyes, the same wavy hair—though this latter was matted and compressed through the body's submersion in the Tiber. The skin had a gray taint, the mournful color reserved for death, but there was no mistaking the similarity.

No, not similarity, Alexander thought, *identity*. As far as he could perceive from the small screen, the dead man looked exactly like the stranger.

"I don't understand. The man who walked into the Vatican's been found dead?" There'd been no coverage of such a discovery on the radio, and news this big would be headlining everywhere.

Gabriella took back the phone and stared at the photograph again.

"This body was discovered in the river this morning. So far, it seems to have been kept quiet—in the knowledge only of the force. No idea why, but Tonti sounded like he was taking a risk sharing it even with me." She scanned a few notes the junior officer had texted after the photo. "The precise cause of death is still unknown, but murder is the running theory. There were chains around his ankles. It looks like someone hadn't wanted him to be found, but they were too amateur for the chore."

Alexander raced through the possibilities. "There have been no announcements of the stranger leaving the Vatican." A memory reaffirmed the point. "I spoke with my uncle only an hour ago. I think he'd have mentioned something if the stranger had gone."

"So this can't be him. Every entrance and exit to Vatican City has been surrounded by reporters since yesterday morning. And there's no access to the river from within its walls."

"But it's . . . it's him," Alexander persisted.

Gabriella fidgeted with his phone, scrolling beneath the photo and typing a reply to its sender: *Explain. Is this the man from St. Peter's?*

She clicked send and simply stared at the screen, waiting for a response. To her relief, the bubble indicating that the recipient was typing immediately came to life, and a few seconds later the phone chimed as the reply came in.

"*No,*" she read aloud. "*We've phoned the Apostolic Palace and they've confirmed he's still with them.*"

Then who is this? Gabriella typed back.

A pause, then, *Identity unknown.*

Gabriella peered up at Alexander.

"If it's not him," Alexander said, "that leaves only one possibility." He waited for Gabriella to nod in agreement. When she didn't, he continued. "These similarities of features can't be coincidence. Not to this degree. Not to this extent of likeness."

Gabriella turned her eyes back to the photo. The image of the stranger glowed there. Slowly her expression changed as she came to the same realization as Alexander.

"It's a twin," she whispered.

"It has to be. It's the only explanation. Identical twins," Alexander confirmed.

Gabriella's white face went whiter. Suddenly the man who had appeared in the Vatican, whom so many were calling divine, was looking eminently human. Angels weren't known to have twins, and every Catholic child knew Christ didn't have a brother.

"And if this is the man's brother," Alexander added, "then it's clear that no one was supposed to know about his existence. Murder a man and dispose of his body . . . it's a pretty good way to conceal an identity."

Gabriella blanched. "But why?" She reflected during the silence that followed her question. "Could this be a red herring? A trap to throw us off?"

"Do you think your junior admirer would be up to that?" Alexander asked back. "Does this photo look faked to you?"

Gabriella shook her head. She didn't know Tonti well enough to answer the first question, but the photo looked genuine.

"I still don't understand why anyone would do this. If it's real. If it is his brother."

"Because Crossler was right," Alexander answered, "and so was Tosi. What's happening at the Vatican is a fraud. Someone desperately doesn't want the world to know the identity of the man who's gained the Pope's ear. And they're willing to go to whatever lengths are required to keep it a secret."

The Apostolic Palace: 10:45 a.m.

At precisely 10:45 a.m., Pope Gregory XVII made his entrance into the Sala di Constantino, dressed in his customary white attire and walking without aid. The chatter of the reporters and their cameramen halted instantly as the pontiff moved into the room followed by the Cardinal Secretary of State and two priests of the curia.

The Sala di Constantino, one of the four Raphael rooms, so-called because of their frescos by the great master and his students, was a space often used for public receptions within the papal apartments. This morning it had been converted to a press room, filled with traditional umbrella lighting and sound equipment. Two television cameras had been permitted, both positioned carefully. Space for the twelve invited reporters had been cordoned off with red velvet rope. As was traditional, the Pope would not speak from a podium but from his seat, *ex cathedra*, where a microphone had been hinged to a wing mount and made ready.

A few seconds later he was in position. Cardinal Viteri stood to his right, piped in crimson, the two priests in their black cassocks to his left. Behind him was the monumental depiction of St. Constantine's vision of the cross in the skies above the Milvian Bridge, painted by the hand of Raphael himself. It was artwork to rival Michelangelo's adornment of the nearby Sistine Chapel.

"I thank you for coming," the Pope said calmly to the reporters. Then, turning toward the cameras, "and I greet all of you who are watching this broadcast with the peace and the love of God."

He paused for what seemed an eternity, his eyes closed, before finally opening them again toward the cameras.

'In the past hours and days, my beloved brothers and sisters, our world has been given new signs of hope. We who are men and women of faith call them miracles. Others may call them merely inexplicable phenomena. But whatever title one gives them, in these days we are witnessing events to stir us all with wonder.

'The world now knows of the precious children born without sight like the man born blind in the gospels, who yesterday awoke to something that medical science had long deemed impossible: vision. I have spoken today by phone with the doctor who oversees their care, and even to one of the girls who, for the first time in her life, could see the ward around her. And as I heard the wonder in her voice, my heart rejoiced.

"The world has now also heard of the men and women here in Rome suffering such terrible sorrows from cancer who today were discovered to be free from that plague of a disease. Again, I have spoken with their chief physician and with a few of his patients. Can I ever express to you the awe one feels at hearing the hope in the voice of a woman who knew as an absolute fact that death was only weeks away, and who suddenly finds herself restored to health?"

The Pope paused. Every reporter noted the glassy wetness to his eyes. None doubted the sincerity of his emotions.

"And then there is my own condition," he continued a moment later. "You are all well aware of the effects I've borne my whole life, carrying a childhood condition into middle age. It's a reality that has kept me bent over and in constant pain. So many of you have written to me over the years with your words of encouragement and I have felt the prayers that millions have offered, especially since I was charged to wear the ring of the fisherman."

Suddenly the Pope stood upright.

"And today I stand before you. *Stand before you*. I bear witness to a miracle that can only have its source in God." He allowed the cameras a moment to take in his fully upright form before again sitting in the red-cushioned chair.

"We have been visited," the Pope said, and instantly the ears of every reporter perked forward. Was this it? Was this the moment he would mention the stranger?

"We have been visited," Pope Gregory continued, "by the unexpected mercy and grace of God. Of this there can be no doubt. And in this visitation we see the signs of hope for a world that needs it so desperately. And so I exhort you, my beloved flock, who struggle with so much confusion and fear: do not be afraid. Press forward in faith, never forgetting that the Lord stands in our midst. Allow the miracles of God to fill your hearts with the fervor of virtue, and do good."

He gazed into the blank stare of the cameras, as if willing the peace and consolation of his heart to be transmitted through them with his image.

"Finally," he continued, "I would leave you this morning with one further thought. It is a line that was brought to my attention earlier today, and one that I would share with you all."

He reached into his cassock pocket and extracted a small slip of paper, folded once down the middle. He opened the page, smiled gently, and read aloud.

"The lost child returns, and the dead are restored to life."

Pope Gregory looked back to the camera. 'Is not this image a fitting metaphor for the spiritual condition of our fallen world—a child that is lost? But that precious child, our hope for good, returns to us; and the peace that was dead in us, by God's power, returns to life.

"May this promise of resurrection fill your hearts with the same hope that stirs anew in mine. May God bless you."

Invoking the apostolic blessing with the sign of the cross, the Pope rose once more and walked silently from the room.

Piombino, Italy: 10:59 a.m.

Two hundred and fifty kilometers north of Rome, the expansive, luxurious mansion of one of Italy's most renowned film directors, Gianni Zola, clung to its hillside outside Piombino. Its interior was as quiet and mournful as its exterior was beautiful. To the famed celebrity, perhaps the most famous director in all of Italy, the Pope's words sounded shallow as they beamed live on to his oversized plasma-screen television. He was tired of hearing promises he knew would never be fulfilled.

The mahogany coffin in the center of his sitting room was proof, final and terrible, of that.

"Resurrection." He said the word with distaste in his mouth, as if it were poisonous and sour. "Not likely, my dear Holy Father."

Before him, the coffin of his daughter lay open on the funeral home's portable bier. It was surrounded by lilies and yellow orchids. Her favorite flowers. She had finally been pronounced dead at eight minutes past midnight the night before. The moment hope had died, along with Gianni's precious girl.

He pulled a set of old beads through his fingers. Saying of the traditional rosary, with family and close friends gathered together around her at home, would begin soon. For now he needed his moment alone with . . . with what was left of Abigaille.

Gianni didn't attempt to hold back the tears. His daughter had been his deepest, purest joy. She was beautiful, talented, filled with life. She'd starred in two of his films and developed a celebrity all her own. It wasn't yet of the caliber of his, of course, but Zola's daughter had only been nineteen years old. Just starting out.

Nineteen years old.

He downed a mouthful from an overly full glass of imported cask-aged Tennessee whiskey that sat next to him on the sofa. The wooden beads of his rosary clanked against the crystal. He willed the liquor to deaden the pain, knowing it wouldn't.

Abigaille had been surfing with her friends on a small beach near the Località Falcone eight days ago, as she'd done almost every weekend since she was old enough to carry a board. She knew that beach from edge to edge. She knew the water of the temperamental Ligure Sea. She knew the rocks.

But it was the rocks that had taken her from him. She had caught a wave "of unexpected trajectory"; that was how the investigators had described it. It had taken her at an angle toward an outcropping that lay just below the tidal surface, smashing her fragile body against it with overwhelming force.

She had been rushed to hospital as soon as her friends had brought her body to shore, but she was unconscious in the ambulance and pronounced comatose shortly after arrival. Zola had visited her every day since. Indeed, he'd spent nearly every moment of the past week at her bedside. Outside the hospital, the public outpouring of grief had been immediate and tremendous—a nation of fans in shock, expressing their sorrow, sharing their love. There had been candlelight vigils each night. Flowers flooded the walls of the hospital complex. Masses were said in churches and fans stood outside, waiting and hoping for the best. But none of it helped.

Zola swallowed another long dram of his drink. It seared this throat, and somehow that pain was a comfort. He cast aside his rosary beads. In this moment, there was no consolation there.

It had been last night, in the darkest hours when his body had demanded that he depart from the hospital to take some rest, that she had died. Alone.

Ten hours ago. That was all. That was how recently his world had ended.

The hospital and funeral home staff had worked gently and efficiently to have her body moved into the Zola mansion for the traditional rosary service prior to the funeral. The crowd of fans had moved too: from the hospital to the outskirts of his property, now keeping vigil of a different kind.

Zola peered up. The coffin looked so cold and final. He took another drink, his eyes blurry with tears, then abruptly stood and walked to the open head of the casket. His daughter's eyes were closed, her face slightly bruised from the accident that had claimed her life. On his instructions she'd been brought directly to the house. No embalming, no make-up or decoration. Not yet. There would be time for that before the funeral. In this moment he needed just to be alone with her, as she was. Untouched. His little girl.

The Pope's message continued to broadcast on the screen at the side of the room. He'd kept the set live to watch the coverage the press was giving to his daughter. It was touching to see how she'd impacted on those around her, even in her short life. A few minutes ago the feed had cut to the pontiff—a special broadcast from the Vatican. Perhaps that was fitting. Abigaille had never really been religious, but the Zola family were dedicated Catholics through and through.

Gianni closed his eyes. Suddenly it was all too much. He could feel his heart, his hope, failing him. Everything, *everything* was gone. Emotion came in throbbing, violent surges from deep in his belly. He wasn't sure he would be able to remain standing.

And it was then, in that moment, that he heard it.

With agony clouding his senses, he didn't at first trust his ears. He froze his sobs and stood still.

It came again. He could make it out clearly now: a distinct creaking of wood. A strange sound, in this place.

He opened his eyes, trying to make sense of what he was hearing. He looked around him, seeking the source, but he was alone in the room. He brought a sleeve to his eyes to wipe away the tears, clearing his blurred vision—but no one was there.

He sighed, chided himself. Hope: it had the power to make liars of even the senses.

But then the sound came again, and this time there was no doubt of its reality. Wood creaked. Fabric rustled. And there was only one direction that it was coming from.

Gianni spun back toward his daughter's casket, and beheld the impossible.

In a singular heave of motion, Abigaille Zola's chest swelled. Her muscles tensed, and her eyes snapped open.

An instant later, Gianni Zola's dead daughter sat up in her coffin.

The world seemed to halt. Gianni struggled for breath, afraid for an instant that he was himself dead, or asleep, and this was just a vision. But Abigaille turned to face her father. Her eyes blinked. Her face was confused and endearingly childlike. And then he could not contain himself: he lunged at her, wrapped his arms around her. It was not a dream. It was not a vision. Abigaille was beautiful, radiant, *alive*, and he pulled her as deeply into his breast as he could.

And from the television set that blared at his side, the Pope's words resonated in the air.

"The lost child returns, and the dead are restored to life."

SECONDO

39

In all his years serving in Rome, Cardinal Rinaldo Trecchio had never seen anything like the disarray currently consuming the most senior administrators of the holy mother church.

These were men, himself included, who were used to predictability. Having functioned continuously for almost two thousand years, the Church was an institution that rarely operated on the unknown. Non-believers and the secular world as a whole might regard the spiritual realm as something ethereal and void of concrete substance, but to the men who led the Church it was known territory, firm and absolute. They were comfortable with it and cherished it.

Rinaldo had known Pope Gregory for nearly nineteen years. They had been made cardinals within a year of each other, had concelebrated together more times than either of them could possibly remember. Rinaldo considered the new pontiff a close friend as well as spiritual brother and father.

And that made the events of the past twenty-four hours all but impossible to understand.

Of the veracity of Pope Gregory's healing there could be no doubt. He had been a cripple; now he walked upright. It was a miracle, as sure as any recorded in the Bible or in the centuries-long annals of church history. Even the skeptical bones in Cardinal Rinaldo's body—of which there were only a few—could not fail to be persuaded of it.

But it was still a surprise, and surprises were never good. Moreover, it had come as the first of a chain of surprises that were threatening to destroy the peaceful equilibrium in which the Church preferred to operate.

And then the Pope had spoken to the press. *What the hell was Gregory thinking?* The conference had launched the curia and assembled cardinals into its current state of uncertainty. Why was the Holy Father speaking to the press, to the world, when so little was yet known about what was going on? Why was he speaking to cameras and reporters more readily than to his own bishops and advisers?

And why, in the Lord's holy name, had he talked of resurrection? The angels in heaven might be able to see some good in the strange words of the Vicar of Christ, but Rinaldo could only see danger. The Pope had all but given ecclesiastical endorsement to the healings in Pescara and Rome. Before they'd been understood. Before they'd been investigated. God knew the media wouldn't hesitate to stand in for the Congregation for the Causes of the Saints and the famous Miracle Commissions normally set to verify the seemingly miraculous. What if they should find something untoward, something scandalous?

All this, and without any public mention, yet, of the source of it all: the stranger whose arrival in the Vatican had been the catalyst for this worrying cataract of miraculous activity. The man remained within their closed walls, gathered together with the pontiff. A man that none of the princes of the Church had yet met face to face, though there were whispers that the Pope was planning to introduce them later in the morning. *A man unknown, unexamined, just like the miracles.*

Cardinal Trecchio was well aware that faith had once been defined as the substance of things hoped for and the evidence of things unseen, but he had been in the Vatican long enough to know that what was unseen in this place was all too often sinister. There were forces at work who wore faith only as a banner under which to exercise their interests, and whose plottings in dark corners far exceeded the scope of the works they undertook in the translucent light of day.

The outward appearance of current events was all positive. Suffering was being alleviated, the sick were being healed. And this strange man, whoever he was, seemed to be at the heart of it, working not evil, but good.

It was perverse that the presence of such goodness brought Cardinal Trecchio no peace. It only made him nervous. It felt like the rise before the fall. And as every good Catholic knew, when man fell, he fell hard.

Two minutes later, he could sense the fall beginning.

A clergy assistant walked into his office carrying a single sheet of paper. A worried look stretched across the whole of his face.

"Your Eminence," the young priest said, deferentially but in a voice plagued by anxiety, "the Holy Father has called for a meeting between the senior members of the curia in his study in five minutes' time. I think he means to introduce you to . . . to . . ."

It was clear he didn't know how to finish the sentence. Absolutely no one in the Vatican knew what to call "that man." Rinaldo, however, understood his meaning perfectly. His heart raced. The meeting was not just a whispered rumor. He was at last going to meet the stranger. He stood abruptly, anxious and ready.

"But before you go, Eminence, I feel you should read this."

The priest handed the single page to Cardinal Trecchio—a printout from his computer. Rinaldo, hardly the world's most technologically literate ecclesiastic, nonetheless recognized the visual pattern of a blog entry.

"It's from a site run out of Piombino by a teenager with an eye for local news," the assistant explained. "Given its subject matter, I thought you'd want to . . . I thought you'd . . ."

Rinaldo barely heard him stumble his way to a mute, confounded halt. The cardinal's eyes were on the page and his world was changing yet again. The headline of the blog entry ran in capitals along the top of the short text:

RESURRECTION: DECEASED DAUGHTER OF FILM LEGEND GIANNI ZOLA RETURNS FROM THE DEAD, MINUTES AFTER THE POPE SPEAKS ON LIVE TELEVISION OF THE DEAD RETURNING TO LIFE.

40

Headquarters of La Repubblica newspaper: 11:38 a.m.

Alexander stepped into the bullpen on the fourth floor of *La Repubblica*'s main offices, Gabriella in tow, with an apprehension he'd never felt in the years he'd worked there. He knew he was unwelcome now in a way he'd never been before. Laterza would be sitting in wait, relishing the opportunity to pounce on the man who'd formerly been his least favorite reporter. Formerly, because Laterza had given him the boot the previous night—something Alexander still hadn't shared with Gabriella. And he'd given it remotely. *Bastard.* Moreover, since he hadn't yet seen him face to face, Alexander knew his former editor would be cherishing the opportunity for that confrontation, and he hoped more than anything that he might be able to avoid it. He scanned the broad space carefully before leading Gabriella inside, moving toward his cubicle in the far corner.

"This place is buzzing," Gabriella noted as they walked. The room was packed. Every desk was occupied and the air was electric. "Is it always like this around here?"

"Hardly ever."

"What are they all doing?"

"What do you think? They're working on the same story we are, though I doubt from quite the same angle."

"They're all allowed just to step into your territory?"

"It's not mine anymore. My editor dropped me yesterday, by tweet," Alex said, dodging between desks. He tried to avoid her glance, feeling a certain embarrassment at having to admit he'd been sacked. "Apparently I was too busy getting shot at to do my job, so he gave it away."

"I'm sure he'll reconsider once he learns what we've been working on."

Alexander shook his head, stepping into his cubicle and motioning for Gabriella to join him. Right now his future employment was the least of his worries. He wanted to get into the paper's network and gain access to its databases before he was removed from the system. One thing he knew about the administration of *La Repubblica*: it might move stories quickly, but internal business was managed unpredictably. He might have access for weeks, but there was no point in cutting it close. He needed information now.

"Sit low," he instructed Gabriella. He motioned her toward a small chair as he crouched before his desk. "I don't want us seen in here."

"You're going to be that unwelcome?"

"I wasn't exactly my editor's favorite before this began. I don't particularly want to be seen by others who might let him know I'm here."

"I'm willing to bet he changes his opinion of you the moment you show him the photograph of the body from the river. It's still being kept under wraps downtown, but that's front-page material if ever there was any. You'll go from pariah to favorite son in a flash."

Alexander swiveled toward her, his face suddenly serious.

"Gabriella, that photograph—for the moment, I think we should keep it to ourselves."

She was startled. "It could debunk the whole fraud in an instant. I thought you'd be as eager as possible to get it into the hands of your colleagues."

Alexander shook his head. "It will definitely raise questions about the man at the Vatican, but I know how the press cycle works. That will become the sole focus and everything else will get shoved aside. We'll do better to sit on it until we can prove a definitive link between the stranger and whatever is going on with the IOR and the medical firms. Material like this is far more powerful when it's exposed together."

Gabriella dwelled on his suggestion a moment. "Fine. Your call. Of course, that's assuming nobody knows about the body yet, outside the precinct office."

"I'll go with that assumption till we're proven wrong. For the next few minutes, our sole focus is the financial questions."

She nodded in agreement. A few seconds later, Alexander had extracted his laptop from his rucksack and connected it to the office's internal network.

"We've done plenty of investigating on the Vatican Bank here at the paper, before and since I came on board. I should have access to all the filed stories as well as a good number of research notes. And the business section has probably profiled at least a few of the companies on that list."

"We could start with knowing precisely what those companies do," Gabriella said.

Alexander was already typing, searching the paper's records for whatever facts they could disclose about the mysterious partners of the Vatican Bank.

It took several minutes to begin collating information from the archived articles and stored research. When at last he had worked his way through everything likely to be relevant, he started printing off the most important files.

Amongst the institutions in the IOR's listing, several were invested in medical research and considered to be at the cutting edge of their fields. Few specifics were available. A common trait of medical research groups appeared to be their attachment to secrecy: concealing the precise details of their work from rival companies until they were ready to announce their next big breakthrough, patented and profit-protected. But what Alexander was able to discover was enough to reinforce his previously held suspicions.

The projects detailed in public records included Cygna-Gen's advanced research on treatments for genetic blindness, and Alventix's work on pharmaceutical treatments for various cancers thus far deemed terminal by the medical community.

Blindness and cancer.

But there was nothing yet that directly related to the first miracle: the healing of the Pope.

"I'm trying to search for any connection between the research of the firms on our list and . . ." Alexander hesitated. "It's aggressive spinal stenosis, right?"

Gabriella nodded. She, along with the rest of the Roman Catholic world, had learned the name of the Pope's condition in the days following his election. Every news program in the world had featured little medical moments on the new pontiff's "crippling ailment"—a narrowing of the spinal canal that could range from causing minor aches and pains in its sufferers to crippling disfigurements of the spine and extraordinary, constant pain.

But at least as far as the materials databased in the paper's collection were concerned, there were no links to the condition. Even orthopedic ailments more generally seemed absent from the remit of the firms linked to the IOR.

"Nothing there," Alexander said, "but what we've got on the others is damning enough. Two of the companies attached financially to the Vatican Bank engage in research that directly connects to the healings that have taken place since the stranger's arrival at St. Peter's."

"I understand that, but don't jump to conclusions. These are broad realms of research. Even you have to admit that. What large-scale medical companies *aren't* doing research on potential cures for cancer? Or looking to cure blindness?"

Alexander wagged his head. Gabriella had too much faith. She was resisting the obvious.

"It's circumstantial, Alex," she added, "though I'll admit it doesn't look good. But we need to get something more concrete."

Alexander sat forward. "This is the extent of what we've got on file here. Any suggestions?"

She was already moving, fidgeting in her pocket until her phone emerged.

"We first got on to this track through money," she said. "Money's going to be where we find more specifics."

"Who do you suggest we call?"

"My admirer down at central. Officer Tito Tonti, of he's-willing-to-overlook-my-being-blacklisted-and-provide-us-with-photos fame. Maybe he can pull up more detailed financial information on these three firms." She paused, then, with a grin, "I'm sure he'll be responsive to a little . . . feminine flirtation."

Alexander grimaced as Gabriella dialed. There was a glimmer in her eyes. In amidst the humor, the fire of a police officer's zeal was doing battle with the faith of a believer and, for the moment, winning. *Damn, I've missed her.*

A second later, his attention was pulled away. A colleague peered over the top of the cubicle wall, his face a smile. He'd been discovered.

"Alexander, wasn't expecting to see you here! Heard you were sacked."

"Not sure it's official until I get it in writing," Alexander answered, smiling back. He'd always liked Donald Branson, a particularly forward English nineteen-year-old interning at the paper on his gap year.

"What you in for?" Branson asked, eyeing Alexander's open laptop. "Trying to gather up your old files before you're cut off the network?" A devious wink contorted his left eye. With his penchant for bluntness and general lack of reserve, Branson would last fifty years in this industry if he survived his internship.

"Just pulling up a bit of information. Sacked or not, I'm following through with some leads on the medical miracles from yesterday—the ones being associated with the arrival of the man at the Vatican."

"Medical miracles? You mean the blind kids and the cancer lot? Fuck, Alex, that's old news!"

Alexander pinched his eyebrows. "Old news?"

"Hell, yeah. Haven't you been keeping your ears open? Our stranger's doing a whole lot more than healing the sick."

Alexander didn't know what to say.

"Come on, Alex, you're really in the dark?" Branson shook his head, floppy hair bouncing boyishly, tut-tutting with the joyful expression of someone who had the privilege of sharing big news. "Zola's daughter, the up-and-coming teen star, the one who was crushed out surfing last weekend . . ." He watched Alexander for recognition, and when he didn't see it: "Abigaille Zola. In a coma since the accident, pronounced dead last night. Seriously, it's been huge."

Alexander's face started to whiten. He remembered seeing news of her death pop up in his search engine when he'd started in on his investigation, hogging the top of the search results. Celebrity did that. But he had been entrenched in his new work all morning. He hadn't seen anything else.

Finally Branson simply came out and said it.

"Alex, she's alive. The girl just—I don't know, sat up in her own coffin. Her father was out on the balcony of his house a minute later, proclaiming the miracle to thousands of fans who had gathered in mourning, announcing that it took place at the precise moment the Pope read out his statement about the dead returning to life on live television."

Branson seemed to consider the strangeness of it all, then laughed.

"Healing the sick is small potatoes," he continued. "Our stranger's graduated to raising the dead."

41

Head office of Alventix Ltd., Rome: 11:45 a.m.

Oberst Raber walked into the office of Arseniy Kopulov, the publicity-loving director of the massive Alventix medical research firm, awash with conflicting emotions. The head of the Swiss Guard was not a man accustomed to this state of inner turmoil. There was duty, there was honor and virtue. In his world, their parameters were generally clear. But in the past twenty-four hours he'd felt the increasing presence of this new sensation, unwelcome and uncomfortable.

There was going to be hell to pay for the Pope's comments. The public interest and media obsession had all been over the red line before the statement. Now there would be a circus, especially with news coming in that the Holy Father's "prophecy" of resurrection had come true in Piombino. That meant new security concerns for Raber's men to handle.

But the Guard were trained to deal with such situations. The need for increased public protocols didn't worry Raber. Rather, he was concerned with precisely what was going on within the fortified walls of the Holy See. And the first step in resolving that question lay in the meeting he was about to have: a meeting with the man he'd spotted on the CCTV footage from yesterday's Mass.

"I'd say welcome to my office," the enormous Russian said, his expression half-sneer, half-grin, "but I think we both know you're hardly that." Kopulov was well over six foot four, which made him an imposing figure even when seated. His precise age was hard to determine behind the hair dye and skin treatments, but Raber knew it was fifty-eight, which made him almost eight years the *oberst*'s senior, though he appeared just as fit as Raber himself.

"I'm grateful you were willing to meet with me."

"When the Church beckons," Kopulov answered, his words syrupy with irony. He motioned toward a seat and indicated that Raber should take it. "Besides, it's not every day I meet the man at the helm of an entire military."

Kopulov said the last word with a full accompaniment of air quotes and a tone that suggested he viewed the Swiss Guard to be as much a military as a pre-school snowball brigade.

Raber sat, looked the Russian squarely in the eye, and decided to be blunt. "What were you doing at St. Peter's two days ago?" He allowed his words to take the tone of an accusation, which was precisely what they were.

The suddenness of the challenge seemed to catch Kopulov off guard. A stencil-perfect pair of black eyebrows rose, compressing the broad wall of his forehead into rolling furrows. But the Russian's composure was affected for only the most fleeting of instants. The twin brows fell back earthward, his features hard.

"Rather a direct line of approach, wouldn't you say, Commandant Raber?"

"I would appreciate a direct answer." Raber didn't break the locked gaze.

"I can be wherever I want to be, do whatever I want to do, whenever I fucking feel like it!" Kopulov barked his words with sudden anger. "And I sure as hell don't have to explain my choices to you."

"You were in church. In *my* church—at a papal Mass. Am I meant to believe that the great atheist critic has found faith?" Raber asked, deflecting the Russian's emotions dispassionately.

Kopulov eyed him, but Raber wasn't finished.

"Your contempt for the Church is well established, Mr. Kopulov. You cannot have thought I wouldn't notice you suddenly sitting in one of our pews, your hands folded and your lips muttering prayers."

The Russian looked uncomfortable. "Know your enemy," he muttered, though there was less bite to his words than a moment ago. His sneer, however, quickly returned. "You obviously do your due diligence in knowing yours."

Raber allowed a few silent moments to pass. Kopulov clearly wasn't going to open up and share the reasons for his sudden churchgoing impulse. It was time to press him with the other piece of information he had gained from his research during the night. His smoking gun.

"Fine," he said. "If you don't want to be forthright about your presence in St. Peter's, why don't you tell me instead about the twenty million euros that have suddenly appeared in your personal bank account."

Gun, fired.

For the first time, the Russian man looked truly flustered. His face reddened, anger clearly a customary and automatic reaction. But Raber noticed, through the mounting look of aggression on Kopulov's features, the glimmer of something else. *Confusion.*

"What the fuck are you doing looking into my personal accounts!" he finally boomed, wagging an enormous accusing finger at the head of the Swiss Guard.

"As you said, due diligence," Raber answered calmly.

"Bullshit! This is spying. It's entirely unjustified. You can bet I'll be taking this up with the authorities."

"Take it up with whomever you wish." Raber waved a dismissive hand. "You'll have to explain the same thing to them. Twenty million is a noteworthy sum, even for you."

"I'm a wealthy man," Kopulov answered, "and my personal finances are nobody's business but my own."

"That's one approach you can take," Raber said, "but I want you to consider how things look to me at this precise moment. Twenty million euros are wired into your account—I don't yet know from whom, but you can be quite certain I'll eventually find out. Twenty million, two days before a stranger invades a Vatican service. A service you, an avowed hater of the Church, spontaneously decide to attend. And then lo and behold, the whole world discovers that a flock of terminal cancer patients a few miles away have suddenly and mysteriously been healed."

The Russian glared at him, his face deepening to the color of a ripe tomato.

"The world starts to cry out 'Miracle!'" Raber continued. "But I just can't get away from that twenty million, and your face on my CCTV feeds. A massive payment to a man whose company has made remarkable advancements in," he leaned toward Kopulov, "the pursuit of pharmaceutical treatments for precisely the type of cancer in question."

Raber's pulse was thumping in his ribcage. Despite his rank and experience, directly challenging secular men of power was not a normal experience for the commandant of the Swiss Guard. But he kept his accusing gaze fixed on the Russian.

"Tell me, Kopulov," he added forcefully, "how you think that ought to look to me."

The Russian seemed wholly consumed by a rage that Raber knew, if allowed to emerge, would be explosive. His neck was bulging with such engorged fury that it threatened to burst the pearl button hovering above the loose knot of his tie.

But instead of exploding, the Russian took a long breath, leaned back in his chair and slowly raised a hand, pointing to the far side of the room.

"Get the fuck out of my office."

Five minutes later, Christoph Raber was on the phone to his closest officer. As the connection passed through the requisite switchboards, he ruminated on the one fact he'd held back during his conversation with Arseniy Kopulov.

The fact that Raber knew precisely where the twenty million had originated.

He'd left it out because he still didn't understand what it meant.

The source of the funds had been the Istituto per le Opere di Religione. The Vatican's own bank. The Church had paid Kopulov, and that didn't make any sense.

The line connected.

"Klefft, sir," a regimented voice on the other end answered.

"I want you to tap all the finances of Arseniy Kopulov's Alventix Ltd. Get me details on every transaction with outside corporations over the last six months."

It was a tall order, but Raber knew his men could do it.

Whether or not they could do the next was a different question.

"And get me a full accounting of all the IOR's external transactions as well. Without letting them know we're looking."

*

Kopulov sat in his office, his whole body churning with rage. The visit from the tall cop from the Vatican had insulted him in every way possible. He'd wanted to strike the man. Hell, he'd wanted to kill him, to rip the pretentious head from his twig of a neck and bowl it full force into the wall. *Who the hell do these people think they are! Don't they know who I am?* Everything in him wanted to show those bastards who they were really up against.

Everything, except for one fact.

Arseniy *had* been at the Mass. He hadn't known, and he still didn't know, what had drawn him there. He hadn't been to church since he was a schoolboy. But that morning he'd risen, certain somewhere in the depths of his core where he had to go. It was a feeling he hadn't experienced since his youth, and he wasn't entirely sure he'd even experienced it then. A draw, powerful and potent. He'd dressed in his finest. He'd walked to St. Peter's, unsure even as he'd walked why he felt such a strange and unfamiliar urge to go there. He'd sat in a pew and, by God, he'd actually prayed. As if he were being drawn to the foreign act by a magnet. He'd closed his eyes, interlaced his fingers, and a dimension to his being he hadn't thought he possessed had opened up. He'd felt, for the first time in his life, like he had a soul. That he wanted it purified. That he wanted redemption.

He'd left St. Peter's almost at a run, sweating, terrified by the strange zeal that had possessed him. But it had been there. It had been real, and he had no idea how to explain it.

And now, to add mystery to mystery, he'd learned even more confounding news. He leaned forward and pressed a small buzzer on his phone. A few moments later his personal accountant entered the office—a lanky man who withered beneath the obvious fury of his boss.

"Get me a printout of all my personal accounts," Kopulov demanded. "I want it on my desk in ten minutes."

"I'll need some time to—"

"Get me my fucking accounts, *durak*!" Kopulov roared, slamming a massive fist down on his desk. "And then explain to me what the fuck twenty million euros is doing there—twenty million that I know nothing about!"

42

The Apostolic Palace: 11:49 a.m.

Cardinal Rinaldo Trecchio emerged from the Pope's private study feeling like a man transfigured. In all his life he had never felt like . . . like *this*.

The Holy Father had called the curia's senior-most members into his study for the express purpose of finally meeting the man who'd been cloistered there since the previous day. Rinaldo had walked toward the great wooden doors of the room with intense trepidation. Whoever this man was, he was upsetting the normal order and drawing Pope Gregory into events that threatened the Holy Father's very credibility. The closer Cardinal Rinaldo got to the study, the more forceful his emotions became. He was suspicious. He was angry. He was resentful that a perfect stranger should arrive in their midst and threaten so much damage to the Pope and the Church.

And then he had walked through the doors and everything had changed.

When he emerged ten minutes later, Cardinal Rinaldo Trecchio's world had been transformed. All his anger was gone. There was no more resentment, no more suspicion. *No more fear.* Rinaldo was a man at peace, filled with the most profound intensity of love. And the man he'd met had said almost nothing. It had been enough just to be with him, to sit with him. To sense that the world was right, that God was in his heaven and that the sorrows of the world would be overcome.

As he had departed the study at the end of the brief meeting, Pope Gregory had placed a hand on his old friend's shoulder and peered into Rinaldo's eyes. The long glance shared between the two friends said everything that needed to be said. There was no longer anything to be afraid of. Things were as they ought to be.

But then Rinaldo had left the study. The door had closed behind him, he'd walked away through the corridors of the Apostolic Palace, and his fear had begun to return.

What they had on their hands was real, of that he no longer had any doubt. That meant those who were their enemies in times of peace would be more strongly their enemies now. And with that fact in hand, only one thought filled his mind.

He had to warn his nephew.

Central Rome: 11:58 a.m.

Alexander guided Gabriella through the main doors of *La Repubblica*'s offices, back toward the busy Piazza dell'Indipendenza and their parked car. They had barely spoken a word since learning of the return to life of Gianni Zola's daughter. That event had, over the past hour, migrated out of the realm of blogs and tweets and was now the stuff of special television bulletins and interruptions to radio broadcasts. Italy was spellbound at the news.

"It's not clear there's any connection between the girl's return and the Pope's words," Gabriella finally blurted out as they walked along the pavement. This time it was she who was the voice of doubt. Healing the sick was one thing, something to be praised and thankful for. Raising the dead, however, was territory so miraculous she found it almost off-putting. It might have been beautiful in ancient Galilee, but it was too much for the modern world.

"Just because Gregory talks about the dead coming back to life in a press statement," she continued, "it doesn't mean that . . . in his words . . . he spoke as if it were a metaphor." She was fumbling.

"There's nothing metaphorical about a nineteen-year-old girl sitting up in her casket," Alexander answered.

Gabriella let her breath hiss out between pursed lips. She was at once repulsed—death, corpses, coffins, resurrection. And yet there was also a powerful impulse toward hope. *Could it be true?* She was deeply devoted to a religion built around the life of a man who had risen from the dead and promised that he would raise others. Was it possible this promise was being fulfilled?

"But," Alexander continued, shaking his head, "I still don't like it. Let's set aside for the moment that raising the dead is *impossible*. We can't overlook the fact that the other miracles the world has witnessed since yesterday morning now look deeply suspicious."

"Suspicion is a cagey thing," Gabriella cut in. The roles of skeptic and believer alternated between them, reflecting the state of confusion of both. "The links we've drawn are tenuous."

"But one thing isn't. Everything began with the arrival of the stranger at St. Peter's. He's at the heart of all of this, Gabriella. And though the whole world seems eager to call him an angel, or Christ returned, you and I seem to be among the very few who know the truth."

"Do we?" Gabriella queried, genuinely surprised. She stopped their progress. "Just what do we really know, Alex?"

"That he sure as hell isn't divine, for a start. I may have left the Church, but I'm still fairly certain that angelic beings don't have dead twins floating in Italian rivers."

The twin. Gabriella still didn't know what to make of the photo of the body in the Tiber.

"It can only mean," Alexander continued, "that the stranger is part of something far more dangerous than just a manipulation of funds or religious convictions." He turned to face her more directly. "Somehow this man has planted himself at the heart of the Church. He's caught the ear of the Pope, and through him the world. He calls himself 'the one' and he has all the right features for the role: the flowing hair, the right posture, the charismatic eyes. But he can't allow anyone to find out he's actually just an ordinary man, with a brother who looks all but identical. And then we happen to find this brother—dead!"

Gabriella stuttered for a response. "Alex, he healed the Pope in front of the world. You saw the video. That wasn't a parlor trick."

"I saw the Pope stand upright, I don't deny that. And no, I can't explain it. But there are reasons it could have happened."

"He's been crippled all his life!"

"Maybe he's been receiving treatment. Maybe this was simply the first occasion the results of his treatment have been manifest."

"You think the Holy Father is lying?"

Alexander shook his head emphatically. "No, Gregory's an honest man. But Gabriella, the power of suggestion can be strong. Think about it: he undergoes therapy, maybe just daily exercises for God knows how long. Then on this morning a man with extraordinary charismatic gifts stands before him and commands him to stand upright. The Pope is filled with religious fervor. He's standing at the high altar, there's angelic music. The man has captivated the crowd and walked right up to him, and Gregory's caught in the inspired moment. For the first time he really *tries* to stand, believes he can—and all that therapy has its effect. He stands, but not because the man has healed him. He's only drawn out a healing with a quite earthly explanation."

Gabriella was silent, but slowly started walking again toward their car.

"You have to admit," Alexander persisted, "it's not outside the realm of possibility. It's surely more likely than the idea that this man is Christ, walking around central Rome healing the sick."

"But the sick *are* being healed, Alex. And what about the girl? That's more than a healing."

They arrived at the ugly Opel. Alexander walked to the passenger side and opened the door for Gabriella. It was unlocked, which surprised her. She couldn't think of the last time she'd left a car without instinctively locking the doors behind her. The day's events were obviously distracting her focus.

"I don't have any idea how to explain this morning's resurrection," Alexander admitted. Exasperation sounded in his voice. "But at this stage, with everything else we know, I'm sure it's as fraudulent as the other miracles."

Gabriella harrumphed her way into her seat as Alexander made his way round to the other side of the car. An unfamiliar creak came from his door as it opened, as if it were sitting improperly on its hinges. Gabriella shook her head. She'd have to make a note for her aunt. The old lady would want it fixed.

As for Alexander, he made a compelling case. But still, in the midst of it all, something hopeful lingered within her. She wanted to be suspicious, but she also wanted to believe. Not necessarily in the identity or powers of this man, but in the possibility that miracles did happen. That the sick were truly healed. That resurrection was more than just a dream.

Lord, I believe. Help my disbelief. The words of the gospel returned to her.

A telephone rang from the driver's seat. Alexander reached into his pocket. The screen of his phone was lit up, his uncle's number flashing on the display. He slid his finger across the screen eagerly.

"Alexander." The cardinal spoke the instant the line connected. "We have to meet."

43

Headquarters of Global Capital Italia: 12:04 p.m.

Very few things made Caterina Amato nervous. She was a woman far too accustomed to being in control to experience that emotion with any frequency. Yet this was almost too much. Too much going her way, being delivered into her hands. It was almost as if she were being offered her every need on a platter, and Caterina wasn't used to being given anything. She was used to taking.

Abigaille Zola had come back from the dead in Piombino. She'd done it almost half a day after the public pronouncement of her death had sent a nation of fans into mourning. She'd done it in the presence of her father, who'd proclaimed it to the masses. And she'd done it, to all intents and purposes, simultaneously with the Pope announcing to the world that the miracles that had followed upon his visitation would pinnacle with resurrection.

Caterina could not have plotted a better course of events had she designed it herself and manipulated its every contour, as she'd done with the healings at the two medical centers. But it was precisely that which made her nervous: she hadn't. Her hand hadn't been involved in Piombino at all.

She took a deep breath, calming herself. D'Antonio was already en route. He would find out what was really at play there, and how they could use it to their advantage. Whatever its source, the situation would be put to good use.

But then . . . then there was the discovery that was the greatest gift of all. A body, found in the Tiber. One that looked identical to the stranger who'd appeared in St. Peter's. D'Antonio had emailed her a photo the moment it had been discovered. Then he had ensured that the police investigation into the apparent homicide remained entirely under his control. That in turn had ensured that details of the corpse's discovery had not been released.

Who was this man? Caterina had no more idea how to answer that question than she did of the identity of the man in the Vatican. It seemed clear the two must be related. In fact, it appeared that the man in St. Peter's was likely the twin of the deceased, and that meant that he was a manipulator all his own. A like-minded soul, a vicious soul, though with motives she couldn't yet fathom.

But it didn't matter. She would be able to link them together by visual appearance. Discrediting the visitor was going to be far easier than she'd anticipated. Flash this image on a television screen and the whole facade would come tumbling down. If she didn't believe they were solely the inventions of idiots and the gullible, she would say it was a gift from the gods—because whoever the man in the Vatican was, whoever the man in the river was, she now had everything she needed. On a platter.

Yet Caterina swallowed, a strange tightness in her chest. Nerves tingled her skin. Few could hate the Church more than she. Still, she'd been at Catholic boarding school long enough as a girl to remember that the last man who'd been given everything he asked for on a platter had found that it tore his world apart.

44

Central Rome: 12:07 p.m.

Alexander's phone conversation with his uncle was brief: a warning followed by an insistence upon meeting and practical arrangements as to a place and time. Nothing extraneous or emotional. He disconnected the call only moments after it had begun.

Gabriella had overheard and was already nodding her confirmation of the plan when he looked over at her. He reached his hand forward to the ignition, the key pinched between his fingers as he made to start the Opel. Suddenly she lunged at him, grabbing his forearm and yanking it back violently.

"Alex, stop!" she cried. He turned to her, completely uncomprehending.

"Gabriella, what're you doing?"

"What are those?" she asked, pointing frantically to the car's ignition cylinder. Her eyes were as wide as Alexander had ever seen them.

He glanced to the slot meant for the key. It appeared normal to him: a slotted metal rotatable disc framed in the plastic steering column, a few scratches around its edges.

"It's the starter," he answered, baffled at the obvious question. "Gabby, what's going on?"

She was shaking her head fiercely. "Around it, the scratch marks." Her breath was short.

Alexander looked again, but there was nothing even remotely surprising about what he saw. "Every car has those," he said. "Mine's got them in droves. You don't always aim the key just right. Vinyl gets scratched."

"No, not in this car." Gabriella's head was still shaking. "My aunt's obsessive about keeping the interior unmarked. Look around you, Alex, there's not a spot or scratch anywhere in here."

Alexander took closer note of his surroundings, for the first time becoming aware of just how pristine the interior of the unassuming car really was. But he still couldn't comprehend the panic in Gabriella's voice.

"Gabriella, what are you trying to suggest?"

"Those marks, they weren't there when we drove here," she answered, turning toward him. "I'd have noticed." Her eyes shot back and forth, racing through her memories and observations. "And my door was unlocked. And yours . . . the groaning from the hinges."

She bored her eyes directly into his.

"Alex, someone has been in this car."

Umberto watched his two victims from a position fewer than eighty meters down the street on the opposite side. He and Maso sat side by side in their small hatchback, waiting for the inevitable.

In a way, it was disappointing that these targets hadn't been a more difficult challenge. They'd been clever enough to rid themselves of the mobile phones he and his brother had used to track them to Trecchio's apartment last night. But that had apparently been the extent of their post-assault precautions. That was unsatisfying. One a reporter, the other a cop. Did neither of them think that their pursuers would check for family in the region? That the existence of Fierro's aunt wouldn't remain a mystery to them? Or the make and number plate of the woman's car? Or the office where Trecchio worked, and the likelihood of his returning?

Pity. The chase was so much more rewarding when the prey had a bit more skill. But no matter. At least the job was done. The ball of fire about to consume their two victims would leave barely an identifiable feature on either.

At Gabriella's urging, Alexander slowly slid himself sideways in the driver's seat and crouched down so he could look beneath the steering column.

It took only an instant for him to realize that her fears were well founded. Tapped into the ignition system was a small silver box, clearly a recent addition to the surroundings and just as clearly a detonator. Packed behind it was a wad of what appeared to be gray putty, but which Alexander immediately knew was some type of explosive.

"It's a bomb," he affirmed. He suddenly felt afraid to move. He'd only ever seen bombs in films.

"Alexander, sit up," Gabriella instructed, her words suddenly drawn out and commanding. She tugged at his shoulder. "Slowly."

He obeyed, carefully avoiding contact with the explosives he now knew rested just above his right knee.

"If this was added here while we were inside," Gabriella said as he rose, "it was done fast, only a few minutes ago. Chances are whoever did it is still nearby, waiting to confirm that this device . . . does what they want it to."

Alexander started to crane his neck sharply to the right, ready to scan the street and surroundings.

"No!" Gabriella clutched at his knee, driving her finger-tips in hard. "Don't. Keep looking forward, or at me. Look natural. Smile."

He turned slowly toward her. She had a forced smile on her face, but her eyes were steady. "If they're out there, watching, then we need to let them think we're still just talking. We can't let them know we're aware of the bomb."

"Do you think it's the same men from last night?"

"Right now, our only question is how we're getting out of here. If they're outside somewhere, we can't just go walking down the street." Her eyes were darting right and left, her mind seeking a solution.

"Downstairs," Alexander suddenly blurted. Gabriella peered at him quizzically. "The basement of the newspaper's building," he continued, "it feeds directly into the metro station. If we can make it back inside and downstairs, we could take any of three lines that call there."

Gabriella glanced out of the window at the building they'd just left. It was at best forty meters away. Even if they were chased, even if they were shot at, they would have a chance. Not a great one, particularly if guns were involved, but a chance.

"That'll have to do," she said. She gripped Alexander's knee again, this time in encouragement.

"Are you ready?"

He forced a hesitant smile. "Since I don't think we have any other options, I guess I am."

Gabriella smiled back. "On three."

Umberto twitched a finger anxiously. It should have been over by now. What were these two doing?

But the explosion he'd intended didn't come. And in an instant, Umberto realized that it wouldn't.

Suddenly, in perfect synchronicity, the driver- and passenger-side doors of the orange Opel flew open and his prey launched themselves out, aiming for the building from which they'd come.

"Fuck!" Umberto shouted.

An instant later, he and Maso were out of their car, racing across the street on foot.

Gunshots didn't start to pepper the pavement, which was a good sign. Gabriella had half expected them both to be shot the instant they opened their doors. But as she and Alexander sprinted toward the *La Repubblica* building's glass entry, no firearm reports sounded through the air.

But she knew they were far from safe. At the edge of her peripheral vision two men appeared at a distance. Unlike the rest of the crowd, these men were running—just as fast and ferociously as she and Alexander, and aiming directly for them.

And she recognized the taller of the two men's faces.

"Inside!" she shouted to Alexander. They burst through the double doors and he started to slow, but she pushed him along. "It's them. Get us down to the station, now!"

Umberto slammed the full weight of his torso into the glass doors as he reached the entrance to the building. A woman on the opposite side caught the edge of the door and went flying to the floor, but Umberto barely noticed her existence.

He scanned the foyer. Trecchio and Fierro weren't there.

He ran to the security desk. The rent-a-cop guard was already rising, preparing to scold him for his violent entrance. Umberto silenced the encounter by unholstering his Glock and aiming it at the man's face. He might not be willing to open fire on two victims in the middle of a crowded street in broad daylight, but he sure as hell had no problems with using his weapon to get his way in here.

"The two people who just ran in here before us, a man and a woman. You saw them?"

The guard looked terrified, sputtering, glued to the spot.

"Answer!" Umberto shouted, pushing the muzzle of his weapon into the man's forehead.

"Y-yes!" the guard finally cried. "They went that way." He pointed toward the stairwell. "It leads downstairs."

"Downstairs?"

"To the metro station. Two flights!"

Whether the guard said anything more Umberto didn't know. He was already running for the stairs, Maso a step behind.

At the bottom of the stairs, a crowd mingled on a small platform that shone with industrial-grade tile and white fluorescent lighting. It smelled of the unique mixture of oil and recycled air that marked out underground stations everywhere.

There was also the sound—the sound that clenched Umberto's stomach as he rounded a corner and found himself facing the platform for the only line active at the moment.

The sound of metal wheels scraping along tracks. The sound of a train in motion.

"Damn it!" he roared. He signaled Maso. "Get to them!"

They raced across the platform, slamming waiting passengers out of their way, trying to get to the cars. But the train was already moving, its doors sealed, its interior crammed to capacity. Its speed increasing. It was beyond stopping.

As it pulled away from the platform and into the darkness of the tunnel beyond, Umberto cursed loudly.

In the final window, he saw his targets huddled together, moving deeper into the center of the crowded carriage. Alive.

45

Near Piombino, northwest of Rome: 12:14 p.m.

Deputy Commissioner Enzo D'Antonio had pointed his car toward the Piombino precinct station the moment news of Gianni Zola's daughter's resurrection had hit the media outlets. For the first time since he'd bought it, the Alfa Romeo 4C into which he'd poured the better part of his life savings the year before hadn't seemed anywhere near fast enough. He braked hard for the speed cameras when he knew they were coming—he could hardly classify this as an official excursion with a connected exemption from violations—but the moment he was past them he pressed the metal pedal hard to the floor and kept it there.

He had to get to the girl. He had to get to the father. He had to find out what had happened before it destroyed everything they'd been working to construct.

The news that the daughter had "come back to life" had made it into the public eye immediately, and from there the story had simply caught fire. It was the most sensational event in a week already marked by the extraordinary. The fact that the Holy Father had gone on live television and all but predicted the girl's return was more than the public could bear, especially when a celebrity was involved.

And it had all been going so well!

The media had begun to do the work that D'Antonio's true employer had known they would. He'd been in the pocket of Caterina Amato for years, feeding her information since she'd first approached him with requests for "a little bit of sharing" in return for more money than a police commissioner would make in a decade. It was an arrangement with which he had no problem. Hers was a pocket lined with cash, which suited D'Antonio just fine. He certainly wouldn't be calling an Alfa Romeo like this his own if it weren't for her. Besides, the woman was brilliant, almost prescient in her wisdom. She knew what would attract hype, and that what was hyped would be doubted and researched. And she knew it was precisely there that she and her people could take control.

Even the heavens seemed to be on her side. D'Antonio had grabbed control of the investigation into the body in the Tiber the moment his beat officers had reported it. He'd recognized immediately that it was another powerful tool Amato could wield. How such good fortune could fall upon one who was almost the definition of sinister and conniving, he didn't know. But the body was there, the face the spitting image, the whole situation superlative.

But then this. Resurrection. *What the fuck are we going to do with that?* D'Antonio asked himself nervously. *You can fake a healing. You can't bloody fake raising a girl from the dead.*

And if they couldn't manage to make it look fake, then things were poised to go terribly wrong.

Café Barberini, central Rome: 12:31 p.m.

After their escape from the second attack on their lives in as many days, Alexander and Gabriella both felt as if they could barely breathe. They'd seen their two pursuers arrive on the platform beneath *La Repubblica* as their train had pulled away, and they'd changed lines twice afterward in an attempt to muddy their trail. To their relief, there had been no further signs of their being followed. Neither of them, however, felt safe any longer. The men who had tried to kill them last night were not going to give up.

Which made their scheduled meeting with Alexander's uncle all the more important. He'd called to warn them of danger, told them they needed to meet so he could explain. It was an explanation that now seemed essential.

Given the speed with which their escape had pushed them through the metro system, they arrived at Café Barberini early and quickly approached a small booth that was familiar to Alexander from many a frequent meeting here in years past. The café, which Cardinal Rinaldo had selected when he'd phoned his nephew insisting that they meet, was a bustling city affair, popular with locals, students and more and more tourists with each year. It was fashioned in the old Italian style: long, narrow interior with a tiny glass shopfront, booths lining one side with two-seater tables along the other and row upon row of seating outside, spilling into the street beneath a broad yellow awning.

After they'd both scoped out the entirety of the small interior, Alexander saw Gabriella into a booth then walked to the rear of the shop and ordered three double espressos. The thick aroma of the coffee filled the cramped space, deliciously bitter in the midst of the sweet scent of pastries being baked in the back.

"You come here often?" Gabriella asked as he slid back into the booth. The absurdly mundane question felt like a necessary tool in restoring some sense of calm after what they had just experienced. Alexander took the place next to hers, leaving the opposite side free for his uncle.

He slid close to her.

"I used to. My uncle and I met up here at least twice a week in the month before my ordination. To discuss my reservations."

"You were nervous?" she asked, sipping from the small white cup, which immediately browned at the lip with the thick liquid. For the moment it seemed she didn't want to talk about the attack they'd just escaped. It was a sentiment Alexander shared. His memories might be unpleasant, but at least they didn't involve bombs or would-be assassins.

"I was terrified."

"Lifelong celibacy's not an easy pill to swallow," Gabriella said, traces of a smile at her eyes.

"Surprisingly, it wasn't that. It was the . . ." Alexander's voice faltered, his fingers tapping a tiny silver spoon against the edge of his cup. It was as if he still wasn't sure how to finish the sentence after all these years. Even with her. "I guess it was the notion of that level of commitment to something so great. To lay there, prostrate, flat on your face on the floor of St. Peter's. To pledge that your whole life will be given to God and the Church." He shook his head. "That was terrifying."

"But you overcame your fear."

"Mostly due to my uncle. It was his example more than anything. The man's been working in the Church longer than I've been alive, and every day of it with dignity. I've always admired that. I sat right here, in this very seat, shaking with fear. Opposite me, he looked so calm and peaceful. So certain that this life was holy."

A few wordless moments lingered. The background noises of the café bustled around them.

"Your uncle sounds like a good man," Gabriella finally said, "and with everything going on around us, a man of peace is just what we need." She took a deep breath, exhaled it slowly. She finally began to look something close to calm.

When, a second later, a man in street clothes slid deftly into the opposite bench of the booth, he looked nothing like the man of peace Gabriella had hoped for.

Piombino Hospital: 12:45 p.m.

Enzo D'Antonio sat at last in Abigaille Zola's small room at the Ospedale Piombino. The girl had undergone a battery of medical tests since her remarkable return to the living. Thus far they had all come back strong and clear. She was in perfect health, despite having been declared dead by two of the finest doctors in Italy less than half a day ago. Despite nurses and funeral home directors moving her limp dead body from hospital bed to gurney to coffin. She was alive and well, as the same doctors now described her, with only one area of abnormality. It was precisely that area D'Antonio was here to explore.

"My name is Deputy Commissioner Enzo D'Antonio," he said, taking a seat in the tan vinyl chair next to her bed. He'd received the doctor's assurances that he could have up to fifteen minutes alone with the girl for the purposes of a preliminary police interview about her sudden restoration. That the force in Rome had no idea he was here was not something the doctors could possibly know, and his warrant card was enough to convince them his presence was legitimate.

"The whole world is happy to have you back," he said to the girl, forcing a smile. He wasn't used to talking to teenagers, and wasn't sure what tone to take.

"I'm happy to be back," she answered. Her face was warm and grateful, but there was a patina of confusion across her features. Her words came in hesitant clumps.

D'Antonio waited a few seconds. "Have the doctors spoken to you about what happened?" *I really need you to tell me just what the fuck happened.*

The girl considered her answer before she spoke. Her face was intense with concentration. "They said I was . . . dead. But that can't be true, can it?"

"The whole country heard about your death. You'd been in a coma for a week. Finally slipped away."

"I don't remember anything." She shook her head, her eyes glassy. "Anything at all."

This was the territory D'Antonio needed to explore. "What are the last memories you have, Abigaille?"

"I was at the beach with my friends. We were surfing. It was a normal day."

"Do you remember what happened while you were surfing?"

She tried to focus. "There was wind, lots of it. I wasn't in control of my board anymore. The currents were shifting. Then . . ." Her voice trailed off.

"Then?"

"I don't know. I woke up in what I thought was my bed, but my hands were folded across my chest and my legs were cramped. It was like I was trapped. I sat up as fast as I could. I had a terrible headache." She took a deep breath. Her eyes were wet pools. "My father was standing next to me. I was in a . . ." She hesitated, as if she couldn't bring herself to say the word "coffin." Her words returned to the memory of her father. "He looked terrible. And when he saw me, he looked so *scared*."

"You don't remember anything between the beach and waking up? You were in a coma for seven days, but you make it sound like an instant. And you'd been pronounced dead ten hours before that moment with your father. *Ten hours*."

Abigaille shook her head. "Nothing. The only images in my mind are vague. Not really memories."

D'Antonio leaned in toward her. "What kind of images?"

"Just . . . light. Tremendous light. Bright, white. Everywhere. I can't describe it. A few sounds, maybe. Nothing distinct, nothing precise." A tear formed in the corner of her left eye. D'Antonio briefly contemplated reaching out to wipe it away, but thought that would be too much.

Inside he sighed, a tremendous relief.

"That, my dear, is very interesting," was all he said aloud.

Enzo D'Antonio interviewed Abigaille Zola for another ten minutes before departing her room and the hospital. His face was beaming as he left. It had all gone perfectly.

He was on the phone to Caterina Amato within minutes of being back in his car.

"The girl remembers nothing," he said as soon as the line connected.

"Nothing?"

"Nothing at all. No green pastures or white clouds. No walking in the presence of the saints. Just—nothing." D'Antonio knew that had been Caterina's biggest fear as soon as she'd heard of the girl's return. If Abigaille came to saying she'd been in heaven, or that she'd walked through the pearly gates with *that man*, their plan would have been destroyed.

"It gets better," he added.

"Better?"

"She remembers only indistinct, shapeless light. And a few sounds she can't identify. Background noise."

There was a long pause on the other end of the line. But after a few seconds Caterina had pieced together the implication of the police commissioner's report.

"Sounds that . . . that might have come, for example, from medical equipment? Amorphous white light that could be, let's say, the glow of fluorescent bulbs seen through closed eyes?"

"She didn't say."

"But . . ."

"But it could be." D'Antonio was smiling into his phone. "It could very well fucking be."

"Then we don't need to be worried about Abigaille Zola after all." D'Antonio could hear the pleasure, even relief, in Caterina's voice. "Let her speak about her experience all she wants. It will fit together nicely with everything else we've got in play.

"We couldn't have asked for a better recollection if we'd written her a script."

46

Café Barberini: 12:46 p.m.

Cardinal Rinaldo Trecchio slid into the center of the bench opposite Alexander and Gabriella, gazing around him as if he were concerned with being followed. He looked nothing like a prince of the Church. In gray trousers and a blue-checked button-down shirt with a navy sleeveless sweater, he looked like a tourist's lost grandfather. Inconspicuous, uninspiring, forgettable.

"Uncle, it's good to see you." Alexander reached across the table. He grasped the man's wrist and squeezed firmly. Warm smiles forced their way past both men's nerves. Rinaldo's features curved, but his eyes remained wary.

"And you, Alex." The cardinal looked toward Gabriella. "You must be Inspector Fierro. A pleasure to meet you. I wish it were under better circumstances."

Gabriella took note of the man's behavior. This was the great Cardinal Rinaldo Trecchio. She'd heard of him often as a bastion of confidence, but behind the forced smile he looked worried. No, it was something beyond worry. It was fear.

He took up his small cup and downed the double espresso in a single swallow. The crema was still spotting his lips as he turned to his nephew.

"I can only assume, knowing you as well as I do, Alex, that you've continued with your investigation despite my warnings."

Alexander tilted his brow in the affirmative. "We couldn't stop, especially since what we were discovering was so monumental. Your warning was vague."

Cardinal Rinaldo nodded, affirming that this was the answer he'd expected despite it not being the one he wanted.

"What have you discovered?"

Alexander sat back in his seat, his torso pressed against the green leatherette padding. "I think it's better that we take things in order. I still have questions for you. How did you know what I was doing? And what were you afraid was going to happen? Because I have to tell you, a hell of a lot *has* happened."

Offering answers, however, was not paramount in the cardinal's mind. In an instant his gentle meekness was gone and his expression grew firm. "No, I don't think it's better that we start there. I'll get to that in due time, Alex. Right now you need to trust me. Tell me, now, what you've discovered."

It was strange to see the cardinal, who had a kind of grandfatherly tenderness to his features—an unassertive inward-sloping chin, skin wrinkled to the texture of a well-tended leather glove—in this moment look so harsh. Gabriella could see the surprise cross Alexander's features too, and stepped into their exchange.

"Alex and I were dropped into our current project rather bluntly, Cardinal Trecchio. Two gunmen came to his apartment while I was there. We barely escaped alive." She briefly recounted the story of their chase into the Roman night.

Cardinal Rinaldo raised his brow, but Gabriella noticed that it wasn't an expression of surprise. It was sad understanding. The cardinal was disappointed that this had happened to his nephew. The fact that he seemed quite unshocked by a story of executions and attempted murders struck a note of increased fear in Gabriella's stomach.

"And after you escaped?" Rinaldo asked, his voice steady.

"We regrouped and tried to find a connection between the two professors and the Vatican. As they'd both written stories on corruption at the Vatican Bank, that's where we went next."

"You were there when I called you the first time? After your text?"

"We'd just left the building," Alexander answered.

Rinaldo shook his head slowly. "Going there has put you in grave danger."

"The president of the IOR was very forthright," Gabriella interjected, "even helpful."

"I'm sure he was. But he's not the man in charge."

"What's that supposed to mean?" Alexander asked, but his uncle held up a palm to quiet the question. He turned back to Gabriella.

"That's the extent of your progress?"

"Apart from almost being killed again on our way here to see you," she answered, anger rising in her voice, "that's it. The two men from last night came after us again. This time it was a bomb in our car. To be quite frank, Your Eminence, I think it's pretty impressive we've got as much as we have."

Alexander reached a hand to her arm and tried to calm her, but Gabriella was on a roll. "Holtzmann gave us a listing of the bank's partner agencies. From that we were able to make our first direct connection. Something we don't yet fully understand."

"Money has been going out of the IOR to medical firms and corporations," Alexander cut in, "and the major transfers of funds began to take place just as . . ." He hesitated. "Just as the miracles started to happen with the stranger you've got in the Apostolic Palace."

Cardinal Rinaldo looked confused for the first time in their conversation. His eyes were suddenly probing. "What's the connection?"

Gabriella took back the reins of the conversation and explained to him what they'd been able to piece together. Gradually, understanding started to dawn on the cardinal's face.

"You think—"

"We don't have enough concrete information to confirm anything at this stage," Alexander interjected quickly, "but from the outside, it's looking a lot like the Vatican, or someone within the Vatican, is staging a rather impressive show, designed to hurt the Pope. And it all centers somehow around this visitor."

Rinaldo shook his head. "The medical issues, these firms, I know nothing about any of that. But this man. Alex, I've been with him. He's . . . he's not what you assume. And I can assure you he's not part of a Vatican plot."

"You've actually met him, face to face?" Gabriella queried, leaning in to the table. Her eyes were as wide as the cardinal's had been a moment before. *Tell me*, they probed, *tell me everything.*

"Only briefly," Rinaldo answered. "He's remained almost exclusively with Gregory since we were cloistered. But a few of us were brought into the Pope's study to meet him for a few minutes, just before I called you to arrange this meeting." He turned toward his nephew. "Alexander, you have to believe me, that meeting was something extraordinary. This is not an ordinary man."

Cardinal Rinaldo's demeanor changed as the memory resurfaced. He drew in a long breath. His body seemed to gain an inch in new height. His eyes glistened, suddenly warm and wonderful. "To be in this man's presence, how can I describe it? I've rarely felt such peace or calm. Such confidence in the goodness of life. You can fake a lot of things, Alex, but this is something else. This is something that can't be concocted."

His eyes were filled with wonder and he let them linger on his nephew's. Then he turned and drove his hopeful stare into Gabriella. *I believe*, they cried out, *and I want you to believe.*

For a moment it seemed as if the sheer power of his conviction might win them over. But the moment passed. Alexander and Gabriella knew one fact about the man that the cardinal didn't. Something that trumped feelings of peace and goodness and supernal calm.

"Uncle," Alexander began, "I'm afraid there's something else. One other thing we discovered today. Something that is going to force you to reassess these . . . these things you're feeling."

"What are you talking about?"

He extracted his phone from a pocket and called up the photo that he knew was going to shatter his uncle's confidence.

"There was a body found in the river today. Not long dead."

"Bodies are found in the Tiber all the time," Rinaldo answered. He looked suspicious.

Alexander shook his head, and even Gabriella's eyes were filled with compassion. What was coming was not going to be easy on the cardinal.

"Not like this," Alexander said. "But it's best I don't explain. It's something you need to see."

He passed the phone to his uncle. As the old man gazed at the small display, his face was suddenly transformed in disbelief. All the peace and tranquility were gone. There was only disbelief. And then, far worse for a man of faith, doubt.

Rinaldo Trecchio didn't look up. He slowly closed his eyes. His words came out as a pitiful whisper.

"Oh my God."

47

Vatican City: 12:56 p.m.

Cardinal Viteri picked up his telephone and prepared to dial a number that very few people in the world knew he possessed. The Cardinal Secretary of State was an individual who maintained relationships with hundreds of men and women across the world: heads of state, ambassadors, nuncios, leaders of charity organizations and corporations. But Viteri had always assiduously avoided any public contact with Global Capital Italia and its CEO. Firstly because it was a financial conglomerate with an ethical record that would make even the most mercenary of Catholic insiders balk. And secondly—and far more importantly—because he could not allow any opportunity for his true connection to the firm to be discovered.

The truth of that relationship was one that he and his compatriots in the Fraternity would never be able to justify were it to come into the open. They'd partnered with the devil, because the devil had dirt on them all. Their weaknesses had been discovered, documented, and used to chain them in servitude to this firm and its leadership. Because if that dirt were ever to become public . . .

The mere thought raised a flutter of fear in Viteri's throat. He swallowed it away like he always did, refusing to contemplate the scenario. Instead, he scrolled through the contacts listed on the tired LCD display of his blue plastic phone. Three screens down he clicked "CA," and a few seconds later Caterina Amato answered the line.

"I have bad news," Viteri announced the instant they were connected. He'd always been pleased that Caterina abjured the use of names during phone calls. He was almost certain that the Swiss Guard didn't have his private mobile tapped, but it was still a risk.

"Bad news," Amato answered, her voice cold and hard as usual. "I'm not surprised. This is the only kind you tend to have." Her tone was almost flippant. There was no hint of anger or retribution, which Viteri took to mean that Caterina hadn't already been informed of what he was about to tell her. That was unfortunate. He knew his next words would change her tone entirely, and he took a deep breath as he prepared himself for the rage that was undoubtedly to come.

"One of the inner ranks has broken the cloister." He dropped the words, shaded though they were, like a mortar shell, fully expecting them to do just as much damage. "He's left the walls. We caught him making his way out, all done up in civilian clothes. We weren't in time to stop him, but we had him followed." Viteri hesitated. "He met with outsiders."

Christ, why do I have to be the one to tell her? She's supposed to have people everywhere. She should already know.

There was a long, tense pause. Viteri swallowed, a thin sheen of perspiration sticking to his brow.

"This isn't just bad news," Amato finally answered. "This is a disaster." He could hear the anger surging beneath her drawn-out vowels.

Unfortunately Viteri wasn't yet finished. "It gets worse." Now the sweat was forming into droplets that cascaded down his nose and dripped on to the surface of his desk.

"Worse? How the hell could it get worse, Donato?"

She's using my name. She must be ready to kill. Viteri had never heard the CEO drop her own protocol before. She'd been a woman marked out by an absolute self-control as long as he'd known her.

"The individual who broke the cordon," he continued, blurting out the words, "is Cardinal Rinaldo Trecchio."

Another pause. "That name doesn't mean a great deal to me."

"Rinaldo Trecchio is the uncle of the man your assassins have not been able to eliminate. And he went to speak with his nephew."

Viteri could hear the in-draw of Caterina's breath. When her words were delivered, they barely constrained her fury.

"The reporter? The one working with the cop?"

"Yes."

"His uncle's a fucking cardinal? And you let this man *talk to them*? At this stage in our operation! What the hell's wrong with your Fraternity? I thought you controlled the curia!"

Cardinal Viteri forced himself not to react to the insult.

"He left covertly. Even we can't keep absolute tabs on everybody. At least we saw him on the way out and know where he went. I've just asked for a papal blessing to call an extraordinary meeting of the cardinals, ostensibly to discuss the particulars of church administration while we're closed up here. We'll send out a college-wide page, and assuming he doesn't want us to know he's broken out, he'll return swiftly. We'll keep tabs on him till then."

For the next tense moments Viteri simply listened to the angry breathing of the woman at the other end of the line.

"I simply don't know how your institution has made it two thousand years," Caterina finally said. "If I ran as loose a ship as yours, my firm wouldn't have lasted two months."

"This isn't the time for insults," Cardinal Viteri answered. He wanted to bark out that this bitch might have tremendous power, but he was the Secretary of State of the oldest nation state in the Western world and she should show at least a modicum of respect. But she owned him, through and through, and he knew it. There was nothing he could do to change that.

"This can be fixed," he said instead. "We'll find a way to—"

"You'll do nothing." Caterina cut him off, her voice dropping. Viteri felt a shiver rush up his spine at the emotionless manner in which she delivered her next words. "I've had enough of your help. Get your missing cardinal back into the Vatican. I'll take care of the rest myself."

48

Café Barberini: 12:59 p.m.

Cardinal Trecchio reopened his eyes and stared again at the photograph on Alexander's smartphone. "Tell me what this is," he finally demanded, a twist of despair in his voice. "What are you showing me?"

"The body of a man our forces discovered deceased this morning," Gabriella answered. "He was found by two officers in the Tiber, after it was reported by a local."

"But he looks identical to . . . to our . . ." Cardinal Rinaldo faltered.

"To your visitor at the Vatican." Alexander finished the sentence for his uncle. "We've noticed. Which means that others will have spotted the resemblance as well, though by some miracle nothing's leaked to the press yet."

"Who is he?" Rinaldo set down the phone, pushing it across the table with a sudden revulsion. He kept his eyes averted, as though it might somehow cease to exist through sheer force of will. "And why haven't I heard anything about this? This should be . . . news."

"We don't know who he is," Gabriella answered, "but I'm sure our labs and forensics are running prints and dentals now. As to why you haven't heard, it appears the central force is keeping a tight lid on this discovery. No one's been made aware. I don't know why, but even I was only able to find out through some intra-office schmoozing."

The cardinal's jaw moved, words almost on his tongue. But the sounds didn't come.

"Uncle, it's time to tell us what you know," Alexander pressed. "We've shared what we've learned. Why did you call me? What do you know?"

"I know nothing about *this*," Rinaldo answered. Anger made him turn his attention back to the device he had been avoiding so assiduously, the photograph glowing on its display.

"Your call and your warning came before we found out about this," Gabriella interjected. "Why were you so nervous?"

The cardinal shook his head. He looked to his nephew.

"Since the moment the stranger arrived and the Holy Father was healed, I knew something was wrong. I've suspected the situation would be, how shall I put it, taken advantage of."

"Meaning?" Gabriella asked.

Rinaldo glanced around, looking even more nervous than he had a few moments before. "Both of you need to understand, there are more forces at play in Vatican City than just the curia and its official offices. To know who these men are, you need to know . . ." He stuttered to a halt. After a moment he began again. "I trust you're both well aware that Pope Gregory has made enemies since he was elected to St. Peter's throne?"

"I thought he was a deeply loved man," Gabriella answered. "Respected almost universally. Even Alex likes him."

At any other moment Alexander would have raised the corners of his lips at her combination of truth and sarcasm. Maybe even shot back a retort. In this instant, however, he only wanted to know his uncle's response.

"It's true," Cardinal Rinaldo answered, "but it's not the whole story. Pope Gregory is a man on a mission. That mission has a single point of focus: clean up the Church and everything over which the Church has an influence."

"A noble aim," Gabriella muttered.

"You and I are in agreement on that point, young lady. But not everyone shares our opinion. Noble aims are inspiring if you don't have any skeletons in your closet or anything to lose by upsetting the status quo."

"You're saying there are groups within the Vatican that do?" Alexander asked.

"Of course there are, Alex. Don't be naïve. The Vatican has operated in its own world for centuries. There are men who are answerable to none, accountable to no one but God. One can get used to those kinds of freedoms."

"So who precisely is against the Pope's reforms?"

"I can't give you names because I don't know them. But it's a long-held belief within the walls of the city that there exists a brotherhood of high-ranking Vatican officials who work to preserve the old ways in the face of threats of change and reform."

"The old ways?" Gabriella asked.

"Ways that don't involve asking questions, that don't include holding people to account. Ways that allow things to happen under the table as they've done for a very, very long time."

"And this group would threaten an individual involved in such change? Even if he's a pope?"

"Especially if he's a pope," Rinaldo affirmed. "The Pope might not have the kind of absolute power within the Church that the world assumes, but he's definitely got the highest pulpit and the loudest voice. Therefore he poses the greatest risk."

"This brotherhood—you don't know any names at all?" Alexander asked, pushing his uncle in the hope of more details. The cardinal only shook his head.

"I've known Gregory too long and am far too close to him. I'd be the last person such a group would let into their circle." He leaned in to the table. "But these men are extremely dangerous. And if the rumors are true, they're allied with others. There's talk of them being arm in arm with groups outside the Church. Groups who, let's just say, do what they need to do to get their jobs done."

Alexander processed the information. "The kind of groups that might send hit men after us?"

"Or after a couple of professors who threatened to expose them," Rinaldo affirmed. "The brotherhood itself wouldn't dirty its hands directly with those sorts of actions. There's a modicum of a moral code in place, however flimsy. But others would have no problem with bloodshed."

"But why were you so worried about us going to the IOR?" Alexander asked.

"Because, Alex, the old saying holds true: money breeds corruption. However this group is organized, it's somehow connected to the bank. Traipse around there, you're going to step on somebody's toes."

Before the cardinal could continue, an electronic beeping began to emerge from his pocket. He reached down and extracted a pager. The device looked like it had emerged directly out of the 1980s. He glanced at its tiny display and his features immediately changed.

"We're being summoned to a meeting of the College of Cardinals. Twenty minutes."

"Can't you skip it and stay with us a little longer?" Alexander asked. "There's so much more we need to know."

"I have to go," Rinaldo answered. He was already sliding toward the edge of the booth. "We're cloistered, remember? I had to sneak out to get to you. If I don't show up at the meeting, they'll know I've gone. Worse, they'll send someone to look for me."

He stood peering around the café, his nervousness returned. After a moment, he glanced back to his nephew.

"Please be careful, Alex. These are not people who play games, you know that now. With what's at stake after what you've shown me, they're going to be at their most aggressive."

"What will you do back inside the Apostolic Palace?" Gabriella asked him.

"I'll try to feed you what I can from the inside, about this . . . this *deceiver*." He seemed genuinely pained to admit that the stranger was not the holy man he'd previously sensed.

"And I'll pray for you." He glanced back to Alexander. "I'll pray for us all."

Central Rome: 1:11 p.m.

Caterina Amato shut the door to her office behind Umberto and Maso. The two men had arrived only minutes after the ten-second phone call through which she'd demanded their presence. Umberto looked annoyed—hardly unusual—and Maso looked nervous. He generally was.

"I'm not a religious woman," Caterina announced, "but I don't at all mind playing God. And in my limited understanding, God's commandments are generally expected to be followed. Are they not?"

The two men stood silently, the tone of the meeting having been quickly set. Umberto's annoyance gave way to trepidation. Maso looked like his legs might give out beneath him. The few crow's feet at the corners of Caterina's eyes seemed to deepen.

"Your failure to eliminate the two targets last night, then again today, less than an hour ago, has opened the door to the biggest risk of this whole operation," she said flatly. "You're supposed to be the best. Is there a reason you come to me bearing the kind of news I'd expect to receive from a pair of amateurs?"

"We're—"

"That wasn't a question requiring a response," Caterina spat out. She waved a dismissive hand. "There's no excuse for failure." Her breathing was deep and angry, but gradually she straightened her back and slowed the pace of her words. "There is, however, the opportunity for repentance. I'm going to give you the chance to repair what little remains of your reputation."

Umberto looked outraged, but held his tongue.

"I've had a call from Cardinal Donato Viteri inside the Vatican. Our friends there have a leak. A leak that needs to be plugged." She returned to her glass desk and leaned over it, her palms flat on its surface. "The man's name is Rinaldo Trecchio, and he wears a red hat."

Umberto's expression began to change as he recognized what this instruction meant.

"He's the uncle of the little bastard you keep failing to kill. A man who's working, if I need to remind you, with a police officer." A long, ominous, accusing pause. "You're to take the nephew and his associate out immediately. Then I want you inside the Vatican, by whatever means are necessary. I want the cardinal eliminated."

She paused, dressing down both men with stony eyes. Then she reached into a drawer of her desk and drew out a vicious-looking handgun of a make Umberto didn't recognize. But he couldn't fail to recognize that when she laid it on the desktop, its barrel was pointed directly at him.

"This time," Caterina said, "I will allow no excuses."

49

Headquarters of the Swiss Guard: 1:31 p.m.

Christoph Raber laid four single pages on the black surface of his desk. Despite his fluency with the technology the Swiss Guard used in their investigations, at a certain point he always felt more comfortable with paper and ink. This afternoon, he'd come to that point.

The first three sheets each contained details of medical firms for which his men had drawn connections to the Vatican Bank. The first was a company called CygnaGen, which performed research into cures for various genetic conditions, including child blindness.

The second was Arseniy Kopulov's Alventix Ltd., whose chairman Raber had interviewed earlier in the morning. The man had had no explanation for the twenty million euros that had arrived in his account only days ago. Moreover, he'd seemed genuinely shocked to learn of the sum. Raber had seen men fake surprise many times and he could usually spot the signs—a certain twitch at the temples, a subconscious straightening of the back, a repositioning of the eyes. He had seen none of these with Kopulov. Despite his inherent dislike for the man, he suspected that he had been telling the truth when he said he knew nothing about the funds.

The implications of that realization had only caused more questions for Raber. Questions that he had been investigating in the hours since his meeting with Kopulov. Was something going on behind the scenes at the IOR? Did the people heading those connected companies know as little about what was going on as the Russian seemed to?

The third page suggested that might be the case. Dr. Marcello Tedesco, head of the Lisa Tedesco MCL Research Unit, had announced the previous day that his cancer treatment group had been healed. Tedesco had been legitimately working on the disease for years, but his links to Alventix were deeply suspicious. These suspicions had only been reinforced when Raber and his men had started looking into the doctor's financials. His primary personal account appeared clean. A second private account, however, had received a wire transfer of twenty-five thousand euros three days ago, and another twenty-five only hours after his announcement.

Connections, clear as day.

Raber stood. He'd summarized his conclusion, as tentative as it was, at the bottom of the third page. *Kopulov and his company are connected to, or responsible for, the curing of Tedesco's patients.* There was no other conclusion to draw. *CygnaGen must be responsible for the healing of the blind patients in Pescara,* he'd written just after it. He didn't have a direct connection to the doctor there yet. But the firm itself had been involved in suspicious funding transfers, just as Alventix had. Then again, Kopulov *had* seemed genuinely surprised about the money. As if he had no idea . . .

Raber suddenly froze. Numbers and tracking routes flashed through his mind.

These "miracles" are the manipulations of the medical firms themselves, or some group behind them. The thought came like a revelation. *They're companies with the technology, power and ability to effect these cures. They've created the appearance of individuals being paid off, so that if there should be any investigation into the cures, it will look as if these men have propagated a fraud—keeping the companies' involvement hidden.*

But why? Why effect healings and stage them as miracles, taking pains to make it look as if individuals had been behind them if they were ever discovered? Raber could see no clear motive, or how anyone could benefit from such a plan.

And he still didn't know what to make of the IOR's involvement. Two of the payment tranches he had tracked down had immediate ties to the Vatican Bank. He peered at the fourth sheet on his desk: a printout of financial transactions his men had covertly snatched from the IOR's computers. There was no question: someone inside Vatican City was manipulating these events.

But that was not all the information meant. While two of the payments had been routed through the IOR, the others that Raber had been able to identify had not. And that meant that whoever was operating within the Vatican was working with someone outside it.

50

Café Barberini: 1:42 p.m.

Alexander stared at the empty space where his uncle had been seated. They'd hugged as Rinaldo departed, and a few seconds later Alexander had sat back down, numb from the encounter. Gabriella remained beside him in a long silence.

"Alex," she finally said, "we need to figure out what we're going to do."

He nodded slightly.

"The group your uncle spoke about . . . if he's right, they're aiming at nothing less than taking down the Pope. He's a man dedicated to reforming the very kind of irregularities that give them their influence. And yet there's something I still don't understand." She hesitated. "How does staging a healing of Gregory work against him? It seems instead like the whole world is more devoted to him than ever. He's become the suffering servant, cured for his labors."

Alexander had a hand at his chin. He'd shaved in the morning at her aunt's, but already the dark roughness was returning beneath his fingers.

"How do you take down a pope?" he asked abruptly. "What would it really involve?"

Gabriella pinched her eyebrows. The question wasn't one she'd been expecting. "You can't just oust him from power," she offered. The concept seemed to offend her piety, but it was also a puzzle. "The Roman Catholic hierarchy isn't designed like that. Popes hold their positions for life."

"With little option for removal."

"We always said at school that the only one with the authority to remove a pope from office is God."

Alexander didn't take the statement as a joke. "Which means death is the only way out."

Gabriella's eyes went wide. "You're not thinking that—"

"It's not as if it hasn't been tried before," he interrupted. "John Paul II took a bullet in 1981."

"He lived. God protected him."

"Maybe. But that was only the most famous attempt. There have long been rumors that another, made not long before, was more successful."

Gabriella knew immediately what he was referring to. "You're talking about John Paul I?"

"Or Albino Luciani, as he'd been only a month before. He died just thirty-three days after his election. Rumors have persisted ever since that his death was not accidental."

"The nuns at school used to joke that the cardinals had made their choice for the right man to succeed St. Peter, but God had disagreed."

"God maybe," Alexander answered humorlessly, "but there were plenty of other candidates. There have been speculations of poisoning, of plots by the Vatican Bank, by the Masons and the Italian P2 Lodge. By members of the curia who were worried over his theological reforms."

Gabriella hesitated. "You think we're looking at an assassination attempt?"

Alexander turned to face her more directly. "It's a possibility. We can't rule it out. Though if my uncle is right about the motives of this group, the death of the Pope would probably work against them."

"It would eliminate their enemy pretty effectively."

"True, but with the legacy of suspicion since John Paul I, any assassination would provoke conspiracy theories and investigations. For people trying to avoid scrutiny and attention, it's not the best way to go."

"So what do you do instead?"

Alexander pondered the question a few moments before answering. "If killing the Pope isn't a realistic option, discrediting him is."

Gabriella sat silently, waiting for more.

"Think about it," Alexander continued. "Pope Gregory is generally regarded as a moral light for the Church. He's universally respected. He's admired and seen as a pillar of spiritual stability. More importantly, he's used that foundation as a starting point for radical reforms of the curia. And he's extended those reforms outward as well, beyond the borders of the Church. All of this would make the individuals in the fraternity nervous."

"As well as their partners outside," Gabriella agreed.

"So if you can't simply get rid of him, what do you do? You take away that moral mandate. Eliminate his spiritual stature and the sense that he's a capable leader."

Gabriella looked only partially convinced. "Fine, discredit the Pope to destroy his power. I still don't see a connection to what happened in St. Peter's. His being healed makes him seem more spiritual, not less."

"You have to look at it in the light of what else we've learned," Alexander answered. A confident energy was creeping into his voice. "That one event looks good, yes. But it was only one. And significantly, it was the first. Say that word 'first' and it's going to bring up connections to the second, to the third. And just how long has it taken us to find details putting miracles two and three in a questionable light?"

"Not long, all things considered."

"That's the plot, Gabriella. All that remains, once the deception of those later miracles is unearthed, is to connect them back to the first. Fraud there must mean fraud here."

Gabriella didn't answer. Once again, Alexander's logic was hard to refute.

"And it gets worse for Gregory," he continued. "He's taken this stranger into the Vatican. He's spoken to the masses about love and hope in terms that pretty much everyone has connected to his experience of this man's presence."

Gabriella's breathing started to grow shorter, gaining in speed. "His press statement. He didn't mention the man by name, but it was essentially an endorsement."

"And not just of the man, but the miracles. He *called* them miracles. That makes his downfall a simple affair. All his enemies have to do is reveal the truth."

"Which is?"

"That the stranger is a fake. You and I know it's true, and that fact will be enough to topple Gregory. The Pope has been duped by a con man. He's given official endorsement to criminal deception. He can't tell medical science from an act of God. He's been deceived at the most basic level of faith and belief."

Gabriella sat back, deflated. "His credibility would be destroyed."

"Pope Gregory would have all the spiritual authority of a schoolboy," Alexander affirmed.

That was it, they both now realized. That was how to eradicate a pope when you couldn't kill him.

"What do you suggest we do?" Gabriella finally asked.

"There's only one thing we can do," Alexander answered. He set his palms flat on the table, his torso rigid.

"We have to get inside. We have to get to the Holy Father."

51

Central Rome: 2:01 p.m.

Most people live their lives in complete ignorance of the ease with which their every motion can be tracked, their location pinpointed, their activities exactly known. Not just by governments or major corporations: this is a possibility for any individual with enough know-how, persistence and, from time to time, cash.

It had taken Umberto fewer than thirteen minutes to pinpoint the location of Alexander Trecchio and Gabriella Fierro once he and Maso had left Caterina's office. Both targets had abandoned their original phones, so that method of tracking was out until the brothers could learn their new numbers. But Trecchio still had his laptop in his pack, and that device had background Wi-Fi geolocation enabled. Even when the computer was asleep, it pinged nearby Wi-Fi routers for background updates and downloads—one of the features of the newest machines. And one that made them trackable.

Umberto had traced the MAC address he'd obtained for Trecchio's office-issued computer—a remarkably simple task that had taken nothing more than a phone call to *La Repubblica*'s technical support office, claiming to be Trecchio to a disinterested phone support technician who clearly hadn't ever met the one amongst a thousand reporters, and asking for the number "so I can register my laptop on my network when I'm at home." He'd had it seconds later. Then he'd located its latest stationary coordinates and simply fed them into Google Maps on his Android phone. There was no need for advanced tracking software or expensive mapping programs. Within seconds he had zoomed in to Street View and familiarized himself with the awning and front windows of the café where the pair were seated. The café's own website provided a layout, and with just a little additional finessing and precision he was able to determine that they were in one of the establishment's three booths, probably the second.

It had been 1:14 p.m. when Caterina Amato charged him to find and definitively eliminate the two thorns in their collective sides. By 1:32 p.m. he'd known exactly where they were. Now, half an hour later, he and Maso were positioned outside the Café Barberini, awaiting their prey. First the two troublemakers, then on to the cardinal. As instructed.

Maso was seated at a small round table just outside the café's sole exit, sipping an espresso, with a leather hat partially obscuring his face. He held the morning's paper in his hand, still a favorite resource for covert surveillance. Beneath it he artfully concealed a small directional microphone whose feed went straight to his and Umberto's earpieces.

Umberto himself was on a public bench on the opposite side of the street. In his fashionable attire he looked wholly ordinary in fashion-sensitive Rome, clutching a bundle of freshly cut flowers from a nearby kiosk, watching the traffic go by with a mild look of contentment on his features. An apparent lover, waiting for his beloved.

He'd instructed Maso to pick up Alexander and Gabriella's conversation as soon as they emerged. He wanted to know where they were going. While neither man was willing to fail in their mission, they both knew that gunning down two people in the middle of a busy coffee shop was out of the question. They would follow their targets at a distance and kill them in a location a little more discreet. And then finally they'd be done with them.

They didn't have long to wait for the operation to begin.

Gabriella Fierro emerged first, Alexander Trecchio immediately behind her, their eyes squinting slightly in the bright sunlight. Their lips were moving.

"Can you get them?" Umberto asked through his hidden mouthpiece.

"One moment, boss." Maso fiddled with his controls. At first the device yielded only silence, then static. Then, at last, voices.

"Do you really think it's possible?" Gabriella asked. Maso tightened the controls so that her voice came through more clearly, cutting through the background noise. *"The whole place is locked down. No one's being allowed in or out."*

"That doesn't mean there aren't ways around those hurdles," came the man's voice.

Umberto had no idea what they were talking about, a fact that annoyed him.

"St. Peter's Square is out of the question," the woman continued. *"I've seen the cordon of officers surrounding it. And there just aren't that many other ways in. The main entrance is only for the curia and staff, and that's fully guarded even in ordinary circumstances."*

The subject matter began to dawn on Umberto. *They're speaking of Vatican City.* But why?

Trecchio's voice clipped back into the field of range of Maso's microphone. *"You're thinking like an outsider."*

"I've lived here all my life, Alex, thank you very much."

"But you've never lived on the inside. I have."

Umberto tensed on his bench as he strove to remember the rushed details he'd pulled on Alexander Trecchio. Nephew of a cardinal who had spent a short time in the curia at Vatican City. The man had inside experience.

"What I can tell you about living inside the Vatican," Trecchio's voice continued, *"is that while you're there, you learn a few secrets."*

"Like?" Fierro asked.

"Like how to get out without being seen."

"The way your uncle did today."

"And equally important, how to get back in."

Umberto nearly dropped his flowers. Trecchio and Fierro were planning to break into the Vatican. It was a spectacular act of bravado, whatever was motivating it. And Trecchio was right: if anyone had the knowledge to make a real go of it, it was probably him.

Their motivation was irrelevant. To Umberto, this new piece of information meant only one thing: he could use them. He and Maso needed to get in to Vatican City to fulfill the second part of Amato's orders: the killing of Cardinal Rinaldo. But they weren't Vatican insiders, and short of a full-scale assault, he'd not yet figured out how he was going to get past the walls of the most heavily fortified state on earth.

Now he knew.

52

2:18 p.m.

"You realize that no matter how much of an insider you may have once been, no one will just let us walk into the Apostolic Palace," Gabriella protested as she and Alexander made their away along the busy Roman street. Locals as well as tourists were out in their usual droves, the pavements little rivers of contrasting currents and constantly moving obstacles.

"I know," he answered, "but there are more ways in than just the one. It's a huge place. More than a hundred acres, surrounded by a wall that has gates for staff access, emergencies, deliveries, connections to former buildings. It may look like a fortress, but its walls are full of holes."

"Still, I don't think we're going to be able to—"

"Leave the getting inside to me." Alex cut her off. His face was hard, determined. "What's more important is figuring out our strategy for the other side."

"I doubt anyone's going to be too keen to listen to us."

"Everything will depend on our preparation. All our theories will need to be spelled out with evidence, and we'll have to enter with those materials in hand. Materials that leave no room for doubt."

"Just who will we be showing them to?"

"If we can get as far as my uncle's office, hopefully we can show them to him. He's already got a basic idea, and he can get us to the Holy Father."

Gabriella swallowed hard. She'd never met the Pope. She'd seen his predecessor in person once, at a massive gathering in the Piazza San Pietro after a feast day. He'd been a little white dot in a window high above, visible across a sea of bodies. And here she was, pondering breaking into his house.

"You think he'll believe us?" she asked. "The Pope?"

"He'll believe what his eyes see," Alexander answered. "Which is why it will be absolutely essential that we have every detail to hand. Specifics on the companies. The IOR. The medical research. And most importantly, the body."

"Right now, all we've got on the body is our photograph," Gabriella answered. "I don't think that will be enough."

Alexander agreed. "That will have to be down to you. Can you get in touch with the junior officer who sent us the file? He can probably help. And asking in person is probably better than by phone. We need everything he can give us: who this man is, where he comes from, how he died. And when."

Gabriella felt confident that she could manipulate the fawning attention of Assistente Tonti and get at least some of the materials Alexander had listed, despite her being blacklisted.

"And we'll need full details on all the medical firms for which we've found links. Who runs them, what research they've been up to," Alexander continued. "I can work on that. I can't go back to the office, but our English intern fancies himself as an investigative journalist. Maybe I can shake some work out of him the way you can out of Tonti."

They fell silent as they walked. A tall, slender tree was planted at the corner of the street ahead, a fashionable cluck of slender women smoking beneath it. Alexander craved a cigarette. He put a hand gently on Gabriella's shoulder and drew her to a halt.

"We need to split up. There's too much work to do it together."

"Absolutely not." Gabriella shook her head. "Not after what we've been through." There was more than just practical concern in her eyes. There was emotion. Care.

"We'll both be on our guard," Alexander insisted, keeping his hand on her shoulder, "and we'll be apart for only a few hours. I'm fairly sure you can handle it."

Gabriella's words weren't boastful when she answered. "It's not me I'm worried about."

"I'll stay low, I promise. As I told you, I do know a few back channels around Rome. All I really need is the ability to find somewhere secure where I can get online, on the phone and with access to a printer."

Gabriella was still shaking her head, but Alexander let a gentle squeeze on her shoulder emphasize what they both knew was true. "It's the only way. Without these materials, all of this will be for nothing."

He looked long into her eyes, trying to broadcast comfort as well as necessity. "Can you do this? Can *we* do this?"

She drew in a deep breath and answered with resolve. "I expect you to be at the end of your phone constantly. I want you to check in with me while we're apart. Let me know you're all right."

Alexander sighed his relief. He didn't like this plan. He didn't want to be away from her for an instant. But it was the only option they had.

"We can meet up at five p.m.," he said. "Will that give you enough time?"

"Assuming I can get Tito to cooperate, just."

"Then we'll meet outside the Taverna Due Alpini, just beyond the northwest wall of the Vatican."

Gabriella peered into his eyes. In that instant, both of their minds seemed to echo with memories of gunfire, car chases, bombs. Separating was a risk. The fact that they might never see each other again was hard to ignore, even if only forty-eight hours ago neither had ever thought they'd be a part of each other's life again.

"Assuming we can get inside, Alex," Gabriella suddenly interjected, "do you think this is really our best option?" She hesitated, then asked the real question on her mind. "Are you sure you want to go through with it?"

Alexander pondered the lifeless face of the stranger's twin. "I don't think we have any choice."

Across the street, Umberto called Maso to his side. They'd listened in on the whole conversation between Trecchio and Fierro and it only confirmed the wisdom of changing their plans.

"Maso, you follow the woman," he instructed. His brother looked momentarily disappointed but quickly washed his face of the emotion.

"Make sure she gets everything she needs along the way. And watch out for her. She's not to be harmed. We want them both back for their rendezvous so they can lead us into the Vatican."

Maso nodded, and without a word was off.

Umberto had no worries about Trecchio. Whatever he found in his little quest online could only help them.

Now all he needed was to clear his new plans with Amato, then make ready to follow their prey into the Apostolic Palace.

53

Headquarters of the Swiss Guard: 2:27 p.m.

Oberst Raber called his four most senior officers into the semi-darkness of his office. The mood was tense, electric, the moment they arrived.

"What do any of you know of Global Capital Italia?" he asked directly. He allowed his hard eyes to pass from one to the next with deliberate slowness. No one spoke.

"Global Capital Italia," Raber continued, "is a capital investment firm centered here in Rome. They maintain financial partnerships with banks, companies and organizations all over the world." He paused, allowing the possibility of some recognition, but his men were hardly trained in the world of global finance.

"I've never had occasion to explore the firm before today. But a link of financial irregularities emerging out of our current circumstances has brought them to my attention."

His men stood a little taller. So this had something to do with what was going on upstairs.

"I'll cut to the chase," Raber said. "One of those financial partners is us. Our Vatican Bank has been involved in funding partnerships with medical research firms who specialize in the kind of conditions we've seen cured over the past twenty-four hours." He watched his men's eyes, which slowly began to dawn with recognition. "Not only do we have evidence of partnership with such companies, we have evidence of pay-offs made to doctors and researchers in those firms—large pay-offs, in the tens of thousands and more—in the days just before these miracles took place."

Raber's officers were now rigid, the magnitude of what they were hearing lost on none of them.

"And Global Capital Italia is somehow at the heart of this. We've spent the past hours hacking into their computers and found connections to these firms, as well as others, and monies going in and out of personal accounts with little explanation." He paused, catching his breath and smoothing his uniform. "This is a conspiracy, gentlemen. The fact that it has involved the healing of our Holy Father and a stranger taking up residence in the palace means that men on the inside are part of it." He paused. The existence of the Fraternitas Christi Salvatoris was a suspicion long harbored by the Guard, though they'd never suspected them of crossing into something this serious. "Global Capital Italia seems to be their connection to the outside, extending their reach into outer Rome, Pescara, even Piombino. Though I don't know yet whether they are the initiators or merely the helpers."

Raber paused, but knew that he didn't need to soften his words with these men. They were his best, and they needed to know his thoughts completely. "We have to assume that whatever is happening isn't going to end simply with the staining of the Pope's credibility." He reached down and opened a folder on the middle of his desk.

"The CEO of Global Capital Italia is called Caterina Amato. She's earned a reputation as an efficient businesswoman and tycoon. But off the press sheets and behind the glossy-magazine interviews, she's known for absolute ruthlessness and the brutality she's willing to employ to have her interests served."

Photographs peeked up from Raber's open file.

"I take it those aren't from the public record, sir?" one of his officers asked.

Raber shook his head. "These are some of the figures who've gone up against Caterina Amato and her Global Capital Italia." He flicked out the first photograph.

"That's François Daniau, vice president of Paris-based Imperia Financiale, who resisted a hostile takeover in 2007."

A second photograph. "David Bryx, COO of Bryx Management Industries, who wouldn't allow a merger to go through without a full audit of Amato's firm."

A third photograph. "That's Lila Borea, the head of research for London's TriTechnica. She'd been charged with performing a thorough background investigation into Global Capital Italia's overseas networks prior to authorizing a local contract."

Raber halted. The folder contained several more photographs, but the three now on the desktop were sufficient to make his point.

They were all captains of financial industry. Men and women of significant power, fortune and ability.

And they were all dead. Individuals with no links to each other except through one person—Caterina Amato. A link so tenuous it would never have raised suspicion in an investigation. But a link that Christoph Raber was convinced was concrete, and deadly.

The commandant gazed up at his men. "I want the Guard posted everywhere. *Everywhere*. Someone is trying to take down the Pope."

54

Headquarters of Global Capital Italia: 2:44 p.m.

Caterina Amato's fruitful relationship with the brotherly team of Umberto and Tommaso had lasted for several years. They were the type of men whose loyalty could be bought and who considered it noble to do the dirty work others required with a degree of honor and dignity. Fine. She'd take them for what they were worth. They'd performed admirably many times in the past, and she still had confidence they'd be able to eliminate Trecchio and Fierro, despite recent setbacks in that particular project.

But Rinaldo Trecchio was a different matter. The brothers had a plan to get inside the Vatican, one they'd developed on the fly. But even if they were successful, she wondered now whether having two outside hit men kill the cardinal might represent a lost opportunity. It would look bad, yes. That was a plus. She wouldn't stop them from making the attempt, even though she didn't have high hopes of their success. But by God, more was in her reach.

She straightened her back, sat a little taller in her chair and ran her fingers along her cheeks. It was a pensive gesture that felt both comforting and contemplative. The wrinkles at the edges of her eyes were the only ones on her face—a remarkable fact for a woman in her mid-fifties. Caterina never wore make-up. Her skin was smooth, uniquely elegant and firm. Almost a physical affirmation of her power.

Umberto, Tommaso, the attack . . . The Pope would likely recover from the blow their assault would deliver. He would be stained by the mark of getting himself involved in affairs that brought hit men and assassins into the Vatican, but he would recover. And that prospect was no longer satisfactory. Neither was simply finding a way to take him down more permanently. Why destroy only the Pope, when it was now within Caterina's grasp to bring down the Church as well?

Her fingers caressed the fine point of her chin, her skin like silk beneath her fingertips.

To bring down the Church, she needed to make the action internal: that was the strategy that would do it. The hit against the cardinal must come from within the Church, not without. She would assign it to the Fraternity's ranks—force the men with their black dresses and white collars to get their saintly hands dirty. Then, when the curtain fell, the den of the old guard would look just as corrupt and inept as the den of the new.

Caterina let her fingers rest on her red lips, the edges of which were rising in the tight curves of a smile. The brothers could still make their way in, serve as back-up in case this new action failed. But it wouldn't fail. It was perfect, and all it was required was issuing a new command.

She'd already made the call.

Vatican City: 3:08 p.m.

Deep within the walls of the Vatican, Father Taylor Abbate, "the American," sulked quietly as he walked through dark,

empty corridors. The cardinals had been recalled by the Secretary of State for their meeting. They'd gone over organi-
zational and administrative matters, then they'd been sent
back to their chambers to rest prior to the None prayers and
an evening meal in common. Most were now sealed behind
wooden doors, praying and planning.

Father Taylor had never felt quite so purposeful while
walking the corridors of the Vatican. He usually felt a little
sinister, of course. These were the avenues of ecclesiastical
wheeling and dealing in which he'd always been keen to
play a part. That meant keeping secrets and twisting truths. It
meant manipulating people and events to suit the outcomes
the right men required. His comfort with that interior flex-
ibility of virtue had earned him a place in the Fraternity after
only two years in the curia.

But today, at this moment, sinister took on a new level.
He did not object to the task he'd been given. He understood
it needed to be done and perfectly comprehended why he'd
been chosen for it. The last person Cardinal Rinaldo Trecchio might suspect of wrongdoing was his own secretary, a
post that Father Taylor had held for eighteen months. The
two men had a strong working relationship, even a friendly
social banter.

So there should be no problems. Especially as Cardinal
Rinaldo always took his tea a little early, just after three.

"Your Eminence," Father Taylor said softly as he rapped a
foot against the cardinal's office door. His hands were filled
with the silver service of the cardinal's usual tea for one.

"Come in, Taylor," an older voice answered. The priest
pushed open the door and entered the softly lit room. Cardinal Trecchio had a penchant for Aztec-style rugs and
warm furniture, giving his office a vaguely Central American flavor.

"That's rather good of you," the cardinal said, looking
up from a small pile of paperwork and catching sight of the

tea. "You can bring it here." He shoved aside some papers to make room for the tray.

"A working tea today, Eminence?" Father Taylor asked.

"A lot to get through. I thought I might as well keep at it."

Father Taylor set down the tray and arranged the cup and saucer as usual. He added a splash of skimmed milk before pouring in the darkly brewed Darjeeling blend the cardinal favored.

"I trust all is well, Your Eminence?" he asked politely, as he always did.

"All is . . ." Rinaldo sounded like he wasn't quite sure how to finish the statement. "All is in the hands of a loving God, Father."

"Isn't that the way it always is?"

The cardinal smiled. He lifted the teacup to his nose and took in a long draw of its rich scent. "Indeed." The familiar smell seemed to relax him. His shoulders dropped slightly.

"Then may his holy will be done," Father Taylor answered, standing upright. With nothing left for him to do, he gazed at the cardinal for a pensive, reflective moment. His face was a mixture of respect, sorrow and duty.

"May his holy will be done," he repeated as he turned and walked to the door. His hand slipped into the black pocket of his slacks. Between his fingers he rolled the tiny vial of poison. It was empty now, its contents steaming in the tea that Cardinal Rinaldo Trecchio was even at this moment bringing to his lips.

TERZO

55

Taverna Due Alpini, northwest of Vatican City: 5:00 p.m.

When the time of their appointed meeting arrived, the sun was already beginning to move toward a traditional Roman evening. The light of the city, always ancient and other-worldly, began to brown around the edges, turning its rays orange as they dimmed toward dusk. It could be romantic, it could be haunting. In this as in so much else, everything depended on perspective.

The Taverna Due Alpini sat on the busy street of Via Angelo Emo, just a few streets away from the northwestern section of the great wall that enclosed Vatican City. Alexander stood outside, wearing the same attire he'd been in since yesterday. He had contemplated changing, but the memory of the previous attacks was sufficiently fresh to keep him from returning to his flat. The only difference now was the abandonment of his suit jacket, which he'd set aside somewhere between the office and the café. For what he knew would lie ahead, he wanted to be as unencumbered as possible.

He stood within as much cover as he could find on the street corner—a clump of trees near a street lamp. His eyes constantly scanned about him. Ever since he and Gabriella had parted, he had felt as though he was being watched. He knew that the men who had tried to kill them twice already could be round any corner.

Gabriella approached, walking at a brisk pace down the pavement. She too was cautious in her movements. She kept one shoulder close to the side of the buildings, moving at an angle that increased her outward field of vision and allowed for easier backward glances. Her eyes moved in a constant sweep over everything around her.

Despite the situation, Alexander soaked in the sight of her approach. In all that had happened over the past twenty-four hours, she was the one thing that brought him some comfort. Gabriella Fierro, the woman who had stood at the threshold of his departure from the clergy. The woman he'd once thought was forever relegated to his past. A memory, broken and disjointed. Their split had seemed so definitive.

Yet for the past two days, their lives had been thrust back together. The reunion hadn't been the kind Alexander would have imagined. Car bombs and photos of floating corpses had figured little in their previous experiences together. But one thing didn't surprise him, as much as he tried to deny it: the feelings he'd felt for her before were still there. Four years had passed. His priestly life was further away. He'd changed. His heart felt . . .

Gabriella stepped up to him, finally reaching the front of the taverna.

"You look lost in thought," she said softly, a smile on her face in spite of the nerves she must be feeling.

Alexander looked warmly at her. Was he lost, he wondered, or was he being found?

He noticed a bundle of papers tucked into a plastic folder under Gabriella's armpit. "Were you able to get anything useful?" he asked, bringing himself out of his reverie.

"More than I thought I'd manage," she answered. "I met Tito outside the precinct office—it was the only way he'd agree to see me. But he produced the goods."

"Kid's got the hots for you."

"Whatever it takes," she answered, a devious twist to her eyes. She tapped at the folder. "Full details on the body. You want to read them yourself?"

"Give me the highlights."

"His name is Benedetto Dinapoli. Identified from fingerprints in the birth registry of a small hospital in Portici, near Naples." Gabriella had clearly gone over the details multiple times in her head. "Born the twenty-fifth of March 1982. Educated in his home town through to the end of primary school. Then at work ever since as a shipping hand for a local canned goods producer."

She paused, but Alexander could tell from the glimmer in her eye that she was saving something.

"And?" he asked, eager.

"And he was born the slightly younger of a set of identical twins. His older brother, named Ottavio, was as close a match for facial identity as the doctors in the town had ever seen. There's a side-by-side photo in this file that you'd swear was just the same picture duplicated."

"Where's his brother?"

"That's just it. Ottavio was always the rebel of the two and left home shortly after school. He's popped in and out over the years, usually to ask for money from the family. But he's essentially been off the radar for the past eight years. No employment records. No medical records. Nothing. Just . . . wandering."

Gabriella had finished her report, and for a moment Alexander stood silently.

"No one knows where he is now?" he finally asked.

"No one's seen him in at least six months."

Alexander turned slowly, gazing toward the wall of the Vatican that loomed beyond.

"I think they have," he said. "And now we need to let the Pope know exactly who he's dealing with."

56

The Apostolic Palace: 5:03 p.m.

Christoph Raber pulled closed the door behind him as he entered the pontiff's private study. At his request, the stranger had been led into a separate area, leaving the commandant of the Swiss Guard free to speak privately to the man he had pledged before God to protect.

"Your Holiness, I am duty-bound to inform you that we believe your life to be in immediate danger."

Gregory's brows rose slowly. The spoon with which he'd been stirring his tea came to a stop.

"Danger?" He was calm, but looked surprised.

"Yes, Holiness. We have reason to believe you and your office are currently under attack."

"Who's the 'we?'" The Pope's expression widened.

"Me, together with the full resources of the Guard. There is . . . evidence, Your Holiness."

Gregory set down his teaspoon and waved Raber closer. His previous surprise gave way to his more usual demeanor.

"Let's do away with formalities, Christoph. Speak frankly. What are you talking about? As you can see, my office is perfectly secure. I trust your men are outside the door, as they always are."

Raber nodded. "Of course. I'm referring to the office of the pontiff. We now have information that makes absolutely clear that the miracles of the past twenty-four hours are the result of manipulation."

"How do you manipulate a healing, Christoph?"

"By staging a scientific treatment in the guise of a religious event." Raber stepped forward, pulled out a chair and sat opposite the pontiff. "By funding a medical firm, for example, that deals in genetic blindness and has been working on a cure for that condition for decades. By paying them off to apply this cure in a way that makes it look like a spontaneous act. An act people will interpret as divine."

The Pope looked puzzled. "That seems a bit of a stretch—"

Raber interrupted him. "Or by paying off a doctor who works at a cancer research firm, convincing him to treat his patients covertly with a new regimen developed by a multibillion-euro company. A company you also control. We know the doctor's name. We have his account details and clear evidence of payoffs. Everything in place so that he could announce a healing that the world would interpret as a miracle."

"Why would anyone want to do this?" the Pope asked. "Medical firms aren't known for keeping their discoveries secret. If they could cure this cancer, surely they'd announce that fact, not hide it."

"Why indeed, Your Holiness? It's a question I've been asking myself since yesterday." Raber hesitated, but he knew he had to be direct. "I wouldn't have an answer if it weren't for you."

"For me?"

"Yes, Gregory." For one of the few times in his life, Raber spoke with personal informality to a pontiff of the Church. "I have before me a clear set of data. We have fraudulent miracles taking place within hours of your recovery. We have the arrival of a man in the Vatican who many people are considering a divine agent, if not Christ himself. We have no reason to presume his innocence, given these circumstances. There's only one conclusion I can draw. Someone is out to discredit you. To destroy you."

Slowly the pontiff's color began to match the white of his garments. "This is a very serious charge, Christoph."

"I wouldn't be here if I weren't certain. We've identified the companies involved. We've tracked money changing hands. It's not a theory, Your Holiness. This is a fact."

"Who would do such a thing? Manipulating the faith and belief of millions . . . just to get to me?"

Raber gazed firmly into the Pope's eyes. "You know full well that you have enemies, Gregory."

The Pope nodded, but it was an affirmation of the obvious. "Every pontiff has them. Every world leader."

"Yours are . . . closer to home."

Now the Pope leaned in toward the commandant. "You're suggesting this deception is being wielded from inside the Vatican?"

"I know it as a fact," Raber answered. "Some of the funds we've tracked have come from our own Istituto per le Opere di Religione. It would appear that the Fraternitas Christi Salvatoris is no longer a myth with a whiff of substance behind it. They are real, active, and they're at work."

The Pope sat back, dumbstruck. "Our own people?"

"With outside help," Raber added. He extracted a photograph from his valise and set it on the pontiff's desk. "This is Caterina Amato. She's the CEO of Global Capital Italia, a financial firm you have no reason to know anything about. But she's been at odds with us before. The more I've looked into these interactions, the more I've see a pattern of consistent aggression toward the Church, though I've yet to determine its origins."

Gregory paused, contemplating the details. "What's her connection to all this?"

"Her company is linked to payments to the same medical firms, Your Holiness. She's working together with whoever's betrayed you here within the Vatican. And . . ." Raber's voice faltered.

"Spit it out," the Pope demanded.

"This woman is deadly. Men who go up against her wind up one of two ways: either obliterated in the public sphere, ruined and defamed . . ."

"Or?"

"Or deceased, Your Holiness. A surprising number of her former opponents have had conspicuously short lives."

Gregory pondered the details. Then, finally, "I must speak to this woman. Get her on the phone, bring her over. I'm sure I can come to some sort of peace with her."

"I'm afraid that's not going to be possible," Raber answered.

"Why not?"

"Because the threats we've assessed are simply too great to allow for any outside interactions. From this moment, Your Holiness, I'm placing the Guard's highest security protocols into effect. I'm going to have to insist that you remain in this room until we've apprehended the people who are threatening your life, and that you speak to no one while you're here."

"You would make me a prisoner in my own office, Christoph?"

Raber tried to convey a polite regret, but his features were firm. "I do apologize, Holiness. It's for your own protection."

57

Northwest wall, Vatican City: 5:18 p.m.

Gabriella peered up at the wall before them. The whole of Vatican City was ringed by the enormous fortifications begun under Paul III nearly five centuries ago, building on earlier walls that dated almost seven centuries earlier. In most places the walls were at least two stories tall, rising as high as five in some places. All were constructed of solid stone that ranged from two to a remarkable ten meters in thickness.

"Alex, it's inconceivable that you think we're going to get inside if they don't want us to," she said. In the deepening shadows of early evening the wall seemed even more forbidding than it did in the bright light of day.

Alexander merely gazed at the seemingly impenetrable facade. The edges of his lips were curved in a confident smile. "Trust me, there are ways through this wall."

They were standing just off the Viale Vaticano, which ringed Vatican City, in a small triangle of grass and trees that met the street and abutted a series of right-angle bends in the great wall.

"As I said before," he continued, "people inside the Vatican have needed escape routes over the centuries."

"I thought the wall was meant to keep people out."

"Out, in—sometimes intention is a fine line. Life inside can be stifling. Members of the curia have had millennia to ensure that there are enough passages to provide for a quieter departure than walking out the Bronze Doors. Surely you've heard of the *passetto* viaduct?"

"The one that leads into Castel Sant'Angelo?"

Alexander nodded. "Inside the Vatican it opens into a small library in the Apostolic Palace. But that's only one example, and that one was designed for safety rather than secrecy."

Gabriella looked again at the structure before them. "You're suggesting there's a passage here that will lead us undetected into the heart of the Apostolic Palace?"

Alexander grinned. "Not quite. But I'm suggesting there's a section of the wall, just over there"—he pointed to their right, to a patch of wall partially concealed behind a series of bushes—"that will provide us with a way into the grounds, emerging just behind the Città del Vaticano, the headquarters of Vatican Radio."

Gabriella was incredulous. "And I presume this door will just be standing open for us?"

"It's got a keypad," Alexander answered. "That's the only bit of this plan that's not certain."

"The only bit!"

Alexander ignored the sarcasm. "I'm counting on the code not having changed. I know that sounds unlikely given that it's been a few years since I qualified as an insider. But on the flip side, the code stayed the same the whole time I was in the curia. And it's worked every time I've used it to sneak in and out to visit my uncle since. All in all I'm fairly confident."

"So we type in your code, the door swings open, and we just stroll on into Vatican City, undetected?"

"Oh no, we definitely won't be undetected," Alexander answered. "They'll know we're coming. There's a camera just there," he pointed high up to the corner of the wall, "and another just like it on the other side. And I'm pretty sure the door is monitored electronically. They'll know we're here the moment we get anywhere near it."

Gabriella looked dumbfounded. "I'm not sure it's in our power to fight our way past the Swiss Guard."

"Neither am I," Alexander answered. There was a devious smile on his face. "I was thinking we'd just let them arrest us."

Less than forty meters away, across the street in the room of a white stucco house with a red slate roof, Umberto and Tommaso huddled behind a narrow window. The elderly inhabitant of the ground-floor bedsit lay awkwardly in the corner, blood slowly oozing from the two bullet holes that a silenced Glock had delivered to her forehead.

The directional microphone Maso had used earlier in the afternoon was mounted at the base of the window, which he'd opened less than three centimeters. Though the noise of traffic made clarity difficult, it was enough to monitor the conversation currently taking place on the other side of the road, beneath the shadow of the Vatican wall.

Umberto rolled away from his crouch at the window and leaned against a nearby radiator, removing an earbud from his left ear.

"Well," he said, "that's our way in." He set down a camera, with which he'd snapped a few photos of the scene to send to Caterina. She'd asked for visual updates on everything they encountered. And after their failure to eliminate Trecchio and Fierro earlier, Umberto wanted to ensure they stayed on her good side.

Maso turned toward him, his face disbelieving.

"Didn't you hear what the man just said? There'll be guards on the other side of the door!"

He paused, as if his point were self-evident. Umberto didn't respond.

"*Guards*," Maso repeated more emphatically. "They're not just going to let us waltz in after them."

Umberto grunted, rolled his eyes. He pointed to Maso's hip. "What is that you have holstered there, brother?"

"A gun."

"And you have others?"

"You know I do."

"And you know how to shoot them?" Umberto asked.

"Of course I bloody well know how to shoot them!"

"Then, Maso, I simply don't understand why we're having this conversation."

58

Swiss Guard central command center: 5:24 p.m.

"Oberst Raber, you need to see this."

Raber quickly moved from his position at a central monitoring station to the control desk of one of his officers. He'd already stationed their full complement of patrols throughout the Apostolic Palace and at all major points of access and vulnerability across the city. The command center was double-staffed with officers monitoring the three hundred video cameras that fed into their central computer system.

"See what?"

"A trigger at the Unknown Gate." The Unknown Gate was the sarcastic name the Swiss Guard gave to the tiny door leading from the Viale Centro del Bosco, which stood within the city just behind the radio tower, out into central Rome. The name had been given in homage to the foolish belief of members of the curia that the Swiss Guard knew nothing about it and so it could be used with impunity. In reality, it was just as closely monitored as every other point of access to the Vatican.

"Is the movement in or out?" Raber asked.

"The keypad's been accessed from streetside. Someone's trying to come in."

"One of ours?" Raber knew that a full shutdown of Vatican City didn't mean that members wouldn't sneak in and out. The possibility that it was a cardinal out for a covert meeting or a priest seeking a few hours' respite would not be a surprise.

"I don't recognize them. Have a look for yourself, sir."

The officer fiddled a moment with his keyboard and two feeds appeared before them. The first was an external camera, which caught only the motions of a small stone door, swinging on its hinges in the great expanse of wall.

The second feed came from the inside and clearly showed a male and female emerging from the entry point into Vatican City grounds.

"They're not ours," Raber confirmed instantly. "Get our men to them now."

"They're already on their way," the officer answered. At the edge of the screen, the coordinated motion of a troop of guards could already be seen sweeping toward the dark premises of the Unknown Gate.

Northwest wall, Vatican City: 5:29 p.m.

"Careful," Alexander announced to Gabriella, reaching up to take her hand. "There's a bit of a drop down to the grass on this side."

She took his hand, grasped firmly and pulled herself through the tiny passageway in the stone. It barely qualified as a door, but it provided a way through. A second later, a soft thud, and she'd landed on the soil of the only nation in western Europe whose reigning sovereign was listed as God himself.

It took less than three seconds for the distinctive rattle of cocking firearms to replace every other sound in Gabriella's consciousness. She looked up to find that they were entirely ringed by Swiss Guardsmen in full tactical dress, indistinguishable from any other city's SWAT team save for their lopsided berets bearing the ancient seal of the Pope.

The mix of SG 552 Commando and Heckler & Koch MP5 assault rifles in their hands, however, was entirely modern.

Without taking her eyes off the guards, Gabriella whispered to Alexander from the corner of her mouth.

"Well, you said we'd be arrested. Here's hoping these men are willing to limit it to that."

59

The Swiss Guardsmen who had Alexander and Gabriella at gunpoint spoke with a politeness that was unexpected coming from men whose hands were clutched around enough firepower to obliterate them both in an instant.

"Sir, madam, you have broken into the sovereign territory of the Vatican in violation of international law." The man who spoke stood at the center of the semicircle that had them penned in. He looked indistinguishable from the others but seemed, by mere authority of voice and posture, to be their ranking member. "I am advising you that we are placing you under arrest on suspicion of terrorist activities."

"Terrorist activities?" Gabriella began. Alexander shook his head firmly. *Don't*, he mouthed.

"Two of my officers will now step forward to search you," the lead guard continued, "but I am asking you in advance whether you are carrying on your person any weapons or dangerous objects of which we should be aware."

"No," Alexander answered calmly, "we're not."

"I do hope that is indeed the case," the guardsman said. He nodded, and two of his soldiers stepped forward. The frisking they gave Alexander and Gabriella was severe and efficiently thorough.

"They're clean," the pronouncement finally came. "The only items on them are personal, and two dossiers of files." The soldier speaking handed the two folders to the officer in charge.

"Please," Alexander pleaded, "we're not here to do anything but help. The Pope's in danger, and we need those files to be able to assist."

The guards' expressions didn't change. "The Holy Father is well protected," the lead officer said sternly, "and your possessions will be returned to you only after they've been examined in holding." He motioned to another of the guards. "Place them both in cuffs. Then take them to the cells."

Gabriella understood the way apprehension protocols worked, and saw the signs of men working through well-rehearsed security patterns. She had to convince them to break with that normal order.

"Before you lock us up," she said, "we're not here totally uninvited. We spoke earlier with Cardinal Rinaldo Trecchio." She hoped the name dropping might do some good. "We need to see him now."

The guard was unmoved. "Whatever your motivation, breaking in here was a very bad move, madam. You won't be speaking with anyone until your arrest has been fully processed."

Cuffs were being locked around her wrists. Those at Alexander's had already been secured. Yet Gabriella had to protest. These men had to listen. They couldn't come this far only to—

The thought remained incomplete. A barrage of gunfire overtook everything, transforming the surreal scene into one of pure chaos.

It wasn't gunfire like any Gabriella had ever experienced. There were no explosions, no reports of firing rounds. But she knew at once what she was beholding: the avalanche of rounds blasting into the earth at her feet was coming from suppressed weapons, bullets slicing silently through the air with deadly force.

"Shit!" one of the Swiss Guard shouted, polite phrasing and decorum immediately abandoned. "Someone's shooting at us!"

"Not at us," another guard yelled. "At *them*!" He pointed downward and all the guardsmen saw the same thing. The rounds were not landing at their feet.

They were landing around the two captives they'd just arrested.

"Cover them!" the leader shouted, and two of his men ran forward, slamming their bodies into Alexander and Gabriella and heaving them out of the line of fire.

"And take out whoever's doing the goddam shooting!"

60

Unlike those of their attackers, the Swiss Guard's firearms were not suppressed and the unleashing of their return fire transformed the scene. Flashes of light blossomed in the semidarkness while the booming report of gunfire echoed off the trees and the stone of the Vatican City walls.

"Get behind us!" one of the men shouted, ordering Alexander to his left. Beneath his feet, a clump of earth exploded, a silent round from the men outside landing centimeters from his left boot.

He fell, more than ran, in the direction indicated. Gabriella was at his shoulder and the two of them kept pushing until they were finally out of the direct line of fire.

"The same men from my apartment? From the car?" Alexander barked through the noise.

"Who else could it be?" Gabriella shouted back.

There was a slight lull in the gunfire, then a quick resumption. As five of the guards kept firing toward the source of the attack, two sidestepped from the main action and advanced to the interior of the wall itself. Keeping visible to their own men to ensure they didn't inadvertently end up casualties of friendly fire, they inched toward the open door.

"Now!" the commander shouted when they were close enough. His men ceased firing and the two guards covered the rest of the distance swiftly. One grabbed the open door, applied his full weight and swung it toward the closed position. As it slid into place, the second guard slammed it firmly shut, listening to ensure the lock had clicked into place. He entered a code that caused the keypad to flash red, a sign that it was locked down and would accept no more entries.

Suddenly the scene was other-worldly quiet. The only sounds were the muted thumps of bullets slamming into the far side of the wall. But so many feet of solid stone wasn't going to budge before ammunition of that caliber.

"Get a team on the outside," the leader commanded his men, "and apprehend whoever's out there."

"Control's already got men moving."

"Then take up positions here, and there, and there"—he signaled key locations around and behind them—"and ensure they don't make any move toward incursion."

The men stepped silently into motion.

The commanding guard finally turned to Alexander and Gabriella. They stood, hands cuffed behind them, huddled into each other. The officer glared at them.

"It's time you told me just who the hell you are."

Explaining oneself at gunpoint is never the easiest of tasks. Alexander was completely outside his zone of comfort. He tried to speak, but the words thumped and got stuck somewhere in his chest.

"We're here to see Rinaldo Trecchio," Gabriella kicked in, repeating the cardinal's name. She wasn't used to being interrogated in this way either, but she had more familiarity with tense, gun-bearing scenarios than Alexander.

"What do you want with the cardinal?" the guard demanded.

"This is his nephew," Gabriella answered, nudging Alexander. "The cardinal contacted us earlier today regarding an investigation we've been working on together." She paused. "I'm an inspector with the Polizia di Stato."

"I'm unaware of any work being undertaken with the Italian police," the guard interrupted. "Our territory is sovereign. So are our investigations."

"I'm not here in an official capacity," Gabriella continued. "We've been looking into a series of deaths that have taken place in Rome since the arrival of the visitor you've had within these walls."

At the mention of the stranger, the guard's features changed subtly, but remained unreadable.

"Two men have been killed." Alexander finally spoke, the Twitter photo of Professor Tosi colliding in his memory with the gruesome image of Marcus Crossler's mutilated body. "We think probably by the same people just outside that door."

"And their intentions aim far higher. We've brought everything we could dig up in the way of proof," Gabriella added, signaling the folders the guards had taken from them. "Proof of an attack against the Pope. We need to get to Cardinal Rinaldo Trecchio and provide him with what we've found."

The guard appeared to consider their information for a few silent moments, but then his face hardened. This was not his job. These were intruders; protocol was clear. They'd be taken to the cells and processed.

He opened his mouth, but before a word emerged a chirping began in his ear.

"*Ja, Herr Kommandant.*" He spoke into his mic. The two-way feed between his team and control had been live since their operation began. On the far side of the connection,

Oberst Christoph Raber spoke a short series of commands to his officer.

The communication ended swiftly and the man turned back to Alexander and Gabriella. With a nod, another man stepped behind them and removed their cuffs.

"Stay between my men at all times," the lead officer said. "I've been instructed to take you to Cardinal Trecchio immediately."

61

Caterina Amato had gathered her board of directors around her for an evening meeting. The day had been fruitful, but it was time to swing the next phase of their operation into action.

"The Pope's statement this morning worked in our favor beautifully," she said. "Though he didn't endorse his visitor, he sure as hell endorsed the miracles."

The men around the table smiled. The world was so eager to believe. A little manipulation of money, a little modern science, and it saw miracles everywhere.

"Captain D'Antonio has made a trip to Piombino to interview the girl," Caterina continued. "You'll be relieved to know she remembers nothing."

Sighs of satisfaction.

"But nothing *of what*?" the man with the slick appearance asked. "Do we have any idea what actually happened to her?"

"Does it matter?"

"She was . . . in her casket," he protested.

"There are ways to fake a death," Caterina snapped. "Perhaps her father was hiding something. God only knows. An insurance scam, maybe a publicity stunt."

"But the whole nation watched the announcement of her death. It was on every news report," another board member protested. "The public is only going to read this one way: a return from the dead."

"Then there's nothing to be complaining about. Everything's to our advantage. Her only memories are the kinds of things that could easily be the results of a faked experience. Blurry lights, indistinct voices." Caterina paused, allowing the implications to sink in.

"You're suggesting she was drugged? That she was kept in a coma and her death was staged? Whatever for?"

"More irrelevant questions!" Caterina boomed. "Are none of you paying attention? The only thing that matters is that her situation can easily *look* like a fraud. Who cares what the real story is? We can make her return appear illegitimate, and that's enough. Once the world has caught miracle-deception fever, illegitimate is all they're going to see."

She was right. They'd staged the medical events in Pescara and Rome themselves, so everyone in the room knew that proving them to be hoaxes was not going to be a problem. Abigaille Zola's strange return to life in Piombino had happened without them, just as had the Pope's restoration; but at the end of the day, that really didn't make any difference.

"It's time for the campaign to begin," Caterina announced firmly. "We need to transition the people from faith to doubt."

"Why the rush? I thought we'd agreed to wait until the Pope more clearly aligns himself with his guest."

Caterina's angry face reddened. "Because that bastard reporter and his cop girlfriend have been able to find out too much. With his family connection inside the curia, it's too risky to wait. If they know something, and they share it," she continued, "all our work turns against us." Her glare conveyed the understood details. The miracles they'd produced needed to be exposed from the outside, so the world would discover that its great spiritual leader was a feeble toy caught out by fraudulent deception. If the discovery came from within the Vatican, the whole plan would go the other way: the Pope would come out looking adept and more insightful than ever, moved by apparent miracles but industrious enough to recognize when he and his church were being manipulated.

"Can we stop them?" one of the board asked.

"It's already being taken care of. I've ordered Trecchio and the girl removed from the scene once and for all. The cardinal is being dealt with from the inside."

Caterina looked slowly over the collection of associates. Her features were stone.

"It's time to step it up," she said. "Release the photograph of the twin. Get it on every television station, internet blog and magazine in the country. Within the next twenty minutes, I want it to be the most recognizable image in Italy."

62

The Apostolic Palace: 6:01 p.m.

At Oberst Raber's instruction, guards had been posted every twenty meters along the main corridors of the Apostolic Palace. The progress made by Alexander and Gabriella toward the door of Cardinal Rinaldo Trecchio's study, flanked by their team of guardsmen, was undertaken in a kind of rigid silence. There was little that could happen in a compound so well guarded as this. And despite the dangers and stresses of their arrival here, neither Alexander nor Gabriella could be entirely unmoved by the resonant antiquity of the space. These were corridors that had been crafted by some of the finest architects and adorned by some of the greatest artists Europe had ever known. Pinturicchio had painted here. Michelangelo. Raphael. Their spirits seemed to hover in the cloistered spaces, stuck close to the ornate images they had bequeathed to the centuries.

"My uncle's just down at the end of that corridor, then on the left—"

"We know the location of Cardinal Trecchio's rooms," the head guard grunted dismissively. It was apparent that he remained unhappy with these intruders being led into the Apostolic Palace rather than immediately arrested. Orders, however, were orders, and he had never questioned one before. Instead he marched ahead of the two captives while one of his men walked behind them and two others held flanking positions. All with their hands fast on their weapons. Everything about their demeanor suggested that if Alexander and Gabriella's motives for being inside the palace were not quite as pure as they'd let on, the guards were going to give them no opportunity for escape.

"Wait here," the leader instructed as they reached the end of a long marble-floored corridor, its walls covered in elaborate red and orange oil frescos speckled with every color of the rainbow. He stepped carefully into the three-way intersection where a corridor of equal length and grandeur crossed perpendicularly. Despite the video coverage and the presence of guardsmen everywhere, he made a visual inspection of the space before instructing his men to move their small diamond formation forward and to the left.

Ten or fifteen meters later, they'd arrived at a wooden door, bold and imposing, waxed to a mirror-like shimmer. It, like every other door in the wing, was unmarked. It was assumed that anyone who had business being in this part of the palace knew which doors he needed to access.

Alexander stepped forward, a hand already extending, ready to knock on the familiar door of his uncle's office.

"Back away," the lead guard ordered, holding out an arm and blocking Alexander's way.

"He'll know it's me."

The guard merely stared him down. Alexander finally stepped back.

The guard turned, straightened his flak jacket and beret, then knocked firmly three times on the wooden door.

"Your Eminence, this is Hauptmann Remo Deubel of the Guard. I have with me a man claiming to be your nephew, as well as his companion."

The announcement boomed through the air of the long corridor, stone and polished wood granting it a ghostly reverberation.

Alexander stood impatiently. He knew Gabriella would be unhappy with being described as his companion, so he tried not to look at her.

No answer came. The whole group stood silently a few moments, then the captain knocked again.

"Cardinal Trecchio, I'm ordered by Commandant Raber to present these individuals to you. It is imperative you receive us."

Silence again, after the echoes faded. No footsteps from beyond the door. Alexander began to feel a constriction in his chest. Something here wasn't right.

After a few moments, Deubel spoke into his shoulder mic.

"Control, give me the location of Cardinal Rinaldo Trecchio." A pause, then the chirped response in his ear, audible to all in the otherwise complete silence of the space.

"The cardinal's in his office. He entered at 2:56 p.m. and hasn't left since."

The group's tension increased. Deubel's earpiece chirped once more, and this time a new voice crackled into the waiting space.

"Remo, this is Raber. Break down the door."

The guard's eyes went wide, but an instant later he furrowed his brow with the intention to comply.

"Move away," he instructed the others, already taking a step backward himself. Then, his handgun raised before him, Deubel swung a leg hard and fast, his right boot coming into contact with the door only a centimeter from the knob and lock.

The wood groaned, there was a distinct crack—but the door didn't give. The guard drew in three swift breaths, tightened his muscles and kicked again.

This time the wood beneath his boot shattered, splinters flying away from the frame. The door didn't swing open, but the lock was gone. The guard pulled out his foot, righted himself, then shouldered open the door.

There was no need to cry out in search of Rinaldo Trecchio. The cardinal's body was slumped across his desk, face down, his arms limp at his sides and the shattered remains of a teacup littering the floor beneath his dangling fingers.

Alexander lunged forward. This time the guards didn't stop him. He raced to his uncle's side, horror on his face.

"Uncle!" he shouted, groping for the man's shoulders. He tried to lift him, but the cardinal's frame was heavy and stiff.

Captain Deubel was at his side almost as fast and thrust a finger deep into the cardinal's neck. A silent pause, and then he announced what everyone already knew.

"The cardinal's dead."

"No!" Alexander shouted, genuine emotion tearing at him. "He can't be!" Gabriella moved to his side, placed a hand on his back, trying to provide a comfort she knew couldn't suffice.

Deubel was on his radio again, muttering quietly and swiftly up the chain of command. A moment later he stood before Alexander and Gabriella.

"I'm sorry for your loss," he said emotionlessly. "May your uncle's soul find rest. For now, we're going straight to central command."

63

Headquarters of the Swiss Guard: 6:20 p.m.

Christoph Raber was livid. Somehow a cardinal, a prince of the Church, had been killed on his watch. Not just that, he had been killed inside the Apostolic Palace—the very heart of his jurisdiction and the most secure section of Vatican City. And he knew Rinaldo hadn't died of natural causes. Not like this, not today, not under these circumstances.

Raber's worst fears were coming to fruition.

He'd immediately ordered a third cohort of guards to move to the papal apartments. Two were already stationed at every access point, on every staircase and in every passageway that led anywhere near the pontiff. But this third he instructed to enter the apartments themselves and stand guard alongside the Pope within constant line of sight. Gregory wouldn't be pleased, but there were rare moments when even the Holy Father simply had to accept Raber's professional decision. The Pope might be a man accountable only to God, but the Lord had appointed Raber over a group of men whose sole duty was to protect God's earthly vicar. He didn't mind incurring the pontiff's displeasure if it meant he could keep the Holy Father safe.

Raber would join them shortly. He would explain the situation to the Pope himself. But first he wanted to know exactly what Alexander Trecchio and Gabriella Fierro were doing breaking into the city.

From the moment of their arrival at the central office, Gabriella's nervousness increased dramatically. Everything about the Guard's headquarters spoke of the kind of technology-orientated, hyper-vigilant security service that modern society had been programmed not to trust. NSA surveillance networks, CIA enhanced interrogation practices, military rendition—the emotionless atmosphere of this underground complex struck her as resonating with them all.

She and Alexander were led further into the complex until they reached the etched-out glass door of Commandant Christoph Raber. There they were told to stand still while a digital eye scanned them from above. When the glass finally slid aside, they were pushed into the room.

The interior was an office, sleek and modern, and the man who sat behind the central desk was immediately hard to read. He wore civilian clothes: a dark-blue pinstriped suit beneath which a firearm was obviously holstered at his chest. His hair was cropped short and neat, the wrinkles in his face more those of experience than age. He looked friendly and forbidding at the same time.

"Mr. Trecchio, Inspector Fierro," he began as they entered, "my name is Christoph Raber and I am the head of the Papal Swiss Guard. I want to begin by impressing upon you how little I enjoy anyone breaking into Vatican City."

Alexander tried to speak. "We were—"

"Even if," Raber cut him off, "one of the intruders is the nephew of a cardinal and an ex-priest who used to wander the grounds with a degree of freedom." He glared into Alexander's eyes. The man clearly knew everything about him. A moment later he turned to Gabriella. "Or a mid-ranking police officer who, my sources tell me, has been removed from active duty for insubordination."

Gabriella sensed there was no point in making a response.

"But," the commandant finally said, turning back toward Alexander, "you are indeed the nephew of Cardinal Rinaldo Trecchio, a man I respected greatly. And I happen to know he respected you. You've told my men that the Pope is under attack. Right now the only thing keeping you out of a holding cell is that you say you've brought proof."

Gabriella suddenly found a charge of courage. "We need the files we brought with us. The proof is there."

Raber nodded and one of the guards handed her their confiscated dossiers. She tossed the first, the material that had been collected by Alexander, on to Raber's desk.

"That folder contains full details of three medical firms we believe have staged the healings of the past two days. It highlights their connection to pay-offs originating here in Vatican City, at the IOR. It also links them to an outside source we've not been able to pin down."

Raber sat back slightly and shrugged his shoulders. "This is not news to me. Our investigation has found the same."

"There are men inside the Vatican helping with this deception," Gabriella continued.

Raber waved aside the revelation. "The curia is hardly white as snow. We suspect everyone, including our own, as a matter of course."

"Even of murder?"

Raber's features hardened. "Cardinal Trecchio's death will not go unpunished. Of that I can assure you."

"That's not the murder I'm talking about," Gabriella countered, and for the first time, Christoph Raber looked surprised.

"You're referring to the two professors." The commandant had obviously found his way to the same information she and Alexander had.

"Not those murders, either."

Now Raber stood. "Then just what murder are you referring to, Inspector Fierro?"

Gabriella stared at him, then turned to Alexander. He nodded his support and she turned back to Raber. "You really don't know, do you?"

"Don't make me ask again," he warned.

Gabriella reached down and opened the snap on the second plastic folder.

"One other death has come to light today. So far it's been heavily concealed, which is suspicious by itself. But once you see the body . . . well, you'll understand."

Raber waited as she leafed through the pages until she found the one she wanted.

"I know you all experienced something in the presence of the man you're housing here with the Pope. I saw the video footage of the Mass. I watched you all kneel. But whoever you and others believe him to be, I can assure you this man is not a divine visitor. He's the troubled runaway brother of a set of twins, whose other half washed up in the Tiber earlier today."

She flung the photograph down on Raber's desk. Even in the dark lighting of the office, the paling of his features was obvious and immediate.

"Whoever you've got upstairs," Gabriella continued, "he's a plant. Whether he's planted himself or been manipulated by others I don't know. But there is an attack in progress, on the Church and on the Pope. He's a part of it, whoever else may be involved. And so far, those people have left a trail of blood and death in their wake."

A tense silence lingered in the office. Then, all at once, Raber snapped into action. He grabbed the photo and slid it into his jacket pocket. His eyes flew to Gabriella, then to Alexander.

"Gather your things together."

"Where are we going?" Alexander asked.

"We're going to see the Holy Father."

64

Throughout Italy: 6:31 p.m.

On ten thousand televisions in ten thousand homes it began.

On wall-panel displays on shopfronts in the heart of Rome.

On LCD billboards lining the way to chic city centers in the Tuscan Riviera and the more discreet public television displays that cornered classic boulevards in Florence. In every city, in the towns, all the way down to the tiniest villages.

One image, everywhere, flooding the consciousness of a confused public: the face of the stranger.

The one they had seen walking down the central corridor of God's cathedral.

The one who had called silence upon the masses.

The one who had felled the Swiss Guard in synchronized obeisance.

The one who had ascended the high altar and spoken to the Vicar of Christ.

The one who had healed a pope.

The one whose mere presence in their midst had given sight to the blind and bodily health to the diseased. The one who had raised the dead.

But this wasn't him. The whole world knew that man was in the Vatican, but this image had come from outside. From a river. A body. *A dead body, identical in its features to the face they knew so well.* And every heart, every mind and soul knew what this horrifying image meant. They had wondered, some scrupulously, some piously, about the identity. Now they knew.

A fake. *A fraud.*

The newspapers hadn't had time to run new issues yet, but the day's headline was written on the shocked faces of millions of Italians, whose surprise, anger and rage began to spread around the world.

One word, vile and poisonous.

DECEPTION.

Vatican City: 6:36 p.m.

Cardinal Viteri dreaded this phone call more than anything else he'd dreaded in this dreadful day. Secretary of State to the Vatican, head of the Fraternitas Christi Salvatoris, confidant of pontiffs and anti-pontiffs. But it was a second phone call to Caterina Amato, a second call with bad news, that filled him with real fear.

"What is it, Donato?" she asked as the line connected.

"It didn't go as planned."

A pause, then fiery anger. "What the fuck is that supposed to mean?"

"It means your hit men weren't able to eliminate Trecchio and the woman. They tried, but—"

"You're telling me that the two individuals with full knowledge of our work have escaped our assassins, *twice*, and are now inside your supposedly sacred city?"

"They're in the custody of the head of the Swiss Guard now."

"How could you let this happen!"

"I wasn't . . . They were supposed to be . . ." Cardinal Viteri fumbled for words.

"Shut up," Caterina spat back at him. "This could destroy everything I have worked toward! It's a good thing you're not here in front of me, Donato. With news like this, I'm not sure I could guarantee your . . . personal safety."

Viteri knew it must be his mind, but he could have sworn he could hear a gun being cocked and holstered on the far end of the line. He caught his temper and sat silently. Then, as calmly as he could: "Tell me what you would like us to do."

"I want you to get yourselves ready," Caterina answered. On her end of the line, she was already in motion. "Use whatever power you've got in there, Donato, the full influence of your Fraternity. Because what has to happen now can't be delegated to others."

She paused, then spoke flatly. "I'm coming in myself, and I'm bringing my own team with me."

Headquarters of La Repubblica newspaper: 6:38 p.m.

Antonio Laterza didn't often beam. Almost never did he exult. But the anonymous telephone call he'd received two minutes ago had evoked these foreign reactions in him. He felt radiant.

La Repubblica, along with every other media agent in the nation, was already pushing the news of the moment: the fact of the unknown twin to the stranger in the Vatican, whose image had been leaked only half an hour ago. Everyone was scrambling to figure out who this man was, how the two were connected, and what the hell all this meant for whatever the fuck was going on in the Church.

But now, now Laterza had something no one else in the world had. Something that would win him editorial prizes and garner his paper awards. And a happy additional gem in his new-found crown: it would help him crucify Alexander Trecchio.

The phone call had come two minutes ago from a woman he didn't know. She didn't identify herself. But by God, she said such beautiful things.

"Are you the senior line editor for the paper?" she asked.

"Who are you?"

"I'm the person who's going to give you your next story."

Laterza had been suspicious. Lots of people promised stories.

"I'm sending you a series of emails, with attached photographs," the woman continued. "They're coming to your private account."

"How do you know my private emai—"

"It's better if you don't ask questions," she interrupted. "Go to your computer and confirm that you've received these messages. Do it now."

Laterza had walked to his computer and done as instructed. Three messages were there as promised. Their return addresses were the kind of garbled alphanumeric gibberish that indicated a temporary address created and deleted as soon as its messages had been sent.

"I have them," he confirmed.

"Open them and have a look," the woman instructed.

Antonio clicked open the first email and began to read. His eyes widened from the first line. There was a single subject: Alexander Trecchio. A man bitter with the Church, angry at having been rejected from his life of service. A man infuriated by what he saw as a corrupt institution, headed by a corrupt man, feeding the world lies and false hope.

A man intent on taking down the Church by whatever means he could.

He clicked to the second email with its string of attached photos. Alexander leaving the scene of a murder, as yet unsolved. An annotation detailing his attempts to explain to the police that the victim—his victim?—held secrets that could destroy the curia. Alexander co-opting a police inspector known for her deep, almost excessive piety to help him in his cause. Photographs of the two of them gaining entry to the IOR during the lockdown of the Vatican. Evidence of them stealing financial data.

Laterza's pulse thrashed in his chest. He clicked the third email. It contained only a single photo: Alexander Trecchio and Gabriella Fierro breaking into Vatican City through a small door in its wall.

Laterza couldn't breathe. "I trust these materials are sufficient to give you something new to write about," the woman on the phone said. "You'll find enough detail in the documents to justify publication." She paused. "I suggest you run with it immediately. Get it in your online edition now, then share it with everyone. Your name will be made forever. You'll be the editor who saved the Church."

65

The papal apartments, Vatican City: 6:43 p.m.

Two Swiss Guards in full ceremonial dress stood outside the door to the Pope's private study, halberds angled slightly inward and eyes forward. They stood at post as the Pope's innermost guards had done for centuries, though in reality they were only the visible face of a much larger team that surrounded him. A team that Christoph Raber had already augmented. There were men stationed on the other side of the door who held MP5s instead of halberds. Every quadrant of the interior had a guard posted, leaving no section of the study, office or apartments without immediate manned line-of-sight protection.

As Raber approached the embossed wooden doors, Alexander and Gabriella behind him, together with a small group of his core team, the two uniformed guardsmen drew their halberds straight. Raber followed the protocol and knocked three times, solemnly. Then he broke with that protocol by opening the door without waiting to be summoned.

As they entered, the pontiff was already standing. He looked at Raber, his face reddened and not its usual picture of serenity.

"Christoph, I know you are concerned for my safety, but is all this really necess—"

"Your Holiness, your life is now in immediate danger," Raber cut him off.

"So you've already said." The Pope's response was tinged with a faint annoyance. "And I've told you that threats against the papal office are not uncommon and will not stifle us with fear. You of all men should be aware of this."

Raber took another step forward. His stance was forceful but his face belied this with a more sympathetic expression. He seemed to know that his next words would wound the Pope.

"Cardinal Rinaldo is dead." He stood his ground, peering into the pontiff's eyes. Gregory was stunned.

"You're . . . you're sure?" he finally asked. There was genuine pain in his voice.

"He was discovered in his office less than an hour ago, by his nephew." Raber motioned to Alexander, who took a step forward. The pontiff didn't turn to face him.

"Rinaldo was," the Pope stuttered, his eyes glassy, "he was my friend. Of many years." Suddenly he lifted his hands to his face, covered his eyes and wept. Gentle tears, then one great mournful sob. Then he drew in a long, controlling breath. He lowered his hands slowly and his reddened eyes stared forward hard.

"Who did this?"

"We don't know," Raber answered. "It took place in his office. Poison."

Suddenly the pontiff's eyes were on Alexander and Gabriella. They were neither warm nor tender.

"How did these two get in here?" he demanded. "I ordered the Vatican sealed."

"We broke in, Your Holiness," Alexander answered honestly. "It was the only way to get to you."

"We were hoping to speak to the cardinal," Gabriella added. "We have information for you, but it's not as if others were lining up to help us get it to you."

"So I understand!" the Pope retorted. He reached down to a black remote on his desk and aimed it at a small television on the far side of the room. They had barely noticed its muted images since they'd entered, but suddenly the sound made its presence a focal point.

"We repeat," a newsreader announced over a backdrop of the northwestern wall of the city, "two individuals—one a former priest and recently sacked newspaper columnist, Alexander Trecchio, and the other a suspended Roman police inspector, Gabriella Fierro—are reported to have broken into Vatican City within the past hour. Nearby residents report hearing a volley of gunfire before order was restored."

"My God," Gabriella gasped.

The Pope motioned for her to be silent. "Just wait."

The report continued, flashing old head-shot images of Alexander and Gabriella on the screen. "Trecchio and Fierro have different reasons for acting so violently against the Church. Trecchio, embittered by ecclesiastical scandal, is reported to have long been on the attack against his former employers. Fierro, pious to a fault and known by her colleagues as a woman possessing religious belief, is believed to have been bribed by Trecchio into collaboration."

"This is outrageous!" Gabriella exclaimed.

"To push that relationship beyond any doubt," the newsreader continued, "a sum of over ten thousand euros was transferred from Trecchio's personal bank account to Fierro's only two days ago, in what appears to be clear evidence of securing her cooperation."

"Ten thousand!" Alexander erupted. "There's never been that much in my account to begin with!"

The Pope muted the display. His face betrayed his mistrust as he turned to Raber. "I may indeed be in danger, Christoph, but it seems you've brought the people responsible for it right through my door."

Raber considered this a moment, but shook his head. "Your Holiness, I've personally checked into the backgrounds of both Alexander Trecchio and Gabriella Fierro. As of twenty-four hours ago, their bank accounts were clean. What you've just heard could only be true if those accounts have been manipulated since. And manipulation of funds is precisely what we've been investigating. You'll recall the firms I discussed with you before."

The Pope reflected on the information, hesitant to accept it.

"Gregory," Raber said, softer and more personally, "they're being framed."

Gabriella took a tentative step forward. "Your Holiness, neither I nor Alexander have anything against you. I'm a devoted child of the Church, and Alex is too, though perhaps he has a few scars from that childhood."

At this, the Pope's features softened slightly. He appeared able to relate to the scabs and scars sometimes borne by those who held the Church dear.

Gabriella continued. "We have nothing but respect for you. But we've made our way here as we have because we do have something against—"

She was cut off. A door at the side of the room opened with a click. The whole space fell into an immediate, captivated silence.

The stranger entered, looking directly into Gabriella's eyes. "Against me."

66

Central Rome, en route to Vatican City: 6:47 p.m.

Caterina Amato spat into the car phone of her S-Class Mercedes as her driver barreled through the evening traffic of the city. The man on the other end of the line had fast become the individual she despised most in the world. Amato was not someone accustomed to failure, and had never been one to allow it in those who worked for her.

"If you want to avoid a bullet in the back of the head the next time you let down your guard, Umberto," she said to the thrice-failed assassin, "you'll be at the entrance to the Apostolic Palace in ten minutes."

"We're already en route," Umberto answered. "Maso's got a slight wound in his arm but should be okay for the mission."

"A wound?"

"He took a bullet from one of the guards during the exchange outside the wall. Only a scrape."

Caterina's instinctive reaction was immediate. *He's a dead horse. Shoot him in the temple and move on.* But personnel was at a premium for what had to come next.

"Can he still fire a gun?"

"Of course."

"Then bandage him up and get him fit for action. I've already called together as large a team as we can manage from D'Antonio's men." The side benefit of having the police deputy commissioner in her pocket was that every corrupt officer he had in his—which included marksmen, sharpshooters and incursion team members, all willing to do just about anything for the right price—was also at Amato's disposal. She needed them tonight.

There was a slight delay before Umberto replied.

"What, precisely, is the change of plan?"

"Discrediting the pontiff is no longer on the cards," Caterina answered. "We can't pull it off, not like this."

"I'm not sure about that," Umberto answered. It was the first time in his life he'd ever directly countered his employer.

"What's that supposed to mean?"

"It means you've already succeeded. Whether or not Trecchio and Fierro expose our involvement, the scandal alone will be sufficient to accomplish what you wanted. Even if the Pope is exonerated of responsibility, in this day and age it's enough just to be involved in scandal to be mistrusted forever. You'll still have ruined him."

Caterina fumed. "I don't pay you to think about these things," she spat back. "I pay you to do what I tell you." Her rage was well past anything that would be sated simply by tarnishing the papal reputation. And what would be the satisfaction in ruining the Pope, if her own company was ruined in the process? The object of war was not mutual destruction but to come out the winner.

Another silence. Umberto recognized he'd been put back in his place. "What are our new instructions?"

Caterina sank back into the cushion of her seat.

"We are taking things to their next logical step, Umberto. It turns out it may be possible to kill a pope after all."

67

The papal apartments: 6:53 p.m.

The sudden appearance of the stranger in the papal apartments silenced all conversation. For Gabriella and Alexander, this was the first time they had directly seen the man who had started off their whole quest. Prior to this moment he had been an image in video clips, recycled newsreel and grainy photographs in newspapers. Now he stood in their midst. The man that Crossler and Tosi had been convinced was part of a devious plot. The man whose origins were suspect and whose powers were a mystery that seemed bound up in fraud, his intentions completely unknown.

Yet the man didn't impose. He didn't threaten. He didn't appear defensive. Nothing in his demeanor suggested an appetite for power. He looked only . . . peaceful.

An almost ethereal silence hung over the room as he stepped softly toward the group.

"You are here," he finally said, returning to Gabriella's exchange with the pontiff, his words soft, "because you think

I am manipulating the Pope. That I am manipulating the people."

Both Alexander and Gabriella wanted to speak, but both seemed held in silence. Alexander, the great doubter, couldn't break his stare from the man's eyes. They were like pools, drawing him in.

"Well, aren't you?" the stranger asked again. There was no malice in his voice, no accusation. It was a simple question.

"Your presence here," Gabriella eventually said, "it's tied into things we know to be fraudulent." The last word came out of her mouth as if it saddened her to say it.

"Fraud," the stranger said. There was something like a pitying smile on his face. "Yes, there is always fraud. I have no doubt it's around us in abandon. It's always been so. But what has that to do with me? Have I committed some fraud?"

"There's nothing that links you directly to the scandals we've seen in Pescara or the clinic in Rome," Raber said, a strange protectiveness suddenly in his voice.

Alexander wanted to attack, wanted to be aggressive, but he couldn't manage anything more than a surprisingly meek tone. "It's the timing that's suspect. Your arrival is the key."

The man looked at him with something resembling sympathy in his eyes. "Timing can be a strange thing, don't you think? It was time for the Pope to walk, that much is now clear to the world. It was the Lord's doing, and these things happen when they are willed. But such timing can also be taken advantage of."

"What sort of advantage?"

"The arrival of good," the stranger answered, "often stirs up intentions of evil."

"You're saying you had nothing to do with those healings— the children, the cancer patients?" Alexander demanded. His voice was now more forceful. "That it's mere coincidence?"

"Neither I nor you believe it's coincidence at all," the man answered calmly. "Everyone in this room knows that others have had their hands in those affairs."

Alexander's eyes went wide. "He admits it!"

"Though I ask you," the stranger continued, "are those healings any less miraculous just because they were caused by the machinations of men? Even evil men? The blind still see. The sick are still healed."

"What about the girl?" Gabriella asked. "Abigaille Zola? Is that also a fraud?"

The man turned tenderly toward her. "What do you think, Gabriella? Do you believe this precious child has been restored to life?"

Gabriella hesitated. Her heart suddenly felt torn. Unsure. "But she was . . . There could be other explanations."

The man smiled. "There can always be other explanations—for everything. Faith rarely exists in the absence of other possibilities."

Gabriella's eyes moistened. They looked ready to brim with tears. But Alexander's visage was bolder. He was unsatisfied.

"That's all well and good, but I'm afraid none of your philosophical talk can answer this." He reached over to Raber, who instinctively handed him the small photograph. Alexander laid it down on the Pope's desk. The whole group, save the stranger, stepped closer.

"I suppose that is the famed photograph?" he asked. "The one of the unfortunate soul found in the river." Once again his tone was mystifyingly non-defensive. There were only hints of sorrow in his voice, without any echoes of self-justification.

"It's damning," Alexander answered. "We know this man had a twin who's been on and off the grid for months. We know he disappeared weeks ago. Then you appear, lone and spectacular in the midst of miracles that aren't miracles."

"Why don't you simply say what's in your heart, Alexander?" the stranger prompted calmly. "You believe I am this man's twin. That I killed my brother to cover up who I really am."

"Or had someone else do it."

Alexander's full accusation was laid bare, but in this moment what shook his confidence was the fact that the stranger only nodded his head knowingly. It was as if the charge laid against him were an expected and reasonable idea. Yet at the same time he looked sorrowful that Alexander had given it voice. As if he had been betrayed. As if someone he loved had rejected that love. That seemed to wound him more than the accusation of murder and duplicity.

"And if I were to tell you," the stranger finally answered, "that this man's brother would be found, within a few days, hiding from his creditors in a run-down boathouse somewhere in the north, trying to avoid being captured for murdering his own kin, would that satisfy you?"

"You're saying you're not him? You're definitively claiming that you're not this man's brother?" Alexander questioned back.

"I'm asking how you would respond if you discovered that his story and mine are not connected. That a man with similar features to mine was found dead at a time when men are looking to explain away something they cannot comprehend. And so similar becomes identical, and mystery becomes deception. I'm asking how you'd react if it turned out that coincidence could be just as heavily manipulated as design."

Gabriella's voice was suddenly anxious. "Do you have proof of the whereabouts of this man's brother?"

"Oh Gabriella, we've spoken before of faith," the stranger said, turning again toward her. "Why ask me what I know? It's what you believe that will give shape to what comes next."

"I believe what I can see," Alexander answered accusingly, pointing again to the photograph, "and I see the face of a man who plugs the gaps of a story filled with holes."

The stranger's eyes were back on him. He smiled. "We see what we want to see."

He took a gentle step toward Alexander. His voice remained soft.

"I am standing here before you, normal and usual. There's nothing beautiful before your eyes, no majestic appearance. I imagine I look like many other men." Alexander made to speak, but the stranger gently held up a hand. "But then so do you," he continued. "So do we all." He took another step closer. "That's the way of human perception. We see what we want to see, when we want to see it."

He pointed to the photograph on the Pope's desk. "You want to see deception, to see liars and deceit. So you look at that man's features, you know his story, and you see me. Because doing so will help . . . explain me away."

He picked up the photograph and looked at it a moment contemplatively. Finally he took the last remaining step to bring himself alongside the man who was, in this moment, his main accuser.

"Alexander," he said, "this man in the photograph, this man with golden-brown hair, green eyes and gentle cheeks. It could be me. It could be anyone. It could even be you."

At that moment, with profound gentleness, the stranger reached out and turned Alexander to his left. An enormous mirror was mounted on the west wall of the papal study. He positioned Alexander so that they were both facing it, then held up the photograph between them.

Alexander's breath caught. When the photograph was held next to his face, something in his perception changed. Side by side, he could start to see his own features in the deceased twin's face. Their hair was a similar color. Their eyes were nearly the same shade of green. It wasn't an exact likeness by any means, but if one were determined enough to look for it—determined in the way that Alexander and others had been to find a likeness to the stranger—one could see a profound resemblance.

"We see what we want to see," the stranger said again, softly, "and especially when we want to see deception and lies, we find them everywhere." He waited a moment, then slowly lowered his hand, leaving Alexander to gaze only at their two reflections, side by side in the mirror.

"The question is not always what you know, Alexander," he finally said. "Sometimes it's what you believe."

"I believe," said the Holy Father, the first time he'd spoken in several minutes. He turned toward the stranger. "So tell me, what would you have me do?"

The man smiled gently. "What must always be done for the sake of truth. You must speak out against the lies."

68

The Apostolic Palace: 7:12 p.m.

Breaking into Vatican City is significantly more difficult when one is not welcomed at the door by the Cardinal Secretary of State in all his crimson regalia. In the absence of such an escort, the chances of unexpected entry are almost nil. With it, there are very few in the Vatican equipped with the authority to stand down the second-highest-ranking figure in the Church.

Caterina Amato's Mercedes was met at the famous Bronze Doors by Cardinal Viteri. He was flanked by a small entourage from the curia. Each was a member of the Fraternity, each aware that this was no normal reception. Behind Amato's car were two large SUVs, and as the ranks of men climbed out of them looking like anything but ordinary visitors to the Vatican, Viteri gave every visible impression of having expected them all.

"Ms. Amato, I'm so glad you could join us," he said, stepping to the curb and extending a hand in traditional episcopal style—palm down, fingers slightly curled, ring ready to be kissed. He noticed the instantaneous glimmer of resentment in Caterina's eyes, but she bowed and brought her lips to within a few millimeters of his hand, deftly avoiding actually kissing his ring.

"We're glad we could get here so soon," she said, righting herself and keeping up the scripted charade. "It is gratifying to think that in this time of trials, the Holy Father should feel us useful."

"Indeed, indeed," Viteri muttered, smiling and glancing over the troop of men who had accompanied her. He didn't give a shit what silly utterances Amato gave. The only question that any of the guards stationed here would ask was whether she was invited, whether she had clearance, and whether Raber had authorized her breaking of the general cordon.

All of which the Secretary of State could assure them of. And because of the cardinal's stature, none of them would question the lie.

"The pontiff has requested a private session with Ms. Amato and her colleagues," he announced to the nearest guard. "Check the duty log, I'm sure you'll find the visit indicated."

Because my men have planted it there. The Fraternity knew how to pull on the strings of the great puppet show that was Vatican City protocol when it suited them.

The guard disappeared into a booth, stared at his screen a few seconds, then returned. "Everything checks out, Eminence," he said. "The visit has been approved by the commandant himself."

Like hell it has, Viteri thought. Raber would rip Viteri's throat out if he knew how the cardinal had forged his credentials.

But rough as his thoughts were, his words remained the picture of political formality. "Then please see that this lady and these gentlemen are escorted in quickly." He gave a faint smile—the kind old bishops give that wax paternal and wise.

The guard nodded, and within seconds he and his counterpart were escorting Caterina Amato and her group into the heart of the Vatican.

Inside the Bronze Doors, a broad flight of steps led from the ornate foyer up to the main corridor that tunneled into the heart of the Apostolic Palace. Viteri and his companions from the Fraternitas Christi Salvatoris assisted the members of the Swiss Guard in escorting their guests—thirteen, by the cardinal's count—up the steps.

It was when they were all there, standing under a crystal chandelier that hung beneath a fresco of the assembled angelic ranks, that Caterina Amato nodded to one of her companions.

It took less than two seconds for the swarm of men to produce weapons from hips and shoulders, each suppressed, each expertly handled. The two ceremonially dressed Swiss Guards were dispatched each with two bullets through the chest and one through the head. A third in a connected control room had two shots through his skull before he realized anything was happening. A few steps down the corridor, a page awaiting his function of guiding the group toward its meeting place was taken out with a bullet through the side of his neck, spraying a crimson mist across a white brocade collar and on to the stone floor.

Three more shots took out the cameras—the Fraternity had provided Amato's team with the locations long ago. And that was it. They were alone, unguarded, in the house of the Vicar of the Lord.

"Christ, Caterina! Was that really necessary?" Cardinal Viteri protested, disgusted. "They were barely more than boys!"

"Grow some fucking balls, Your Eminence," she answered, looking at him as if he were a frightened teenager cowering at a fight meant for grown-ups. "And don't think it'll be the last of it."

She turned toward her men, signaling four of them. "You know the route to the apartments and the office. Sweep ahead. Kill everyone, *everyone*, you encounter, until you get to the door to the Pope's office."

As she completed her command, they were already in motion.

Caterina turned back to Cardinal Viteri. "So, this is your 'state.' Be a good secretary, then. Take me to the man in charge."

69

The papal apartments: 7:14 p.m.

Within the papal study, Christoph Raber leaned close to Pope Gregory. At last the stranger had spoken words with which Raber agreed. The Pope had to speak out against the lies, and not in some diplomatic or pastoral way. The time for such things had passed. Raber's task now was to convince Gregory that it was no longer simply the truth that was in danger, it was his very person.

"Your Holiness, I beg you to think carefully about what's coming next. The plot to discredit you has failed. Too many people found out about it: I did, these two did . . ." He motioned to Alexander and Gabriella. "But your enemies are not the kind of people to give up. They won't have abandoned their plot. They'll have changed it."

Finally realization dawned on the Pope. "To my life," he said, slowly.

Raber nodded. "It doesn't seem that was their wish at the outset. Why risk exposure, or stirring up conspiracy theories?

Much better to implicate you in spiritual deception and financial scandal. Make it seem you'd destroyed yourself."

"But," Alexander stepped in, "now that we can show the scams to have come from other groups, that discrediting won't work. They could still embroil you in scandal, but only at the cost of their own involvement being exposed. I don't think going down with your ship is something they're willing to risk."

"They're going to kill you, Gregory," Raber insisted. "It's the most logical plan now. You end up dead, and those who had wanted to discredit you pass the blame on to someone else." He nodded again toward Alexander and Gabriella. "Scapegoats. The real culprits will appear as horrified as the rest of the world at what these 'fanatics' have done. Then they'll quietly go about their business as usual, you and your desire to clean up the Church forever off their charts."

"What's the solution?" Gregory asked. "What can we do?"

"You have to act," Raber answered. "Expose them, expose it all, right now. We have the means here in the Vatican. Go on live television, attack the deception, and name those involved in this plot."

The Pope was pale. "But who, Christoph? I can understand forces on the outside wanting to get rid of the Church's influence. But who within our beloved Mother Church would do this to me?"

The answer came from outside the walls of the study.

A series of thumps were the only reports of suppressed rounds being fired into the bodies of the guards who stood post outside the papal office. A moment later they were followed by the sickening thuds of bodies collapsing to the ground.

Then silence, and then a voice.

"Your Holiness." It sounded from beyond the wooden entry. "Please, it's important that you open your door. I have urgent need to speak with you."

Gregory blanched, his eyes bulging with recognition. "Cardinal Viteri?"

A long pause filled the tense air. Then: "Yes, Gregory. I'm afraid it is time that we put a stop to this."

The Pope stuttered, staggered by the betrayal.

"Were it any other man who betrayed me," he muttered, quoting the scriptures, "but it was you, my own familiar friend . . ."

There was a moment of silence, of broken, shattered communion between the two men who had worked together for so long.

Then a woman's voice claimed authority.

"Screw this," was all she said. A second later, the gunfire began.

70

7:22 p.m.

It didn't take long for the firefight outside the papal office to have its effect. The guards who had been stationed outside had been dispatched with ruthless efficiency, the element of surprise offering them little chance to fight back. Now the firepower of Caterina Amato's men was concentrated not on opposing forces but on the ancient frame of the door. Holes began to pierce the wood immediately, splintering a ring around the lock and in equal measure around the hinges.

"Your Holiness, take up a position at the back of the room," Raber ordered. The men he'd stationed inside the office moved immediately into action. Two took the pontiff to the corner of the office furthest from the main door. Sliding out a massive armoire, they positioned him behind it, providing a bare modicum of cover.

The other guardsmen took up key positions in the room: two on either side of the entry, weapons drawn and ready to cut down anyone who stepped through the door, which looked ready to disintegrate at any second. Two more were a few paces back at oblique positions. Raber himself pushed Alexander and Gabriella as far from a projected line of fire as he could, then stepped backward. He took a position immediately in front of the armoire that was the only barrier to the Holy Father.

It was his post. Captains stood firm on the bows of their ships. Generals held up standards when their men could no longer fight. The commandant of the Papal Swiss Guard stood before the Holy Father, ready to sacrifice everything before he let the head of the Church come to harm.

At the side of the room, the stranger stood calmly.

The door exploded. Shards of Renaissance woodwork flew to the ornately carpeted floor and two men with legs as thick as tree trunks kicked in the remaining panels.

Raber's men were firing before the splinters came to rest. The two guards at either side of the door sawed through the intruders' kicking legs with a spray of fully automatic fire. Behind them the other men, standing back at forty-degree angles, obliterated their chests with fusillades of unrelenting fire. Medieval swordplay this was not. The air rang with the non-stop report of the powerful weapons and the smells of sulfur and cordite filled the normally incensed surroundings.

But outside the door, Caterina Amato's troop had also positioned themselves carefully. The two men who forced the door were a calculated sacrifice. Somebody had to be at the front line, and such souls rarely lived to tell of the experience. But behind them, armed men had been placed at angles similar to those the Swiss Guard inside the room had taken. As they calmly watched the source of the fire that took down their comrades, these gunmen sighted their targets and, with only a few trigger pulls, passed 10mm full metal jackets through their heads.

Which left only the two guardsmen directly to the interior sides of the entryway. There was no way to get an angle on them, so only one other possibility presented itself. Stealthily, one of Amato's men slid along the wall to the edge of the door. The low-yield grenade in his hand had a destructive radius of only ten feet: plenty to knock out the two gunmen without risking the others deeper inside the room.

He pulled the pin, counted, then gently rolled it a few inches to the center of the empty door frame and lunged out of the way.

The blast was like a ball of white light, at first silent and peaceful. A millisecond later came the thunder—a blast that seemed to deliver a blow to every organ, every bone in every body in the room. But it only did real damage to the two of Raber's men stationed at the entry: they were knocked completely backward, dazed. In that instant of disorientation, two of Amato's men stepped in, fired three rounds into each man as he lay sprawled on the floor, then stepped back to safety.

The only remaining guards inside were the two men nearest the Pope, and Christoph Raber himself.

71

Once the gunfire had subsided and Caterina's men had clearly gained the upper hand, a new silence fell over the shattered scene. Particles of wood frame littered the floor; plaster from ancient wall moldings crumbled on all sides; Persian rugs were shredded. And on top of it all were bodies, a few of hers but mostly those of the outgunned Swiss Guard, bleeding a crimson paint on to the abject disarray.

Caterina's remaining men—nine of them—swooped swiftly into the room as the dust began to clear, taking up strategic positions around the space. Their threats were few: two remaining guards at the back of the room and their commander. A small huddle. Three guns. Absolutely no chance of overwhelming them with an attack. If any should be so foolish as to fire, they would all be dead in under a second.

For an instant, time seemed to linger rather than advance. The dust in the air caught the soft light that streamed through the antique glass of the study's high windows, almost dancing in the oddly serene moment. All that could be heard was the heavy breathing of the men and the occasional metallic jostling of their weapons.

Finally, another man entered.

Cardinal Secretary of State Donato Viteri stepped into the papal office with an oddly casual demeanor. He was dressed in his customary finery: crimson-piped simar with red zucchetto, a large gold cross at his neck, a scarlet sash around his waist. The tufts of hair peeking out from the edge of his skullcap looked a little out of place, much as they did on every other day. The only thing that distinguished him from his usual appearance was the unconcealed hardness in his eyes.

"Donato, how dare you!" the Pope exclaimed, stepping out from the bulky wooden furniture behind which he'd been thrust. Raber's frame tightened, but the Pope wasn't being stopped. "You of all people. A leader of the Church!"

"This isn't the time to pontificate with me, Gregory," Viteri answered. There was venom in his voice. "And you, you're not a man to talk about leading anybody."

The Pope was genuinely stunned. "What's come over you? You've always been a loyal son of the Church. How can you betray her in this . . . this vile manner?" He motioned to the bodies littering the floor.

"I'm more loyal to the Church than you've ever been," Viteri answered. "A son protects the legacy of his fathers, he doesn't try to destroy it."

A flash of realization crossed the Pope's features. "All this is because you're upset with my reforms? Donato, I'm only trying to clean up the mess that our curia has become. To free us of scandal!"

Viteri spat on the floor, his face contorted in disgust. "Always so fond of platitudes, Gregory. But you've never understood what you were dealing with. Some things can't be changed. *Shouldn't* be changed. There are ways things have always been done. Some of us hold those sacred."

The Pope's tone was now indignant. "Your hands are stained with blood and you dare speak to me of the sacred! Your only desire is to protect your territory, Donato. Your influence and power. You're a betrayal to everything the Church has called you to!"

"Junior bishops shouldn't lecture their seniors, whatever color hat they wear." Viteri hissed out his words. "You've been pope less than a year, a cardinal less than ten. I was a prince of the Church when you were still an assistant priest figuring out which end of the chalice was up. And you presume to tell me what needs preserving and what needs changing!"

Gregory suddenly sighed. Through Viteri's angry tirade a new realization had hit him. "The Fraternity. The group mentioned in whispers. It's you. You've been behind this all along. Plotting against me."

"Don't be arrogant. It's never just been about you. We work against anyone who threatens what the centuries have created. If it takes a brotherhood of a few dedicated clerics to ensure that the Church's ancient traditions are preserved, then so be it. We're willing to do what needs to be done."

Their exchange might have gone on, but behind Cardinal Viteri a bold feminine cough cut through the volley of words. A woman, middle-aged but bearing a regal composure, stepped through the chaos. She was tall, her height enhanced by heels, and in her suit she was a commanding presence. Her blue-green eyes were filled with disdain.

"Excuse me, gentlemen," Caterina Amato said, taking another step forward, "but as touching as this is, I haven't come here to listen to the two of you dispute competing ideologies of the Church." She smiled wryly for only a second, then forcibly shoved Cardinal Viteri out of her way. She stood face to face with the Pope.

"Mr. Antonio Pavesi," she said spitefully, using the pontiff's secular name without any religious titles, "a man of many offices. Of new roles. Even a new name." She eyed him up and down. He was a man who bore the kind of power in his world that she seemed determined to bear in her own, and the resentment on her features was plain.

"There is a difference between your Secretary of State and me," she finally said. "In some twisted way, he actually cares for your church." Caterina leaned in until her face was only centimeters from the pontiff's. Their breath flowed into each other's nostrils.

"I, I can assure you, do not."

72

"What is it you want?" the Pope asked, holding his ground before Caterina Amato's seething stare.

"Only what any professional would want," she answered. "The freedom to do what I wish. To run my business as I wish, without the interference of institutions like yours."

"Are you not free?"

"I've amassed wealth, influence, all the trappings. But real freedom means being unencumbered. Unhindered. And there, Mr. Pavesi, you have posed a problem for me."

"I've never done anything to stop you," the Pope answered. "Until today, I didn't even know who you were."

"Your attacks aren't personal, Your Holiness," she answered, mocking. "Yours is a much more manipulative control. You talk about moral mandates, you hinder the free exploration of scientific advancement. You issue statements condemning financial freedom and you define what's ethical and what's not in terms that billions listen to." She glowered into the face of the pontiff, and for an instant she could almost see her mother's controlling features there.

"We only seek to preach what is good in the world," he answered.

"What *you* dictate to be good in the world." Caterina paused, her neck flushing red, then suddenly stood straighter, her eyes hard. "But I think we can be entirely frank, can't we? If it were just your political and economic interference that was at stake, I wouldn't be here. What you really have to answer for, *Holiness*, is the fact that your sanctimonious palace of righteousness is a hornets' nest of liars, cheats and far, far worse. And you have the unrivaled audacity to tell others, to tell *me*, what I can and cannot do, based on your personal visions of right and wrong."

"The Gospel is pure. We all know men can be corrupt, but I've worked tirelessly to change tha—"

"Change isn't good enough! When you have men who take innocence and destroy it, who take boys—who take my brother—and *desecrate* them." She wagged a finger at Cardinal Viteri, keeping her eyes fixed on the pontiff. Viteri's face was suddenly as red as the piping of his simar.

"Caterina, don't! You said you wouldn't—"

"When that happens," she yelled, ignoring the cardinal's protestations, "when men like *that* are allowed to wear robes like those, then the time has come not to change, but to eliminate."

Caterina spoke the last word with fire in her voice, her chest heaving. She scowled at the Pope, hatred radiating from her every feature. And then, a moment later, in an almost instant shift, she'd regained her composure.

"The simple matter is, I've had enough. If it brings you any peace, I hadn't intended for things to go quite this way. I'd intended your destruction to be less physical. Some man shows up on your doorstep unannounced, God only knows who he is"—Caterina signaled toward the stranger, still standing silently at the side of the room—"and fuck only knows what causes you to suddenly stand upright that morning. Maybe you've been exercising, taking some better meds. But by damn if it wasn't the opportunity I'd been waiting for."

"So you staged the rest." Alexander stepped in. "You saw an opportunity and ran with it. Fake a few miracles, get the Pope to believe, get the people to believe, then expose your own fraud. The Pope is left looking a fool."

"A moral authority no more." Caterina nodded.

"If you want to discredit the Holy Father," Raber finally interjected, "just do it. You don't need to employ such violence."

"You and I both know we're well past that," she answered. She stared Raber down a moment, then turned back to the pontiff. Her next words came slowly.

"We all know what has to happen now."

Gregory stood silently, motionless.

"You're going to kill the Pope," Alexander said aloud, his words barely a whisper.

"No," Caterina laughed. "I'm not going to kill anyone." Then she looked straight into Alexander's eyes. "*You're* going to kill the Pope."

Gabriella gasped, but Alexander stood firm with a new resolve. "That's never going to happen," he said. "Gregory is a good man. The kind of corruption you speak of—it's in the hands of men like this that it's done away with. That things become different. Don't let the past destroy what could be good in the future." It was ironic, the ex-priest defending the Pope and the nobility of the Church despite the sinfulness of some inside it. These were the very things that had stirred his own loss of faith.

Caterina shook her head, vaguely disappointed.

"No bother," she said. "We can always make it look like you did it." She turned to Cardinal Viteri, grabbed a gun from one of her men and held it out to him.

"Your Eminence, it's time you killed the Holy Father."

Cardinal Viteri blanched. His eyes fixed on the gun dangling before him.

"This was never part of the bargain!" he cried out. "I'm not a killer! The agreement was for you to frame him, to destroy his reputation!"

Caterina glared at him, her features hard.

"Plans change," she said firmly. "But don't worry, you'll be blameless in the end. The guilt will fall on the crazed ex-priest and his woman, whom you'll also shoot. A perfect story: they kill the Pope, you kill them. You come out the hero." And Viteri would remain in her clutches, entirely within her control. "I'm not offering you an option."

"This is madness!"

Caterina thrust the gun closer to his face. "I'm losing patience. Take the fucking gun and shoot the goddamned Pope!"

The world seemed to collapse to only a bubble between them. The cardinal stood in his regalia, sacred and authoritative. The woman was an embodiment of power, anger and command. There was nothing else. No Vatican around them, no past or future—only this moment. Every eye in the room was on them.

And Viteri knew he could not comply.

"I will not do thi—"

Caterina didn't let him finish. She pulled the trigger twice and pierced two perfect holes through the cardinal's forehead. Viteri's face didn't even have time to register surprise. He hovered a split second, muscle memory holding him upright, and then the longest-serving Secretary of State in the history of the Vatican collapsed on to the floor.

Plans change.

"Well, Your Holiness," Caterina continued, turning to face the Pope, "I guess I'll have to do this myself after all."

But as she turned, Caterina's heart missed a beat. Where the Pope had stood was only an empty space. He was gone—and so were Raber and his guards, as well as Alexander, Gabriella . . . and the stranger.

"Where have they gone?" she shouted. She turned to her men. "Weren't you watching them?"

And then she saw the inexplicable. Her men were standing where they'd been positioned before, but they were surreally still, as if frozen in place. All their eyes were on Cardinal Viteri's fallen body.

"What the hell are you lot doing just standing there?" she shouted, walking over to the nearest one and kicking him in the back of the leg. He buckled, and motion began to return to the others.

What was with these men? Had they been so captivated by her exchange with Viteri that they'd not noticed their main captives fleeing? How could so many trained men be so distracted? The scene was close to surreal. Almost supernatural.

"They've got away!" Caterina cried. She started searching the room frantically as the realization hit the men, who immediately started in on the same project. Behind the large armoire—nothing. The bookshelves—standard, no hidden doors. Then the nook to the side of the room where the stranger had been standing, with a large mirror in gold framing with—with hinges.

Hinges.

Caterina grabbed the side of the mirror and it pulled silently outward, a dark passageway behind it.

"They've gone this way!" she shouted to her men. "Follow them. And kill them all."

73

Corridors behind the papal apartments: 7:52 p.m.

"This way, Your Holiness. Watch your step. The descent is a little steep." Raber guided the pontiff through the ancient corridor that led from the papal study to a small library a floor below. Behind them the stranger followed, along with Gabriella and Alexander. Raber had ordered his two remaining guards to stand watch behind them in the corridor, certain that their means of escape would be noted soon enough.

"Are you all right?" Gregory asked the stranger, who was just behind him. The man had not lost the sense of serene calm he'd had since the moment the Pope had first met him. Even the chaos of the last few minutes had not changed his demeanor.

"I'm fine," he answered, giving the Pope a gentle, encouraging smile in the dim lighting.

"What happened back there?" Alexander asked from behind. "What kept that woman's men from challenging us as we left?"

Gabriella tapped his shoulder gently. "Just accept that we made it out," she whispered. "Have a little faith."

Alexander bit back a response. This wasn't the moment for discussions of piety. And yet, whatever had distracted their captors, whatever had held their eyes elsewhere as they made their exit, was well beyond anything he could comprehend. Or explain.

It was something close to a mirac—

"We go left here," Raber suddenly announced as they came to a fork in the tunnel. The group followed his lead.

Shots behind them broke through the quiet space. First the violent report of the Swiss Guards' unsuppressed firearms, then the lighter pings of the suppressed weapons of Amato's men. The exchange lasted only a few seconds, then silence returned.

"It's over," the stranger said softly. "Your Holiness, your men are gone."

The Pope made the sign of the cross over his breast as they continued to move. The two guards behind them had been their last line of defense. Now they were on their own.

"Which way did they go?" one of Caterina's men asked as their group reached the fork in the passageway. Neither direction bore any distinguishing marks—just stone walls curving off into the distance.

"Half of you to the right, the other half with me to the left," Caterina instructed. She let her men divide themselves along the two corridors, then took up a position at the back of the three men speeding to the left, kicking off her black heels so she could keep pace more easily. The man immediately in front of her was Umberto, the sole remaining brother from the pair of assassins. She couldn't help feel contempt for the man who'd failed her repeatedly over the past two days. If it hadn't been for his incompetence, they wouldn't be in this mess at all. At least his idiot brother, Maso, was dead in the pathway behind them. Before the evening was out, one way or the other, she'd make sure Umberto joined him.

"Up ahead—light," the man at the front of their troop announced, his voice low. They slowed, and in the distance the glow of electric light bored through the tunnel's darkness.

"Keep your weapons up," Caterina ordered. "If that's the exit, I expect you to do what must be done on the other side."

Raber pulled the Pope out of the corridor and into the minuscule library to which it led, then assisted the stranger and their two companions. Within a few seconds they were all in the brightness of the mahogany-and-leather space.

"Get away from the bookshelf," Raber instructed, motioning toward the hinged contraption that served as the hidden door into the tunnel. "The safety lights we saw from the other side will guide our pursuers to this exit, and you can only lock it from the inside."

"That seems foolish," Alexander said.

"It's designed not to let people in who shouldn't be there," Raber answered, "but the whole point of these tunnels is to give the Pope an escape route, not to keep him locked inside."

Gabriella quickly scanned the room. The only door was on the opposite wall, closed. "That way," she said, pointing toward it.

"Wait." Raber shook his head and held up an open palm in warning. "Where we turned left, the men behind us may have turned right. If they did, they'll emerge only a few dozen meters down the corridor outside. If we head out that door, we could walk right into them."

"So what are we supposed to do?" Alexander asked.

"Just give me a second to thi—"

Raber didn't manage to finish his sentence. Automatic fire began from the tunnel behind them, the bookshelf serving as the concealed door erupting in a cloud of shattered paper and shelving.

Raber drew his weapon, adopted a corner position and pointed toward the door. Then he reached to his back and withdrew a second firearm which he passed to Gabriella.

"No choice now!" he shouted. "Go. I'll fend them off as long as I can."

Alexander grabbed the pontiff by the shoulders and pushed him toward the door. Gabriella pocketed the small gun and took the stranger by the arm, and they both moved swiftly to the exit. Alexander kicked it open and poked his head outside. No one in either direction.

"Move." He nodded quickly to Raber, and before he could pull the Pope to safety, the head of the Swiss Guard reached down to a holster at his ankle, extracted another handgun, and tossed it to Alexander. A moment's glance connected the two men, Raber's face broadcasting a single command: *Keep him safe.* Then Alexander, ensuring that Gabriella and the stranger were behind him, led the group out before slamming the door closed again.

Inside, Raber aimed his weapon at the speedily disintegrating bookshelf. The gunfire stopped, and the commandant of the Swiss Guard used the brief silence to do what he had not done in a long time. He said a prayer.

God protect His Holiness, and deliver us from evil.

As the broken door to the corridor swung open, he began to fire.

74

8:03 p.m.

Oberst Christoph Raber was dead within seconds. The small library offered no tactical positions that could give one man's skill, however refined, a chance against the kind of onslaught Caterina Amato's men had brought. A single low-yield grenade was thrown into the room. The concussive force of its explosion knocked Raber off his feet. It was all that was needed. A second later two men stood above him, half their clips emptied into his chest and forehead.

"They're in the corridor," Caterina said, emerging from the passageway. "Get them."

"Which way?" Alexander asked as they left the library behind and found themselves confronted with one of the vast hallways that led through the Apostolic Palace. High above, Renaissance cherubs hung from clouds and bearded saints peered down from the columns that lined the long corridor.

"To the right," the Pope answered. "A dozen or so doors down is a stairway that leads to the ground floor. From there we can get to the gardens."

The group was already in motion. Alexander took the lead, the Pope and the stranger behind him. Gabriella brought up the rear: the most dangerous position. Hopefully they would have time to get out of the straight line of attack before their pursuers came through the door behind them.

In the end, it didn't happen the way she envisaged. Twenty meters ahead of them a door in the wall burst open. Two men moved out into the space. From their movements they seemed disorientated, their heads swiveling rapidly as they tried to get their bearings.

Alexander knew he couldn't hesitate. He raised his handgun and fired. The first shot missed, ricocheting off ancient stonework. The second also missed its mark. Ahead, the two men realized they were under attack. The weapons slung at their shoulders came up, they began to turn—and Alexander fired again. This time his weapon found its mark, a round slamming into one of the attacker's shoulders. It wasn't enough to kill, but it threw him off his feet and he flew backward into his companion. Alexander fired again, and this time a bullet pierced the skull of the second man. He ran forward, sighted the gun between the eyes of the terrified first attacker, and pulled the trigger again.

Then explosions began to come from behind. Spinning around, he saw that the exit they'd taken from the library was now open and men were emerging there as well.

"Gabriella!" he shouted, giving warning, but she'd already spotted the danger. He ran in her direction, trying to put his body between the attackers and the pontiff, as Gabriella raised the weapon she'd received from Oberst Raber and started to fire.

She was more practiced and far more accurate than Alexander. She double-tapped two rounds that felled the first man out of the library, then stepped back to shove the stranger to the ground behind her, making him a less open target.

"Get the Pope to the floor!" she shouted to Alexander, who immediately complied. Gabriella was firing again, but the second man out of the door was expecting the attack and moved agilely to the opposite side of the corridor, where a large decorative vase sat on a waist-height solid stone pedestal. He took up cover behind the stone and began to fire back, his first shots narrowly missing Gabriella's shoulder. She forced a deep breath, calmed her focus and fired back, shattering the vase. But the man had already ducked. The round careened off the wall behind him as he raised his weapon again and loosed another shot.

This one caught its mark, and the bullet tore through Gabriella's right shoulder. She emitted a pained cry as the impact spun her off balance.

"Gabriella!" Alexander shouted, horrified.

He tore his gaze away and aimed for the man who had shot her. He pulled three times on his trigger. The man's head was ripped back as the third round caught him in the forehead, his body flying backward and slamming into the floor.

But Alexander's moment of revenge had distracted him. Another man had emerged from the library, and by the time Alexander noticed him, the man was facing him full on. Alexander recognized the face at once: he'd seen it staring down at him from the window of his flat as he and Gabriella had fled down the fire escape. Now, as then, it was a face devoid of emotion. No hatred, no rage—only cold, hard dedication.

The man's gun was leveled, and Alexander realized there was no way he could get his own firearm up in time. No way to defend himself from the shot that was to come. He who had believed, who had doubted, who had served, who had fallen—he was to die here, executed by a man with no heart, mere feet from the white robes of the chief shepherd of the church he had left.

The icy man fired. It was over.

But the bullet was not meant for Alexander. In a split second, he realized that this moment was to be far, far worse.

Gabriella was on her knees, facing him, as she worked to right herself from the gunshot to the shoulder that had dropped her. Her eyes met his, and they contained a resolve, a willingness to fight. Alexander knew his own contained nothing but sorrow.

The icy man's gunshot hit her squarely in the back, its round piercing flesh and bone and organ and tearing its way out of her chest in a violent, grotesque spray of blood.

Her consciousness lasted only another second, but her eyes—those beautiful eyes—recognized what had happened. They pleaded with Alexander. *I'm sorry. I'm afraid. I'm . . .*

And then, in an instant, they were lifeless and pleaded nothing at all. She fell forward, her face slamming into the marble tiling that was already stained with her blood, her life gone.

Alexander's rage and pain and grief consumed him. He lifted his handgun to the man behind her and fired until it would fire no more. The well-dressed figure of Gabriella's executioner convulsed with the riddling of bullets, slammed back against the wall, and finally slid lifeless to the floor.

75

8:07 p.m.

Alexander Trecchio had never known grief like he felt at this moment. It was as if everything in him were being torn apart. Gabriella was gone. All at once, he realized she was more than a friend, more than a flirtation or a memory. She was *his*: not a possession, but something, some*one*, he had truly treasured in his heart. He hadn't fully realized it before. He'd been attracted, he'd been afraid; but he'd never known that something of himself was bound up in her. That he needed her, that . . .

That it couldn't possibly matter anymore. She was gone, and Alexander had the horrifying, soul-crushing sensation that he would never be whole again.

"I'm so very sorry about that." A voice suddenly cut through his grief. Alexander looked up, his eyes red and watering. Caterina Amato had emerged from the library, the last member of her group still standing. Her shoulder-length hair was ruffled, its streaks of gray standing out in the strange light as she wiped the strands from her face. In her other hand, her pistol was aimed squarely at him. "I realize it's hard to see a partner die."

Alexander could barely form his words. "She wasn't just a partne—"

Caterina waved off his comment. "Please, Mr. Trecchio, I really don't care. I was just being polite. I couldn't give a fuck that she's gone. She was going to die today in any case. Just like you, and just like them." She pointed her gun toward the Pope and the stranger before bringing it back to Alexander. He was the only one of the three that had a weapon, and he still had it in his grasp.

Alexander bore within himself only fury, and had nothing left to lose. He drew the gun toward Caterina's face and pulled the trigger over and over again, a bestial yell emerging from somewhere deep inside him. Every cry he'd ever wanted to let loose, every pain that had been stored up inside him, every decibel of a soul tortured and wild and lost—they emerged from his lips in a singular peal of agony and rage.

But each time he pulled the trigger, only an impotent click came in response. Eventually his guttural cry ceased and Caterina was still standing, smiling.

"Only so many rounds one of those will hold," she said. Her grin was wide, satisfied. "I'm afraid you've done all you can. A gun that still has rounds inside sounds like this." She raised her weapon and without a second's hesitation pulled the trigger. The aim was so close to Alexander's position he was sure the shot would end him, but it flew left of his body and on into the corridor. A warning. A sadistic act of pre-execution torture.

What came next happened so quickly, and was so unexpected, that Caterina was caught off guard.

As Gabriella had fallen, her Beretta had slipped from her lifeless fingers and slid across the floor. There it had lain until it was picked up by a man who had never in his life held one before. A man whose whole body was clad in white.

The Pope sat upright, the gun clasped in his hand and his arm surprisingly steady.

Caterina stared at him, incredulous. "This is rich! A pastor of peace with a gun in his hand! But we both know you won't do it. You're the fucking Pope! Turn the other cheek was tattooed somewhere on your consciousness at birth."

The Pope's breath was heavy, but he did not lower his arm.

Caterina glowered at him spitefully. "Give it up. We both know you're not going to kill me."

"That's right," Gregory said calmly. "I'm not going to kill you."

He pulled the trigger only once. Caterina's expression widened in utter disbelief, but the pontiff kept his word. The single round slammed into her left knee, shattering bone and tearing cartilage. Caterina wailed in pain, falling backward. Her gun flew out of her grasp. Before she'd even hit the floor, Alexander had charged her, knocking her fully on to the marble tiles and grabbing the gun that only seconds ago she'd aimed at him.

Caterina's body quivered, shock and terror combining. Alexander knelt beside her, cocked the weapon and held it to her temple.

"As you've already proved," he said coolly, "this one still has a few rounds left in it." Then his voice grew colder still. "But I'm only going to need one."

Caterina closed her eyes. There was nothing left to do— no resistance, no fighting. Her fiefdom was over, her empire fallen. She had lost.

Alexander tightened his finger around the trigger, began to pull.

"Stop," a voice suddenly commanded. He froze, then slowly turned to look behind him. Pope Gregory was standing, his white garments covered in the blood of his guards, of Amato's men, of Gabriella. "You cannot do this, Alexander."

"She deserves it!" he cried, his voice a newly tormented plea. "Of anyone in all the world, she deserves it!" His hand shook around the gun.

The Pope's eyes were soft. Alexander stared into them. In the midst of everything, they were two gems, peaceful and tranquil.

"There is more to life, to your life, than this," Gregory said softly.

Alexander was weeping, the first time he could remember doing so in years. "What?" he asked helplessly. "What could there possibly be?"

The Pope smiled softly. His answer was a single word. "Hope."

Alexander wasn't sure if he believed the Pope's message. He wasn't sure if hope could ever exist for him again. But in the pontiff's peaceful surety, he knew this had to end. He breathed deeply. He exhaled until his lungs were completely deflated.

Then he let the gun in his grasp drop gently to his side.

76

Pope Gregory himself walked into the library, to the fallen body of his faithful head of the Swiss Guard, and extracted a pair of handcuffs from the man's belt. He made the sign of the cross over Christoph Raber, uttered a silent prayer for his soul. There would be many funerals in the days ahead, many prayers offered. Raber's would be one of the hardest. The man had done what he had sworn to do the day he'd stood beneath the brocaded banners and kissed the papal ring in the San Domaso courtyard, repeating the ancient oath: *I swear I will faithfully, loyally and honorably serve the Supreme Pontiff and dedicate myself to him with all my strength, sacrificing if necessary also my life to defend him. This I swear! May God and my holy patrons assist me!*

Assist him they had. The Pope was safe, though it had cost Raber his own life to accomplish it.

Gregory rose and exited the room, his back straight and his resolve firm. Raber's work had to be finished. He walked over to Caterina Amato's fallen position and cuffed one of her hands to the heating pipe that ran along the wall. It wasn't the world's most secure binding, but she was disarmed and severely injured. In this setting, the defeated woman simply looked old and worn out.

The Pope pondered their position a moment longer, then stepped back into the library and took the radio from Raber's shoulder. It was a simple device and he called in for support without trouble. Every remaining member of the Guard would be at their location in moments.

But there was nothing to be done for the tragedy that tore at the pontiff's heart. It was one thing to grieve over the loss of a man who every day had been willing to give his life in an act such as this, but what faced Pope Gregory at this moment was . . .

Lying face down on the floor, Alexander Trecchio now again at her side, was the body of Gabriella Fierro. The Pope had been told she was a pious Catholic, that in her youth she'd considered being a nun. Today she'd died trying to save him. And more than him: the Church, her friend, and a man she didn't even know. God would grant her rest in the abode of the righteous, of that the pontiff felt absolutely certain. The stranger was already crouched beside her, drawn up close on the floor. He, more than Gregory, could offer words of comfort.

But the grief emanating from Alexander Trecchio was overwhelming. He'd been a priest, Gregory knew. He was the nephew of Cardinal Rinaldo, one of the Pope's dearest friends—another loss he'd hardly had time to absorb, that he would mourn in the days ahead. And Alexander had supposedly lost his faith, struggled to retain in his adulthood what had sustained him in his youth. What would this do to him now? What fragments of faith could survive such tragedy and sorrow?

For the first time in his life, staring at this broken man and hearing his agonized cries echo down the long, ancient corridors of the Apostolic Palace, the Pope felt truly helpless.

Alexander crouched over Gabriella's body. Carefully he reached out and turned her over. He knew it would expose the repellent wound in her chest, but he had to see her face. He had to look into her eyes.

He laid her as gently as he could on her back. Her eyes were still open. He couldn't bring himself to close them. He couldn't bear to think she had seen her last sights, that this woman of such strength and hope was now . . .

Alexander's quiet sobs choked in his throat. He was a man utterly unprepared for the emotions he was feeling.

And then, without his noticing its arrival, he felt a presence at his side. His closed eyes were holding back tears and he did not open them, but somehow he knew that kneeling beside him was the stranger whose arrival had sparked all of this.

"Do you know," the man softly asked, his voice like a sea of calm, though more hesitant than it had been before, "what her favorite verse was? The single line she uttered over and over again, that sustained her through her life?"

Alexander couldn't answer. He didn't know. Gabriella had never shared it with him. They hadn't had the time.

"It was from a moment in history a long, long time ago," the stranger's voice continued. It was raspy, its phrases shorter, but it spoke with the same serenity as always. "A man had a son who was possessed by a demon. The creature tormented him; the boy foamed at the mouth, raged, did himself constant harm and could not speak. Nothing could be done for him. He was a lost cause."

Alexander wished the man would be silent. He did not need stories now. He did not want them. But when he finally opened his eyes and looked up, what he saw caught him unprepared. The stranger was there beside him, but he was not kneeling in a pious posture of compassion. He was propped up next to Gabriella's body, his own shirt dripping with blood. Alexander noticed a rosette of red on the left side of the stranger's chest. A much larger gash of crimson covered his right side, dripping dark, thick blood down on to the man's jeans.

Every muscle in Alexander's body tensed. The first shot, the warning Caterina had fired so close to him as an act of extra terror before execution—in an instant Alexander understood that it hadn't been a warning shot at all. Her bullet had struck the stranger, though the man had reacted without a sound. And now, blood pouring from his side in quantities that made it clear his wound was fatal, he'd brought himself to Gabriella's side and was trying to speak words of comfort.

Alexander made to let go of Gabriella and reach for the stranger, but the man held up a hand and gave a subtle shake of his head.

He was not seeking to be eased of his suffering. He wished only to continue his story.

"The son was a lost cause," he said again, and Alexander could see specks of blood forming at the corners of his mouth, "but the father of the possessed child brought him before the Lord, begging for him to be healed. Begging for the impossible. And the Lord replied to him, 'All things are possible for those who believe.'"

Alexander's eyes were newly wet with tears that broke over his lids and flowed down his blood-streaked face. He gazed into the serene eyes of the stranger, shining the more brilliantly amidst his paling skin. The man's hand had settled tenderly on Gabriella's brutalized chest.

"That was it?" Alexander asked. "That was her favorite verse?"

The stranger coughed, more blood appearing at his lips and his chest beginning to quiver, yet he smiled all the more peacefully. "No, Alexander. Her favorite verse was the father's response." He reached out his other hand and closed Alexander's eyes again. Not knowing why, Alexander let his hand remain, the man's warm palm covering his face. He could feel blood, which Alexander now knew was the stranger's own, warm and slick against his eyelids.

"The sorrowing father cried out to the Lord from the depths of his heart: *O Lord, I believe. Help my disbelief.* And those, Alexander . . ." the stranger paused, "those are the words that Gabriella recited every day of her life."

Finally, Alexander's heart broke. Only in her death had he learned that Gabriella's faith had been as fragile as his. Only now, here, covered in blood on the floor of the Apostolic Palace, did he realize that he did believe, despite it all—but that his belief could not sustain itself. It had needed his uncle. In some way it had needed Gabriella. And now, now it needed . . .

He lingered in that embrace a few seconds longer, his eyes closed beneath the palm of this strange man. And then he heard a sharp inhale, and a long, completing exhale, gurgled and fading, which he knew could only be the man's last breath—the sound of the spirit departing the flesh and life fading away. His eyes still closed, he felt the stranger's hand fall from his face and heard the soft thud of a body collapsing on the cold floor.

Alexander kept his eyes closed, his fingers clutched tenderly around Gabriella's arm, and he whispered her verse a final time—for her, and for him, and even for this stranger.

O Lord, I believe. Help my disbelief.

77

The gasp of air was tiny, barely audible in the massive space. It almost didn't register. But then there came another, a little stronger. Then a third, full and complete, and Alexander felt motion beneath his fingertips.

He opened his eyes. On the marble floor before him Gabriella lay prone as she had before, his hand still gently wrapped around her arm.

Beneath his gaze, her hazel eyes blinked.

And she breathed.

Her chest rose, and her body was filled with life.

Alexander looked up in wonder. The Pope knelt across the hall, his eyes still closed in fervent prayer.

Alexander's gaze fell again to Gabriella, her chest slowly rising and falling. *Alive.*

But beside her, the stranger had fallen. The hands that had covered her heart, that had covered Alexander's own eyes, were open. His arms were outstretched on the marble floor. The blood from his wounds slowly spread out from beneath his body, flowing on to the ancient tiles.

The paradox struck Alexander like a wound in his own heart. Gabriella was alive. She was back.

But the stranger was dead.

FINALE

78

The Apostolic Palace: Tuesday

Morning broke over Rome with its usual grace. The rising sun was oblivious to the horrors the evening had wrought within the sacred city. Traffic was at its usual loggerheads by 6:30 a.m., the bustle of business and tourism unabated. Life, it seemed, pressed on.

Under stringent advice that he must issue a statement as soon as possible, Pope Gregory had scheduled a press briefing for 10 a.m. The gunfire at the northwestern wall the previous evening had been widely reported in the media, and ongoing reports of automatic weaponry from within the Apostolic Palace had been picked up by the parabolic microphones of the news vans stationed around Vatican City. The world knew that something had gone down inside those ancient walls. The longer it was left to speculate as to what it was, the worse those speculations would become.

Gregory had prepared for the event as he'd prepared for nothing else in his life. He'd felt real trepidation the first time he'd stepped out to speak to the public as pope, and he'd never fully enjoyed media engagements of any kind. But this was something different. For the first time he felt genuine confusion, yet it was mingled with an undeniable sense of responsibility. Terrible things had happened, and the leader of his flock had the duty to speak.

There was still blood beneath the pontiff's fingernails. It was caked brown, hardened, crumbling on to the white paper he'd used to write up brief notes for his remarks. Normally this would have been the job of his Secretary of State, but some of that blood was his.

Gregory hadn't had time to shower since the events of the night before. He'd barely had time to change out of the white cassock he'd been wearing, now streaked crimson with the blood of . . . by God, he couldn't even remember how many individuals' blood was on him by the end of that day. Christoph Raber, Cardinal Viteri, Gabriella Fierro together with the man who'd shot her.

And then there was the stranger.

His blood, too, stained the floor of the Apostolic Palace. The Pope hadn't seen him shot. He'd only recognized that his visitor had fallen when he'd seen his collapsed form next to Alexander Trecchio, Gabriella's lifeless body gripped in the former priest's arms. At that moment Gregory had known that the only thing he could do was pray. And so he had fallen to his knees, folded his blood-soaked hands, and done as he felt God was bidding him.

When he'd opened his eyes, the mysterious gift that had been given to him had been taken away. The woman was alive—the Pope beheld it himself, that extraordinary wonder—but the stranger was still. The wound he had sustained was too much. His life had been stolen from him, yet he had given it up willingly. Silently. In peace.

And in that instant, for the first time, Gregory wished he'd asked him his name.

The Pope televised his press statement from his office. His legs were weak and he did not know whether he could stand for his remarks, but he did not want to sit *ex cathedra* for these words. Instead, he called a small news crew into the office, allowed them to set up their equipment and station two reporters at the sides of the room to take down notes as he spoke. That would be enough.

When the time came, the light on the camera went red and the television aide signaled his three-second countdown. Gregory reported the details factually, calmly, and with as much dispassion as he could muster. There had been an incursion into Vatican City in the early hours of yesterday evening, though the individuals whom the media were reporting as its instigators—Alexander Trecchio and Gabriella Fierro—were in fact nothing of the kind. They were studious investigators who had selflessly forced their way into the midst of danger in order to offer assistance. They were both now safe, alive and well and under the protection of the Holy See.

Gregory choked slightly on that last phrase. He had seen the bullet tear its way through Gabriella's chest. It was only he and Alexander who knew what an earth-shattering miracle it was to say that this woman was "alive and well."

But some things were not meant for the media. Not now.

He summed up, in broad terms, what was known of the incursion. He saw no need to lie or conceal the truth from the public. A group within the Church, the very kind he'd been working to rid it of since his pontificate began, had joined arms with an outside corporation. They had attempted to manipulate and distort the public perception of events in a manner that discredited him personally, as well as the Church as a whole. Their aims were malicious, motivated by personal gain and the increase of power.

"Not all the miracles we have seen in these past few days have been divine in origin," he announced. "Men have tried to play God, to masquerade as God, to call into question all of us who believe in a God. And that plot ended in violence, as such things too often do. But it was thwarted. Truth has had a louder voice."

There were furious scribblings on the notepads of the two reporters in the room, penning the questions that would consume the media and the public in the days ahead. Which miracles had been false? Who was this outside company that had been involved? What group within the Church had acted in this way? There would be questions and conspiracy theories and rumors and doubts to fuel a generation. Despite his apparent innocence, the pontiff was revealing scandal, and scandal always tarnished everyone. He would never be looked at in the same way again.

But then the Pope came to the most difficult section of his statement—the portion he'd forced himself to write out so that emotion didn't cause him to lose his way midstream. He forced a stalwart posture and spoke calmly.

"I must also report," he read to the camera, "that the stranger who had appeared in our midst, in whose presence we had seen so many wondrous things come to light, was killed in the gunfire within Vatican City last night. That gunfire was ultimately part of an attempt on my life. In the process it mercilessly took the lives of many others. Including his. I have had his body moved to my private chapel, to await a burial befitting a man who gave so much."

Even the minuscule news crew found it impossible to keep their composure as the Pope directly mentioned the stranger for the first time since the man had arrived in St. Peter's. They noticed, as millions of viewers on the live television feed also noticed, the glass that came over the pontiff's eyes as he spoke.

One of the reporters at the side of the room was overcome and broke protocol, interrupting the pontiff's broadcast with a question.

"Your Holiness," she asked, "who was he? This stranger? Can you tell us directly, at last, who it was that you had in the Vatican?"

It was the question the world had wanted to know since the Pope first stood upright beneath the great baldacchino of St. Peter's. It was the question with which he himself had grappled, if only for the wonder of what every conceivable answer might mean. It was the question he'd never felt it appropriate to ask the man who had healed him and who—though he'd done so by evoking an envy in the hearts of those with medical resources and stirring them to action—had none the less given sight to the blind and health to the suffering. The man who had raised the dead.

But finally, the pontiff knew the answer.

"It is written in one of our sacred texts," he replied, "that a man can show no greater love than laying down his life for a friend. You will continue to have questions. I will continue to have them. But what I can tell you is this: this man laid down his life. He was an example of perfect love."

The Pope choked back tears, but for an instant his face beamed a strange, comforted joy.

"And, I think, he was my friend."

It took a matter of minutes for the pontiff's address to stir the public to new levels of frenzied questioning and debate. The world had hardly been ready for the stranger's appearance, but it seemed even less prepared for his departure. It was as if it had come to accept that there was something exceptional about this man, if for no other reason than that he stood in the midst of events that had so quickly shaken society.

There had been ardent debate in the public forum as to whether he was what many believed: the return of Christ, an angel, a divine visitor. Millions of faithful were ardently pro, millions of dissenters adamantly against. But everyone had expected that the man's story would go on; that they would have more time to deliberate, to debate, to fight. Not that it would end so suddenly, with so many questions still unanswered. The stranger's arrival had divided the country, had divided society; but his sudden death had united them, at least in this.

His funeral was to take place in private. He had touched the world, but the Vatican had decided that in keeping with the man's quiet humility, his departure from it would not be made a public spectacle. Rumors were already spreading over the reasons for the decision. Did the Vatican know who he truly was? Were they hiding something? Why wouldn't they allow his body to be seen? There were conspiracy theories stacking up upon conspiracy theories. But the Vatican, in keeping with its reputation, was still keeping some secrets.

The day finally passed, and when night descended on the Eternal City it brought with it a different sort of darkness. With that night there seemed to descend a great shared sorrow that extended far beyond Rome's hills and towers. A sorrow that something had been given; a sorrow that something had been lost. A sorrow that something was forever changed, and the world might never know why.

79

Gemelli Hospital, two miles north of Vatican City: Wednesday

Alexander stood at the side of Gabriella's hospital bed. Under the influence of the Holy See she'd been given a private room that was lush and comfortable, almost hotel standard. Her condition was closely and constantly monitored.

Only moments after her return to life, the remaining Swiss Guard had arrived on the scene, and among the pontiff's first instructions were that she was to be taken immediately to Gemelli Hospital. In under ten minutes she was in Vatican medical transport. In under thirty she was on a gurney in the care of some of Italy's finest physicians.

The Pope had not been permitted by the Swiss Guard to leave the Vatican, but he promised he would shortly be at the hospital to visit. While Caterina Amato was taken into custody and given medical treatment, while her executive board was rounded up by the police and questioned—during all this, the Guard wanted the pontiff under constant protection. He would be permitted to leave the confines of the Apostolic

Palace only after they could, in some small measure at least, ensure his safety.

Alexander, however, had not left Gabriella's side. She had come to, breathed and blinked her way into her new life there on the floor of the palace. Shock and blood loss, however, quickly took their toll as she lost consciousness. Alexander wouldn't let go of her hand and walked with her, rode with her, stayed with her at every moment in the hospital.

Gabriella was thoroughly examined, but apart from being unconscious from shock, there were no signs of life-threatening trauma. The bullet wound that Alexander had seen shatter her chest was nowhere in evidence. She was bruised, and had a degree of blood loss the doctors could only presume came from the shot she'd taken in her shoulder. That shot had fortunately missed her bones and pierced only muscle and tissue, and so it, like all her other injuries, was easily treatable. Her prognosis was excellent.

Alexander had waited by her bedside as the hours of Monday night became those of Tuesday; as the Pope addressed the world and the world responded with its new fever of interest. There was a television in Gabriella's room and he'd monitored the coverage, but only for a few minutes before switching it off.

For the first time in his life, he didn't have questions. He wasn't curious. He was only waiting.

When Tuesday became Wednesday and Gabriella finally came to, he was there to behold it.

Her eyes had opened slowly, blinking in adjustment. Their hazel light was foggy, but it was strong. She was with him.

"What . . . what happened?" she asked, her voice groggy from the pain medication dripping into her veins from an IV.

Alexander opened his mouth to speak, but he didn't know what to say.

"I'm not sure," he finally answered, reaching out to intertwine his fingers with hers. There was a smile at the edges of his eyes. "But I think I'm finally ready to admit I've seen a miracle."

Gabriella remained in the hospital ward throughout the day. She regained strength and stability quickly, and Alexander sat at her bedside filling her in on the story of what had happened in those final minutes at the Apostolic Palace.

The Pope came to visit as he'd promised he would. He brought flowers, a warm and protocol-bendingly long, tender embrace, and a small gift.

"I could have brought you anything from the Vatican treasury," he said with a gentle smile, taking up a seat next to her bed, "and I'd gladly have done so. Anything for what you did for me, for the Church."

Gabriella made a slight motion with her hand, waving away the suggestion that any gift was required or expected. The Pope signaled her to be still.

"However, I believe I've found something that will mean more to you than a first edition of Galileo or a Raphael original to hang on your wall." He paused. There was a deviously pleased smile on his face. "Someone told me that you have, all your life, carried a cheap purple plastic rosary in your pocket."

Despite herself, Gabriella blushed. Cheap and plastic it truly was. When her grandmother had presented it to her on the day of her confirmation, she'd confessed its charity-shop origins and price. But Gabriella had loved it her whole life.

"In the blood that covered the floor of the corridor where that gunfight took place," the Pope continued, "my staff found a scattering of plastic beads. I had them collected, I washed them as well as I could, and had one of my assistants, Sister Pearl, restring them."

He reached into his cassock pocket and retrieved his gift: Gabriella's plastic rosary, refashioned and only slightly the worse for wear.

Gabriella's eyes were suddenly moist, matching the Pope's. She raised a hand and the pontiff wrapped the rosary around her fingers, then clutched her hand in his.

"It's hardly enough," he whispered.

She shook her head. It was more than she'd expected.

"You know," the Pope continued, drawing his lips close to her ear, "what we've seen, what we've experienced, you and I . . . the world will never understand it. They will only see the lies, the manipulations, the hurt."

Gabriella turned to face him. "Don't tell me, Your Holiness, that you're beginning to doubt?"

"No." He smiled back at her, but there was sorrow on his face. "It's not doubt. Only fear. Fear that no matter what I say or do, the world outside will never accept any answer to the questions they have. Who am I to say who this man was? I can no more answer that than I can explain how he arrived, or what he did."

Gabriella now lifted her other hand and wrapped it around the Pope's.

"My dear father," she said, "sometimes even the successor to St. Peter can't provide all the answers."

"Then what am I to do? After all we've been through, I feel I ought to know."

The plastic beads of Gabriella's rosary were interwoven between her fingers and those of the Supreme Pontiff.

"I can't say I know either," she said, "but as I was recently taught, the answer sometimes has less to do with what we know than what we believe."

80

Beyond the windows of Gemelli Hospital, out on the streets, Rome's breath was tense. The city's pulse did not beat with its normal rhythm. A crowd had gathered in the Piazza San Pietro, though the Pope was not there and no audience or service was scheduled for the day. Still they trickled in by twos and threes, till there were dozens, then hundreds. They crowded around the obelisk and stared up at the monumental Renaissance facade.

Waiting.

The wait wasn't for news. That had been coming in droves since the assault on the Vatican. Caterina Amato's company was now the source of investigation by every agency in government and every news crew in the country. Its manipulation of the past days' events was being laid bare. The miracles that had captivated the nation at the medical clinics in Pescara and Rome were now known for what they truly were: the application of incredibly advanced medical research the company had held back from the public, funded by the same kinds of sums that had been planted to forge the impression of wrongdoing and concealment. They hadn't been miracles, but they were still miraculous. The medical world was rejoicing, even as conspiracy theorists proclaimed victory. And the trail of the money was being followed.

Still the public gathered in the square, waiting.

Of the two other events that had shaken the world, what had been uncovered since only made them more mysterious than ever. Neither Amato's company nor the secretive group within the Vatican had been involved in the Pope's extraordinary recovery. While the former was now the source of rampant public scrutiny, the mysterious Fraternity seemed to have been swallowed whole by the Vatican machine. The Pope had revealed that there were those within the Church who had been involved in the week's events, but no more than that had come from the curia. Whatever investigation was to follow on that front, the Swiss Guard had made it clear they would be handling it internally. The buzz in the ears of those with access was that the calm exterior the Church was maintaining concealed a flurry of activity within. The Guard was acting to break up the group that had wreaked such havoc, but as yet, there was no connection between what they'd discovered of that group and the recovery of the pontiff.

The same was true of Abigaille Zola's return to life. Doubters were sure it must be connected to the firm's machinations, insiders wondered whether corrupt men in cassocks had had their hands here too; but the forensic investigation of files and records could not forge even the remotest connection. The event was simply unexplained.

And the crowd in the piazza grew.

The Pope had submitted to a thorough medical examination. The complete absence of any sign of spinal stenosis baffled every specialist who participated. As for the girl, there were cries of fraud and deception on all sides, but the staff of the Piombino hospital reaffirmed what they knew to be true, publishing charts and electronic monitor logs as proof.

Abigaille had been dead. How she now lived, no one could explain.

St. Peter's Square began to resemble a sea of people.

The man whose face had raised cries of deception when his body was found in the Tiber remained in the city morgue. His very existence had roused the nation to doubt. But fourteen hours ago, his twin brother had been found in a small village ninety kilometers north of Rome. Ottavio Dinapoli had been hiding in a run-down boathouse. When the police came to arrest him, he broke down within minutes and confessed to the murder of his brother, Benedetto, during a trip to the capital only days before. An ongoing family dispute gone horribly wrong. Ottavio had been drinking heavily when a meeting between the brothers had taken a predictable turn and transformed into a fight. What hadn't been predictable was the force with which a direct chest blow had thrown Benedetto back against the guardrail of the ugly modern suspension bridge that crossed the Tiber north of the Roma Urbe airport. In that desolate setting, on an expanse of concrete and cable leading from a highway to a water treatment facility, Ottavio had ended his brother's life. It had been an accident, but he'd known no one would believe that. Not with his past. So he'd wrapped his brother's feet in chains from the back of his van and dropped him into the flowing waters below. Then, conforming to a habit he'd had for years, he'd fled.

The great deception was deception no more. What remained was only a mystery. Whoever the stranger had been, at least in this regard he wasn't the fraud the world had temporarily believed him to be.

And so the square outside the great basilica where he'd appeared filled up. The city knew the funeral was to be private, that they wouldn't be allowed into the Pope's personal chapel. They knew they wouldn't be able to see the body, perhaps even the grave. But still they came.

For more than a few, the stranger's death had come as a blow. But in the way of a people who'd had faith stirred into their blood for centuries, they had not failed to notice that this was the third day since he'd been killed.

The third day.

The day of resurrection.

Acknowledgments

I want to thank Luigi Bonomi for this book. Without him, I never would have written it, and for his prompting and persistence I'm tremendously grateful—not to mention the fact that he is a unique combination of a superlative agent, literary wizard and genuinely good person. To him and to all the people at LBA, I'm greatly indebted. Profoundest thanks, too, to the hardworking, supportive and energetic team at Headline, who have taken to my writing with such enthusiasm: first and foremost Emily Griffin, Commissioning Editor, who has a superb eye for the fast-paced and suspenseful and has been a tremendous help both here and with *Genesis* and *Exodus*, as well as Darcy Nicholson, Beth Eynon, Jane Selley and everyone else on the Headline team. The US ensemble at Quercus has been equally delightful and enthusiastic in bringing the book across the Pond: Jason Bartholomew, Nathaniel Maru, Anna Hezel, Elyse Gregov and Alex Knight. It's a real joy to be drawn into such a dynamic team.

I put a raw and terribly rough version of this story into the hands of Kate Atherton and Miles Orchard some months ago, and their keen eyes and feedback helped make it better. Sincere thanks to you both—and Kate, I'm just delighted that I managed to make you cry. The Chianti reference is for you. I also can't fail to mention Thomas Stofer, my initial editor for this book, about whose skills I can hardly say enough.

Two priests were kind enough to assist me both in my research and in editing, and both have humbly asked to remain anonymous. So I offer my deep gratitude to the anonymously exceptional figures of Fr. A—and Fr. I—. Thank you so much for your kindness, insight and openness.

Finally, thanks to the readers of Genesis who have found their way here to Dominus. There's more on the horizon!

ABOUT THE TYPE

Typeset in Meridien at 11.5/15 pt.

Inspired by his study of a sixteenth-century typeface, Swiss designer Adrian Frutiger created Meridien in the hope that it would make readers feel as though they were wandering through a forest. Meridien was released by the French foundry Deberny & Peignot in 1957.

Typeset by Scribe Inc., Philadelphia, Pennsylvania.